Yankee
Reconstructed

Yankee Reconstructed

Carolyn P. Schriber

Published by Katzenhaus Books
P. O. Box 1629
Cordova, TN 38088-1629
Cover Design by Avalon Graphics

ISBN-10: 0990797554
ISBN-13: 9780990797555
Library of Congress Control Number: 2015918229
Katzenhaus Books, Cordova, TN

Contents

Chapter 1

A Flicker of Torches

October 1867

*J*onathan breathed deeply as he stared at the western sky. He had always loved South Carolina sunsets. Their purple clouds swirled across a background of gold, followed by curtains of navy blue. Darkness settled slowly over a city that seemed to be at peace, if only for a few nighttime hours. If he had ever had doubts about the wisdom of bringing his family back to Charleston after the war, they faded away in the soft, scented air. Flowers still bloomed, even in these months of autumn, and the night birds still chirped their sleepy calls. He closed his eyes, holding the memory against whatever challenges the next day might bring. Perhaps that was what made him miss the first flicker of torches from behind him.

"Damnation!"

"Sh-h-h-h!"

"Roses got thorns."

"Hush!"

The mumbled comments, added to the shuffle of boots, jerked Jonathan from his reverie. Turning from the sunset toward the other end of the piazza, he was almost blinded by blazing torches carried by indistinct figures robed in dark clothing. He moved toward the door, open to catch the night breezes. He had left Susan sitting near the door with her tatting, and his first instinct was to protect her from whatever this invasion portended. But he was not quick enough to move back into the house.

"Grenville?"

The challenging voice froze his movements, his hand still on the latch. He eased the door closer to the frame as he turned to face the group of men now stomping up the gentlemen's staircase. At the top, they stopped. "You Grenville?" the same voice asked again.

"I'm Jonathan Grenville, yes. What do you want with me?"

The ringleader took a single step onto the piazza. "We don't want you. We want your nigger."

"There are no Negroes here."

"So you say. That's not what we hear."

"Who are you? Why do you come in darkness with your faces covered? I am an honest man, and I expect others to be honest as well. Identify yourselves, and then we can talk."

"Our disguises are for our own protection. There are those who would prevent honest Southern gentlemen from doing everything they can to protect their families, their state, and their heritage. We hide our faces until we know the people we are talking to are not scalawags, carpetbaggers, Yankees, or nigger-lovers. Do you fall into any of those categories, Mr. Grenville?"

Jonathan tried his best not to react to the question. Truth be told, he thought to himself, I probably fit into all four groups. "You are Klansmen, then." It was a statement, not a question.

"Ah, you have heard of the noble Ku Klux Klan, I see. Why is a fine, upstanding Southern gentleman like yourself not one of us?"

Jonathan refused to be baited. "I've heard of you, but I didn't know you were active in South Carolina. We've never needed your kind of interference to manage our affairs. I repeat—What do you want with me?"

"We're looking for Hector Moreau. Recognize the name, do you?"

"There's no one else here, except for my family. We hire a woman to help with the cleaning and the children, but she goes to her own home every evening."

"We're not after a housemaid. We want Hector Moreau. He's a fugitive from justice, and we understand he might be heading here to seek your protection. You do know him, although by his former name—Hector Gresham." It, too, was a statement, not a question.

"Yes, I know Mr. Gresham, but I haven't seen him in over a year, and I was not aware he had changed his name . . . He has never been a criminal, and he's certainly not my . . . 'nigger.'"

"Used to be your slave, didn't he? That's what we've been told."

"Long before the war, yes. But I freed him, and he moved his family far south from here to start a new life."

"Sure. Moved south to cause more trouble, more likely."

"No, Hector's not the type to cause trouble. Surely you have the wrong man."

"Didn't you own a plantation on Edisto Island?"

"Yes, but—"

"And that's where he went—to join his father-in-law in stealing your property from you."

"You're wrong. His father-in-law, Thomas, purchased a piece of our land at the end of the war, as General Sherman's Field Order #15 provided, and Hector went to help him turn it into a proper farm. They bought the property fairly. You have the story confused."

"No, you are the one who is behind the times, Grenville. South Carolina no longer recognizes anything that damnable Sherman had to say. General Howard came to Edisto last October at the order of President Johnson and told the slaves they had to give their land back to its former owners. In February, agents of the Freedmen's Bureau arrived to assure the peaceful transfer of land, only to find a bunch of sullen, defiant niggers standing their ground, armed with sticks and hoes. Your fellow Thomas was one of the ringleaders, until federal troops forcibly removed the protesters. Thomas and some of his lot armed themselves and declared they would die before they surrendered their land. So some of them did."

A chuckle came from somewhere in the darkness. "Served them right, too, those damned niggers."

Jonathan felt a chill ripple across his back, and although this was a conversation he certainly did not want to have, he could not help but ask, "You say you're looking for Hector, so he was not one of those involved in the incident?"

"No, but that don't say much about what'll happen to him when we catch up with him. He's made his own brand of trouble."

Another chuckle responded, "String him up, I say. Ain't fit to live."

The ringleader held up a hand to quiet his followers and then turned back to Jonathan. "So you haven't seen him?"

"No."

"Well, keep your eyes on the lookout. He's bound to turn up here sooner or later, and when he does . . ." The statement trailed off but left no doubt as to the threat it proffered. "We'll be back, Grenville. We're not through with him . . . or with you."

Jonathan found he could not move as he watched this small band of troublemakers move down the street. They kept to the shadows and peered furtively into empty yards. Then they turned a corner and were gone. Jonathan felt the terror drain from his body, only to realize he was trembling and sweating at the same time. *I can't let Susan see me like this,* he thought. *I must calm down, or I will frighten her beyond reason.* He drew several deep breaths and tried to stretch his muscles.

He froze again as another dark figure emerged from the shrubbery and climbed the stairs. This man had no torch, yet he moved surefooted across the piazza. "You may not be ready to believe this, Mr. Grenville, but I am your friend." He spoke in falsetto, making his voice unidentifiable.

"Do I know you?"

"You've seen me many a time. If you saw my face, you would know me."

"Then take off the mask and reveal yourself."

"I cannot do that. I took a solemn oath to keep my identity a secret from all with whom I have Klan dealings. We don't even know the others in the Klan. That's for our own protection. We are strangers, but we move with a single purpose—to rescue the South from the horrible injustices that have been committed against her."

"There was no injustice. The South started the war by seceding and pursued it long after all hope of victory was lost. The bloodshed of those horrible years must rest on your own shoulders."

"This is not an argument I want to have with you. I like you. I know you to be a good man. I know how many students have profited from their time in your classroom. But I know more about you than that. You are a Yankee—born, raised, and educated in Massachusetts, of all places."

"I've never denied it."

"Some would call you a carpetbagger, although I wouldn't. Still, you came down here to make your living by teaching our young men, and then, as I recall, you lost your teaching job because you taught them some of your abolitionist views. You hoped to change our attitudes and our business practices to suit yourself. You married a young Southern belle to get your greedy hands on her inherited property."

"See here! I had no such . . ."

"I know. I wouldn't say that, but some will, and those who do will call you a carpetbagger. Others—those who believe you once made an honest attempt to learn the ways of the South—will label you a scalawag."

"Which is, according to your definition?"

"A scalawag is a Southerner who turns against his own land and traditions. You have to admit you—"

"I have to admit nothing. I am a simple man only trying to live a quiet life here in my wife's ancestral home. I am not a political creature. I vote as a civic duty but not as an outspoken advocate of one party or another. I do not meddle with such things. Why will you not leave me alone?"

"Because you do not yet understand the gravity of your position. And as your friend, I want to help you to do that."

"You have a strange way of showing friendship."

"This is the only way I have. But I pray you will listen to me further. The Klansmen who were here tonight also call you a nigger-lover. The story of you freeing your slaves on the night of the Great Fire is well-known. A certain judge who helped draw up the formal emancipation papers for you now moves with us. He will speak against you, if it should ever come to that."

"Why should it ever come up? I have done nothing wrong, while you—you have invaded my property and brought threats against me and my family. You have come under cover of darkness and in disguise. I challenge you once again to stand and reveal yourself if you are so sure of the rightness of your cause."

"And I have told you I will not do that. Ever. I may never have another chance to speak to you so freely. I'm risking punishment as it is. But as I told you, I am your friend, and I would like to see you avoid further difficulty with the Klan. I urge you to take this warning to heart—if Hector Moreau comes to you for protection, you must turn him over to the authorities. If you do not, the Klan will come after him with a rope. And then, my friend—and then—they will come after you. Take care!" With the same light-footed step that marked his arrival, he moved down the piazza stairs and was lost into the darkness.

Still stunned by this turn of events, Jonathan moved to the door, determined only to reclaim the safety of his home. As he closed the door behind him and dropped the heavy safety bar, he heard Susan's voice, as if from a far distance.

She stood in the doorway to the dining room, down the hall from the twin parlors that flanked the front door. In the flickering gaslight, her eyes were huge, and her hands cupped her cheeks as if to hold herself together. "Jonathan?"

"Everything's all right, Susan. You don't need to fret yourself."

She shook her head. "No, you don't understand. They're here."

"Who's here? That unruly mob has gone on their way. I'm sorry if you heard part of their accusations, but they're gone now."

"No, not them. Him. Hector's here—and Sarah. They're belowstairs right now. What are we going to do?"

Chapter 2

Welcome Home

October 1867

Jonathan stared at his wife. Most of the time, he was sure he knew her well, but now and then she mystified him. "They're here? Since when? What are you talking about?"

Susan shook her head and touched her lips to hush him. Nodding toward the dining room, she led the way to a pocket door in the far wall. It slid open to reveal a steep stairway leading down to the old warming kitchen. She indicated he should precede her, and then she closed the door behind them.

At the foot of the stairs, Jonathan looked around with some curiosity. This was a part of the house he almost never entered. He knew Susan now cooked their meals down here, but he usually saw only the finished dishes when she and the girls carried them up to the dining room. A huge fireplace dominated the far wall, its opening bristling with hooks for pots and skewers for holding roasting meats. At this time of night, the fire had been banked, so that the hot coals glowed only at their edges. The sides of the room featured shelves and cupboards, including an elaborate pie-safe, its door decorated with screening and fancy scrollwork designed to discourage pests from investigating dessert. And in the middle of the room stood a great slab of scoured wood. The tabletop was almost white except for its ridges, and it showed several long gashes, as if someone had taken an axe to it. Distracted by its unexpected appearance, he asked, "Do we need to replace this work area?"

"What? Why would you ask that?"

"Well, look at it. It's gouged and splintered, and someone's been hacking at it."

"Splinters happen when you make scrapple."

Now it was Jonathan's turn to ask, "What?"

"Scrapple, dear. You know, that delectable fried mixture you enjoy with your breakfast? You've never seen anything but the end result. Scrapple starts with a whole raw pig's head, and to remove the nasty bits, one has to take an axe to the top of the skull. But pig heads being what they are, they start to slither across the table when the axe hits them. The worktable tends to get the worst of it."

It was a bizarre image, and Jonathan shook his head to dislodge it from his memory. "Forget I asked. But where are Hector and Sarah? I thought you said they were here."

"They're asleep. I bedded them down in one of the old storage rooms where we had several cots from the sleeping porch."

"They're asleep. Then why did you bring me down here?"

"I'm trying to tell you, dear, but you keep interrupting with strange questions."

"Proceed, please. I won't speak again."

"Well, it was around three o'clock this afternoon. I remember the time because the whistle blew for the daily departure of the mail ship in the harbor. It always announces it is leaving in case anyone has to run up with a last min—"

"Susan!"

"You promised not to interrupt."

"And you promised to get on with it!"

"As I was saying, it was around three, and I was tidying up the dining room and thinking about what dishes I would need for our evening meal. There was no one else in the house, so when I heard a door shut, I jumped, as you can imagine. I waited, listening, and then I could hear soft steps on the stairs. I was terrified. And a voice whispered my name. For a minute I thought it was Sarah, and then I remembered she was long gone."

"But it was?"

"Yes, but let me tell the story. I walked over close to the pocket door and whispered back, 'Is anyone there?' And Sarah answered, 'Yes, it's us.' They had slipped in through the door over there that leads out into the old slave yard. I usually leave it unlatched during the day because the children are in and out, and I often need to get water from the cistern for one chore or another.

"Oh, Jonathan, you should have seen them! They were bedraggled, their clothes ripped and worn through in spots. They were pale, their eyes red-rimmed, their hair wild, and both were completely caked in mud—not just mud, but that nasty pluff mud that smells so bad."

"The pluff mud whose aroma you once told me always reminded you of home?"

"Well, yes, but not when someone has been bogging around in it. They said they had been traveling during the day but hiding out in the marshes at night to avoid being captured."

"Did they say why they were on foot instead of driving here in the wagon we furnished them when they left?"

"No. And I didn't ask, either. I figured no one gets himself into such a condition by choice. Their clothes were beyond salvage, so I fetched them some old things from up-stairs. Sarah is so frail that one of my housedresses hung on her, until I tied an apron around her tiny waist. And Hector fit into a shirt and trousers from our Johnny's college days. They both needed shoes, too. The soles were falling right off the ones they were wearing. Then I helped Hector carry their old things out on the end of a stick and add them to our rubbish heap. Once they finish drying, they'll burn nicely.

"They were starving, too. They didn't say so, but Sarah's eyes kept wandering toward the pot bubbling on the stove. I served them a couple of heaping bowls of stew and the rest of last night's cornbread, and they practical-ly attacked it. And once they were warm and fed, they started to doze off, sitting there at the kitchen table. I told them explanations could wait and showed them where the old cots and blankets were kept. They've been asleep ever since."

"They were right here—asleep beneath our feet—and you didn't think to mention it all through dinner? When, pray tell, were you going to tell me? Or were you planning to keep them hidden away for your own personal . . ."

"I planned to tell you as soon as you came back in from the piazza. I know you enjoy having a peaceful time to yourself. But then those horrible men with their torches showed up, and . . ."

"So you saw?"

"Yes, and I heard part of what they had to say, too. Their lights drew my attention, so I peeked out from behind the parlor draperies. But when they mentioned Hector, I drew back from the window and went to make sure the pocket door was closed. I didn't want Hector coming upstairs and walking right into their arms!"

"I should think not. But we can't keep these people hidden away in a storeroom, for heaven's sake. Go wake them up so we can find out what this is about."

"No, Jonathan, please. They're exhausted, and you're upset because of the visit of those thugs. Let it rest until morning, and then we can sit down and start to figure out what's going on."

"There's no time in the mornings around here," Jonathan protested.

"Tomorrow is Saturday, dear. You don't have to go to work, and the children will be off on adventures of their own. It's the perfect time. It's never wise to deal with a crisis when everyone is exhausted."

"But what if they take off again in the middle of the night?"

"They won't be able to."

"Why not?"

"I'm going to steal their new shoes!"

"Sometimes, Susan, you are absolutely incorrigible."

Later, Susan woke to find Jonathan sitting on the edge of the bed. After watching him for a few moments, she whispered, "Are you all right?"

"No, but I didn't mean to wake you."

"What's wrong?"

"I'm worried about this Hector situation, but I'm not sure what disturbs me most. I hate to think he's in trouble, but if he is, I don't know what I can do about it. As I told the Klansmen, he's not a slave any more, and he doesn't belong to me."

"Yet he came to you."

"Yes, he did, but why? I have no rights or power over his behavior."

"Ah, but you do, Jonathan. Look—in some societies, if you save a man's life, he becomes your responsibility from then on."

"That's the opposite of what's going on here. When he was a slave, we assumed responsibility for him. We fed him, we clothed him, we housed him, and we controlled his actions. But then we freed the man. By doing so, we made him responsible for his own life. Apparently, he has even changed his name in order to distance himself from his past—a past which includes us, by the way."

"And when he was in trouble, he came back—and I fed him and clothed him and gave him a place to sleep. Why? Because he is still my responsibility. My family made him a slave. I have no right to say, 'Go away. You don't belong here any more.'"

"I think you took him in because he is also family— because he is married to your cousin, a black woman with whom you share a grandfather."

"Yes, as far as I'm concerned, that's probably true, but it goes deeper. There are some relationships you can never change."

"Family ties? Yes, of course. You still see Johnny as your little boy, and I'll be Charlotte's Papa until the day I die. But slavery is different."

"Is it? This afternoon, Hector was still calling me Miz Susan, and so was Sarah, just like the old days. We'll still be their owners, and they will still think of themselves as our slaves. You can't make a relationship go away with a piece of paper that says it's no longer so."

"Why not? Couples separate. In some states, husbands become ex-husbands, and all it takes is a piece of paper."

"But the bond—once it is forged, it's not easily broken. Emotions don't pay attention to pieces of paper, and neither do the habits of a lifetime."

Jonathan pounded his pillow in frustration. "I don't want to be responsible for him. There—I've said it. I argued slavery was wrong, but perhaps what I really meant was I did not like what it did to me. It placed the weight of those lives upon my shoulders, and I knew I was not strong enough to bear the burden. I didn't like it. I wanted them to go away. I still want them to go away and quit interfering in our lives. I don't want the Ku Klux Klan paying me visits whenever a former slave does something they don't like. I want to be free. Free of the burden. Free of the responsibility."

"So you see yourself as somehow enslaved by it? How ironic!"

Jonathan stared at Susan with something close to hatred blazing in his eyes. Oh, he loved her, but he hated her, too, for turning him into the kind of man he never wanted to become—a Southern slave owner. And he hated her for knowing, as he had not, that the condition was an incurable one and for understanding that once you claimed ownership over another human being, he became yours forever.

Chapter 3

Hector's Tale

October 1867

onathan rolled over in the gloomy half-light of dawn and peered at his pocket watch propped up on the bedside table. Already 7:30? It couldn't be. He felt as if he hadn't slept more than an hour or so. He stretched out both arms and reacted with a start when he encountered another sleeping lump on the far side of the bed.

Susan stretched and glared at him. "What? You're ready to get up so early? It's still dark."

"Actually it's late, and I thought I smelled coffee."

She sniffed, paused, and then grinned. "You're right. It's coffee, and frying sausage, too, if I'm not mistaken."

"But you're still here."

"And luxuriating in the realization Sarah must have the kitchen well in hand. How lovely to have her home."

"Well, there is that to be grateful for. But from the way you described them last night, I'm still surprised she's up and about."

"I'm guessing it's a real treat for her to be back in a well-equipped kitchen with ample food supplies. They've been living in the rough for a long time. Come on, let's get dressed and go see what she has waiting for us. The children are going to be excited to see her, too. We're maybe missing out on a family reunion."

"The children! I'd forgotten . . ."

"Forgotten we have children? With the sounds of all those running feet in the house?"

"No, of course not, but I'd forgotten that having them aware Hector and Sarah are here may be a problem. Maybe we should have taken steps to keep them hidden. One careless word from a child and we could have the Klan pounding on our front door again."

"We'll have to trust them to keep a secret. Anyway, it's too late now. Once they get a whiff of this breakfast, there will be no hiding the truth. They know I don't cook like that on Saturdays."

In the dining room, their four youngest children were already milling about the sideboard, exclaiming over the sight and smell of freshly baked biscuits, thick sausage patties and more sausage crumbles swimming in a creamy peppered gravy, along with shimmering fried eggs and a buttery pan of grits. "Look, Mama!" Jamey cried when he spotted her. "It's a real breakfast!"

"And Sarah's back, too. Did you know?" Becca's eyes looked suspiciously wet. "Oh, how I've missed her."

"Yes, we knew." Susan ruffled the hair of her youngest daughter. "They arrived late, and we thought it would be fun to surprise you." Jonathan frowned at her for telling a fib, but she shook him off.

"You said 'they.'" Mary Sue was watching her parents carefully. "Is Hector with her?"

"Dat he be!" a voice boomed from the doorway.

"Hector!" Robbie was usually the quietest of the Grenville children, especially now that his voice was beginning to crack, but he might have been eight years old again as he threw himself across the room to wrap his arms around the big man's waist.

"Whoa! Hold on a second, I's got muh hands full uh jam an stuff. An you bin grow lak uh weed!" Laughing, he handed the jam pots to Susan and grasped the twelve-year-old by the shoulders. "You be lookin good, boy!"

Robbie flushed with pleasure but found himself tongue-tied, not knowing what to say.

Susan took the chance to go to the door and call down the stairs. "Sarah? Breakfast looks wonderful, but we're not going to eat it without you. Quit fussing in the kitchen, and come up and join us. There's enough food already for a family twice this size."

As they filled their plates and settled around the table, a bolt of lightning flashed and a sharp clap of thunder shook the window panes. "Oh!" Susan exclaimed. "It's raining, isn't it? I was so drawn by the inviting aromas of breakfast I never looked outside. So that's why it still felt dark when we woke up," she remarked to Jonathan.

"Yes'm," Hector said. "Some shrimp fishers we run into yesterday, dey say dere be a late hurricane lurkin off de coast. It probly gwine rain all day and all night."

"Well, I can't think of any group of people I'd rather be penned up with in a storm than all of you."

"But, Mama. Me and Robbie was gonna go downtown today and meet up with some of the other kids. What'll we do all day?" Jamey glared at the window, as if his personal displeasure could make the rain stop.

"'Robbie and I were' . . ." Susan corrected automatically. "Actually, I have an idea. Your father and I have some business to take care of with Sarah and Hector, and the details and paperwork would bore you to death. But . . . remember when we first moved back here? You begged to be allowed up in the attic. Instead, I locked the door and told you there would be no explorations up there until we were well-settled with everything in the lower house. Are you still curious as to what your Grandmother Dubois has hidden away?"

"I remember she told us your old toys were up there and lots of stuff from the family history, too. I'd love to get into it," Becca said. "And Mary Sue, you would, too, even if you do think you're all grown up, now that you're seventeen."

"Dolls and books?" Robbie looked doubtful.

"Don't you remember the Christmas early in the war, when Grandma found our gifts up in the attic? That's where your telescope came from, Robbie, and the great ceremonial sword she gave Johnny."

Now Mary Sue was excited, too. "Come on, let's go see what we can find!"

"Mary Sue? I'm counting on you to make sure nothing gets accidentally thrown out. You might want to designate some piles—one for letters and family papers, one for old clothes, one for books—that sort of thing. Here—take the key and have fun."

As the sound of pounding feet died away, Jonathan looked at his wife with a slow smile. "You, my dear, are brilliant."

"I know. That's why you married me."

⁓

"No," Jonathan said as Sarah began to clear the table. "Leave the dishes be. There are more important matters afoot, and we need to talk while the children are out of earshot. I am, of course, delighted to see you both. However, last evening while you were asleep, I had a disturbing visit from the Ku Klux Klan. They were looking for you, and I'd like to know why."

"Oh, Massa Jonathan. I'm sorry dey disturbed you. I dint mean to bring trouble to your door."

"I'm sure you didn't. And, please, quit using that old 'Massa' title. You sound like a slave, still. My name works quite nicely. Now, what's going on?"

"I'm getting to that, and I'll try to talk like you taught me. When I'm around most white folk, I can speak as well as they do, but somehow when I get back here, the old Gullah-speak I was raised with comes tumbling out of my mouth."

Jonathan and Susan exchanged glances, both knowing now they had been right about the continuing links between master and slave. "We haven't heard from you since you left here on your way to Edisto Island," Jonathan reminded Hector. "I want the whole story, however you choose to tell it."

"We expected to find Edisto a black island. People had told us the white folks were gone and their freed slaves had taken over the plantations, like General Sherman said."

"You're referring to his Field Order #15, which said no whites could live on the Sea Islands and former slaves had a right to buy plots of land up to 40 acres."

"Yes, and they were supposed to get help, too, and maybe a mule."

"So?"

"Well, as soon as we crossed the Edisto footbridge, we started seeing white folks, and some of them looked mighty familiar. We were headed to Harbor View Plantation to find Thomas, 'cause we knew he bought himself a big chunk of your land. But the fields around there looked empty and overgrown. When we stopped and asked a black fellow on the road where we could find Thomas, he stared at us and then took off running. We knew something was wrong."

"You'd been hearing from your father regularly, hadn't you, Sarah?" Susan asked.

"Yes, 'cause he knowed . . . knew . . . how to write. But we hadn't heard . . . not for a while." Her eyes began to leak tears, and she touched her husband's arm. "You tell them, Hector. I can't."

"All right. To make it short, we finally found somebody we knew, and the whole story came tumbling out. The former slaves were allowed to move back to Edisto at the end of the war, and the only white folks that went with them were a fellow named John Alden, who was to be the government supervisor, a Mr. Hunn to open a general store, and his daughter to be the schoolteacher. The freedmen went right to work. They fixed up the old cabins to live in till they could build better houses. They planted their food crops, and they built fences to show off the land they owned. Everybody was happy. Father Thomas claimed the house at Harbor View, and he was fixing it up to keep it nice, like you did.

"Then in October, when the crops were getting ripe, here came Mr. Howard from the Freedmen's Bureau, and he called everybody together. He said President Johnson had changed his mind about the land purchases. He wanted to put everything back the way it was before the war. He called his plan 'Presidential Reconstruction.' So he pardoned the Confederate soldiers, so long as they would say they were sorry for making all that trouble. And then he'd give them back their land. Mr. Howard said it was not his idea, but everybody had to move out and let the white folks come back. He said the black men could stay around and work for wages for their old owners, if they wanted to. But they would have to sign a contract to stay on the job for a year at a time and do whatever the white men said. The old owners have managed to get some laws passed that set up Black Codes we have to follow. The contracts are one part of that law.

"Well, everybody started yelling, 'No, no,' and the women started singing spirituals, and the meeting broke up. But afterward, the men elected four freedmen to speak for them, and they wrote a letter to Mr. Howard, arguing that if they lost their land they would not be free any longer. Then they worked quick to get more crops in the ground, so they could show they deserved to own the land because they were the ones taking care of it.

"In February, Mr. Howard came back with some other white men, and he said it was time to leave. But the freedmen stood in a line with their hoes and sticks in hand, and they said they were not going anywhere, because they did not have anywhere else to go. Father Thomas was the leader, which made me proud."

"Not me," Sarah whispered to Susan. "He should have known better than to challenge the white men."

"The next week, the white men came back again, and this time they had soldiers with them. They said everybody had to put down their hoes and go away, and Thomas said, 'Never!'"

Sarah was weeping openly now, and Susan held her hand, feeling helpless and ashamed at where the story was leading.

"Was Thomas armed?" Jonathan asked.

"Only with a hoe. But the soldiers aimed their guns at him anyway. And they shot him dead."

Jonathan slammed his palm on the table. Shoving his chair back, he stood and strode toward the door—then stopped, as if he realized that he, too, had nowhere to go.

Chapter 4

Good Plans Gone Awry

October 1867

Susan realized the room was close to bursting with pent-up emotions. To break the tension and give everyone a chance to compose themselves, she stood and began to clear the table. This time, Jonathan said nothing. Sarah blew her nose and then joined in carrying the dishes down to the kitchen, while Hector followed them with the heavier trays and serving pieces. No one had anything to say. They simply worked, as if putting things to rights in the dining room would somehow keep their world from shattering around them.

When Jonathan returned to his seat at the table, the others joined him without comment. He turned to Hector. "You still haven't explained why you and Sarah have been on the run, why you've changed your name, and why the Ku Klux Klan is after you."

Hector resumed his story, but took his time in answering those crucial questions. "After we got over the first shock of realizing Thomas was dead, we went to see Mr. Alden, the island overseer, to find out if there was any way we could claim Harbor View. He was polite and sympathetic, but not encouraging. He pointed out the new presidential rulings were designed to accomplish the opposite—to keep black men from being treated as citizens. That's what the Black Codes and the contracts they require are about."

"Did he tell you what is going to happen to the property?"

"Yeah, it's pretty clear. The only one who could claim it would be Mrs. Dubois, and she would have to come down to Edisto from Flat Rock, confess in a court of law that she had supported the Confederacy, and then apologize and ask for a pardon. If she did that—and I think we know she's not going to—she could get the plantation back, and everyone else now living on the acreage would have to move off. Then she could start hiring them back to work for her, provided they were willing to sign one of those Black Code contracts that recreate the conditions of slavery."

"And if she refused to act?"

"Then after a while, the land would be confiscated by the government and sold for back taxes, with the usual result—black men working the fields almost like slaves."

Jonathan had no further comments. He listened, shaking his head in disgust at the whole process.

"Mr. Alden did have a few suggestions," Hector added. "First, he said he thought Annie ought to be in school, but when Miss Hunn came by to test her, she was so impressed she suggested we send her to a school on St. Helena Island. Mr. Alden arranged to have some men row us over there to meet with a Miss Laura Towne, who runs the schools for black children in the area. She is a plain, dowdy-looking woman, but when she spoke, she was so warm and caring we forgot she isn't beautiful. She offered to let Annie stay with her until the end of the school term. Then, she said she might be able to hire her to teach in the lower grades of her school. So that meant Annie was settled, and she was excited about the books she was going to get to read.

"Next, he recommended we go by another name. Seems the name 'Thomas Gresham' has become something of a symbol for a rebellious slave, and he thought we would be wise to avoid being connected to him. I chose the name 'Moreau' because I remembered hearing about a decent white man who treated his slaves well back in Martinique. I wanted my new name to link me to my past but with a connection only I would understand.

"Then Mr. Alden said there was a fair and kindly government official in Beaufort—a General Rufus Saxton. He was head of the Freedmen's Bureau for a while till he and the president clashed over policy and he got himself fired. He's still in the Army, though, and nobody can much overrule him. He earned one of those Honor medals early in the war, and he's been in the Lowcountry ever since the Union Expedition arrived in Port Royal back in 1861."

"He's a Medal of Honor winner?"

"Yes, that's what it's called. So, anyway, we went down to Beaufort and knocked on his door, bold as you please. He invited us in, listened to the whole story—like I've been telling you—and promised to help in some way. He was impressed to find out I could read and write, and he said I had no business working the land—that educated Negroes were badly needed to help get the country straightened out. Then he took us down the street to meet a friend of his.

"We were surprised to find his friend was a black man. I wasn't expecting that. His name be—uh, was—Robert Smalls. I never heard of him, but I guess he's pretty famous. They say he stole a gunship from the rebels and turned it over to the Union Army back in 1862. That earned him a trip to Washington, D.C., and they gave him a reward, too. There was enough money to let him buy the big house on Prince Street where he was raised as a slave and, with what was left over, he opened a general store for freedmen right on the main street of Beaufort. That's where General Saxton took us. Mr. Smalls was a nice-looking young man, well-dressed and prosperous-looking. He explained that he was getting ready to run for political office."

"A black man?" Jonathan could not hide his surprise.

"Yes. Isn't that a wonder? He said he became a Republican because it was the party of Lincoln and because Republicans in the U.S. Congress passed the Fourteenth Amendment, which gave black men full citizenship. And if we're full citizens, we should get to vote and hold office, too. Smalls is the Republican candidate there in Beaufort for a seat in the South Carolina House of Representatives in the upcoming November election. He explained that black men far outnumbered the old southern Democrats around Beaufort, and if they all voted, he'd be sure to win. The upshot was he needed help with the paperwork in the store while he campaigned, and he also needed campaign helpers to talk to voters about supporting him. When he learned I was an educated Negro, he hired me on the spot. It wasn't gonna get Thomas's land back, but it meant that we could have a home and a steady income, and maybe be doing something important, too."

"It's an incredible story. Sounds like you had friends in high places, so how'd you end up in so much trouble?" Susan posed the question she knew was bothering Jonathan.

"I was out working the campaign late one evening. My job was to find Negroes who didn't know much about politics and convince them to vote for Mr. Smalls. But the Ku Klux Klan had other plans for me. They came out at dark, wearing hoods and carrying the torches they held close to my face so as to dazzle my eyes. They surrounded me in the street and started pushing closer and closer to me. They said it was bad for my health to be supporting a Republican candidate, and I should go home and quit campaigning. I said I couldn't do that because I believed Mr. Smalls would make a good representative.

"Then one fellow showed me he was carrying a noose. He held it up and asked if I knew what it was for. I didn't answer. So he came closer and stuck that noose right in my face and told me to take a good look because it was going to be what killed me. I was sure he was trying to get it over my head, so I shoved him away, not hard, but to let him know that he wasn't going to hang me without a fight.

"And then . . . I don't know what happened . . . it was dark . . . maybe he couldn't see where he was going because of that hood. He stumbled and tried to turn around. Then he fell forward, and he hit the side of his head on the corner of a tabby cement hitching post."

Susan heard Jonathan gasp, just as she herself drew a quick breath. "Did he . . . was he . . . ?"

"Dead? Yes, ma'am. He never twitched again." Hector sat staring at his clasped hands on the table. "I didn't mean to kill him, but I knew how it looked. I should have run right then, but I couldn't move. The Klansmen started shouting about murder, and that brought the local constable running. All those hoods disappeared like magic, and there I was, surrounded by middle-aged white men with a dead one at my feet. I suppose I was lucky the constable was there. He dragged me right off to jail before the others could take their revenge. At the jail, they asked me if I needed to notify anyone, and I sent a note off to Sarah to get help from General Saxton."

"You must have both been terrified."

"I know I was!" Sarah said. "I was afraid to go out, but I understood Hector needed me. I didn't remember where to find the general, so I walked over to Prince Street and told Mr. Smalls what had happened. He came out right away. He took me to find the general, and then the three of us went to the jail. I was so relieved to see Hector still alive that I started crying and couldn't stop."

"You did exactly what I needed you to do," Hector assured her. "My two friends bailed me out with their own money, and then we went back to Saxton's office because it was on Army property, and we knew the Klansmen couldn't follow us there. But the news wasn't good. Everybody knows that in South Carolina, black men don't get trials—they get ropes. Saxton's advice was to run, right then, without stopping to pack our things or make any plans—just run for our lives."

"How did he expect you to survive?"

"Well, Mr. Smalls went out and came back with some fake papers. I still have them next to my heart in this waterproof case. One of them says my name is Jacob Rivers and my wife's name is Betsy. I'm a hostler for a white man named Toby Conway, and I'm making a round trip to Tennessee to see about buying some horses for my master. The other one says our names are Pete and Jenny Jones. I'm a bricklayer under contract to a fellow named Ralph Masters from Savannah, and he's sending me to Virginia to help his brother build a house. Both papers look legal. They meet the requirements of the Black Codes. Hostlers and bricklayers are other names for slaves, I suppose."

"Have you used either of them?"

"Not yet. Nobody's asked for my papers. But either one of them should keep me from getting arrested for vagrancy, which is what usually happens if a black man is out in public without a contract. Anyway, we've been careful not to run afoul of the authorities. When we're passing through towns, we move about in broad daylight, because that's when other freedmen are taking care of their business. In the countryside, we slip through the marshes at night, trusting the dark to hide us. That's why we smelled so bad when we arrived."

Jonathan still looked worried. "The Klan knew you were headed here. This is the first place they looked."

"Which is why we're not staying any longer than necessary. We'll be gone by tomorrow's dawn, I hope. I won't risk going today because no honest man would be out in such a deluge, but we'll leave as soon as this rain lets up a bit."

"But where will you go?"

"We're heading for Aiken first. We want to see our son, Eli, and make sure he's taken care of. I have some cash here, too," he said, tapping the waterproof case. "My plan is to buy train tickets and ride to Aiken in style. That's the last place the KKK will think to look for us. And then? We head west and keep going until we get beyond the old slave states of the Confederacy. I'm thinking Kansas or Missouri or maybe even further. We'll mark out a homestead somewhere where there's no old owner waiting to pop up and drive us off."

"What can I do to help you?"

"A little fib wouldn't hurt. I don't want anyone harassing you on my account. If somebody asks, you can tell them we're headed to Louisiana or someplace like that, while we head in another direction."

"Do you think that will work?"

"Of course it will. Most Klansmen aren't very intelligent. They're pathetic little men trying to make themselves feel important. And to deal with them, you have to be smarter than they are—which isn't that hard."

Jonathan still did not look convinced. "One thing we've been worried about—none of our children would hurt either of you, but they may not understand the importance of keeping your visit a secret."

"Then we lie to them, too, Jonathan," Susan said. "We tell the children the same story we tell the Klan. If they keep the secret, all's good. If they forget and let the secret out, no harm done."

"Except that you will have lied to them."

"It won't be the first time. And when this is over and we can talk about it openly, they'll understand."

Chapter 5

Those Left Behind

October 1867

Susan awoke slowly, one sense at a time. The sound of chirping outside her window was a surprise. She had fallen asleep to the pounding of rain on the roof and the gushes of water in the corner drain spouts. Now all was quiet except for the birds. She breathed deeply and caught the scent of damp ground and crushed foliage. It, too, was soothingly fresh, but she sniffed curiously, remembering the day before, when the morning air had been fragrant with the scents of coffee and sausage biscuits. She opened one eye and then closed it quickly, as bright sunlight slipped through the crack in the curtains and announced that morning was well underway.

She rolled toward the center of the bed and took pleasure in seeing that Jonathan, too, was still asleep. Gently, she reached for his hand and entwined her fingers with his. From long habit, he turned his palm to meet hers, and for several satisfying minutes they lay joined together in that simple gesture. Jonathan smiled sleepily and whispered, "Good morning, Slugabed."

She squeezed his hand and then shook herself loose. "It's late. Sarah and Hector will be wanting to get on their way."

"And so they have. Hours ago."

"What?" Susan pushed herself into a sitting position against the pillows. "They're gone? Already? Without even saying their good-byes?"

"Sarah said to tell you she knew it would be too painful to say good-bye again."

"You were up? Why didn't you wake me?"

"I told you. They didn't want to make an affair of their departure. They slipped out the back way around four o'clock, when even the most diligent watchmen have given up their posts in anticipation of the coming dawn. They plan to catch the train to Aiken at one of the first stops up the way from the central station, so they needed a head start."

"But . . ."

"They'll be fine, Susan. Hector knows exactly what he is doing. He's planned every step, and he needs no advice from you or from me."

"But . . . do they have enough money? Are they going to be able to ride the train as passengers, or—"

"The less we know, the less the danger to them. We can't reveal their plans if we have not been made privy to them.

When it's safe for them to do so, they will get word to us. Until then, I'm afraid we'll have to have faith in their own good judgment. Now, Mrs. Grenville, may I remind you that you are back to cooking breakfast this morning?"

"You men! All you ever think about are your stomachs."

"You might say the same about your ever-hungry growing children. Think you can come up with something to fill them?"

"Well, chances are it won't be much beyond porridge," Susan grumbled as she swung her feet from under the covers. "But you don't get off scot-free, my fine pompous husband. I'll do the cooking. You get to explain to the children why Sarah and Hector are no longer here without revealing anything about their plans."

"Are we still agreed that they are headed toward Louisiana?"

"It's as good a story as any. But make sure you don't mention Aiken or a visit with Eli."

❧

Downstairs, the children were already milling about but looking more subdued than usual. Susan forced herself to smile as she headed toward the stairs and the kitchen below. "Breakfast will be ready in a few minutes," she promised. "Mary Sue, you could help by setting the table."

Jonathan also tried to put on a relaxed expression, but because he had nothing to occupy his time, he was less successful.

Jamey, as usual, was oblivious to the underlying tension, but both Mary Sue and Robbie watched their father to see if he would break the uncomfortable silence. After a few moments, Robbie cleared his throat and asked, "Where are Hector and Sarah? Why aren't they here?"

"Uh, they . . . they had to leave early this morning. They said to say good-bye."

"No, they wouldn't do that! Something's wrong, isn't it?" Robbie's voice cracked, and he felt his eyes start to water.

"Nothing's wrong, Robbie. They were in a hurry to be on their way."

"Where were they going?"

"They're heading for New Orleans, I believe, to get a fresh start."

"I don't believe you!"

Jonathan's anger flared. "Are you questioning me?"

"No, sir, but . . ."

"But what?"

"I . . . I thought Hector would have wanted to see me before he left. And why didn't he tell me he was going that far away?"

"He had other things on his mind."

"That's what I meant. I could tell yesterday something was bothering him. What is it?"

"Sarah was acting funny yesterday, too," Becca added. "If they're in trouble, shouldn't they be here where you could help them?"

Jonathan caught his breath. "Sometimes, Robbie, grown-ups have to deal with things they don't want to discuss with children. This is one of those times."

Mary Sue took her younger sister by the elbow and turned her toward the china cabinet. "Get me the silverware, Becca."

Jonathan threw her a grateful glance and then headed for the back porch, where he could escape the children and their probing questions.

By the time Susan reappeared with a bowl of porridge and a platter of badly burned toast, the children had lost their appetites. They sat at their accustomed places at the table with downcast eyes and pouting lips. "I know it's not Sarah's cooking, but you could be polite enough to try a few bites," Susan said.

"I'm not hungry." Robbie pushed his chair back from the table. "May I be excused, please?"

"Me, too!" Jamey was quick to mimic his brother, although he grabbed a slice of toast as he departed.

Becca sat frozen, tears seeping from the corners of her eyes. She looked at her mother, lips parted like a little baby bird's beak, until Susan took pity on her and nodded in the direction of the door.

"The porridge tastes really good," Mary Sue said, reaching over to pat her mother's hand. "It's been such a strange weekend that none of us is quite sure what has happened."

"I'm sorry about that. Your father and I have been upset, too. And we do realize we have put you children through a great deal of upheaval because of the war and the disasters we have experienced. I hoped that would all be behind us once we returned to Charleston, but trouble seems to have a habit of following us. I wish—"

"I wish you'd recognize that I am no longer one of your 'children.' I'm almost eighteen, older than Charlotte was when she married. I wish you'd treat me as an adult. Isn't there something I can do to help with . . . with whatever is going on?"

"I'm afraid there's nothing anyone can do." Susan shook her head. "Look, Mary Sue, I can tell you only this much—Hector and Sarah have managed to land in a bit of a pickle. They've angered the Ku Klux Klan, who would like nothing better than to corner a couple of freed slaves and make an example of them. So they are on the run. All we can do is make sure that we don't inadvertently do or say anything to help the Klan catch up with them."

"I'm sure none of us would do that."

"Not intentionally, no, of course you wouldn't. But the surest way to make certain is to keep us in the dark so that we don't accidentally say something that gives them away. If it's any consolation to you, I didn't see them leave this morning, either."

"Really? Sarah's your cousin. Didn't she tell you . . . ?"

"No, and I wouldn't have wanted her to do so. Someday, when this turmoil has settled down, then perhaps we can be a family again. For now, no."

Susan stood and held out her arms to her daughter. They hugged briefly and smiled at one another, both comforted by the quiet understanding that passed between them.

"Let me handle the washing up," Mary Sue volunteered. "You can relax a bit."

"No. That's sweet of you, but I'm more in control if I stay busy. Why don't we do the dishes together?"

❦

Mother and daughter bustled about in the warming kitchen in companionable silence for a while. Then Mary Sue returned the kettle to the stove. "Maybe a cup of tea?" she asked. "There's something else I'd like to discuss with you."

"Another problem?" Susan was instantly on guard.

"No, not a problem, but something I don't understand. You remember when you sent us packing up to the attic to get rid of us?"

"It was obvious, was it?"

"To me it was, although I don't think the others noticed. Anyhow, while the children were playing dress-up, I found an old journal and settled into a corner to read it."

"A journal? Whose?"

"Your grandfather's, I think. 'Pierre Antoine Dubois' is the name inside the cover. The date of the first entry is January 1, 1786. He starts by musing over the fact that the Revolution has been over for more than two years, but the problems that caused the war with England have not found a satisfactory solution. I was struck by the coincidence. His comments could have been written today. Here we are after another great war has wracked this country, and again, more than two years after peace has been declared, the problems of slavery have not lessened."

Susan hesitated for a moment with her lower lip caught between her teeth. "I think you have put your finger on a universal human failing. Whenever people have a problem, they assume they can solve it by forcing others to change. You see it at all levels, whether it's a parent spanking a wayward child or a country declaring war on its neighbor. Unfortunately, violence seldom works."

Mary Sue smiled at her mother's wisdom. "Then, what does?"

"Love, perhaps. No—love, most surely."

"I'm not certain Pierre Antoine would agree with you—at least not about the War for Independence, and probably not about his later problems, either." Mary Sue frowned.

"Which were . . . ?"

"Love itself. Oh, I know, the family seldom discusses the fact that you and Sarah share a grandfather. But your grandfather's journal shows him to have been a deeply tormented man, and I don't understand why he did what he did."

"Why he fathered a child with a slave woman?"

"No, that's easy to explain, and I know many slave owners did the same thing. Obviously, that's why there are so many light-skinned Negroes. But this man says he acted out of love, not lust."

"Really? Are you surprised?" Susan cocked an eyebrow at her daughter.

"Well, yes, I guess I am, because she was a slave, after all."

"I suspect you are judging Pierre by your own attitudes, which isn't really fair. You need to see him through the eyes of his own time. But then, I'm judging you, too, aren't I?"

"Since you haven't read the journal, you probably can't explain it. Maybe we should drop this discussion. We've had enough crises for one weekend." Mary Sue's lips tightened in a gesture so like her father that Susan caught her breath.

"No, wait, I don't want to drop it. You're dealing with an important question. But I also think you are right. Why don't you bring me the journal and give me time to read it? Then I'll be better able to understand what's bothering you."

❦

Later that afternoon, Susan forced herself to pick up the tattered journal her daughter had left for her on top of the melodeon. She paged through it, noting how quickly the years seemed to pass when only their crucial moments were committed to paper. From long habit, Susan turned to the back of the journal first, wanting to know what happened before she read the whole story. The date on the last entry was October 22, 1826:

This has been the most beautiful and most bitter day of my life. Today I marked my 70th year by taking my family to worship at the newly rebuilt Prince William's

Parish Church in Sheldon, South Carolina. The original church, which served all the Lowcountry in those colonial days, was born in 1756, the same year I was, and then it was destroyed by fire during our War for Independence in 1779. Now we have a glorious new church, built to resemble the old one in every aspect of its Greek Revival style, and we are to celebrate our birthdays together again.

The day was glorious—warm, sunny, but tinged with a hint of fall in the air that sends squirrels chattering to store their acorns and migratory birds to fill the sky with their flights to the south. As usual, we set out early in the morning to cover the 23-mile trip before the start of Sunday services. We were a procession of three— I, driving a lovely carriage for my wife and son; a second carriage for my elderly sister, her spinster daughter, and her personal slave, Ernestine, and Ernestine's son, Thomas (my son Thomas); and a wagon for our other slaves and all our accouterments, including baskets containing the food for our Sunday dinner on the lawn.

The services were everything one might have hoped for. The new harmonium filled the sanctuary with music. The sunlit stained glass painted ripples of color everywhere. Prayers of thanksgiving were deep and heartfelt, and the sermon inspiring.

Then came time for dinner on the lawn, and everything fell apart. My wife, Clothilde, was settling herself on the spread blanket when Thomas approached, *carrying a pitcher of lemonade. He tripped on a tree root (a frequent hazard in that grove of ancient oaks) and splashed Clothilde from head to toe. She screamed at him and leaped to her feet, much faster than she had decorously seated herself. "You wretched little bastard!" she screamed at him. "Get out of my sight, and tell your whore of a mother to keep you hidden from decent company from now on."*

The boy, now pale with fear, ran to his mother, who swathed him in her cloak and urged him away. I watched them leave the clearing and cross the road to the shady grove of pines where the carriages were waiting. I stood there, helpless, unable to deny the accusations Clothilde had hurled across the churchyard, unable to comfort the woman and boy I loved with all my heart, and unable to meet the eyes of my friends and neighbors who had watched the scene unfold.

I am a despicable man.

Those were the last words he wrote. They broke Susan's heart.

She remembered that elegant church from her own childhood. It reminded her of everything that had been most beautiful about the antebellum South. She wondered for a moment if those magnificent columns had survived the years better than her grandfather had. I shall have to ask Hector the next time I see him, she thought, before remembering he might be gone for good. With a sigh directed at the heartaches of the world, she turned back to read the rest of the story.

Chapter 6

Remembrances

By Monday morning, the Grenvilles' lives seemed to be getting back to normal. The younger children settled into their first-floor schoolroom with the tutor their father had hired to help them catch up with the lessons they had missed during the war. Their recitations were comforting because they could be trusted not to change. Jamey, of course, did his share of squirming under the necessity of sitting still, but both Robbie and Becca relaxed and opened their books with pleasure.

Mary Sue left for the short walk to her French teacher's house. Usually, she considered those lessons a waste of her time. French lessons were for debutantes and young ladies hoping to catch the eye of an eligible beau. She still hoped to devote her life to raising and training horses, exactly as her grandmother had suggested back before the war. Mary Sue had argued the only French she would need around a stable was a fair command of French profanities, but her parents had insisted on more traditional training. This morning, however, she was eager to resume her studies. There were many French phrases in her great-grandfather's journal she could not translate, and she was now even more curious to know his inner musings.

Jonathan dawdled over his breakfast, waiting for the children to leave before turning to Susan with husbandly concern. "How are you feeling? Are you settling down somewhat?"

"You mean, am I over my fears? No." Susan started to leave the room, unwilling to let him lecture her. Then, accepting the need to talk, she resumed her seat at the table. "I can't help but worry, Jonathan, even though I understand there is nothing I can do right now to help Sarah and Hector. I still worry that they'll be caught, and we won't even know."

"That's possible. I'm not going to deny it. But if the Klan was going to act against them, it would already have happened. Scary as they may seem, underneath their secretive ways, most of them are as Hector described them—pitiful little middle-aged white men trying to make themselves feel powerful. If they had caught Hector yesterday on the way to the train station, we would know it by now."

"What makes you so sure?"

"Because if the Klan had stopped their departure, they would have made sure that we knew. For men like that, there's no satisfaction in winning if no one hears about it. My greatest fear yesterday was that those damned hooded figures would reappear on our doorstep to gloat—maybe even to threaten to string Hector up before our eyes. But by this morning, I'll wager that they are back at their jobs, doing whatever busy work such people do to earn their livings. They don't have the time, nor the ability, to follow their targets halfway across the state."

"I hope you're correct. But you're still a target within their range, aren't you? What are you going to do?" She stared at him with fear in her eyes.

"I'm going to do my best to ignore them. Even if I'm guilty of everything they've accused me of doing, I can put on the appearance of innocence. That's my best protection. I'm headed off to work shortly. We're in the final stages of preparing the Holy Communion Church Institute Day School to open next month. Dr. Porter keeps us busy discussing curriculum and trying to figure out where to assign each of the four hundred little white Episcopalians whom he has accepted. Nothing I'll be doing for the next weeks can possibly interest the Klan, unless, perhaps, their own sons are among our new students."

"How ironic that would be! So there are to be no Negro children in your classes?"

"Dr. Porter would be eager to explain there are now ample educational opportunities for black children. He's worried the white children are the ones being shortchanged. I don't agree with him, but for the moment, the separate nature of

Porter's school is my best protection. So promise me you'll quit imagining the worst. Try to enjoy yourself today."

As she watched him leave, Susan sighed in relief, not even aware she had been holding her breath for fear of the next emotional upheaval. Now the house was hers, and from long habit she turned to music to soothe herself. Her new melodeon was a continuing source of pleasure, one that filled her private hours with its ability to release her emotions in melody. She settled onto the stool and let her fingers glide over the buttery rosewood finish of the cabinet. She brushed a few stray dust motes from the keys and then began the slow, rhythmic pumping of the foot pedals. As pressure built up in the pipes, she picked out a few experimental notes and then launched into the opening measures of her favorite hymn. Soon her entire body was swaying with the notes, and her mind gave over its worries to the comfort of the music.

By the time Mary Sue returned in midafternoon, Susan's optimistic take on life had been restored, and she had also had time to read the rest of the journal her grandfather had hidden away all those years ago. Once again, mother and daughter huddled over steaming cups of tea in the warming kitchen, where they could talk without fear of interruption.

"I've read most of the journal," Susan said. "It's an amazing tribute to a beloved woman."

"Oh, I agree. His journal entries about Ernestine are really moving. When he writes about her, you can tell how deeply in love he is. He talks about her beauty—how her skin is the color of coffee lightened by cream, how her features are finely chiseled, how gracefully she moves.

"In one entry, he describes how he first met her—or rather, the first time he recognized her as an individual rather than one of his slaves. Did you read that one? He was overseeing the cotton pickers, and he had been ignoring the complaints of those who were too hot or too tired. And then he heard someone singing—not the usual lament about the troubles of this life, but a simple song about the beauties of life. He sought the singer and discovered her working side by side with an old woman. She was filling her own basket, but also the old woman's basket, making sure that the woman's arthritic fingers would not suffer overmuch from the hard work.

"She wore a smile on her face and a twinkle in her eye, he says. And he says she had a kind word for everyone she met, including him. Once, he caught her stopping on the way home to play a game with some slave children, and he says she looked as young as they were. Really, Mother, he sounds absolutely besotted."

"Is that what you found so troubling?"

"Well, obviously, I am surprised at how happy he is and how miserable, at the same time. He is scathing in his descriptions of his wife, isn't he? He points up the contrasts—Ernestine was happy, but Clothilde was petulant. Ernestine was grateful for the smallest favor, while Clothilde was greedy for more. Ernestine was kind-hearted, yet Clothilde was meanspirited. When Ernestine gives birth to Thomas, he laments his inability to raise the child in his own household and to acknowledge him as his own son. He knows Clothilde will have no part of such an idea. He also worries that Clothilde is spoiling her own son, Georg, by indulging his tantrums and giving him everything he wants.

"He dreams of what it would be like to be married to Ernestine, raising the two boys as full brothers. And then he dismisses the idea as sheer fantasy. He does not think he could ever be free to marry her. That's what I can't understand. If he felt that strongly, why didn't he do it—send Clothilde away and marry the woman he loved?"

"My dear child, there was no way he could ever have done that. He couldn't easily do it even today, let alone a hundred years ago. You're old enough to remember what it was like around here when people learned that your father was supporting the idea of abolition before the war. He lost his job over that statement, and eventually we all had to learn how to fend for ourselves in a new location. Even now, he is beset by occasional accusations of 'nigger-lover' because he freed his slaves before the war was over.

"The years after the Revolutionary War, as you have noted, suffered as much turmoil as today's political conflicts, and the existence of slavery was a crucial issue even then. The issue of states' rights was a major sticking point in the efforts to come up with a constitution all the states would accept. Southerners understood that their whole economy depended on their ability to employ slave labor. Northerners, even then, pointed to the principle of all men being equal as a contradiction in a slave-based society. Southerners wanted to make sure the northern states would not pass a law to force the South to abolish slavery. That was the basis of the states' rights controversy. But they also wanted to be sure their slaves would not be encouraged by northern support to rise up against their masters."

"Oh, how silly! I can't imagine plantation owners being afraid of a slave uprising!"

"Well, they certainly were—and some still are, for that matter. It's a sign, I think, that deep down they realized slavery was wrong. When you know you've treated someone badly, you assume he hates you for it. And then you treat him even more harshly because he hates you."

"This all sounds farfetched. Are you saying your grandfather was afraid of his own slaves?"

"No, I didn't say that exactly, but it's more common than you would think. You've seen wealthy homes in Charleston with slave yards in the back. Most of them are surrounded by high windowless walls to keep slaves from communicating with neighboring slaves or from getting out and joining a mob of their fellows."

"But what has that to do with Pierre and Ernestine?"

"*Grand-père* would have forfeited both his social and his economic status if he had married a slave. Slave owners depended upon one another to keep all slaves in line. If one master had treated a Negro as an equal, it would have threatened the security of every other slave owner. He would have been cut off from any activity that exposed other plantation slaves to his workers—no visitations, no sharing of slaves, no joint shipments of cotton bales. It would have broken him and destroyed any chance of an inheritance for his white son. And for Ernestine, a mixed marriage would have meant losing all contact with her own people, whom she obviously loved. Could a slave woman become the mistress of the plantation without changing her relationship to the slaves she would have to supervise? Never! Her family and friends would have shunned her completely."

"But he was so miserable without Ernestine . . ."

"Yes, and he was definitely miserable with Clothilde. Theirs was an arranged marriage. She had arrived as part of a business deal—a stranger from Antigua, as I remember, the daughter of a businessman who wanted access to land in America." Susan smiled and shook her head as she remembered herself as a little girl facing that disapproving grandmother.

"I remember *Grand-mère* all too well. No one could ever please her. She would send us small gifts and demand thank-you letters written in her native French. Then she would send them back, marked up with our grammatical mistakes and demand they be rewritten correctly. She was a horror, but I'm sure that *Grand-père* felt responsible for her. He wouldn't turn her out with nowhere to go."

"But he and Ernestine loved one another."

"Yes, but while love may be the only way to end a conflict, sometimes it isn't enough."

"I still don't understand why he didn't . . ."

"Mary Sue, he did everything he could to make Ernestine's life safe and secure. In his will, he arranged for Ernestine to live with my parents. I remember her from the time I was a small child. She was lovely, even in her advancing age. She ran Mother's household for her, acting as a combination housekeeper and social secretary. She had her own quarters upstairs in this very house. She supervised the household slaves, kept track of Mother's social obligations, fussed over her wardrobe, and kept a kindly eye on us children. I don't know if she was happy—one can never know that—but I know she was protected and cherished by us all, right up to her death."

"Wouldn't it have been better if . . ."

"Who knows? Maybe, if they had had to live together, they would have learned to hate one another."

"Mother!"

"All right, I don't mean to make fun of the issue. But I think it best to recognize the good your great-grandfather did rather than criticize him for what he failed to do. He set an example by trying to keep his marriage intact."

Mary Sue was shaking her head in denial, but she was also starting to grin.

"Well, he didn't keep all of his vows, but most of them!"

"Go on, Mother. Anything else?"

"Something much more important, actually. He treated Ernestine and her son with a degree of love and respect that was almost unheard of in the post-Revolutionary South. And by doing so, he taught this family how to be what your father calls 'benevolent slave owners.' So far as I know, no Dubois slave was ever whipped or chained or deprived of his basic needs. No family was ever separated by having some member sold for profit. Slaves received plentiful supplies of food, serviceable new clothes, and sturdy housing. They were always allowed to hold their own religious services, celebrate holidays with time off, and rest when they were injured or ill.

"It was thanks to my grandfather that my father—his white son—learned to respect Thomas as his brother and trusted him to run the Edisto Island plantation. That's why Sarah and I were raised as cousins, with our family relationship known to all. And, although he might never admit it, it's one reason why your father was willing to marry into a slave-owning family. We were more respectable than most slave-owners, according to your father's Northern upbringing."

"I think I understand more now." Mary Sue looked thoughtful. "Do you think there will ever be a time when blacks and whites will marry without facing the kinds of problems that doomed Pierre's love for Ernestine?"

"I don't know. Not for a good long time, I'm afraid. Not in my lifetime—and perhaps not even in yours! Given the current political atmosphere, I'll be happy enough if the time comes when good people like Hector and Sarah can live their lives in peace, without being pursued by those who judge them solely by the color of their skin."

Chapter 7

Too Little, Too Late

December 1867

The letter arrived on a cold, foggy morning. The unfamiliar spidery handwriting and Flat Rock postmark warned Susan that bad news awaited her. For a few minutes, she let the letter lie unopened on the hallway table, while she tried to marshal the bitter emotions a mention of her mother always caused her. Then she grasped a letter opener and slashed the envelope.

> *My dear Cousin Susan,*
>
> *I hope this missive finds you and your family in good health. We are coping with the winter weather here as best we can, but it has brought a downturn in your mother's health. She has asked that we not contact you, but I feel it necessary to go against her wishes.*

Starting last month, Cousin Elizabeth began to suffer a series of small setbacks. They began with headaches and then progressed to short periods in which she would experience confusion or an inability to understand what was said to her. At times, she complained of vision loss in one eye. And most recently, she has had weakness on her left side and periods in which she slurs her words so badly that we cannot understand her. The difficulty always passes, but each time it seems to grow a little worse and to leave some small permanent damage. We persuaded her last week to visit our own Dr. Highsmith, and he has warned her she may be in imminent danger of having an attack of apoplexy.

I am sure that you will understand that Sister Maudy and I are of such advanced years ourselves that we would be unable to care for your mother if she became paralyzed or otherwise incapacitated. Thus I am afraid I must ask you to take steps to arrange more suitable living arrangements for her. We have enjoyed her company and companionship these past few years, but now it is time for her to have permanent and constant medical care and supervision.

Please inform us as to how you wish us to proceed. Will you have her come to you to live out her last days in her family home, or will you come here to find permanent institutional care for her?

We await your instructions.
With fond concern,
Beatrice and Matilda Girard

Susan closed her eyes and covered her mouth to contain the scream she felt rising from her chest. Questions swirled through her mind: What am I going to do? I can't possibly bring her here. She and I have never been able to live peacefully under the same roof. She would be miserable and so would I. The whole family would suffer. I can't put my children through that. But she's my mother. She cared for me when I was helpless. Now I must care for her. I can't put her in an institution and abandon her to the care of strangers. What will Jonathan say? This is her house. True, she gave it to me, but I've always known she might come back one day. How could I turn her out? But what if she is not strong enough to make the trip back here? Then what do I do?

She began to pace through the house, picking up small objects at random and then putting them down as if she were unsure of what they were. She brushed at lint on the sofa cushion and straightened a book lying on an occasional table. She went upstairs and mentally counted and rearranged the bedrooms. Which of the children will have to move in together so that my mother can have her own room? Will she be able to negotiate that winding staircase? Will we need to hire someone to take care of her physical needs? What if? What if? What if?

Susan was still far from finding the answers when Jonathan arrived home from work. One look at her told him she was distraught. "What's wrong, my love? What has you so upset?" He pulled her into a tight embrace as if he could somehow hold her together and protect her from whatever had assailed her.

His embrace was all it took to unleash wracking sobs. "Susan, what is it? Have you heard something from Sarah and Hector? It isn't one of the children, is it? Are you ill?" He was guessing at random, while all she could do was shake her head and cry the harder. At last, still unable to find her voice, she handed him the letter and watched his face as he read.

"Whew!" He let his breath out in a rush. "This isn't so bad, darling girl. We can take care of your mother."

"Of course we can. But I don't . . . don't want to!" The thought escaped from the mental fence she had been building to contain it and set her off into another round of sobbing.

Jonathan waited, knowing there were no words that could help. When the sobs gave way to sniffles, he took Susan's hand in his. "Of course you don't want this to happen. No one would. What do you think is expected of you? Should you say you are happy your mother is sick so that you can take care of her? Of course not. None of us ever wants to see our parents sick or growing old. Your feelings are natural. We have a terrible situation on our hands, and we're simply going to have to figure out the best way to handle it. So blow your nose and take some deep breaths. Then we'll solve this thing together."

It took some time for Susan to gain complete control of her emotions, but at last she gave Jonathan a watery smile and nodded. "I think . . . I think I want to decide for myself about Mother's condition. I heard a lot about how wonderful

Bea and Maudy were while Mother was planning her move to Flat Rock. But I had never met them or even heard of them. So I have no way of judging their opinions. Perhaps they are saints, or perhaps they are crotchety old ladies who have grown tired of having Mother underfoot. Heaven knows it's easy enough to grow tired of her, even when you love her."

"That's a wise attitude to take, my dear. I've been wondering the same thing. This need to get Mother Dubois constant medical care may be legitimate, but it seems to have arisen too quickly. Do you want us to go up there, or—"

"No, I'll be better off going on my own. I trust your judgment, Jonathan, but I'm not sure I can trust Mother to be honest with me if you are around. And I'm going to go right away, if you can manage things here. No sense in dawdling around and worrying about it."

"We'll handle things here. Mary Sue is old enough to run a household, and the younger ones are probably fully capable of doing more than we've ever asked of them."

"Then I'll catch the morning train."

On the train ride to North Carolina, Susan reassured herself that her quick response would take care of the problem before it had a chance to escalate, but she had not taken into account the three weeks it had taken the letter from Beatrice to reach her. She took a hackney carriage from the station and knocked at the door with rising eagerness to see her mother for herself. There was a long wait before a tiny lady opened the door a crack and said, "Who are you and what do you want? We don't need to be disturbed at this late hour."

"I'm Susan Grenville, Elizabeth Dubois's daughter. I've come from Charleston to see her. Is she here?"

"Of course she's here. How would she get anywhere else? You'd best come in." This was hardly the greeting Susan had been expecting. Nor was the house particularly welcoming. Only one small lamp illuminated the living room, and the parlor fire had sputtered itself into ashes. From above the stairs, a voice called out, "Is it the doctor, Maudy?"

"No, it's Lizzy's girl."

"What?" A second old woman came into view at the top of the stairs. "A servant? Or . . ."

"Lizzy's daughter, she says. Don't rightly remember her name."

Susan spoke up. "I'm Susan. Where's my mother?"

"You'll need to come up here. She's not in any condition to come down there."

Since no one seemed in a mood to offer her any help, Susan dropped her valise in the middle of the floor, shrugged off her cloak, and hurried up the stairs.

The second woman was waiting at the end of the hall. "Took your time getting around to coming, didn't you?"

"No, actually, I didn't. I received your letter yesterday. Today I'm here. I couldn't have done much better."

"What took the letter so long?"

"I'm sure I don't know. I wasn't delivering it," Susan snapped at her. "Is this my mother's room?"

She pushed her way in and then stopped short at the foot of the bed. The tiny woman in the bed scarcely made a bump in the coverlet. Her hair, now streaked with gray, spread out on the pillow in a dirty-looking tangle. Her eyes were sunken and her mouth half open. In the silence of the room, Susan could hear each raspy breath she took, although the covers did not appear to move with the effort.

"What has happened to her?" Susan demanded.

"She had that bad attack the doctor predicted. Apoplexy. She's paralyzed on her left side, and she can't see anything on that side, either. Go round to the far side of the bed and she may notice you. Or she may not. Hard to know how aware she is. She hasn't said a word since her legs gave out from underneath her. Doctor carried her up here and put her in the bed, but there's nothing else to be done."

"When did this happen?"

"Two, three days ago."

"How are you feeding her?"

"She can't eat. Can't even manage a sip of water."

"But she'll die!" Susan's voice was close to cracking.

"Yes, she will. That's what I told you in the letter weeks ago."

Tired of arguing with a woman she didn't even know, Susan moved to the side of the bed and lifted her mother's hand. Her skin was thin and crinkled, the veins looking like thin blue ropes under the surface. Susan squeezed the hand gently, hoping for a response, but there was none. "Mother, I'm here. I've come to take you home," Susan whispered. Slowly, the old woman's right eye flickered open, and what might have been meant to be a smile twisted the side of her face. Then she sighed, and all movement stopped.

Chapter 8

Painful Transitions

December 1867

The old lady in the doorway shouted over her shoulder. "Send Jonah out to fetch the undertaker, Maudy. Lizzy's done died."

Susan stared at Cousin Beatrice, the enormity of her mother's death clashing against the casual, almost rude, reaction of these two women with whom her mother had spent her last years. "Wait! It's Saturday night and everything is closed. Surely there's no need to rush. I'd like some time to sit with Mother's body. I . . . I had so much I wanted to tell her."

"Too late for that now, Missy. Should have thought of that earlier."

"But I came as soon as . . ."

"So you said." Beatrice shrugged. "It's past our bedtime around here, but I have no intention of sleeping in a house with a dead body in it." She stomped to the window and raised it to let a cold blast of air fill the room. "That's to let any evil spirits out of the house. And as soon as the undertaker's man arrives, you can take your mother out of here and make whatever arrangements suit your fancy. Come back tomorrow if you want to sort through her things."

"Or we could put them in the poor box," Maud suggested. "It'd be quicker that way."

Susan felt her mouth working, but no sound came out. She waited numbly until two scruffy-looking men pushed their way into the bedroom and roughly gathered her mother's body into an oilcloth wrapper. She followed them downstairs and out to their wagon.

"You going with the body?" one of the men asked.

"Yes, please . . . I don't know . . ."

"Here, give you a hand up." He lifted her up to the front bench. "Any question you got, you can ask Mr. Strawbridge when he meets us at the store."

After a short ride, the wagon drew to a stop at the back of a warehouse. One of the men hoisted the body onto a wheeled cart, while the other helped Susan down and led her into a cluttered office. "Find yourself a chair in this mess. The boss will be in to talk to you before long."

Susan had no idea how long she waited—a few minutes? an hour? She had lost all sense of time and place.

At last a small, wiry man bustled into the room, stirred the papers on the desk, and then grabbed a pencil. "Here we go, then," he said. "I'm Charley Strawbridge, furniture maker and undertaker in these parts. I need some information. Name of the deceased?"

"Elizabeth Anne Gresham Dubois."

"Age?"

"Seventy-one."

"Address?"

"Ah . . ." Susan fumbled for a piece of paper crammed into her pocket. "304 Market Street."

"And you are?"

"Susan Dubois Grenville. Her daughter."

"I see." He made another note. "Cause and time of death?"

"Oh, dear, I wasn't paying attention to the time. Around eight o'clock, I suppose. And she died from the effects of a stroke she suffered a little while ago. Her doctor—Highsmith, I believe his name is—could tell you more."

"Ah, yes, I know the man. Fine fellow. I'm sure he'll sign the death certificate. Now then, what are your desires?"

Susan felt a hysterical giggle fighting to take over. *My desire is that this wasn't happening!* she thought. "I . . . I don't know how to answer that. What are you asking?"

"I'm sorry, I assumed . . . Never done this before, eh?"

"No, sir."

"Well, then, one thing at a time. Are you from here?"

"No. I arrived on the late train."

"Right. Then I assume you're not planning to have her funeral here."

"No. She was living here with two cousins, but her real home is in Charleston, and I want her to be buried there."

"And which of my services are you in need of?" When Susan again looked at him blankly, he shook his head and went on. "I'm an undertaker," he repeated. "I make coffins and caskets, clean up bodies so they can look presentable for viewing, transport bodies to the graveyard, and take care of some of the paperwork. Will you want me to ship your mother's body to Charleston by train, or will you be hiring a hearse?"

"Oh. Train, I suppose."

"And do you want to let your own people there handle the preparing of the body, in which case we'll leave her in her body bag? Or do you want to purchase one of my caskets and have me lay her out?"

"You can't leave her in a bag! Can you arrange for a casket and fix her up so that she will be ready for viewing when we get home?"

"Well, now." He hesitated, obviously reluctant to upset his visitor. "Ah . . . viewing is going to be a problem, unless you want me to embalm her."

"What? Why?"

"Embalming preserves the body by stopping decomposition."

"Yes, yes, I know that. My husband's a history professor. Embalming is what the ancient Egyptians did, but it took a horribly long time—"

Strawbridge held up his hands to stop the gushing words. "It's not the same process. This is a method that was developed because of the recent war. Many families wanted their boys returned to them, so doctors found a way to treat the body and delay the natural . . . uh . . . eventualities. Even Old Abe had it done, begging your pardon if you're a Yankee."

"Is that necessary for my mother? We're less than a day's ride from here."

"That's so, but I don't ask my carpenters to work on Sundays, so they won't get started on the job for about thirty-six hours. There's a casket to build and legal niceties to be handled. The best we can do is have her ready for the Wednesday morning train, and by then . . . well, you wouldn't want to open that casket, at least not in a closed room."

Susan grimaced and swallowed hard to control the sudden impulse to gag. She nodded. "Do it, then."

"Good. I can get started on that tonight. Now, are you staying at this Market Street address?" he asked, tapping the form he had been filling out.

"Oh, no. They fairly kicked me out. But I don't know where I'm staying. Is there a railroad hotel nearby?"

"Eh, not one I'd want to send a lady to. I'll have one of my men drive you over to the McConahy Inn. It's quite comfortable, and they'll take good care of you tonight. In the morning, I'll have my wife come over and help you get the other matters straightened out."

"You're kind, but I couldn't impose on your wife."

"Nonsense. She married an undertaker. She's used to this."

Susan was still picking at her breakfast in the inn's small dining room when the quiet was interrupted by a short, stocky woman with a huge smile and a wave for everyone in the room. She leaned over the desk at the entrance, whispered a few words, then nodded and trotted over to Susan's table.

"Mrs. Grenville?"

"Yes. Are you . . . ?"

"Thomasina Strawbridge, but call me Tommie. Everybody does. I'm so sorry to hear of your mother's passing."

"Thank you. I'm afraid I'm still somewhat numb. I can't believe she's really gone."

"That's a natural reaction. We're never ready for something like this."

"No, I suppose not. However, I told your husband I didn't want to trouble you, especially on a Sunday morning. You'll be wanting to go to church, and—"

"No, no, I'm not big on churchgoing anymore, not since God let so many fine men die in a foolish war. And this is part of being married to an undertaker. I try to help out Charley's customers whenever I can. But if you would take comfort in prayer, I can take you to whatever church you prefer."

"No, I'm not ready for that. In fact, I have no idea what I should be doing."

"That's why I'm here. May I sit down?"

"Of course." Susan pushed aside her plate. "I haven't managed to do anything but push those eggs around. It seems wrong, somehow, to eat when Mother . . ."

"I'll bet you'd be happier in the parlor. Shall we move in by the fire?" Susan nodded and followed as Tommie led her between the small tables into a cozy side room. "Now, then, make yourself comfortable. Tell me, were you able to get some sleep last night?"

"Yes." Susan was startled by her own answer. "I must have been very tired, or perhaps I was escaping into oblivion."

"Well, the sleep will stand you in good stead. You're going to be very busy for the next few days."

"Doing what? Again, I have no idea . . ."

"Well, you can anticipate a visit from the local constabulary this afternoon. The officials will have a rather long list of questions for you. All deaths, no matter how innocent and expected, must be investigated. And they will expect to see you in full mourning."

"Oh, no!" Susan's fingertips flew to cover her mouth. "I hadn't thought about that! I don't believe I have anything black with me. I wasn't . . . wasn't expecting her to die."

"That's all right. I've brought you a couple of dresses . . . part of my job. We'll find one that fits you. You can use it until you get home and then send it back to me. We'll have you looking suitably solemn in no time."

"You're too kind. What else?"

"I assume you will need to notify your family back home. I thought we could drive the carriage to the telegraph office and get that taken care of as soon as you are properly attired. Then we'll need to talk about her belongings and such. Did I understand correctly that she was staying here in town with relatives?"

"Yes. She came to Flat Rock in 1862 to escape the war, and she's been here ever since. She had two cousins who invited her to share their house."

"Charley gave me an address on Market Street. Oh! That wouldn't be the Girard sisters' house, by any chance?"

"It is. Do you know them?"

"Everybody in town knows them, at least by reputation. They have a long history of . . . I'm sorry. I shouldn't cast aspersions on your family. But I do believe I might have met your mother at one ladies' meeting or another. The sisters have their fingers into most everything that goes on here in town."

"Then I'm sure you know them better than I. I had never met them. When I arrived last night, they were distinctly inhospitable. When we discovered that Mother had passed, all they could think of was getting rid of her—and me. They said I should come back for her things, but I'm reluctant to broach them again."

"I'll be happy to go with you. You'll recognize most of your mother's belongings, and I'll be there to help you pack them up. It will be hard for you, I know, but you'll want to have the items that will preserve her memory. We might want to plan on doing that on Monday. If your mother has been here for five years, she may have accumulated quite a few things. You'll also need to talk to the sisters to find out whether your mother had a solicitor handling her affairs here in town and whether she had a bank account or other legal entanglements. If so, those will be further visits you'll need to make on Tuesday."

Susan reached over to take the older woman's hand in gratitude. "Whatever would I do without your help?"

"The best thing you can do right now is follow my lead. I'll see to it that you get to wherever you need to go. If you can keep from thinking too much, you'll be better off. Concentrate on details as they occur and try to put off your feelings of grief. You'll have the rest of your life to mourn your mother."

Chapter 9

Family Reunion

S usan passed the return trip to Charleston by dozing in her seat and trying to block out the memory of the past few days. Tommie Strawbridge had been an enormous help, of course. The two of them had worked together efficiently to assure the local constable that Mrs. Dubois's death had been a natural one. Then they had packed up her personal belongings, transferred the trunk to the train depot to await the Wednesday train, closed her bank account, and conferred with the bank's business manager. Susan had been relieved to learn that her mother had not made many permanent connections in Flat Rock. She had truly remained only a visitor. Her deeds, her will, and her family records were all in Charleston.

The telegram that Susan had sent to Jonathan listed what still needed to be done:

MOTHER PASSED LAST NIGHT BRINGING CASKET HOME WEDNESDAY HAVE UNDERTAKER MEET AFTERNOON TRAIN TO TRANSFER BODY TO HOUSE BURIAL AT HUGUE-NOTS CHURCH NEXT TO FATHER NOTIFY FAMILY AND SO-LICITOR ROBERT SMITHFIELD

That took care of the formal arrangements. The emotional impact of her mother's death would have to wait.

"Camden Depot next stop!" the conductor announced.

As the train approached the Ann Street station, Susan gathered her few belongings, shook out the wrinkled skirt of her borrowed black mourning dress, and glanced out the window, wondering if anyone was meeting her. The station platform was crowded, and at first she didn't realize what she was seeing. Then she spotted Jonathan and caught her breath. "The children—they're all here!"

She hurried through the corridor and waited impatiently for the conductor to put the steps in place. Then she was in Jonathan's arms, and her family clustered around her, wrapping her in a blanket of comfort she had not felt since she had departed from that same platform five days earlier. As if on cue, the tears she had not shed in Flat Rock now began to flow.

"Poor girl. You've had a rough few days, haven't you?" Jonathan's voice soothed her.

"I'm all right. Really. It's the surprise of seeing you all here." She stepped back for a moment and conducted the kind of family roster check she had done when they were smaller. "Johnny. Eddie. Charlotte. Oh! And the twins! How big you've grown!"

"They're six, almost seven, Mother. You haven't seen them since they were infants."

"I know." The thought of how much she had missed threatened to start the tears again. "And of course, the home crew," she said, as she bestowed a kiss on each of the younger children. "Mary Sue, thank you for holding things together here. Becca, Robbie, Jamey, I've so missed you all."

"Mary Sue's been really bossy," Jamey reported.

"No, she hasn't," Becca answered. "You've just been really annoying."

"Was not!"

"Were, too."

"Children. No arguing. Your mother's not ready for that."

Jonathan's reproach put an end to the discussion, but Susan was laughing through her tears. "It's all right. Now I know I'm really home."

As the Grenville family made its way back to the house on Legare Street, Jonathan filled Susan in on what had been done. "Everything is as you asked, I hope. The girls have set up the gentlemen's parlor to hold the casket and allow for visitors. Mirrors are covered and clocks are stopped. Eddie and Johnny draped the windows and doorway in crepe. The neighbors have been bringing in armloads of early-blooming camellias, and the dining room table is already loaded with cakes and pies and casseroles. Charlotte and I paid a visit to the rector at the Huguenot Church, and they have marked out your mother's plot and are preparing for a Friday morning burial service. Even the stonecutter has been around to carve her birth and death dates on the family headstone as soon as you confirm them."

"Thank you. Everything sounds perfect. People have been so kind to me. I really haven't had to do a thing. Oh! Did the boys get Mother's trunk loaded?"

Jonathan grinned in spite of himself. "I didn't realize she would still have so much stuff with her. But yes, it's on the undertaker's wagon, which is following us. You can relax, or at least take some deep breaths and prepare yourself for the onslaught of visitors. I think you'll be surprised by how many of your mother's friends are still around. We have a full tray of *cartes de visite* already."

⌘

Thus the funeral rituals were observed without a hitch, and although it seemed that time had stopped, the days passed almost too quickly to embed themselves in Susan's memory. On Friday evening, the Grenville family gathered around the dining room table to sample the leftovers from the wake and post-burial reception. After the rush of visitors and the constant murmuring of the same words of sympathy and comfort, the house felt strangely quiet and empty.

"Mother hasn't been in this house for five years," Susan commented. "Why do I now expect her to walk through the door any second?"

"She'll always be a part of this house," Jonathan said.

"What I remember is the Christmas when she gave us those gifts from the attic." Charlotte smiled as the other children nodded in agreement. "She gave me the family Bible to keep up with, but at the time, it never occurred to me I would have to enter her death in that book. I thought she was as permanent as the house itself."

"One of the things I've learned from working with old soldiers is that we all think we change," Johnny commented, "but memories are often more permanent than events in the present. When emotions are high, it's easier to retreat to the past than it is to look toward the future. Right now, I can't imagine this house without Grandmother Dubois. And I think it's helpful to let the memories take precedence for a while."

Susan smiled at her eldest son. "You've grown up a great deal in the past few months, haven't you? It sounds like your position at the church has been beneficial to you as well as to the men you've been working with."

"Perhaps so, Mother, but I don't think I'm really cut out for the pastoral life. Now that most of our veterans have had their citizenship restored, there's less need for our Veteran's Center or for my help with their problems. Reverend Cornish has been encouraging me to study for the ministry, but that's not what I really want to do."

"Are you thinking about going back to the farm?" Jonathan asked.

"No. Look, I really wasn't planning to bring this up yet, but since you asked . . ."

"What?"

"I'm moving to Columbia."

"To go back to college? That's wonderful!" Susan exclaimed.

"No, Mother. College life is behind me. I've told you that. No, I'm going to work for my old regimental commander, Wade Hampton."

"Hampton! What's he doing these days? I remember he turned down the nomination for governor of South Carolina in 1865, but I haven't heard anything about him since then."

"Well, he's been trying to repair the damage done to his family landholdings—hiring immigrants and . . . uh, others . . . to put the land back into cultivation. But more important, he's planning to take over as leader of the state Democratic Party, and that's where he needs my help."

"The Democrats! Aren't they the party that supports white supremacy and the Ku Klux Klan?"

"No, Mother. Hampton has never spoken in favor of the Klan. He simply favors restoring the Old South to its former position of glory. He wants the Southern states readmitted to the Union without punishment, and all the citizens who fought for the Confederacy re-endowed with their former positions and landholdings."

"But, son, that implies a return to slavery, doesn't it?"

"No. Not at all. We recognize slavery has been abolished once and for all. But we object to the efforts of the federal government to go too far in the opposite direction by pushing for Negro superiority. We will not allow land to be taken from its rightful white owners and given to black men who have done nothing to deserve it."

"Done nothing? No, other than working that land for the past two hundred years!" Jonathan threw his son an exasperated grimace, which Johnny ignored.

"And we will not allow the federal government to violate our rights as a state by telling us who can or cannot vote in our state. What's worse—the government is using federal troops to enforce martial law in our sovereign states, and we will not allow that."

"And who are you to think the federal government needs your permission to do anything?" As Jonathan's voice grew louder, Susan touched his arm in an attempt to soothe him.

"I am a citizen. It's my duty to guide my country in the way I think it must go." There was a curious light in Johnny's eyes as he stood and defied his father's interpretation of the politics he espoused. Jonathan did not miss the note of group fanaticism in his son's posture and wisely refrained from pursuing the argument.

"Be that as it may be," he said, "I would hope you would proceed cautiously, keeping in mind that political winds can shift without warning."

"I trust General Hampton. He's a fine man, and I am honored to be given the opportunity to work with him." Johnny jutted his chin defiantly.

Susan, playing her customary role of family mediator, attempted again to shift the direction of the discussion. "What about you, Eddie? If Johnny moves to Columbia, that will leave you alone in that big farmhouse."

"Well, actually, I wasn't going to bring my plans up for a while, either, but since we seem to be making major announcements here . . ."

Susan and Jonathan both looked at him with alarm.

"Oh, nothing bad. But I won't be alone there for long. I'm getting married."

"What? Who? When?" The shouts came like a chorus from all corners of the room.

"Oh, Eddie, don't be silly. You're too young to be getting married."

"I'm almost twenty-two, Mother. And you're going to love her, really. Her name's Gretchen Schwimmer."

"Schwimmer? German?"

"Well, they speak German. Her parents were born in Switzerland. They are Mennonites who came to America in the 1830s, first to Pennsylvania, and then down here shortly before the war. They own a large dairy farm north of Aiken, and her father and his brothers are cheese makers. They have knowledge of old-world cheese-making secrets that will help me improve my own meager attempts. We are an ideal match on all fronts, and her family has already made me feel welcome in their home and in their cheese-making facility."

"Is this purely a business arrangement, then?"

"No, of course not. I met Gretchen in town one Saturday. She was scolding a cat because it was stalking a mockingbird, and I was smitten immediately. In a short time, we became best friends. It was only later that I discovered her family was such a good match for my own ambitions. With your approval, of course, we'll be married next summer, as soon as the crops have been planted."

"And you're planning to live on the farm?"

"Well, see, we haven't decided that for sure. There are other arrangements in the wind that you haven't . . ."

"Really!" Susan took a deep breath to prepare herself for the next bombshell. "And what would that be?"

"That would be me, Mother." Charlotte spoke hesitantly, all the while throwing glances at her younger brother that suggested she was not pleased to be forced into making her own announcement. "Henry and I have been thinking about leaving Tennessee. You will remember, I'm sure, that Henry tried his best to remain neutral during the war, selling his cattle to both sides. That reputation hasn't made him popular, now that General Forrest has made the Ku Klux Klan such a force in Tennessee. The Klan has been harassing Henry a bit, so we've talked about moving down to manage the farm if Eddie and Gretchen want to build their own home somewhere between Aiken and the Schwimmer holdings."

"And then . . ." Mary Sue's voice broke through the momentary silence. "I've been going to ask if I could go up and live at the farm, too. My horse, Sable Girl, is still there, you know, and Grandmother's death has reminded me she really wanted me to . . ."

"To do what?" Susan stared at her daughter in puzzlement.

"To become a horse trainer. There's a big equestrian community developing in Aiken. Eddie and Eli have been telling me about it in their letters. The city has built a racetrack, and there are riding schools and horse ranches. I'd love to see Sable Girl be a part of that."

Susan and Jonathan were both shaking their heads. "This is too much, too soon," Jonathan said. "We are exhausted from the events of the past week, and this is no time for any of us to be making life-changing decisions. You've offered us some interesting scenarios, but I propose we contemplate them privately for a while until our lives settle down. For now, let's get some rest."

Chapter 10

Where There's a Will . . .

December 1867

One last matter remained to be settled. "We are sched-uled to meet with Mother's solicitor, Robert Smithfield, at ten o'clock Monday morning for the reading of her will," Susan announced. "He would like you children to be present."

"Will your housekeeper be here to keep an eye on the twins while we're gone?" asked Charlotte.

"No. The twins should be at the reading as well. It's a mark of respect, as well as a testament that the entire family has been consulted."

Despite some grumblings, the children managed to be ready in plenty of time to allow a leisurely walk to Smithfield's Meeting Street law offices. The day was warm and sunny, with soft onshore breezes strong enough to set the palm fronds waving.

Susan took a deep breath and smiled. "Is it wrong of me to be taking sheer delight in this morning? Everything looks so fresh and alive. Look at the new camellia blossoms. They are making me forget about the darkness and gloom of the past week. I'm feeling ridiculously happy and blessed by having all of you here with me."

"Actually, it's a common reaction. We see it frequently at the church," Johnny said. "Even on the day of a funeral, family members are sometimes quite giddy with delight that in the face of death, they have still survived. You're feeling hope for the future, and that's good."

"Thank you, dear. But I'll try to subdue this giddiness before we hear the reading of the will. I don't want to appear frivolous."

❦

Susan needn't have worried. There was little chance of frivolity as Robert Smithfield led the family into his chambers. Dark paneling and loaded bookshelves lined the walls, and heavy navy blue velvet draperies shielded the windows from sunlight. He had arranged the room with a triple row of straight-backed chairs in front of his desk. "Mr. and Mrs. Grenville in the front row, please. Is the younger daughter, Mrs. Stewart, to be in attendance?"

"Ah, no, she lives in upstate New York and was unable to make the trip."

"Then I will have my clerk come in to make an extra copy of these proceedings for her. Now then, Grenville children in the second row, if you please. There are seven of you, correct?"

"Yes."

"Then the two small . . . uh . . . great-grandchildren, are they? They'll go in the back row."

"Perhaps I'd better sit back there with them," Charlotte said, taking pity on the two tiny faces staring at her with their big eyes and nervously chewed lips. "They are a bit intimidated by these goings-on."

"No, ma'am. Grandchildren of the deceased in the second row; next generation in the back."

Johnny rolled his eyes at Charlotte and nodded from the end of the row. "I can reach them from here," he mouthed. "They'll be all right."

Susan, too, was keeping the twins in her line of sight. She smiled to herself as she noticed that they were tightly holding hands. "Look at them," she whispered to Jonathan. "Remember when Becca and Robbie used to do that every time we had a serious family discussion?"

"You wouldn't know it now," he answered. "They hardly speak to each other."

"They're getting used to growing up. They'll be friends again in a few years."

"Excuse me!" Mr. Smithfield cleared his throat. "If you're quite done with your conversations and chair switchings, we'll get on with the reading." He strode to the office door and shouted through the crack. "Jenkins! Ready for you."

A pale young man with unruly hair scurried into the room, head down, and took a seat several chairs removed from the Grenvilles. Pencil poised over a ragged notebook, he waited for the reading to begin.

"First, I would like to establish that I did not witness the drawing up of this will. That was accomplished in Flat Rock, at the behest of Mrs. Dubois's solicitor there, a Mr. Ronald Davenport. It was, however, duly witnessed, and sent to me under seal for safekeeping. Until this moment, I have not seen the contents. So let us begin:

I, Elizabeth Anne Gresham Dubois of the City of Charleston and State of South Carolina being weak in body but of sound and disposing mind and memory do make and declare this to be my last Will and Testament in manner and form following:

First, I give my soul into the hands of Almighty God my Creator and my body to be buried in a decent and Christian-like manner in the cemetery of the Huguenots Church in Charleston next to the body of my beloved husband, Georg Louis Dubois.

Jonathan winked at his wife. "We did that much right, at least," he whispered.

Susan replied with a grin of her own. "It wasn't all that hard to figure out."

"Ahem." The solicitor frowned at them before he continued.

Next, let it be known that I have applied for, and been granted, from the President of the United States, Andrew Johnson, a full pardon for any support I may

*have given to the former Confederate States of America,
and my citizenship and confiscated properties owned before the War Between the States have been restored to
me. This restoration specifically includes the following:
the house located at 157 Legare Street in Charleston; the
320-acre property outside of Aiken known as Pine View
Plantation; one house on Broad Street in Columbia; the
Harbor View Plantation on Edisto Island; the Meadow
View Plantation on Ashley River Road; the River View
plantation on the Combahee River; the block of three
leased houses on Washington Street in Beaufort; and two
store fronts and a warehouse on High Street in Savannah,
Georgia. All these properties have now reverted to my
estate, together with all their furnishings, outbuildings,
and equipment, any temporary or former grantings of
deeds to such property being thereby revoked.*

Through the reading of this section, Jonathan and Susan
had been staring at one another, reacting to the contents
with puzzlement and surprise but without words, as only a
long-married couple is able to do. At the end of the listing of
properties, Susan raised her hand to stop the reading. "Wait
a minute, please. This pardon she says she received from
President Johnson. That sounds so out of character. Are you
sure that . . ."

"There are several supporting documents that accompany the will. The presidential pardon is one of them. It
was required of her by President Johnson's Proclamation of

Reconstruction because she had inherited from her late husband property valued at over $20,000 before the war. We also have copies of the deeds of the various properties listed here. You may examine them when we are through. May I continue?"

Susan nodded.

> *I do hereby bequeath the following:*
>
> *To my elder daughter, Susan Elizabeth Dubois Grenville and her husband Jonathan Edward Grenville, I bequeath all the properties enumerated in the listing above, to be held jointly by them, share and share alike, and to be retained by the survivor in case one precedes the other in death with the following restriction: that while said inheritors may have and hold full use of all such properties and may collect and use all incomes from said properties to whatever purposes they so choose, they may not sell said properties or any portion thereof. At the death of the last survivor of the two of them the said real estate shall only then be sold at public auction and the receipts shall descend to the surviving children of Susan and Jonathan Grenville and their heirs and assigns forever, share and share alike.*

"What?" This time it was Jonathan who interrupted. "Can she do that? First she takes back a deed duly signed over to me, and then returns it with this new restriction. Can she speak from beyond the grave to stop me from doing whatever I please with the property she has already given me?"

"Yes, of course she can. These are her possessions, Mr. Grenville. She may do with them whatever she pleases."

"But the law does not allow a deed to be snatched back once it has been duly conveyed."

"In this case it does, sir. She has maintained that she granted you and Mrs. Grenville the use of her house and Pine View at Aiken during the War of Rebellion, at which time the protections of the laws of the United States of America were not in effect. Once she had had her citizenship restored, the laws concerning property came back into effect, but they did not apply to what was done outside of their jurisdiction. Therefore, the president restored her ownership of land as it stood in 1860, as he did her citizenship."

"And the law of the United States says she can keep me from selling my property? I can't believe that."

"She has given you what is called a 'restrictive bequest.' That means you get only such privileges concerning the land as she wishes to bestow. She did not wish to allow you to sell off her property. Thus you will receive the use of such land but not a clear title. It's completely legal, I assure you."

As Jonathan shook his head in disbelief, another voice broke the silence. "*Touché, Grand-mère!* Well-played, old girl." Johnny leaned back in his chair and laughed without a hint of true amusement.

Susan whirled in her seat to glare at her eldest son. Jonathan sprang to his feet, knocking his chair over in the process, his fists clenched in anger. The twins began to wail in unison. Johnny grinned back at his parents and chortled at their discomfiture.

"Hear! Hear! This office is at the moment functioning as a court of law. I must insist that you behave in a more respectful fashion. Can someone make those children be quiet?" The solicitor's face was flushed; he yanked the pocket square from his lapel and blotted his sweating face.

Charlotte was already on her knees with an arm around each small child. She refused to move as Mr. Smithfield pounded on his desk to restore order. "You must allow me to continue. If the reading is curtailed, we shall have to start over at another time."

Susan nodded. "Go on."

Smithfield's final words came out in a rush as he tried to finish the reading before another outburst could occur.

To my younger daughter Annaliese Marie Dubois Stewart, I leave my personal effects, the contents of my jewel case and my safe box, and any monies left after all my just debts, funeral expenses and charges of this my will have been in the first place fully paid and discharged.

To my cousins Beatrice and Matilda Girard I leave whatever furnishings I have contributed to our mutual use in their house at 304 Market Street in Flat Rock, North Carolina.

I hereby nominate, constitute and appoint Robert Smithfield of the City of Charleston and Jamison Winchester of the City of Aiken Executors of this my last will and testament, hereby revoking and making void

*all former wills by me at any time made and declare
this only to be my last Will and Testament, In Witness
whereof I the said Testator have to this my last Will
and Testament set my hand and seal this eighteenth day
of July AD one thousand eight hundred and sixty-six.
[signed] Elizabeth Dubois. [seal]*

He dropped the pages onto his desk and mopped his forehead
again. "It would appear that you all have some family matters
to deal with," he said. "Please do so. Then I will see Mr. and
Mrs. Grenville only in my inner office, where I will allow you
to examine the pertinent paperwork that accompanies this
testament. Jenkins! Come with me."

As the two men stomped out of the room, Susan buried
her face in her hands for a moment. "Well, Johnny. You certainly took care of my former giddiness."

The young man shrugged. "Since I don't seem to be in
line for any sudden bestowal of honors and favor here, I think
I shall be moving on. I'll run by the house—figuratively
speaking, that is—to pick up my valise and then go on to
the railway station. I can still catch the afternoon train to
Columbia to join General Hampton. Farewell, all. Good luck
with your so-called great wealth. You're about to discover why
your noble idea of abolition was not such a good plan after all." He sneered for a moment and then limped from the
room.

"Are we rich?" Jamey asked, and Becca responded by
cuffing him sharply behind the left ear.

Mary Sue deftly separated the two. "You'll only make him worse," she hissed at her sister.

Then it was Eddie, always the quiet, serious one of the family, who brought matters under control. "I'm sorry. I owe you all an apology. I should have warned you that Johnny still has major problems caused by what happened to him during the war. Sometimes that artificial leg chafes him something terrible, and he's in great pain. At other times, he simply forgets how to behave in proper company. These outbursts come frequently, and I've found no way to deal with them other than to ignore them and wait for them to pass. Chances are that by tomorrow, he will have forgotten what happened here. If you can find it within yourselves, I recommend that you try to forget it."

"Is he going to be all right, Eddie? This new job with the general—is it a good idea?"

"I don't know, Mother. But you can't stop him, so you might as well let him go and pray for the best. Now, why don't Charlotte and I lead the rest of this troop home, while you and Father straighten out whatever details need to be taken care of here?"

Chapter 11

. . . There Must Be a Way

Susan and Jonathan made a show of examining the papers that had accompanied the will, but neither of them was really taking in the full meaning of any of the technicalities. Jonathan looked back through the stack and then asked, "Will all this paperwork be turned over to us when the will has been probated? Or will it at least be on file and available?"

"Is there another problem?" Mr. Smithfield was still irritated about the disruptions that had occurred in his chambers.

"No problem with the paperwork itself. However, much of this comes as a surprise. We never knew of the existence of several of these properties. I will want to follow up on each one of them, and I'll need recourse to the details."

"Yes, yes. I'll have a clerk make copies for you, but not until after we go through probate. Until then, I don't recommend that you go nosing around."

"I—I—I," Jonathan stammered, barely able to control his surge of anger at the insult.

Susan stepped in quickly. "Thank you. I assure you we will be far too busy in the coming weeks to go 'nosing around,' as you so inelegantly put it. We will, however, expect to be kept apprised of every step in the coming proceedings. To allow matters to be brought to a timely resolution, I suggest you communicate not with us but with our own lawyers at Middleton and Company, and specifically with Mr. Arthur Middleton, our personal solicitor. You do know of him, I presume?" She gave him a frosty smile and led the way out of the office.

"Nicely handled, my dear. I was too angry to find a way to put that pompous ass in his place."

"Language, Jonathan! He's not worth getting yourself worked up over. We'd better let Arthur know, however."

"Yes, I'll take care of that this afternoon."

They walked in silence for a while, Susan periodically scampering to catch up to Jonathan's long strides. "Can we stop for a few minutes, Jonathan? I need to catch my breath, and I'd like to have time to talk before we get home."

"How about the bench in front of The Mills House—or better yet, a cup of tea in their morning room?"

"Perfect!"

Once settled into a quiet corner where they would not be overheard, Susan turned a calculating eye toward her husband. "I won't make any more apologies for my mother. I've always warned you she never did anything without an ulterior motive, but in this case, I'm not sure what she was trying to accomplish. Is it so terrible that we cannot sell the land?"

"It wouldn't be, if there were any real hope of restoring the properties to what our son calls 'the good old days' before the war. Johnny actually put his finger on the problem. We have inherited over 1,500 acres of prime agricultural land, and we have absolutely no way to make it productive. It paid its own way when slaves could be driven to work the fields, but now . . . now we probably can't even hire workers to raise cotton. It's such backbreaking work that no one chooses to do it willingly, and we can't offset the hard work with high wages because the price of cotton has dropped to almost nothing."

"Can the land be used for some other purpose?"

"Not without more expenditures than we could ever afford."

"Can we let it lie fallow for a while?"

"The war already took care of that, I'm afraid, and not to the benefit of the land. To get it ready to work again will require the removal of several years' growth of weeds and brambles. And in the meantime? There will still be taxes to pay. That's the real catch here. Once South Carolina re-joins the United States, which will probably occur within the year, those bureaucratic arms of government will spring back into action to pay for the war by collecting back taxes. And our bill? On 1,500 acres of farmland, nine dwellings, two storefronts, and a warehouse? We're not going to pay for that on my teacher's salary, even if the good Reverend Porter were so inclined to start paying us—which he doesn't seem to be."

"And Mother's money all goes to Annaliese! I don't begrudge my sister her share, but . . . wait! Could we argue that the back taxes fall into that category of 'all her just debts . . . which must be fully paid and discharged'?"

"Hmmm. Maybe. But that would only postpone the problem. Taxes come due every year."

"Yes, but it would give us time to find a long-term solution."

"Maybe so. I'll discuss it with Arthur. I'd better schedule an appointment with him rather than dropping into his office this afternoon."

❧

At dinner that evening, Eddie reminisced about how their parents had always used dinnertime as the stage on which to broach difficult announcements.

"Were we really that obvious?" Susan asked.

"Oh, yes, you'd always send each other little eye signals when it was time to take the plunge. Anyhow, we—that is, Charlotte and I—had been planning to ask you something, and we figured this is the traditional place to do it. A few days ago, we tried to tell you about some planning we've been doing, and we let you put us off for a while because of everything else that was going on. But we'll be heading home soon, and we need to talk about this. Until today, we intended to ask if you would consider selling the farm, either to me or to Charlotte and Henry." Eddie looked around to see his parents' reaction and then nodded at Charlotte to take over.

"But since you can't sell the property, we have a new proposal," Charlotte began. "We'd like you to lease it to The Greater Aiken Grocery Company."

"Who?"

Charlotte giggled. "Sounds impressive, doesn't it? But it's only us, really. We're trying to behave like grown-ups."

"Let me explain," Eddie said. "What we have is the beginnings of a real family company. It starts with me and the dairy business that I've been working on for several years. When I agreed to take over the farm, you granted me the right to sell whatever fruits the orchards produced. At the same time, I've been increasing the size of my dairy herd, and I've been doing a good business selling dairy products like milk, cream, and butter to our neighbors. When I add the dairy income to the proceeds from our peach orchards and vineyards, I'm doing quite well financially. I'm still working on cheese making, but I haven't been very successful except with what Gretchen calls *schmierkäse*, soft-curd fresh cheese for quick use.

"The Schwimmer uncles, however, are expert cheese makers. Their specialty is a white semi-hard cheese with holes caused by the fermentation process. They make it in huge wheels and sell it by the wedge. They can hardly keep up with the demand. So we figured that if we combined forces, so to speak, my milk supplies would enable them to increase their cheese production while I learned how to make the good variety."

"And that's only half the story," Charlotte said. "Now here's how Henry and I fit into the picture. Henry and Eddie started making some trades before the war even ended. When Henry's herd produced some little heifers, he brought them down to Aiken to join Eddie's dairy herd, and when Eddie's cows gave birth to bull calves, he sent them back with Henry to join the steers Henry was selling for meat. Over the years, the numbers balanced out and allowed both our cattle herds to expand. But there's no reason why we couldn't combine our efforts, creating one large herd of cattle without having to chase little calves over half the countryside.

"Then came the discovery that really convinced us. When we met Gretchen, she was bringing Eddie some of her family's cheese, and with it, she had a sausage-like ring that she called circle bologna. One of her uncles had been a butcher and sausage maker back in Switzerland. This circle bologna was his recipe. He makes it from the bits of meat left over after butchering into the standard cuts. It's seasoned, cured, and packed in small casings to be eaten cold. She gave us a sample slice on a small piece of their Swiss cheese, and we became instant converts. The Schwimmers are not producing the bologna to be sold because they don't have a big enough meat supply, but if Henry and I moved down to Aiken, we could supply them with all Henry's trimmings."

"My head is reeling, but I'm following you so far," Jonathan said. "What are you planning to do about housing? That New England-style farmhouse is roomy but probably not big enough for two families."

"Right." It was Eddie's turn again. "Well, for now, I plan to stay at the farmhouse, and Gretchen and I may live there temporarily when we are first married. But I've promised to build her a house of her own. We've even picked out the lot, and I have started the framing already. While we're working on our new place, Charlotte and Henry will be selling their property in Tennessee. When they are ready, they'll come down and take over the farmhouse, while Gretchen and I will move into our new place."

"And there's another part to the plan, too." Mary Sue broke into the conversation. "Charlotte says that if I'm willing to wait until I'm eighteen to look into becoming a horse trainer, I can come live with them. Henry will still be traveling with the cattle business, and she'll be happy to have my company, especially to help with her growing Pickford brood."

Susan raised an eyebrow. "Growing family? Am I missing something?"

"Well, I haven't mentioned it yet, but . . ."

"A baby?" Susan's eyes widened and she swallowed hard.

"No. It's not that. It's . . . well . . . Henry's brother Charles was killed at the Battle of Franklin. Shortly thereafter, his wife died in childbirth, leaving behind two orphaned little ones—the baby, Richard, who has now turned three, and

Martha, who is four. Henry's mother has been trying to care for the children, but they are getting to be too much for her to handle. So Henry and I have agreed to adopt them and raise them as our own."

"Oh, Charlotte, are you sure you can manage this? It's a very heavy responsibility, and what if you and Henry . . . ?"

"Susan, it's not really our business," Jonathan warned.

"It'll be fine, Mother. The twins are fascinated by their little cousins, and the babies adore the older children. It will round out our family nicely. But before any such additions happen, we need to get this business matter straightened out."

"I'm sorry, but when you tell a grandmother something like that, you have to expect more . . . more giddiness, which seems to be my failing today. Go on, dear."

Eddie took over again. "So, if we work together, we can consolidate our operations into one big company—The Greater Aiken Grocery Company, producers of fine fresh meats, cheeses, sausages, and dairy products, with a side line of fruits and wines. We each already have good reputations with our customers. If we put the products together, we'll be feeding most of the area and increasing our various production lines as well."

"It sounds like an ingenious plan, but what does it have to do with us? You're adults. You don't need our permission."

"Yes, but the land we need for grazing belongs to you."

"Ah, so it does!"

"So there it is. We want to make you a part of this operation. If you'll give us a lease to graze the cattle on your land for, say, the next twenty years, with Charlotte and Henry's family occupying the farmhouse, we'll make you a partner in the grocery business, and you'll be pulling in a nice profit from the land without having to work it."

Jonathan was smiling for the first time. He put an arm around Susan and pulled her close. "What brilliant children we have raised!"

Chapter 12

A Fly in the Ointment

December 1867

While the women finished up in the kitchen and the younger children went off to play before bedtime, Jonathan and Eddie moved out onto the side piazza to enjoy the still-warm air.

"I'm proud of you, son. You have a damned fine business head on your shoulders. I'm not sure where you learned it, but I'm happy to see that you are so grown up."

"Thank you, Father. But you did train me well, from those first days when you took me out to Edisto Island with you. That's where I learned to deal with the people who worked for us. You also taught me to keep production records and to think in terms of what my customers might need. Grandmother Dubois helped, too, you know. That famous Christmas, she gave me those plantation books, and I still have them and consult them frequently. I think she'd be pleased with this new plan."

"I think she'd be very impressed!"

"There's one more problem. I didn't want to get into it at the table, but you and I will have to work it out."

"What's that?"

"Hector's land."

"Hector? What? Oh! That piece of land he bought from me to build his own house." Jonathan puzzled over it for a few minutes. "I see what you mean. If Mother Dubois nullified her gift of the farm to me, then by the same token, my sale of that piece of land to Hector was nullified. So it reverted to her, and now it reverts to me, and I can't sell it to him again. Is Eli living there now? How does he fit into your plan? Will he want to stay?"

"Eli's an integral part of this plan. At the moment, he's the hands-on property manager. He keeps track of which fields are producing hay and which ones are ready for grazing. He supervises the barn workers and births the calves. I couldn't have done this without him. He'll have a salaried position in our new company. As for the house, I don't know. Eli often beds down in the barn rather than going home, but now that Hec . . ." Eddie's eyes widened, and he clasped his hand over his mouth.

"Hec? Hector? What about Hector?" Jonathan grasped the boy's shoulders and shoved him back toward the door. "What do you know about Hector? And keep your voice down."

But it was already too late. At the far corner of the piazza, a light flickered, coming in and out of view as the bearer of a torch moved through the garden. When a twig snapped, Jonathan called out, "Who's there?" Then he turned back to Eddie and gave him another shove. "Get inside—now—and don't make a sound. Let me handle this, whatever it is."

Slowly, out of the shadows cast by the torchlight, a figure emerged. The silhouette was indistinct, but Jonathan recognized the determined footfalls as the figure now moved up the steps. "Good evening, Mr. Grenville. We meet again, always out here in the shadows of twilight, it seems."

"You! Again! And still hiding behind that mask and that ridiculous falsetto voice, I see. I've told you before. I will be happy to discuss our differences, but only when you are willing to let me see your face."

"And I've explained why I cannot do that. I am taking a risk by coming here at all. My fellow Klansmen would not approve if they knew I approached you privately. I do so only because I consider you a friend, as we are when we meet in daylight. Your actions have put you in grave danger, my friend."

"I've done nothing to you or your fellows."

"You have made it difficult for us to bring a murderer to justice. A court of law would say that you are withholding evidence."

"But you are not a court of law. By operating in secret and under cover of night, you make that abundantly clear."

"Where is Hector Moreau?"

"I've told you, I don't know."

"You spoke his name, just now, to the person who was on the porch with you."

"That was my younger son. He, too, was asking about him. He misses Hector, as do I. The man was once a part of our family."

"Ah, yes, he was. That's why we hoped to find him here with you on the occasion of the lamentable death of your mother-in-law, a woman who once owned his black hide."

Jonathan's jaw clenched so tightly he could feel the muscles getting ready to pop. "All the more shame to you, that you choose to intrude on our grief in pursuit of your nefarious doings."

"We do what we must. And in some ways I admire your commendable loyalty to a nigger. But I tell you, Mr. Grenville, this nigger of yours is a wanted man. He murdered a white gentleman in cold blood. I watched as that noble blood ran out over the cobblestones of the street. He must pay for what he did."

"Hector was never a murderer."

"We disagree, then. But the facts and witnesses support my version of the truth. You have only your opinion to recommend itself."

"I know the man. You don't."

"I know this—he's going to hang. No matter how long it takes, we will find him, and when we do, he will dance at the end of a long rope as a lesson to all who dare oppose the values of the Old South. He will hang, and if you are not very careful, you may be dangling next to him."

Jonathan snorted. "That's an idle threat and you know it."

"It's a statement of fact. There are great forces moving across this land. The South must be resurrected to regain its rightful privileges in this country. We will win because our great cause is just. You can't stop the Reconstruction of the Old South, and you can't stop us. Beware and tread softly, my friend. Danger lurks all around you." The masked man gave a low laugh, then whirled on a heel and disappeared into the gathering darkness, the fading flicker of his torch marking his passage.

❦

Jonathan realized that his legs were shaking. He sank onto a wicker chair and buried his face in his hands. A short time later, a hand on his shoulder brought him to himself. The sky was now dark, as deep as the darkness that chilled his core.

"Who was that man, Father?"

"I don't know, Eddie." Jonathan stood, as if to prove to himself that he could still rise to his feet. "I'm sorry you had to witness that. Did you hear it all?"

"Not really. I only caught a few words through the door, and my heart was hammering so loudly, I was lucky to do that. Was that a member of the Ku Klux Klan?"

"So he says. But he also declares himself to be my friend, someone I know in the everyday world of work. I never see more of him than his eyes, which look vaguely familiar, but . . . I don't know who he is. I listen to him only because he shows up on his own. Usually the Klansmen travel in groups, for their own protection, I suppose. But this man returns alone to pass me warnings. I tend to take him seriously."

"But I heard him calling Hector a murderer. Surely you don't believe . . ."

"That Hector is a murderer? Of course not. He was protecting himself. But when a white man dies and a black man is there, no one worries about the niceties of guilt or innocence. There is no trial, no presentation of evidence, no presumption of one being innocent until proven guilty. When a white man dies, a black man hangs. And Hector, God protect his soul, had the misfortune to be the only black man present when a white man died. I don't know who the dead man was. It really doesn't matter. It only matters that if the Klan catches Hector, he will hang for the crime. That's why I . . ." Jonathan's voice cracked under the emotional pressure.

"There must be something we can do. A policeman? A lawyer? A judge?"

"Any one of whom might be my mysterious informer. No, son, there's only one way out of this, and that is keeping Hector safe and out of the Klansmen's hands. That's why I reacted so strongly when you suggested that you might know . . ."

Eddie looked stricken as he nodded. "I do. I know where he is. But I didn't know all this. I would have . . . done . . . something to help, something to protect him."

"There was nothing you could have done. But now . . ."

"I wasn't supposed to tell you."

"Tell me what?" Jonathan's voice was a whisper but it echoed in the hall. He checked the door again to make sure it was on the latch. "Tell me!"

"That Hector and Sarah are still in Aiken, staying in their own house. Hector made me promise not to tell you, because he didn't want you to get in trouble on his account."

"Well, I'm already in trouble with the Klan because of him. But why didn't they go on with their plan to find a new life out in Kansas . . . or . . . or Louisiana?"

"He said he didn't feel right about saving his own life while his black brothers and sisters were still suffering in South Carolina. He's working with the Republicans, who are still pushing to get Negroes full rights to vote and own property."

"God in Heaven! And Johnny is working right there for the Democrats!"

"Oh, don't worry about Johnny. I don't think he even knows that Hector is there. He's almost never at the farm. He sleeps on a cot in the back of the church, and, on the rare occasion he does come out to visit, he's usually looking for money. He's not interested in what's going on with the land. And now he's bound for Columbia, so there'll be even less chance of the two of them coming face to face."

"We must make sure it doesn't happen. It's much too dangerous for Hector to stay in Aiken, now that you have been seen here. All the Klan has to do is follow you home, and you'll lead them right to him."

"What can I do?"

"Can you delay your departure a day or so?"

"I suppose. Eli will go right on taking care of things, but how does that help?"

"I'm going to ask Charlotte to go by the telegraph office and send a telegram to Eli. She can make a show of telling the clerk that she wants her husband to know when she will arrive home. But the telegram will also say something like, 'Tell your father to head for Kansas. Can't wait.' I think Hector will understand the Kansas reference. If he doesn't . . . if he's still there when you get home, you can explain to Eli in more detail. The most important thing is you stay away from Hector and from their house. Understand?"

"Yes, sir, but . . ."

"This is really important, Eddie. I'm not exaggerating the danger. If the Klan finds Hector, they'll hang him. No doubt about that. But if they find him somewhere where it appears that we have been hiding him, then they will be coming for us as well. If that happens, no one in the family will be safe."

Chapter 13

Visions of the Past

December 1867

"I'm so tired," Susan said, settling into her chaise longue after dinner. "Having all the children here was wonderful, of course, but I'm beginning to understand why Mother went off to Flat Rock for her retirement years. The energy of the young seems to take on a life of its own. When they were all bustling about, I felt as if I should be keeping up with them. And with the grandchildren around, too, I've been completely frazzled."

Jonathan sighed. "It's partly grief, my love. Funerals are wearing on everyone. They keep you so busy, you don't take time to feel the sorrow. Then it catches up with you later on. We'll make an effort to slow down now and give ourselves time to heal."

"Christmas will be subdued this year. We'll still be in deep mourning, so no one will expect us to entertain or attend the festive occasions in the neighborhood. A quiet Christmas Eve service will be about all I can manage."

"Sounds wonderful to me. You know I've never been one to enjoy the forced gaiety of the holiday season."

"Yes, Mr. Ebenezer Scrooge, I've heard your opinions on the topic often enough. You'll get your wishes this year, but we do still have children at home. They'll have to have some small tokens of Christmas—a few small gifts—and perhaps I can get Mrs. Henderson to do some baking for us. A Christmas cake and a few gingerbread men would be nice. And maybe we can trim the holly bushes and the magnolia trees to bring some greenery indoors. Candles, too. They're not much trouble to set out. And I'll find my old hymnal for caroling music. Maybe we can—"

"Susan, stop it!" Jonathan shook his head and then smiled, despite his best efforts to be stern. "Don't plan. Let's just let things happen as they will. For now, I'm happy to lean back and remember how well our brood is turning out."

"The older children have turned out well, haven't they? Although Johnny's still troubled, I can tell, he's at least doing something he seems to believe in. Joining Wade Hampton's political team is much better than having him moping about the house. We don't have to support his political theories in order to admire his dedication and efforts."

"Humph! Don't get me started on Hampton and his Democrats! Johnny's made a poor choice, I fear, but, as you say, he's an adult, and we don't have to agree with his views in order to love the man who holds them."

"That's true. I'm remembering all the times I thought Charlotte was going off on the wrong track, and look at her now—a contented wife and mother, with well-behaved children, a husband who dotes upon her, and long-range plans for their financial stability. Best of all, she's moving comfortably back into the family circle. I can remember when we couldn't even get her to visit the farm house, let alone make plans to move into it."

"You're right. And Eddie! What a good man he has turned into."

"When I think of him, I still see him as a pale-faced little boy who came home with you the night the Yankees took over our Edisto plantation. His beloved cows had been stolen from him, and he had just learned the brother-in-law he idolized had been killed in battle. I can still see him, eyes wide with terror, every limb shaking, tears running down his cheeks. I thought he might never recover."

"And now he's a man, self-confident, street-smart, and wise beyond his years, getting ready to marry and draw his extended family into a business plan that would confound better-educated men twice his age. He's going to make us very proud, and he just may end up supporting us in our golden years."

"Talk about getting ahead of yourself! Let's be grateful for the present moment and trust the children to stay their course."

"I agree, but I do have to wonder where all their ambition comes from. The whole lot of them seem to have such lofty goals. They want to be leaders and doers. They certainly didn't get that from me, or from you, either, for that matter."

"No, I never really wanted more than I have right this minute. But what about you, Jonathan? When you were their age, what did you see in your future?"

"Do you really want to know? I was thinking about the same question just days ago."

"I do. Did you always want to be a scholar?"

"Yes, from the first time Father took me to visit Harvard. I wasn't very old—maybe twelve. But the atmosphere of the enclave outside of Boston seemed like heaven. The men and boys walked the streets in their black academic robes. I didn't understand why, but I knew it marked them as special somehow. Father took me with him to a meeting with one of his old friends, Theodore Wainwright, who was a professor of religion.

"We entered Harvard Yard through a gate in a solid wall. Behind it was a lovely quadrangle with young trees promising one day to shade the whole area. Massive buildings—plain, solid, geometrically laid out in red brick, each with three stories and a row of dormers above and then topped with massive chimneys—formed the other three sides of the quad. Such a hush lay over the whole area that it made me want to whisper. Father and I entered one of the three buildings—Massachusetts Hall, I think it was—and then found our way to the professor's office. I took one look at the room and knew I wanted it."

Susan watched her husband in wonder as the memory seemed to transform him into someone she had never known. "Was it beautiful?" she asked.

"I wouldn't have called it beautiful. It was just—perfect—in the sense that every part of it was necessary to complete the whole. A small mullioned window looked out onto the quad and the river beyond. On one side of the room, a coal fire smoldered in the fireplace, and two wingback chairs flanked it, inviting an intimate conversation. Opposite the fireplace stood a heavy oak desk with a *bureau à gradin* along the back. It featured pigeonholes, paper slots, and all sorts of mysterious little drawers designed, I suppose, to hold pen nibs and inkwells and other scholarly tools. The remaining walls were lined top to bottom with leather-bound books. And in the middle of the floor was an oriental rug, so worn in places I could imagine generations of students shuffling their feet as they came in and out of the room. And the details: oil lamps with clouded glass chimneys, a wonderful globe that made me want to spin it and travel around its circumference, a jumbled pile of maps on a corner table, a pipe smoking lazily in its tray. I can still close my eyes and see the whole picture. It was everything a professor's office ought to be. And I wanted it. I coveted it in a way I have never felt since."

"Oh, Jonathan . . ."

"Wait. There's more. After a while, the professor took Father and me to visit Gore Hall, which housed the library. The building was some distance away, behind the first street-level quad and on the far side of an open park. I remember I looked ahead at the stone building with its twin towers and Gothic-arched windows and said, 'That's a church, not a library.' The professor laughed and ruffled my hair. 'You have a good eye, son. Gore Hall is modeled on the church at King's College, Cambridge, in England.'

"He took us inside and again, my breath caught in my throat. It was a Gothic cathedral inside as well as out. Impossibly high pillars soared upward and then spread out into elaborate fan vaulting. The center nave was filled with long reading tables, with shaded lamps at each place. Along the side aisles were dozens of alcoves, each lined with books and benches. The walls featured dark oil portraits of long-dead benefactors, and at some of the intersections there were unidentified marble busts. The air smelled of candlewax and old books, a combination of leather, smoke, dust, and papery mold. And again there reigned the silence, broken only by an occasional rustling as someone turned a page. I wanted to sit at one of those reading tables and never move until the knowledge of the world had embedded itself in my brain."

"You did get there—to Harvard, I mean."

"Yes, I did. I had three glorious years as a Harvard undergraduate. I even took a course of study with Professor Wainwright, Father's friend. He gave me my first taste of academia. My shoes got their chance to add a few more scuffs to the old oriental rug in his office. And I spent my share of hours in the library, soaking up knowledge as well as atmosphere. But the longing to be a permanent part of Harvard's hallowed enclave, to be considered worthy of teaching there—that part remains nothing more than an unrealized dream."

"I'm sorry. I took the dream away from you, didn't I?" Susan blinked away the tears that formed as she spoke.

"No, no! Never! I said it was an unrealized dream. I should have said it was an impractical one, maybe even a potentially disastrous one. At the time, I thought I could hide myself behind those ivy-clad walls and thus avoid Hamlet's 'slings and arrows of outrageous fortune' that beset lesser men. Do you hear how arrogant that sounds now? Why should I be so favored? It was simply the hope of a callow young man.

"Today, I know one cannot hide from the troubles of this world. Troubles seek you out whether you are ready or not. Our children seem to understand that challenges must urge us to more effort, not retreat. I'm still learning, but I'm getting better at being ready to 'take up arms and by opposing, end them.'"

"Those phrases come so easily to you. Did you study *Hamlet* at Harvard?"

"Of course, and I played the part in an amateur theatrical group as well. At the time, I hated his character. I thought he was an ass. Little did I realize I was one, too."

By now, Susan was laughing at him. "I can just see you pacing across the stage with poor Yorick's skull in your hands."

"Stop making fun of me. I'm trying to be serious. I learned a great deal at Harvard, but it's taken me a long time to remember some of the lessons."

"You said you were thinking about your old dreams just a few days ago. If you weren't regretting their loss, what prompted you to be puzzling over them now?"

Jonathan sighed. "I read about Wainwright's death in a Harvard publication."

"Oh, I am sorry."

"Don't be. It was all a long time ago, and I've become a different man. In fact, I've become a man who is desperate for some sleep. Can we postpone any more of this discussion until some other evening?"

Later, once the candles had been extinguished and the quilts pulled up to their chins, Susan nudged Jonathan one more time. "Jonathan? How did he die?"

"What? Who?" His voice was muffled by a yawn as he fought to hold onto the edge of sleep that had just eluded him.

"Professor Wainwright. How did he die? He must have been quite elderly."

"Susan, I don't . . . He drank himself to death, if you must know." Jonathan pushed himself up on his pillows, realizing their discussion needed an ending. "One night, he purchased a large bottle of Scotch whiskey from the porter who managed the buttery. He took it back to his beautiful office, stirred up the fire in the grate, and systematically drank the entire bottle. The cleaning woman found him there in his wingback chair the next morning, the empty bottle still clutched in his stiff hand."

"How awful!"

"It gets worse. The college authorities couldn't find anyone to notify. He had no family and no friends left, other than a few nodding acquaintances at the college. He had slept in a tiny rented room in a boardinghouse out at the edge of town. He took most of his meals in the college dining hall and spent his money and free time buying and studying his books. There was not even anyone to claim his body and make the final arrangements. Eventually, the college assumed responsibility. They arranged for him to be buried near Gore Hall, but there were no services held because there was no one to attend. The college claimed his books for the library as payment for his grave, and the rest of his few belongings were sold at a jumble sale to benefit poor scholars.

"Theodore Wainwright lived the dream I had imagined for myself. That's how it ends—in solitude, loneliness, and despair. I have no doubt his death was deliberate, not accidental. In the end, he discovered he had so avoided living that life had nothing more to offer him. It's not an ending I would want for myself." He turned onto his side and fell asleep instantly, while Susan lay wide awake far into the night.

Chapter 14

Problems of the New Year

January 14, 1868

*T*hrough the Christmas season, Susan had poured her efforts into creating a warm and relaxing holiday for her family. She found a precarious balance between too much folderol for Jonathan and enough decorations to reassure the children that Christmas would come on time. There were days when she felt her mother's absence with acute pain, but she did her best to hide her grief. On other days, she suspected Jonathan was having problems at work, but she tried to distract him from them while he was at home. Music helped, as did good food, a warm fire, and a generous helping of unexpected hugs.

Susan had always enjoyed the Christmas season. She loved the scents of candle wax and fresh greenery, the taste of cinnamon and chocolate cakes coming out of the kitchen at the end of every meal, and the sounds of giggling children too excited to remember to speak softly. But she also loved those days immediately after the decorations were dismantled and the good dishes returned to the china cabinet. The house always seemed larger then, with room to stretch one's arms or find a new place to curl up with a book. The frenzied holiday pace gave way to slower steps and time to breathe in and breathe out. Quiet reflection took precedence over excited expectations, and everyone—even the city itself—seemed to settle into restful silence.

This year, however, Charleston did not follow its usual post-holiday pattern of deliberate isolation from the rest of the world. This year—1868—brought with it feelings of both expectation and apprehension as two crucial events dominated newspapers, conversations, and thoughts. In Washington, Congress was getting ready to impeach Andrew Johnson, the first such challenge ever brought against a sitting president. And in Charleston itself, a Constitutional Convention was about to take on the seemingly impossible task of drafting a new basis for statehood that would allow South Carolina to re-enter the Union with its dignity and pride intact.

Susan felt herself growing increasingly short-tempered as she read the daily newspapers. Columnists with diametrically opposing views fought to win over readers by predicting dire results if their political outlooks were not accepted as gospel truth. Almost every week, someone brought out a new study or tally to predict the outcomes of the two controversial events. Counting congressmen was futile, of course, as senators and representatives changed their views depending upon who asked their opinions. Delegates to the Constitutional Convention were even more difficult to pin down, since most of those elected the previous November were completely unknown to the general population. And if it was nearly impossible to predict the outcomes of the final votes, it was even more difficult to make the leap from calling the winner to predicting what a win might mean for the future.

As she had done for most of her married life, Susan turned to her husband for help in understanding the issues. She trusted him to bring his innate wisdom and historical understanding to bear on political matters.

"Jonathan, can you help me make sense of what's going to happen during this new Constitutional Convention? The more I read, the more confused I become."

"What's troubling you?"

"For starters, the makeup of the delegates. There were seventy-one blacks and fifty-three whites elected as delegates, correct?"

"Yes, and it shouldn't surprise you. It's roughly the same proportion as the total population of the state."

"But the local newspapers keep saying those seventy-one blacks threaten the stability of the state, since they will win any vote because they are in the majority."

"Ah! They are dangerous in the eyes of the white population, who, of course, print the local papers you read."

"Are there any black newspapers?"

"Certainly, although you'll never see them. They are free and circulate informally throughout black neighborhoods. And those papers would tell you that the black delegates will vote as a bloc, because they are struggling to hold onto their right to vote."

"So the white delegates cannot outvote them," Susan said. "This writer says the issues are decided on the basis of race before a single vote ever takes place. Without a majority, the white bloc can't possibly win."

"That's where the line of reasoning breaks down. The white delegates do not constitute a bloc as such. Among those fifty-three gentlemen of the minority are a few men who are genuinely concerned about fairness and equality. My 'friend' in the Ku Klux Klan calls them scalawags—Southerners who have betrayed the state of their birth and now intend to vote in support of the black side of the house."

"So that's why *The New York Times* seems so sure the reformers will triumph. Have you seen this quote?"

"No, I haven't read the papers yet this morning. What did the *Times* say?"

"Here it is."

The colored men in the Convention possess by long odds the largest share of mental calibre. They are all the best debaters; some of them are peculiarly apt in raising and sustaining points of order; there is a homely but strong grasp of common sense in what they say, and although the mistakes made are frequent and ludicrous, the South

Carolinians are not slow to acknowledge that their destinies really appear to be safer in the hands of these unlettered Ethiopians than they would be if confided to the more unscrupulous care of the white men in the body.

"They certainly have a point. I would much rather trust my fate to the hands of a man who demands fairness and equality than leaving it up to one who demands privilege determined by the color of one's skin."

"I agree, but I doubt most white South Carolinians would do so. And will it make any difference anyway?" Susan asked.

"Of course it will, and for one overpowering reason. Unless South Carolina can come up with a new constitution the federal government can support, our fair state will not be readmitted to the Union. And if we are left out of that government, the state cannot survive on its own—legally, politically, or economically. Politicians may posture all they like, but in the end, they know there is only one acceptable outcome. The delegates really have no choice. They must guarantee equality for men of all races."

"So you're not worried about the outcome?"

"I'm confident we'll end up with an acceptable constitution. But I do worry the delegates will fail to recognize the tremendous opportunity at their fingertips."

"Which is?"

"The chance to create not just an acceptable state but a forward-looking one. They get to start over, unburdened by the deeds of the past because the war has wiped those out. They can take giant steps toward progress, such as universal education, state-supported welfare provisions for the sick and elderly, financial stability, and economic expansion. South Carolina could become the most advanced state in the Union, if only these delegates would have the courage to look toward the future."

Jonathan stopped, realizing he was making a speech rather than answering his wife's question. He grinned at her and then shook his head. "To be honest, I'll settle for a provision for free public education—enough, at least, to make sure everyone who wants to teach will have a place to do so. If you want to understand the outcomes of this convention, keep an eye on what they say about schools."

Susan's normal way of settling her mind was to turn to her melodeon. She could usually find music to suit whatever mood was upon her, and the dual actions of pumping the pedals and running her fingers over the keys gave her a satisfying feeling of being in control. This time, however, she couldn't translate her feelings into music, so she turned her attention to the long-neglected gardens of the side lawn. She could pretend the prickly weeds were recalcitrant white delegates who needed to be uprooted. Tender young shoots could be educated to grow where she wanted them. And the rich smell of newly turned soil seemed to carry with it a promise of great things to come. Every warm day in January lured her outdoors.

"My, but you're energetic, Mrs. Grenville. It is Mrs. Grenville, isn't it?"

Susan turned at the sound of a strange voice. The house on the other side of their wrought-iron fence had stood empty for so many years she had quit looking to see if anyone was stirring about over there. "Oh!" she gasped and barely caught herself before she tumbled to her knees. "You startled me. Yes, I'm Mrs. Grenville, but—"

"Oh, dear, I should have cleared my throat or something to let you know I was here. I have a bad habit of speaking before I think."

Susan tried to brush some of the dirt from her fingers as she straightened to meet the woman who had spoken. "My bad habit is forgetting to wear gardening gloves when I come out here. Have we met? I'd better not offer my grubby hand."

"No, we haven't met, at least not formally, but I have heard so much about you I feel as if we are already friends."

Susan looked at the woman with a mixture of curiosity and irritation. "I'm sorry, but you have me at a disadvantage. You are . . .?"

"I'm your new next-door neighbor, Henrietta McLeod." As she spoke her name, the woman seemed to draw herself up, with her back straight, shoulders thrown back, chin raised, and eyebrows lifted. Her message was clear: this was a name to be feared.

In contrast, Susan had the distinct impression she was shrinking. "I . . . I . . . I recognize your name, but . . ."

"Oh, be honest. You've never heard of me. It's quite obvious from the blank look on your face. So allow me to help."

"Please do. And while you are about it, how have you heard of me?"

"From my son-in law." When Susan did not respond, Henrietta sighed with the kind of exasperation one usually directs toward a difficult child. "Alex Croft? Your son's college roommate?"

"Alex is married?"

"Obviously! He and your Johnny used to spend most of their free time on my front porch in Columbia, playing at being grown-ups to entertain my fifteen-year-old Rachel and her friends. The boys were classmates of my son Robert—may God rest his soul—so I didn't take Alex's interest in Rachel very seriously. I thought it was just her first crush, but they turned out to be more seriously involved than I thought."

"Wait. Did you say . . . you lost your son in the war? I can't imagine how terrible that must be. My own son lost a leg at Chickamauga, and I ached with his pain."

"Yes. My only son died early in the war, in fact."

"I'm so sorry."

"Don't be. His was a noble death in a noble cause. I do not dwell on it or my grief." The woman's face seemed to solidify, and a small muscle jumped in her jaw, but she continued her story.

"At the end of the war, Alex turned up on my porch again, like the proverbial bad penny. But this time, he had with him two horses, a pair of mules for which he had traded his watch, and a plan to become a famous lawyer and politician. By then, Rachel was old enough to be courting, but it seems she had been holding out for Alex's return. The two of them are so much alike—both headstrong, both impossible to argue with once their minds are made up. Alex returned in May and by July they were wed.

"The Reverend Croft and his wife had moved to North Carolina, so their Meeting Street house was sitting empty. Alex installed Rachel there, sold his mules in exchange for part-ownership in a cotton-ginning mill, and found himself a job as a law clerk. I could see there was little chance of Rachel ever returning home, so I decided to move to Charleston to be near her. She would have been happy to have had me move into their home, I know, but I prefer my independence. Alex found this house for me—no doubt earning a nice commission in the process—and sold me on it, at least in part, by regaling me with stories of the Grenville family when he and Johnny were growing up together."

"That's quite a story. It will be lovely to have the old Benjamin House occupied again, especially by someone with whom we share acquaintances. I shall look forward to welcoming you to the neighborhood more formally, when I do not have a layer of garden dirt under my fingernails."

"Thank you, my dear. I'm sure we'll become great friends, sharing, as we do, our love of this sacred soil and our commitment to the ongoing cause of the Confederacy." Henrietta gave a slight bow, turned on her heel, and disappeared up the path leading to the back of the house.

Susan stared after her, still not quite sure what had just happened. After dinner, she related the story to Jonathan.

"Who did you say she was?" Jonathan interrupted the flow of words with a scowl.

"Mrs. McLeod. Henrietta McLeod."

"God help us! And you didn't realize who she is?"

"I still don't know who she is. As I told her, I didn't even know Alex got married."

"That's not what I meant. Think, Susan. You were quoting that nefarious woman just the other day when we were discussing the Constitutional Convention."

"Nefarious woman? You haven't even met her."

"I've read her words, inflammatory as they are. She wrote the column deploring the unfairness of the black delegates having a majority in the convention. Remember?"

"My goodness! I didn't know women were even allowed to write for a newspaper."

"Well, this one is making something of a name for herself by doing just that. She calls herself Bodicia, in honor of the historical Celtic woman who stood up to the Romans when they tried to take over Britannia. Mrs. McLeod is devoted to the forlorn hope that the South can be restored to its former greatness by putting the Negroes back in their places in the cotton fields. I've heard she is even trying to establish an organization of women who still believe in the Confederacy."

"Oh, dear! And she seems to think I am one of them."

Chapter 15

An Ongoing Struggle for Power

February 1868

Susan was relieved when the weather turned sharply colder in late January and gave her an excuse to postpone any further gardening tasks. She did her best to avoid running into her new neighbor by staying close to home. She read Henrietta's columns regularly now, to prepare herself against any future conversations. She also followed the daily reports of convention activities, but she and Jonathan tried not to draw any early conclusions. "Wait till they are finished," he advised. In February, Jonathan's mood darkened further, and Susan could no longer ignore it. One evening, she broached the subject when the children had settled in for the night.

"What's wrong, Jonathan? Something is obviously bothering you."

"Nothing's wrong. Nothing you can do anything about, at any rate. Sorry to drag it home with me. Have I been a bear to be around?"

"No, you haven't, but I can always tell when you are upset. It's part of being a wife."

"I suppose it is, and I appreciate your concern. It's the school. I'm finding it harder and harder to go to work every day and pretend I'm happy with what I'm doing."

"You've always loved teaching."

"Right now, I'd rather be a phosphate miner or a shrimp fisherman or maybe a carpenter. I might even be good enough at one of those jobs to be able to make those around me happy. I could sell a basket full of fresh shrimp to a housewife and have her tell me how delicious they look. Or I could fix a sticking window frame for a widow and earn her undying gratitude."

"Your students have always adored you. You are a great teacher, and I imagine some of your students look up to you in the same way you looked up to your Professor Wainwright. What's changed?"

"Everything. I'm being asked to teach early American history to a class full of young people who were raised to hate the United States. They don't want to hear what I have to say. They don't want to know the facts—they only want me to reinforce their preconceived notions, and that I can't do. I want them to develop a respect for the wise men who wrote our constitution, and they want to condemn them. There's no one in the current bunch of louts I'm supposed to teach who has an inkling of what I'm talking about." Jonathan's voice was suddenly harsh and tinged with bitterness.

"Are your students at the Church Institute really so bad?" Susan smiled, hoping to jolly him out of his darkening mood.

"The whole Church Institute is a disaster, Susan."

"Already? You've barely started."

"Here's the story. First, the good Dr. Porter, with all good intentions, spent most of his money—some $5,000 collected from his parishioners—to fix up the old Marine Hospital building so it could house 800 freedmen's children in Charleston. He had a really great idea. But then he turned it over to the Protestant Episcopal Church to run as they saw fit. He seems to have lost interest in providing education for black children now. I'm not sure why.

"When he received an additional donation of $1,000, he decided to move in a different direction. It seems he had a son who died of yellow fever during the war. So he decided to build a new school for children who reminded him of his own son. He had an old schoolhouse and a rented house at his disposal, and he set about creating a different kind of school. He looked for young boys whose family backgrounds should have marked them out as elites, the best blood, the children of the best families in the area, but children who were now impoverished, orphaned, and, as he puts it, 'plunged into an abyss of ignorance.'

"He refurbished the empty schoolhouse and used his net-work of clergymen to get the word out to families of moderate means that he was opening a day school at a yearly tuition of $50. That was a price high enough to eliminate any possible black student from the pool of applicants. He accepted four hundred children—mostly young ones— and assembled a staff from the dozens of Charleston tutors who were put out of work by the war.

"Then he decided to use the old house as a specialized orphanage within the school, and he sent out an inquiry to churches all over the Lowcountry, asking them to recommend orphans who should have become the next generation of elite Southern gentlemen. He chose thirty-three of the oldest because they were in the most imminent danger of being lost. He hired a principal, a matron, and eight teachers, one of them me. And to us he entrusted the boys who showed up last week. Our only instruction was to make gentleman scholars of them."

"Why thirty-three? Does that have some mystical religious connection?"

"No. I've heard him say that he hopes to expand to one hundred scholars eventually. That's how many beds he has at the moment. He is determined to fill them all, regardless of qualifications."

"And these boys—they are, what? Unsatisfactory students?"

"For the most part they are ruffians, louts, streetwise con artists, boys who survived the war by brute strength or outright criminal behavior. They have been given a free ride—housing, food, clothing, education, and a promise of scholarship money to take them on to college. Naturally, they took the offer. And just as naturally, they regard the man offering it as a pushover and a fool. They are going to con him out of everything he has, take whatever they can get for themselves, and move on only when somebody has something better to offer. So far, I haven't seen a single one who is interested in his own education."

"But they're boys. Surely they are young enough to be reshaped into good citizens."

"Let me give you an example of what goes on. Dr. Porter called them all together the first night they were there. He told them he regarded the house they were living in as his own home, and they were his guests. As such, he expected them to behave as guests and not to destroy anything that had been provided to them for their benefit. He was particularly adamant that they should never write or draw anything indecent on the walls or furniture. He placed them on their honor to seize any one of their number who did so and force him to clean up the mess he had made. Then they were to clean up the miscreant boy himself by dunking him under the pump. And only then were they to report the guilty student so that he could be dismissed from the school.

"It was some sort of extreme honor code copied from one of the military schools. But with this bunch, it had the effect of encouraging them to bully each other, and they've been shoving each other under the pump ever since. They only stop short of actually reporting someone to Porter, so he tells people that it has been completely effective in curtailing bad behavior. Meanwhile, they're not writing on the walls, but they are stealing and cheating everyone with whom they come in contact."

"They still just sound like boys to me."

"Dangerous boys. I honestly don't think that more than a couple are even capable of being rehabilitated. And even if we could retrain them all, morally as well as intellectually, I don't approve of the purpose for which they are intended."

"And that is?"

"Do you remember the old 'seed corn' argument during the war?"

"I vaguely remember the term, but I never fully understood what was meant by it."

"It arose when the Confederate Army began to run short of volunteers and proposed a draft. There were those who said that college students and the sons of wealthy planters should be exempt from the draft because they would be of greater service to the new Confederate States of America as the next generation of doctors, lawyers, ministers, and statesmen. The argument was that, even in a time of famine, you don't eat your seed corn. If you do, you have nothing left to plant the next year and thus no hope of ever breaking the famine."

"So there was to be an elite class of men who did not have to go off to war but got to stay home safe and sound reading books, while the poorer ones went off to get shot?"

"Exactly."

"But the argument is silly. If everyone's already starving and you don't let them eat the seed corn, they'll die, and then no crops will get planted anyhow."

"You're right, but politicians are seldom as wise as wives and mothers." Jonathan's mood lightened for a moment as he reached over to hug his wife. Then he continued.

"There's a darker side to the argument as well. The men that the seed corn advocates wanted to spare were, by very definition, the sons of the biggest slave owners in the South. They could be counted on to support states' rights, slavery, and all the related issues."

"All right, but what is the connection to Dr. Porter and your school?"

"Well, first, you must understand that the seed corn advocates lost the argument, and the sons of the great slave owners went off to war just like everyone else. And they got themselves killed at a great rate, too, because they didn't have much understanding of what to do in a fight."

"So these boys—the ones Dr. Porter is trying to prepare for college—are the sons of those sons? That's who Porter recruited?"

"Yes. He wants to train them into positions of power, from which they will be able to continue the fight for all the lost causes that started the War Between the States."

"And you didn't know this when you took the job?"

"Actually, I didn't fully realize it until I ran into Dr. Adamson on the street a few days ago."

"Adamson? Your old headmaster at the Apprentices Library School? The one who fired you for being a 'damned Yankee'?"

"The same. He challenged me to explain why I was now working for a man who was trying to rebuild the Old South.

He said he had come to admire me for taking a stand against slavery, but now it looked as if I had turned my coat.

"I told him I had believed Dr. Porter was running a school for orphans, not one designed to create a new class of rebels who would continue the fight to deprive Negroes of their rights and to reinstate slavery, if not by law, then by practice."

"But if you know the difference now, Jonathan, why don't you resign your appointment?"

"That's what Dr. Adamson asked, too. He suggested I would be better off teaching in one of the Negro schools. He even recommended I go and see Benjamin F. Randolph about a new job."

"Who's he? I don't think I've ever heard the name."

"Randolph is a free African from Ohio, educated at Oberlin College, and well-known as an educator and a minister there. But during the war, he served as the chaplain of the 26th U. S. Colored Regiment fighting here in South Carolina. He was even present at the Battle of Honey Hill. What he saw around Beaufort convinced him South Carolina's former slaves needed his help, so he stayed on after the war. In Charleston, he joined the Freedmen's Bureau and took up a position as assistant superintendent of education. He was successful in turning plantations into schools for those who had once worked the land—exactly what I would like to do some day."

"Then why don't you contact him?"

"Well, he's not currently in a position to be bothered with establishing new schools. He's a delegate to the

Constitutional Convention, and he's the one who is drafting the new constitutional requirements for education in South Carolina. That's the most important thing he could be doing right now. He doesn't need to be distracted by a job hunter.

"Besides, I don't like being seen as a quitter. I still labor under something of a shadow because I left my position at the Apprentices Library School abruptly. If I quit a second teaching job, no one is ever likely to hire me for a third."

"Has Porter paid you yet? You've been working for months."

"No, you know he hasn't. He has to use every cent he gets in donations to feed and clothe those thirty-three scruffy orphans."

"Then you are under no obligation to him. I want you to get out of there before you become completely demoralized."

"I have to work, Susan. It's what gives me a sense of who I am."

"You are a teacher, but that doesn't mean you have to work for someone you despise. You can always run your own school or become a private tutor. Besides, you have another job. You have inherited a great amount of property from my mother. Think what you can do with those lands to counteract this seed corn business. You have a chance to use our land for the benefit of the slaves who worked it for so long. Fight back, Jonathan, the way you did when Sherman's ruffians threatened the farm."

"That's a lovely thought, my dear. But it is easier to fight during wartime than it is when you can't be sure who the enemy is."

"Oh, I think you know."

"Maybe it's me. Did you think of that? Maybe I've just lost the will to fight."

"I don't believe you for a moment, Jonathan. You're a good man, and you've always stood for doing what's right. If anything is holding you back now, it's reluctance to put the family in further danger. But nothing could be more dangerous than doing nothing and letting evil have its way."

Chapter 16

Constitutional

Jonathan took the steps two at a time and pushed the front door open hard enough to bang it against the wall. "Susan! Where are you? Susan?"

Usually she met him in the hallway, but today no one responded to his call. Then he heard music coming from the ladies' parlor and smiled as he went to find his wife. But it was young Becca, not Susan, whose swaying shoulders turned from the melodeon at the sound of his voice. She grinned at her father briefly before returning her glance to the keyboard and finishing the melody she had been picking out.

"Uh, Becca?" Jonathan blinked and shook his head in bewilderment. This was not the homecoming he had been envisioning. "Becca, where's your mother?"

"I don't know, Papa. I haven't seen her since breakfast."

"And shouldn't you still be at your books?"

"Not today. Mr. Wilkins said he had a headache from trying to explain fractions to Jamey, so he dismissed us all and went home. I don't blame him, either. You should have heard him trying to tell Jamey that three halves of an apple make one and a half apples. Jamey was looking at him as if he were talking gibberish. According to Jamey, it was impossible because once you've cut an apple in half, you can't put it back together and have a whole apple again." She giggled at the memory.

"So where are the boys?"

"Oh, they said something about going over to the Cartwrights' to see if the twins wanted to go to the park."

"And Mrs. Jernigan? Is she, at least, down in the kitchen where she's supposed to be?"

"I don't think she came to work today. But what about you, Papa? You're supposed to be at work at your school, too, aren't you?"

"I came home early to share some very good news with your mother, but I see things are rather topsy-turvy everywhere—which perhaps is as it should be. Some people will surely say the world has been turned upside down today."

"Why? What's happened?" But before Jonathan could answer, they heard voices coming from the front porch.

"You should know better." The voice was harsh and unfamiliar.

"You're being ridiculous! And I'll thank you not to tell me how to run my life. I've raised seven children—successfully,

I might add. Surely I can be trusted to go shopping without your advice!"

The long-suffering front door banged against the wall again as Susan stormed into the house and then stopped, her eyes wide at the realization she had an unexpected audience.

"Jonathan? What are you doing home in the middle of the day?" she asked.

"And I might ask why you were *not* home in the middle of the day."

Susan's lips tightened for a moment before she forced herself to smile. "Mrs. Jernigan did not come to work today, so I had to arrange something for the family's dinner. Since it was such a lovely day, I decided to walk to the market and see what I could find."

When Jonathan raised a mocking eyebrow at her, she returned a withering glance. "Don't look so surprised. I enjoy walking and getting what my mother always called a constitutional. You're just not usually home to see it. Which reminds me—Becca, would you take these parcels down to the kitchen and see if you can find a bucket of cold water for the big one?"

"Water? What's in it?"

"A fish."

"Ewww."

"Go! The rest of the vegetables can rest on the worktable until I come down."

Jonathan watched his daughter as she headed for the backstairs. Then he turned to Susan. "So, who were you shouting at outside?"

"The insufferable Lady Bodi . . . whatever she calls herself."

"Bodicia? Mrs. McLeod?"

"Yes. She saw me walking up the street and came trotting into the yard to tell me I shouldn't be out and about on a day like today—whatever that means. She also made a point of telling me I looked frazzled and worn out, and then she said something about how I should know what happens when you let the 'Negras' take over the city. None of what she was saying made sense, but she was shaking her finger at me as if I were a wayward child who had just been caught playing in a mud pile."

"Well, you do look a little the worse for wear, my dear. Your neat little bun has some wayward tendrils that weren't hanging out of it this morning, there's a smudge on your nose, and—look—your whole sleeve has been torn loose here in the back. Who have you been tussling with?"

Susan shut her eyes for a moment, as if to block the memory. "Oh, Jonathan, I admit I have had a frightful experience. Once I had made all my purchases, I realized how tired I was and how heavy the fish was. Just then I heard the bell of one of those new horse-drawn streetcars and decided to catch a ride home. I was looking down at my feet to make sure I didn't slip in some gutter sludge as I stepped into the street to board the car. Then all at once, I was looking up at a sea of black faces, many of them grinning or laughing at me, and a chant began: 'No room! No room! Drive on! Drive on!' I was caught in mid-step as the driver clucked at the horses to start them moving again.

"The horses' hooves were splashing me with mud, and I was sure I was going to lose my grip on the railing and fall under the wheels. At the last moment, a strong black hand grasped my arm and pulled me onto the step to safety. That's when my sleeve tore loose. I looked up in shock and recognized Lazarus, who once worked as one of my mother's drivers. But instead of doffing his cap, as I might have expected him to do, he shouted at me.

"He called me Miz Susan, and then told me I was foolish to be out on the streets by myself. He demanded to know why I didn't realize the streetcars would be full of black people today. I still don't know what he was talking about, but he seemed to think I was in danger. He pulled the bell and lifted me down at the corner of Tradd and Meeting Streets. He handed me the bundle of packages I had dropped and told me to go straight home and stay there. Which was what I was trying to do when our nosy neighbor came bustling out of her house and scolded me. And then you wanted to know why I wasn't home, and . . . and . . ." Her voice faltered and she felt angry tears start to form.

"Poor darling. And you were only trying to be a good wife, weren't you?"

"And I wasn't doing anything differently today. What's so special about this one?"

"It is a special day. And I have many things to tell you. But let's go sit in the parlor while we talk—even if you are a little bedraggled."

Susan was shivering a bit as she calmed down, so Jonathan wrapped her shawl around her shoulders. "Now, then. Here's what makes this such as special day. South Carolina has a new constitution! And it's a wonderful one, Susan. The delegates have gone further than I dared hope they would."

"They're really finished?"

"Yes, the morning paper announced the final reading of the signed document would take place at ten o'clock, so I played the truant and went to hear the outcome for myself, as did about half the population of Charleston, by the way. This was the first day the Negro population of the city learned they were really to be treated as equals—they could, for instance, ride the streetcars if they wanted. So that's what they were doing. Yesterday, you could have boarded the car without a problem, but not today."

"I understand now. But what did you do about your classes while you were busy listening to the world get knocked off its rock of complacency? Will you be in trouble at work?"

"No. Dr. Porter is off on one of his interminable fundraising efforts, and my reluctant scholars are not likely to report my absence. But listen to me, Susan. The new constitution completely supports the U.S. Constitution and the Bill of Rights. It establishes three branches of government for both the state and local political organizations. It provides universal male suffrage—and don't wrinkle your nose at me. You know how big a concession that is. It's much more important to give blacks the vote than to let women have their say right now."

"So say you from your side of the house!"

"I won't argue with you. I'm much too excited by the rest of the provisions—equality regardless of race, both in matters of privilege and of punishments, welfare for the poor and disabled, state-run orphanages and mental hospitals, but no more debtors' prisons, and no more property qualifications to hold office."

Jonathan leaped to his feet, as if the chair were suddenly too small to hold him and his enthusiasm. "But the best part, Susan, the best part is the provision for state-supported education! Benjamin Randolph really did it! There will be boards of education at both state and local levels, and every local district will be required to provide at least one free school open to all students, black and white."

"Paid for by . . . ?"

"Both a property tax and a poll tax."

"A poll tax? Won't that disenfranchise a whole lot of people, particularly ex-slaves?"

"No. It's a tax on each individual, but the law specifically says that no man can lose his right to vote if he cannot or does not pay the poll tax. And it goes even further. Each state-supported school is required to stay open for six months of every year, and all children between the ages of six and sixteen are required to complete twenty-four months of instruction. Oh, and there's no separation of races. Every school must be open to all, regardless of skin color. And the provisions disallow any religious control or doctrinal instruction, too. So much for the missionaries who have taken over some of the schools, like the one Dr. Porter financed for black children. Just imagine what it means."

"It sounds like a much-needed change, Jonathan. But how will there be enough teachers for all those schools?"

"They'll be in short supply for a while, but this new constitution even provides for them. It calls for a state-supported university within five years, along with an agricultural college and a normal school for teachers. It's one of the most forward-thinking documents I've ever heard of."

"It's wonderful!" Susan stood and hugged her husband. She hadn't seen him so happy in years. "What are you going to do? Knowing you, I can guess you're already making plans."

"I am. Here, sit back down, because this will concern you as well."

Susan's eyes widened a bit, but she waited as patiently as she could. "You know I support you, no matter what you decide. I just want you to be happy with your work."

"I'm thinking in terms of our property. Once we have titles to all those holdings your mother left us, I'd like to donate—or rather, lease—some of the land for schools: for instance, the plantation on Edisto Island and the one out on Ashley River Road. The houses there could be transformed into schoolhouses easily. I'd like to offer the buildings to the local board of education for a token amount, with the proviso that they use the money they would save to purchase the schools outright when the plantations come up for sale. In the same way, we could divide the rest of the farmland into those 40-acre plots Thomas wanted to see, and lease them to former slaves, with the same arrangement. They would pay only a tiny amount to lease the land and put the rest of the money into a savings account in the new Freedman's Bank, so they could eventually buy the land outright. In return, I'd like to be a part of administering the schools, so I could be sure the students were getting the best education possible."

"You'd want to be a headmaster rather than a teacher?"

"If Mr. Randolph will have me."

"Why wouldn't he, with all your experience? Oh, Jonathan, I think it's a wonderful idea. But we still don't know when those properties will be available."

"True, but the rumors out of Washington say that although President Johnson has been impeached, he has little chance of being convicted and even less chance of being driven out of office. So that particular roadblock is temporary, and it should be removed in the next month or so. We'll be able to get the will settled quickly, and there should be plenty of time to have a couple of schools ready to open in the fall."

"You and your runaway optimism! I'm happy to see it, truly I am, but I suspect you are overestimating the ability of the state to get these provisions up and running."

"If everyone is as pleased with the constitution as I am . . ."

"Which they will not be . . ."

"But if the constitution requires it, they will have to—"

"No. They'll find a way to delay. Before anything can happen, there will have to be elections for a new governor, a new state legislature, and all those boards of education. Those alone could take months—maybe years. Besides, you are going to be too busy to be creating new schools. There will be no time, my dear."

"Busy? With what? I intend to submit my resignation to Dr. Porter the minute he gets back from Baltimore, and then I'm off to a meeting with Mr. Randolph."

"And in two weeks, we are scheduled to move to Aiken for the summer. Eddie and Gretchen's engagement celebration takes place at the end of May, and the wedding itself has to be held before the peach harvest. We'll hardly be back in Charleston before schools reopen in the fall. You're acting like one of your newly enfranchised ex-slaves, jumping on the streetcars as soon as the legal phrases have dried on the paper. They ride because they know they can ride, even though they have no place to go. And neither will you have any firm destination until the voters and tax collectors and legislators do whatever they must do to prepare your way."

Chapter 17

The Tyranny of Conflicting Choices

Spring 1868

Jonathan closed his eyes for several seconds, and tightened his lips into a narrow line as he felt his enthusiasm drain away. Why does Susan always have to be right? he wondered. She can stand there and, without flinching, dismantle my whole plan to turn our inheritance into public schools. She understands the difficulties involved, as I failed to do, and I can do nothing but acquiesce when she says it can't be done in a few months. She's right. I can't make schools burst from the ground without effort. And I can't turn my back on promises made to my own children, whose whole lives lie ahead of them. I can't support both, and if I have to make a choice, I must do what is best for the whole family. But when do I get the chance to do something for myself?

As if she could read his mind—and perhaps she could—Susan wrapped her arms around him from behind and rested her head on his shoulder. "I know how badly you must want to see free public education for the freedmen. Really, I do. But you can't make a dream come true before its time. We'll get our own family settled this summer, because their dreams are ready to be hatched. And while we're doing that, we can let the politicians have time to sort out how they are going to reconstruct the state of South Carolina as a part of the United States of America. That's the big dream, my love, and once it happens, you'll have time to reimagine the shape of free public education for all. It will happen—just not quite as soon as you might like."

"And in the meantime, I'll pray for patience." He turned around and hugged her briefly, then gave her a small but affectionate pat. "Go on now, and deal with your dinner preparations. I'll start thinking about what I may be able to do while we're at the farm. It's not far from Columbia, after all. Perhaps I can make some preliminary contacts."

Drawn by the need to take some deep breaths, as well as a rebellious desire to get away from his family for a few more moments, Jonathan stepped out onto the broad front piazza. He noticed Mrs. McLeod still puttering in her side garden and sneaking little glances toward his house. He stared in her direction, willing her to look up and meet his gaze. When she did so, he glared and took a couple of what he hoped were menacing strides in her direction. She withered under his scrutiny and scurried into a side door. He smiled and then laughed out loud. "Thank you, Miss Bodicia. I feel much better now."

He sat on one of the chaises, stretching his long legs out in front of him. The ups and downs of the day had drained him, and he quickly dozed off, only to be jarred awake by the sound of a muffled voice.

"Don't turn around, Mr. Grenville. I'm masked, but I don't much like being out before the sun sets."

"You again? The speaker for the Klan?"

"Don't make fun. I've simply come to warn you once more. I heard the story of what happened to your wife today on a certain streetcar. She's very lucky to have fallen into the hands of an ex-slave who knew her. Without his protection, she might have suffered much more serious violence. Most black men can't control their lusts, you know, and a white woman enflames them."

"Nonsense! It was only a small misunderstanding. The riders meant no harm to her."

"So you say now. But if the next time it's your daughter, you'll be singing a different tune. If you won't side with the illustrious Ku Klux Klan in their efforts to protect all our white women, you're going to need to keep your own little girls much closer to your protective care."

"I don't believe you for a moment. We now have a new constitution that grants everyone—black and white—full protection of the law."

"A lot of good that will do. It only opens the door to greater violence."

"What is it you want from me? You show up with vague threats and warnings, even though I have done nothing to you or any of your masked cronies. Why do you bother?"

"I bother because I know you and I like you. I don't want to see you or your family come to harm. But I know people are talking about you. They say you're a scalawag. You live in our once-fair city, drawing your living from us and enjoying the benefits of being a citizen of Charleston. Then you side with our enemies. You encourage the Negro population to try to take over the city. You support allowing them to vote and run for public office. You want them to receive free public education. You believe they deserve the same rights as white people. In all issues, you side with the carpetbaggers and the Radical Republicans who want to help turn Charleston into a city controlled by black men."

"And what is wrong with that? They make up the majority of our city's inhabitants."

"It's wrong because we know they are incapable of handling such rights. No black people have ever succeeded in founding a functioning government. They have never had a country of their own. They don't understand what it means to be civilized. And you would turn our own state into their hands, allowing them to destroy everything we have managed to create."

"That's what the Ku Klux Klan believes, is it? Perhaps you all need a little more education yourselves."

"It's not what we believe—it's what we know. Look at what happened today. The so-called constitution that was read out this morning gave black men equal rights to ride the streetcars. Within an hour, they mobbed those cars, keeping all whites from boarding. Your own wife came close to being pushed under the wheels of the trolley. They don't understand what's meant by the word 'equal' and they never will. And they won't rest until they have taken everything we hold dear from us—unless we kill them first, of course. That's our aim, to rid the country of every black-skinned creature who seeks freedom and equality. We're still involved in a war— white against black—and unless you choose to stand with the fine white men of South Carolina, we will be forced to treat you and yours just as we do our black enemies. Be warned, Mr. Grenville. Be warned!"

❦

Jonathan had complied with the instruction not to turn around, but as he heard the footsteps begin to fade, he could not resist glancing over his shoulder. He was too late. The Klansman, whoever he was, had disappeared into the shrubbery shielding the view of the backyard. Only a few shaking leaves marked his passage. "Who are you?" he shouted, hoping his words would reach beyond the piazza. "How do I know you? How do you know so much about me and my family?"

"Ha-ha. No more questions," the strangely disguised voice answered from the yard. "If you discover my identity,

I will stop coming to you and leave you to the not-so-tender mercies of my fellow patriots."

Jonathan clenched his fists in frustration. The visits no longer frightened him, but as usual, the encounter had left him tense. He swiveled his head, twisting his neck to loosen his clenched muscles.

"Damned Kluxer!" he swore under his breath.

"Jonathan?" The softness of Susan's voice startled him.

"I'm right here, Susan. Everything's under control."

"I thought I heard you talking. Was someone here?"

"I've had another visit from my friendly Ku Klux Klansman. He wanted to let me know he was aware of your little adventure this afternoon."

"He knew about the streetcar incident? How?"

"I have no idea. Someone told him. Or he saw it. Maybe he staged it."

"Oh, Jonathan. That scares me!"

"Don't let it. As I've tried to tell you before, this mysterious gentleman means us no harm. If he did, we would have felt the blows long before now. I believe him when he says he is my friend, although I still don't recognize him. He wasn't even threatening this time. He seemed to be on a recruiting mission. He suggested I need to join his band of Klansmen in order to protect you and the girls." Jonathan felt a shudder pass between his shoulder blades. "Ugh! As if I would ever consider such a thing!"

"Why do you say 'girls'? Does the danger not apply to all our children?"

"Apparently not. He was quite clear in his insinuations about what black men think when they see a white woman."

"That's ridiculous. And vile."

"Of course it is. And it makes the supporters of the Klan dangerous in themselves. Oh, let's not talk about them. They exhaust me."

"Jonathan? Are you ever . . . do you ever regret the decision to come back to Charleston? Did we make a terrible mistake?"

Jonathan let the question hang in the air for a moment too long. Then he took a deep breath before answering. "No. It wasn't a terrible mistake. Do I sometimes regret the decision? Of course. When my students are particularly rude or obstreperous, when the KKK shows up, when I see someone treat a black woman disrespectfully . . . certainly, I have a moment in which I wish we were back on the farm. But would I change my decision if I had the chance to do it over? No, I would not. Despite all the ugliness still staining this city, I believe we are where we are supposed to be."

"I'm not sure I understand."

"Do you remember the morning we met in Arthur Middleton's office to discuss the possibility of regaining possession of this house?"

"Yes, and I also remember you really didn't want any part of Charleston. You were simply indulging me."

"I was. I admit it. But then Arthur said something that still resonates with me. I can almost recite it word for word:

We lost five churches in the Great Fire, but we didn't lose the faith that built those spires. We lost buildings, but we haven't forgotten the architectural designs that made them beautiful. We have lost the political battle, but we have retained the cultural heritage that characterized this city. We can still take pride in our educational institutions, our music and art, our shared history, our love of beautiful gardens, our hospitality, our family ties, our warmth and gentility. And I firmly believe that Charleston can bloom again more beautifully than before, provided that good people—like yourselves—are willing to invest their time and energy to restoring what was best about this city.

"When I start to lose faith, when I get a twinge of regret, those are the words I hear in my head. We are here because this city needs us. However, I'm also glad we made another decision."

"Which is?"

"To keep the Aiken farm in the family, to use it as a retreat, as a place we can go to recharge our resolve. I can scarcely wait to get back there and walk through those orchards."

"And meet our new in-law family?"

"That will be interesting, I agree, but at least they won't be wearing masks and carrying torches!"

"No, but I'm a little nervous about it. They are bound to be quite different from us."

"I've been preaching tolerance for a long time. Perhaps this is our chance to discover whether we can live up to our own standards."

Chapter 18

Family: Reassembled

May 30, 1868

As the hired hackney slowed to a stop, the Grenville children could no longer sit still. "There it is! The old farmhouse! Look! Eddie got grass to grow under the old tree!" With a goodly amount of shoving and elbowing, they leaped down the boarding steps and headed off in several directions. Susan was quick to halt the exodus. "You could at least take the time to greet your brother," she suggested, nodding at the lanky figure who had just stepped out onto the farmhouse porch.

"Eddie!" Jamey shouted. He ran headlong to throw his arms around Eddie's legs and then reached up to be lifted.

"Hello there, Sprout. You're getting too heavy to be thrown over my shoulder the way I used to do. How about you learn to shake hands?" He put the boy firmly back on his feet and bounded down the steps to greet his father and help his mother from the carriage. "Oh, it's so good to see you. This old farmhouse tends to echo when it's not full of people. How was the train ride?"

"Full of soot and racket, as usual, and it didn't help to be surrounded with wiggly young people." Jonathan replied. "The children have been all too anxious to get here."

"Can I go now, Mother? We'll have plenty of time to talk, but I haven't seen my horse in almost two years." Mary Sue was talking in the direction of the family, but her eyes kept wandering toward the stables.

"I suspect Sable Girl is out in the pasture by now, but Eli's in the barn," Eddie said. "He'll be able to show you where they are grazing this week."

"Mother?"

"Oh, get along with you, but try not to come back smelling like the stable."

"Girls and their horses! I swear I don't understand that particular attraction," Jonathan grumbled. "Never affected you, did it, Becca?"

"No, horses are much too big—and smelly."

"By the way, Becca," Eddie said, "there's a surprise for you, too, down by the henhouse. But be careful not to get too close if Oscar decides to spread his tail."

"Spread his . . . Oh, Eddie, you don't have a pet peacock?"

"We certainly do. Neighbor down the way bought him for his wife, but she decided he made too much noise. Peacocks make a particularly nasty screech when they are unhappy, so the farmer was glad to give him to me."

Jonathan was shaking his head in bemusement. "The whole place looks prosperous and well-kept, son. I expected you to take care of things, but it looks like you've made lots of improvements. I'm impressed."

Eddie grinned. "Come on in and see what we've done to the house."

Susan was still looking around to keep track of her brood. "Robbie? Where are you going?"

"I want to check on the privy."

"He wants to make sure there's not a porcupine in there." Jamey couldn't contain his giggles as he recalled the story of Robbie's first meeting with the prickly animal. "Come on, Robbie. I'll protect you from any wild animal attacks."

"Quit worrying about the children, Susan. This is Aiken, not Charleston, remember? One of the beauties of this property is that we don't have to worry about the children getting into trouble. This is where they can feel free, and I suspect they need a good dose of freedom. Let them be. They'll show up again when it's time to eat."

Jonathan tried to put his arm around his wife's shoulders to guide her into the house, but Susan pulled away. "Go on. I'll be there in a minute."

She was taking deep breaths, trying to stop the memories whirling in her head . . . the first time she saw this house and proclaimed it a box, which had hurt Jonathan's feelings. The muddy yard. The burned meals when she was learning to cook. Their labored efforts at putting in a vegetable garden, only to watch the bugs eat it or the rains drown it. The day the hawks killed Becca's new baby chicks. The look of the orchard when peach blight forced Jonathan to cut off all the blooming branches. The fears for her son's life and the pain of seeing him as an amputee. The months of her estrangement from Jonathan. The Union army marching up their path, guns at the ready. None of the memories were happy ones. How could the children be so eager to get back here, when all she could remember was the hurt and the anger and the terror?

"Susan?"

"I'm coming." She turned toward the house and then stepped off the path as the hackney driver came back to turn his team of horses around.

"Eeeeek!" She flailed at her face as the sticky tendrils of a spider web entangled her.

"Gotta watch for them webs around here, ma'am," the driver commented. "Of course, the spiders in them bushes ain't dangerous. They're just trying to catch flies. The ones to watch out for are them long-legged brown ones what hide in your shoes. They want to kill you."

"Eww. I'll try to remember that." Still picking the threads off her nose and eyelashes, she fled toward the relative safety of the house. "Hate spiders!" she muttered.

Eddie, grinning with excitement, held the door open for her. "Come in, come in! I want you to see what we've done to the house."

Susan looked around, her lips parted in astonishment. "New furniture, I see, but what are those?" She pointed to the frilly white coverings that lay over the backs and arms of every chair.

"The antimacassars? Gretchen crocheted them for me all by herself. They protect the upholstery from hair oil and greasy hands."

"Ah, I see. They're . . . clever." And hideous, Susan thought, but she tried to keep a smile on her face. "It's certainly an improvement over the old stuff we found when we first moved in here. And my melodeon? How did it get back here?"

"Well, Reverend Cornish said he really appreciated it when you donated it to the church, but now they have a brand new organ, so he thought you might like to have it back."

The sight of the instrument she had offered to God as a bargaining tool for the safe return of her oldest son from the war completely unnerved her. She sank into one of the chairs, accidentally brushing the arm covering off onto the floor. With fumbling fingers, she tried to smooth it back into place before Eddie noticed. "You've certainly done a lot of work around here."

"Didn't take much, actually. Nothing else to do during last winter's snows when I couldn't work on the new house we're building. And Gretchen's such a help. She has all sorts of ideas on how to make everybody more comfortable. But, come on—there are other surprises waiting for you." He offered her a hand and then steered her toward the backstairs.

"Mother? Are you finally here?" Charlotte leaned over the railing and called down from the floor above. "No. Don't bother coming up. The twins fell victim to temptation out in the garden and initiated a mudball fight. We're having something of a wardrobe crisis, and everybody's getting naked—except me."

"Is your whole family here?"

"Yes, of course. We couldn't miss this chance for another clan get-together. Henry's down at the barn with the cattle, as usual, but he'll be up in time for dinner. I'll come down as soon as I manage to get everyone out of their muddy outfits and into something more presentable. Why don't you go see who's waiting for you in the kitchen, and I'll be right down."

Susan took a deep breath and glanced at Jonathan in hopes his face would give something away. He simply shrugged and raised an eyebrow, gesturing to let her precede him into the kitchen. Across the warm and inviting room, the door to the basement stood partially open and the stairs squeaked as someone approached from below. Holding her breath, Susan watched the doorway, hoping young Johnny was here as well. Instead, the figure that emerged was a tiny black woman with an apron full of potatoes.

"Sarah!"

"Oh my, you're home!" Sarah lost her grip on her apron, and potatoes rolled across the floor.

"And so are you!" Susan replied. The two women embraced and then laughed as they bent together to retrieve the potatoes. "Whatever are you doing here? We thought you were in Kansas or Louisiana or someplace."

"Yes, Sarah. What are you doing here?" Jonathan's cold voice cut through the joyful reunion. "I specifically ordered Hector to get as far away as he could."

The smile faded from Sarah's face. She straightened her shoulders, jutted her chin, and glared back at him. "With all due respect, Mister Jonathan, you don't run things around here any more. Hector and I are free now, as you have always insisted we should be. And we don't take orders from you any more."

Jonathan stared at her, astonished. "Of course you're free, but I was trying to protect you. Hector's a wanted man and the Klan was on his trail. They still are. It's not safe for you in South Carolina."

"No black person is safe in South Carolina right now. You must realize that. Hector refused to leave to save his own life when so many of our people were similarly in danger. The murder charge is simply an excuse. One black man we knew was shot because someone mistook him for a bear. Another was hanged for stealing eggs. Healthy Negroes find themselves thrown into jail for failing to step off a sidewalk, and then they come out with broken limbs and battered flesh. Black women are never safe on the streets. They are beaten and whipped and raped."

"But the law says . . ."

"Nobody cares what the law says, so long as the sheriff is a white man looking to re-enslave those he used to own. Hector says the only way we can really protect ourselves is to see to it that black people take over this state and run it properly. So that's what Hector is trying to do. He's out signing up black folks to vote. He's campaigning for black members in the state legislature. He sometimes acts as a bodyguard for black politicians. Right now, he's in Camden helping to protect Solomon Dill."

"Who?"

"Solomon Dill. He was a member of the Constitutional Convention, and then he was elected to a seat in the new State House of Representatives. But now he has decided that he would rather be a county commissioner, so he's standing for election again, with the promise that he will give up his seat in the legislature if he can win this upcoming local election. There are those, as you might expect, who think he overreaches himself, so he doesn't travel alone these days.

"The new assignment meant that Hector would be away from home from April to June. And he left me here because he knew the boys—Eddie and Eli both—would take care of me. So here I am, back in my old job, except now I get paid for doing it. Eddie insists on that."

"Oh, Sarah, I'm so sorry. I don't think Jonathan realized . . ."

"Don't apologize for me, Susan. I'm aware of what's going on in the world around me. You must forgive me if I think of Hector and Sarah as family, not as ex-slaves."

"Of course you do, but you need to let them be grown-ups, too," Susan suggested gently. Then she shook her head in frustration. "I see both sides of this. I'm glad you and Hector are running your own lives, Sarah dear. But at the same time, I worry about you being . . . uh . . . here in particular. You know our Johnny is working for Wade Hampton, who seems destined to be the Democratic candidate for governor sometime in the future. He's bound to object to what Hector's doing. What if he . . . ?"

The question hung over them. Eddie, who had stepped quietly into the kitchen as soon as he heard his father raise his voice, now spoke for the first time. "I still don't think you have to worry about Johnny, Mother. As I told you before, he's hardly ever here. When he does stop by, it's only to get something. Furthermore, his attitude toward Hector and Sarah actually serves to protect them. He tends to look right through them. He knows who they are, but he disregards them. He still thinks of them as family slaves, so they don't matter. I'm sure he would be astounded to know Hector is an active Republican. The image doesn't fit the pigeonhole Johnny keeps him in."

"Well, I hope you are correct. Do you know if Johnny is planning to be here for the wedding festivities?"

"I've invited him and told him when you all were arriving. Will he be here? Who knows? It probably depends on what General Hampton has in mind for him to be doing. That's where all his loyalty lies these days."

Chapter 19

Girls, Boys, and Their Horses

May 30, 1868

Mary Sue tried to control her breathing and her footsteps as she made her way to the barn. She wanted to break into a headlong dash, but she was eighteen now, and everyone expected her to be dignified. At the barn door, she stopped entirely, realizing her heart was beating as hard as if she had really run all the way.

A fuss from inside the barn broke the spell. A horse was restless, whinnying and snorting, stomping and kicking out at the sides of the stall. Cautiously, Mary Sue peered in, hoping it was not Sable Girl who was so upset. She didn't know the horse, and for a moment she didn't recognize the strapping young man who approached the stall with a low whistling sound.

Eli had grown several inches since she had seen him last. His muscles had filled out, and his dark skin glistened from the effort he had been putting forth to clean the stalls. He stopped directly in front of the troubled horse and stood quietly. The sound he was making turned into a soft hum. He closed his eyes and bowed his head, then looked up at the horse and smiled. With one hand, he began to stroke the soft muzzle. When the horse looked back at him, Eli's stroking fingers moved to a soft spot just below the horse's ear. The horse tossed his head and looked again to see if he had gotten away with it. He stomped one hoof and then another but still aroused no response. When he quieted, Eli resumed the gentle stroking of his withers.

After a few more quiet moments, Eli moved to the side of the stall and effortlessly lifted himself to sit on the boards. Then slowly, he swung one leg over the top, a movement that turned him toward the barn door and gave him his first glimpse of Mary Sue standing there, as mesmerized as the horse. He grinned at her and put a finger to his lips to signal for quiet. Then he dropped to the stall floor and resumed his slow massage. The horse heaved a deep sigh and laid his huge head on Eli's shoulder. Eli answered by draping his arm over the horse's neck. They stood quietly, enwrapped in each other like lovers, Mary Sue thought. Eli broke the embrace to reach for a handful of oats and offer it to the now docile horse. Then he sprang up to the top of the side wall again and dropped to the barn floor almost in front of Mary Sue.

"That was beautiful, Eli," she said. "From here, it looked like you and the horse were really talking to each other."

"We were."

"Well, I'm sure I don't know what you said, but whatever it was, it was very effective. I wish I could learn how to do that."

"I can teach you," Eli offered. "How good to see you! The family has arrived, I take it."

"We have indeed arrived. Eddie is giving the parents the grand tour of the house, Becca is hunting down a peacock, and the boys are in the privy, doing something I don't want to know about."

"And you are here in search of Sable Girl."

"Yes, but Eddie said she was probably out to pasture. Do you have time to show me?"

"I'd like nothing better. I'm anxious for you to see her. Come on!" Without thinking, he reached out to take her hand. Hesitantly, Mary Sue responded, and then they both withdrew in embarrassment.

"The rest of the horses are in the south pasture. This way. Watch your step." The awkwardness lasted for most of the way, the two walking side by side and yet separated by a wide social gulf. At the pasture gate, Eli slowed and once again signaled for silence. Mary Sue scanned the field, searching for the first sight of her beloved horse.

"Over there," Eli whispered, jutting his chin toward a low copse of trees, where a small horse was placidly grazing near a dark-colored lump in the grass.

"Oh, I see her. But . . . is that . . . a foal? Eli? You bred her?"

"I promise you I had nothing to do with it. She came up with the idea all by herself."

"She's too young!"

"Evidently not. She handled the birth like an experienced mare."

"Who was the sire?"

Eli shrugged. "Like I said, I had nothing to do with it, except, perhaps, by failing to notice she was about to come into season. I had no idea she was, uh, carrying a foal until her sides began to bulge. And by then, well, all we could do was wait. Several of the stallions using the pasture are dark, so there's no way to tell which one . . ."

Mary Sue had recovered from the initial shock enough now to laugh a little at her own reaction. "I'm only eighteen. I'm too young to be a grandmother to a foal. Do you think Sable Girl will even remember me, or is she too busy now with her own motherhood?"

"Horses don't forget," Eli assured her. "Can you still do that whistle you once used to call her?"

"I don't know. I haven't had much reason to whistle lately." Mary Sue lifted two fingers to her lips and let loose a piercing summons.

Across the pasture, Sable Girl raised her head and looked around curiously before returning to the business of grazing.

"Do it again."

This time, the horse lifted her head with a jerk and stared across the field. She took a few hesitant steps and then turned to look again at her foal.

"Once more, and make it a double if you can."

After another few hesitant steps, the horse began to trot across the field.

"Sable Girl!"

And the horse was racing toward the gate.

Mindless of her skirts, Mary Sue climbed the rails of the gate and dropped to the ground on the other side.

"Careful! She may not know you, apart from your whistle." But Eli's warning came too late and without need.

The little horse drew up within a few feet of her owner and tossed her mane. She whinnied and then leaned forward to nuzzle Mary Sue's shoulder. With tears running down her cheeks, Mary Sue threw her arms around the horse's neck and breathed in the warm, rich smell of her.

Eli might have been a little damp-eyed himself as he watched the reunion, but his main concern now was still Mary Sue's safety. "Don't try to hold her if she pulls away. She's torn between you and the need to guard her foal."

And, indeed, the horse looked over her shoulder and took a few steps backward. She tossed her head again and capered, seeming to invite Mary Sue to come and see what she had produced. And then she was gone, racing toward the far side of the pasture to nuzzle the baby asleep in the grass.

Eli put one hand on the gate and sprang over it into the pasture to stop Mary Sue, who seemed intent on following the horse's lead. He caught her by the shoulders and turned her toward him. "Not yet," he cautioned. "Sable Girl may love you, but you're a stranger to the rest of the herd, and this is their territory. You can meet your grand-foal later tonight, when they come back to the barn."

"Oh, Eli, she's so beautiful, and you've done so well raising her for me." Mary Sue was still crying as she wrapped her arms around the young man's neck. For a moment, he returned her hug. Then he stiffened and thrust her away from him.

"Don't do that, Miss Mary Sue. You'll land us both in big trouble."

She stared up at him, the hurt registering clearly on her face. "Don't do what?"

"Don't hug me. Don't touch me. We're not youngsters any more. I'm a black man and you're a white woman. You're fixing to get me shot."

"I . . . I . . . I didn't mean anything by it. I'm just . . ."

"I understand, but other people wouldn't, not even your big brother. I may be a free man, but I'm still black."

Bile rose in the back of her throat as the full impact of what he was saying hit her. "I'm sorry. It was impulsive and stupid of me. It won't happen again." She turned and began the long walk back.

After a few minutes, Eli caught up with her. Still careful not to touch her, he said, "It doesn't have to mean we're not friends. We're cousins, remember? We just can't . . ."

"I know." She took a deep breath and then smiled up at him. "So tell me about my horse. She's small, isn't she? Shorter than most and not very long front to back, either. She's not as small as a pony, but is there something wrong with her?"

"No, she's fine. I wondered about her size, too, at first, but I've been reading up on horses like her. Turns out she's one of a very special breed—a Carolina Marsh Tacky, to be exact."

"A tacky? You mean, as in cheap?"

"No. Tacky is a Gullah word for horse. Although, the breed doesn't eat anything but grass, which makes them cheap—uh, inexpensive to feed."

"Are they native to this area?"

"No, actually they are direct descendants of the horses brought over by the Spanish conquistadores in the sixteenth century. They were chosen because, among other things, they were small enough to make the journey in those little Spanish galleys. More important, they turned out to be perfect for the Carolina Lowcountry. They thrive on our sea grasses, and they are surefooted in our swampy pluff mud."

"So they've been around for a long time. Why haven't I ever noticed them?"

"Probably because they are too small for a wealthy white planter to show off. Although, as your grandmother did, people sometimes buy them for children or timid women riders because they are easier to handle. Still, the horses your family owned were mostly tall and slender Morgans or English thoroughbred stock, not compact bundles like the Marsh Tackies. The Tackies are now often used by black families to pull their plows or haul their loads."

"Does the distinction between black and white have to come into everything—even horses?" Mary Sue glared at Eli as if he were personally responsible.

"It's not that simple, Mary Sue. But in this case, yes. Black people need a different kind of horse than a white aristocrat does."

"So you like Sable Girl because she's a black man's horse?"

"No, I admire her because she's a wonderful example of her own kind. Please don't pick a fight over this."

"Sorry. It's just . . . all my life, my father has been trying to teach me not to judge people by the color of their skin. And now, when the war has ended and your people have been granted equality, you keep calling my attention to our differences rather than our similarities."

"Well, let's agree on one thing. Let's not ever tell Sable Girl that she's a black person's horse. She's just our . . . I mean, your horse."

"No, she belongs to you as much as to me because you have raised her. She's definitely ours."

Chapter 20

The Formal Betrothal

June 1868

"But what are we supposed to wear? And what kind of betrothal party starts at 8:30 in the morning?" Susan stared at the formal invitation hand-delivered earlier that afternoon. "Did you know about this, Eddie? And do you understand what's going to happen?"

"Mother, I've warned you that the Mennonites take a very different approach to life. I admire them for their enterprise, their virtues, and their love of simplicity. But they are going to seem strange to you. You can't question their choices, any more than they can expect you to adopt their ways. We're going to witness two very different cultures meeting for the first time, and both sides are going to have to make an effort to be tolerant."

"That's all very noble and vague, dear, but it doesn't tell me anything. Let's start with the invitation. Why on earth does it start before breakfast?"

"It doesn't, Mother. The Schwimmer family will have been up and working long before sunrise. By 8:30, they will have eaten breakfast, finished their chores, and taken care of preparations for the festivities, if you can call a three-hour worship service festive."

"Three hours!"

"I'm afraid so. It will be a typical Mennonite worship service, although this one will be held in the yard to accommodate all the guests. Actually, you and the rest of the family probably do not need to be there so early, although I will. They are used to people wandering in and out of their services during the morning. Gretchen tells me there will be several sermons on the meaning of marriage, the creation of a family, and the duties of husbands and wives. The local bishops will all want to have their shot at telling us what they expect of us. And there will be comments from the congregation, too. Every so often there will be a break for a hymn or two, which gets everybody up and moving for a few minutes. You can enter the fray whenever it suits you, so long as you are in time for the betrothal midday meal. And at the very end of the festivities, Gretchen and I will be asked if we still are set upon marrying. Then the presiding bishop will turn to both sets of parents and ask them for their permission and blessing. Assuming permission is forthcoming, he will announce a wedding date, and only then will the service be over."

"And this happens out in the yard? Will there be benches or . . . ?"

"I presume so. There'll be small children and the very old and feeble among the guests. Everyone in the community attends. Some of the seats may be hay bales, but you won't have to stand during the whole time."

"So we'll be home by afternoon."

"Oh, I wouldn't count on that. Mennonites take their food almost as seriously as they do their praying. The dinner will go on for hours, and then there will be games and time for the families to get to know one another, we'll name our witnesses, and then another songfest, and . . ."

"Until dark." Susan's voice was flat with resignation.

"I'm afraid so." Eddie chuckled to himself at her dismay. "And I would suggest you plan to dress for comfort."

"Which means what?"

"This isn't as formal as the wedding itself. So the men will probably all be wearing black trousers and white shirts, but no coats—with their suspenders showing. If Father finds it too informal, he could add a waistcoat, but no neckwear of any kind, not even a collar. And the women will be in their usual plain cotton dresses with white aprons, high necks, and long sleeves. They will wear small white prayer caps over their buns."

"You don't expect us to . . ."

"No, of course not. But you may want to choose a simple dress, the kind of thing you might wear around the house during the summer. No frills or ruffles, no jewelry, no hoops.

Or maybe a shirtwaist and skirt would do, so long as you're not showing, uh . . . uh . . ."

Susan now was the one who laughed at him. "No bare skin? I think I can manage to cover up. But there is one other matter."

"What's that?"

"The Moreaus. Do the Schwimmers know that we have black cousins in our family? Will they be welcome, or . . . ?"

"Mother! The Schwimmers are fond of Eli, and Hector and Sarah as well. They've always known them as part of our family. Mennonites only judge people by what they do, not by the color of their skin. They don't even understand the racial divide in this country. So you need not worry about them. It's you who will be the exotic stranger in the crowd."

⁂

When the day was over, Susan had to admit that she had worried unnecessarily. The Schwimmer aunts and uncles were excited to meet Gretchen's intended in-laws. The younger Mennonite cousins swarmed around the Grenville children, plying them with questions about Charleston and their experiences during the war. Susan and Jonathan were shown to comfortable chairs at the front of the assembled guests, and everyone, even those who spoke more German than English, made an attempt to include the Grenvilles in each conversation. Someone was always nearby to point out the right page in the hymnals. The time passed quickly, and Susan thoroughly enjoyed listening to the fanciful tales and droll accounts of the possible tribulations of marriage.

When the ladies announced dinner by the ringing of the huge barn bell, Mr. Schwimmer led the Grenvilles to the front of a line wending its way past improvised tables supported by sawhorses. What seemed to be an army of cooks bustled back and forth between the yard and the house, bearing platters of ham and roasted chicken, bowls of salads, sliced breads still warm from the oven, and a whole array of desserts. The cooks pressed second and third helpings on them all. Then, as Eddie had promised, some of the men and boys began to organize the afternoon's activities. First came the children to try their talents at three-legged relays and sack races. Then the adults began to stir, and the more competitive guests eagerly sought the Grenvilles' participation in the late afternoon croquet games and quoits matches.

As the evening shadows began to encroach on the sun-dappled lawn, Susan realized that she was terribly proud of her second son, both for his newfound maturity and for his wisdom in choosing this delightful young woman as his bride. There was just one more formality to be taken care of. The two young people stood side by side to face the elders and deacons of the church. And both spoke their intentions with heads held high and voices raised with determination.

Gretchen spoke first. "Father, I ask your permission to marry, and I ask your particular blessing upon this young man at my side. Edward Grenville is an honest and hard-working gentleman. He will become an active participant in our family business, a loving husband to me, and a wise father to our children."

Then it was Eddie's turn. "Father—and Mother—I ask you to grant your permission for this marriage and to welcome Gretchen Schwimmer into our family. She will serve you as she has always served her own parents, with respect and devotion."

But the bishop was not yet satisfied. "Young Mr. Grenville, do you have someone to serve as your witness and your support as you take on this heavy new responsibility?"

"I do, sir. My witness shall be my cousin and lifelong friend, Mr. Elijah Moreau."

Eddie gestured, and Eli rose to join the couple as they faced the congregation.

"And Miss Schwimmer, have you chosen a witness and confidante to stand at your side?"

"I have, Bishop Mueller. Since I have no sisters of suitable age, my witness shall be my future sister-in-law, Miss Mary Susannah Grenville."

It was Eli who showed the first reaction, his eyes widening and his complexion darkening as blood rushed to his cheeks. Mary Sue hesitated just a moment too long before she joined the others. She kept her eyes locked on the ground beneath her feet, avoiding the temptation to look at Eli. But Susan caught her breath at the tableau playing out before her. Was there one couple waiting for permission to marry? Or were there two?

"Mr. Schwimmer? Mr. Grenville? How say you to these, your children?" The presiding bishop gestured for Jonathan and Hiram Schwimmer to step forward. As they did so, Mr. Schwimmer reached out and clasped Jonathan about the shoulders. They stood eye to eye for a moment, then nodded to each other and shook hands.

"Then let the betrothal be proclaimed throughout our land and the marriage date be set for one month hence—on Saturday, July 11." The congregation broke into cheers and shouted good wishes, and the deed was done.

Susan clasped Jonathan's arm as he returned to his seat. "So soon? How will we ever get everything ready in just a month?"

An elderly woman in the next seat leaned forward to answer her question. "Don't you worry none about that, Missus. We've been marrying off our children for centuries now, and we know what needs to be done. You and Bertha Schwimmer will be guests at the wedding. Our community will handle the details."

⬭

The assembly began to break up, but no one was in much of a hurry to put an end to this delightful day. As they lingered over final conversations, Susan noted a horseman approaching. She tugged at Jonathan's sleeve and nodded toward the road. They had been parents too long not to recognize their oldest son as he yanked at the reins and slid to the ground, holding the horse's mane with one hand as he struggled to gain his balance. Then he limped into the crowd.

"Pardon me. Sorry to be so late to the party. Where's my wayward brother?" Johnny's appearance made him stand out among the neatly dressed guests. He was muddy and sweat-stained, looking as if he had spent the better part of the day riding through the countryside. His voice was hoarse and his manner brusque as he looked for members of his family.

Jonathan was the first to reach him. "Johnny, we've been concerned about you. Eddie said he didn't think you would be able to get away, but I hoped you would be here for your brother's sake."

"I've been a little busy, Father. While you all have been partying out here, I've been helping to quell a riot in Camden. We've had people getting themselves shot on both sides of the argument."

"And what argument might that have been?"

"The usual. Some damn fool—fellow named Solomon Dill . . . like the pickle! He wasn't satisfied to be a black man who got himself elected to the state legislature. Then he had to go and decide he wanted to be a county commissioner as well. So he's been running for election again, but there are a lot of white folks who don't want their government in the hands of niggers."

"Watch your language, son. These are peaceful people."

"Sorry. Mustn't step on their pretty little peaceful toes. So, the story is, this fellow Dill . . ."

Sarah pushed her way through the crowd to confront him. "Did you say Dill? Solomon Dill? What's happened? Is he all right?"

"He's dead, along with some of his family and friends. That's what he gets for thinking he's better than a white man. He won the second election and then headed home to Camden, where he was holding a dinner for his buddies. It was hot, so they had all the doors and windows open when some of his political opponents approached the house and fired a few warning shots to let him know he wasn't all that popular. One thing led to another, and it turned into a real gun battle—one of those where innocent people get shot by being bystanders and bodyguards."

"No!" Sarah's piercing cry cut through the voices around them. Susan, caught in mid-discussion with the old woman about wedding preparations among the Mennonites, whirled at the sound and then dashed to grasp Sarah as she began to sink to the ground in agony.

"Hector? Hector was there?" Susan looked frantically between Johnny and Sarah.

"Of course he was. He was Dill's bodyguard, wasn't he?" Johnny's voice carried a sneer. "He got himself shot, too, but he'll live. Bullet hit him in the arm and lodged in his shoulder."

"Where is he?" Sarah demanded.

"Don't yell at me, Sarah. I took care of your Hector. Got him wrapped up and loaded him onto the back of my saddle. We rode most of the night, just trying to avoid the mobs of angry hangers-on. It wasn't easy—him with one arm and me with one leg—but we managed finally to make it to Aiken around noon. I left him at the church, in the capable hands of Reverend Cornish, who was more than happy to bustle around taking care of him. I promised to bring you all back and reclaim the wounded bodyguard by tonight. Can we get on with it?"

Chapter 21

The Heat of Summer

June—July 1868

As Johnny had indicated, the gunshot had not hit any of Hector's vital organs, but the bullet had fractured first his right arm and then his collarbone. Johnny's quick work of wrapping the wound had prevented any serious blood loss, and the care with which Rev. Cornish cleaned and cauterized the wound kept infection at bay. Still, Hector was effectively immobilized. The local doctor had splinted the arm and bound it tightly to his body to prevent him from jarring the broken bones. He could wield neither a gun nor a plow. "I'm useless," he complained whenever someone had to help him with everyday chores or routines.

During the long days of his recovery, he and Jonathan had many occasions to sit on the porch and hash over their views about the future. As usual, Jonathan took the optimistic approach. He concentrated on the broad picture and was sure laws and constitutional changes would eventually secure equality between blacks and whites. Hector, however, saw frightening portents in what was happening to individual black men. For Jonathan, freedom was the end goal; for Hector, it was only a portal opening onto more troubles ahead. Jonathan could be content to rest his heels on the porch railing and enjoy the peaceful vistas of Pine View Farm. Hector wanted to be out and about in Aiken and beyond, lingering on the courthouse steps to hear what travesties of justice had been carried out against his people each day.

When the news that Andrew Johnson had avoided being impeached finally filtered down to the local papers, Jonathan was relieved. "This is very good news for me—and for your people, too," he told Hector. "It means the will Susan's mother left is going to clear the courts, and I can get on with my plans to use the lands we've been given to benefit our freedmen. Black families deserve a chance to get their own land and to have their children educated. I can now make it happen, particularly in the Lowcountry. Thomas's dream of turning our Edisto plantation into a productive black enclave can become a reality."

"And you think it's going to happen during the rest of Johnson's term? Oh, you're wrong, Jonathan. Johnson may have been Lincoln's vice-president, but he's cut from a different piece of cloth. He professes to favor what he calls Presidential Reconstruction, but he doesn't mean he wants to see the South rebuilt in a new direction. Johnson's Reconstruction is a rebuilding of the old South, complete with a return to a form of slavery."

"Surely not, Hector."

"What do you think the Black Codes were, if not a series of laws to bind black men to white ownership? Johnson is not interested in giving black men the vote or educating their children or providing them with the oft-promised forty acres and a mule. He wants them subjugated by the law, and he fully intends to restore the great plantation owners to their former positions. How else do you think Mrs. Dubois got her lands back? If this president's ideas are given free rein, all the gains from the War Between the States will have been for naught."

"I can't believe that. Just look at what's happened this month. Nearly all the southern states have rewritten their constitutions to conform to the federal model. The Black Codes are gone. Arkansas, Florida, Louisiana, North Carolina, and South Carolina have been readmitted to the Union, and soon Alabama will join them. The old Confederate rebels have been removed from power, and new state governments dedicated to enforcing the law will replace them. And best of all, the Fourteenth Amendment is within one vote of being ratified and giving the Negro full rights of citizenship in every state. It's a new day, Hector."

"Tell that to the people of Georgia!"

"Georgia can't hold out for long. It's in their best interests to—"

"Georgia. Pfft!" Hector spat over the railing. "Georgia's where the other states send their troublesome niggers to be strung up. Ain't a sheriff in Georgia who gets upset over the sight of a noose."

"I know there are lots of old Confederate soldiers who resent the coming changes, and they take their anger out on your people, but in time . . ."

"In time? In time we'll all be dead. Look, Jonathan, I respect your position, but for the most part, black men are no better off now than they were under slavery. We may be free, and we may even have the right to vote, but nobody's offering much help when it comes to having a right to eat. The great promise of land didn't last long, did it? And while the Black Codes may be gone, the land is still in the hands of white men. If we want to work the land, we have to become sharecroppers, which means doing whatever the white man says. We have to borrow money from white men to buy food and seeds and farm tools, and then when our crop comes in, we have to give it to the white man to pay what we owe him. So we're stuck in poverty and beholden to the same men who were once our masters. I'm still in South Carolina instead of seeking a new life beyond the sway of the Old South because someone has to fight back. The war may be over for you, but for me, it's just beginning."

❦

Jonathan ruminated over their discussion as he made his way home. Struggling with his reactions to Hector's disillusionment, he let his horse meander wherever it found an extra tasty growth of grass. He hadn't wanted to take their discussion any further, but he couldn't forget about it, either. Was Hector correct? he wondered. And if so, did that mean that emancipation had been a bad idea? Surely not. Freedom for the black man was the necessary first step in reversing the evils of slavery. But perhaps he and his fellow abolitionists had failed by relaxing their efforts after 1863. That thought unleashed a whole new wave of guilt. Have I been wrong all along? Could I have handled the freeing of our slaves in a more benevolent way? Am I still responsible for Hector and his family? Have I betrayed them somehow?

Susan was waiting when he finally arrived home. "Where have you been? I was beginning to think something had happened to you."

"What's the rush? I dawdled a bit on the way home, I admit, but I'm not really late."

"No, I suppose not. But Johnny's coming for dinner, and I . . ."

"Johnny? For dinner? It's been ages since he has been willing to sit down for a family get-together. What's the occasion?"

"He's headed back to Columbia in the morning. I insisted he spend a little time with us before he leaves."

"He'll be back for the wedding, won't he?"

"Apparently not. He says he'll be too busy with General Hampton's plans."

Jonathan shook his head in disgust. "I wish I knew what Hampton does to win such devotion from his men.

If we could figure that out and bottle it, we'd make a fortune."

"Please, Jonathan, just be nice. Johnny's our oldest son, and we can love him without agreeing with his politics."

"I'll try, but shouldn't that advice apply to both of us? I resent having to hide my own opinions just so he won't be insulted and go off in a huff again."

⚮

Despite Susan's determined efforts to smile and keep the conversation limited to pleasantries and family stories, tension hovered over the table. The younger children kept looking from their father to their brother, waiting to see which of them would break first.

"I had a nice visit with Hector today," Jonathan offered. "He's miserable sitting around, of course, but he's healing nicely, thanks to your quick care. I really appreciate what you did for him."

"What did you expect me to do—let him lie there in Dill's yard and bleed to death?"

"No, of course not, but you went out of your way to bring him home."

"That doesn't mean I don't think he's a fool. What does he think he's doing out there, stirring up the blacks to run for office and vote for each other? They're not qualified to hold public office—any of them. That Dill fellow didn't even understand he couldn't hold more than one public office at a time. And right in the middle of his campaign was our Hector, stirring things up. Getting shot served him right. Maybe he'll think twice before he volunteers as a politician's bodyguard again."

"Our constitution now guarantees the right of all men to vote and hold public office, Johnny, whether you like it or not."

"Which is exactly what's wrong with South Carolina at the moment. These new amendments allow all the wrong kinds of people to run the government—ignorant, uneducated, greedy, undisciplined ruffians are in charge of the state, and they don't serve anyone except themselves. Have you seen the latest stunt by Governor Scott and his cronies?"

"Which is?"

"They've passed a bill authorizing the building of a tavern in the middle of the state capitol so they don't even have to go outdoors to get a drink—or a prostitute. Next thing you know, their girls will be dancing on the podium, and the senators will be stuffing money up their . . ."

"Johnny! Your sisters are present!" Susan tried to hush him, but Johnny was having no part of it. "They're hopelessly corrupt, every man jack of them elected by the Republicans."

"Well, then, why didn't your man Hampton accept the office of governor and straighten things out?"

"Oh, he will do exactly that, in time. But first, we need to shut down this whole Reconstruction process, run the carpetbaggers and scalawags out of the state, put the niggers back in the cotton fields, and see to it the Democratic Party can win a fair election. We'll put the old guard back in control, as they are meant to be."

Jonathan slammed his napkin on the table and stood up to tower over his son. "Where are you getting this rubbish? I raised you to respect this country's rule of law and order, to believe in the rights of all individuals to life, liberty, and—"

"Oh, please! Don't start quoting those old ideas to me. The pursuit of happiness means nothing to today's politicians, except, perhaps, a bottle of rye whiskey and a trampy woman with her lungs hanging out."

Then it was Johnny who pushed away from the table and limped out of the room, letting the door slam behind him.

Jonathan slumped into his chair, hiding his face in his hands. "How has it all gone so terribly wrong?"

Chapter 22

The Wedding

July 1868

In the days leading up to the wedding, discussions of politics faded away as the attentions of the women focused on the ceremony to come. Susan invited Gretchen, her mother, and her aunts to come to the farm for an afternoon tea, but at Eddie's insistence, she downplayed the fancy desserts in favor of more substantial and simple finger sandwiches. The Schwimmer women, however, were obviously uncomfortable to be eating in what they considered to be the middle of the workday.

Susan tried to break the silence by turning to the bride. "Tell me about your wedding dress, dear," she suggested.

Gretchen looked toward her mother for guidance but got none. "Well, it's like any other dress, although of perhaps a finer fabric than usual. It's pale blue, with a bit of embroidery at the neck. After the wedding, it will become my church dress."

"Blue? Not white?"

"Yes, ma'am. German wedding dresses are usually blue, although I'm happy I'm getting married in the summer. Winter wedding dresses have to be dark blue, which would make me look awfully pale."

"But dark blue is much more practical, daughter. That's one of the reasons why I disapproved of this summer wedding." Mrs. Schwimmer frowned. "That light gown of yours will show every bit of soil, and heaven forfend that the barnyard is muddy on your wedding day."

"If it is, I'll have to lift the hem a little. And the apron will protect the front."

"You're getting married in an apron?" Mary Sue could not contain her surprise.

"Of course. It's a sign of my housewifely duties."

"I'm sure your bridal bouquet will look lovely against the white apron," Susan said, trying desperately to sound pleased.

"Oh, I won't be carrying flowers. I'll be holding my Bible."

"No flowers? Oh, dear. We don't have many things in bloom right now, but I'm sure I could find some rosebuds."

Mrs. Schwimmer was still frowning. "We have plenty of flowers, Mrs. Grenville. We will use them to decorate the tables for the bridal dinner, of course, but it would be a bit . . . uh . . . suggestive to have the virginal bride carrying them, don't you think?"

Susan opened her mouth and then closed it without saying a word. Mary Sue, for her part, developed a choking cough.

"I assure you, Mrs. Grenville, we have everything well in hand. You needn't worry."

"Oh, I'm not a bit worried about your arrangements. I only wanted to make sure we do not falter in taking care of our responsibilities, such as the ring, or the photographer, or . . . music, perhaps. I could bring my melodeon and . . ."

"We are Mennonites. We wear no jewelry, not even a wedding ring. We do not allow graven images. And we make our own music. You have no responsibilities. You are simply guests."

"Speaking of responsibilities," one of the aunts said, "it is time for us to be returning home. The men will be coming in from the fields soon and they will want their suppers." The Schwimmer women stood as a body and moved toward the door.

"Wait!" Mary Sue cried. "Gretchen, you asked me to be your witness, but you haven't told me what I am to wear."

"Just anything. Whatever you have."

"So long as it doesn't make you appear frillier and fancier than the bride," Mrs. Schwimmer added.

Gretchen grimaced at her mother's tone. "I do have an idea. I was an attendant for an English friend's wedding last summer. My dress was cut from a Mennonite pattern but made out of a gingham material with small checks. I think it would fit you. Shall I bring it over tomorrow? You won't have to wear an apron with it."

"Oh, do, please. I would be most grateful."

As the door closed behind their guests, Susan and her daughter glanced at each other and then began to giggle. "Oh, my goodness! I hope Eddie knows what he's getting himself into."

"Well, I'm glad she won't be my mother-in-law!"

❧

The day of the wedding dawned hot and muggy. Jonathan began grumbling as soon as he tried to fasten his shirt collar against his already sweaty neck.

"Hush, Jonathan. It's your son's wedding day, and you will look proper no matter how uncomfortable you are." Susan grinned and tried to jolly him into submission, but he remained unconvinced.

"Our son's wedding day—and the longest day of our lives!"

In many ways, the rituals were a repeat of the betrothal ceremony, but the tone was more solemn. The presiding bishop read the descriptions of marriage from his huge Bible. "St. Mark tells us there may be no putting aside of a wife. A man leaves his mother and father and cleaves to his wife, and the twain shall become one flesh. What therefore God has joined together, let not man put asunder."

Another bishop read extensively from Corinthians, making sure everyone understood marriage as a part of a hierarchy—God over Christ, Christ over the man, and the man over the woman. A third bishop read from Ephesians: "Wives, submit yourselves unto your own husbands, as unto the Lord, for the husband is the head of the wife, even as Christ is the head of the church."

"Eddie's getting the better part of this deal," Jonathan whispered to Susan at one point, but she refused to rise to his bait. She was too busy watching a silent drama taking place in tandem with the wedding vows being recited by Eddie and Gretchen. The witnesses, Mary Sue and Eli, seemed oblivious to the ceremony unfolding before them. They stared not at the bridal couple but at each other. They didn't hear the words; they heard only the beating of their own hearts. They spoke not a single word, but their emotions were clear to anyone who knew them well. Sarah, too, was watching. She threw a worried glance at Susan and knew they shared the same fear. Their children were taking a fateful step, one that could well land them in the center of the racial tensions fast overtaking South Carolina.

Once the ceremony was over, however, Mary Sue and Eli resumed their responsibilities to the wedding party. Eli led the newlyweds to the center of the long dinner table, while Mary Sue rounded up the children and settled them at their own picnic area at the edge of the yard. Even Jonathan noticed a difference in their demeanor, but he acknowledged their happiness with approval.

"That's the first time I've seen Mary Sue smile in days," he said to Susan. "She's been so serious for the past week, I suspected she disapproved of this marriage. But she's certainly enjoying herself now."

"Perhaps she was just worried about performing her duties as Gretchen's maid of honor."

"Well, whatever has caused the change, she has an unmistakable glow about her now. I hope it's not because she's imagining her own wedding."

Susan was startled. "What makes you say that?"

"Nothing in particular. It's a natural reaction for a young girl, I would think. Her wedding day, whenever it comes, will be the highlight of her life. But I'm not ready to be the father of the bride again. I remember Charlotte's wedding as perfectly traumatic, particularly when I learned what it cost."

He was joking, Susan knew, but she was uncomfortable with the direction the conversation was taking. Desperate to change the subject, she turned to criticism.

"I only hope the rest of our children choose more traditional marriages. This ceremony was inspirational and lovely in its own way, I suppose, with all the hymns and Bible readings. I did like allowing the bride and groom to write their own vows, so they really meant something to them. But so many things were missing. It wasn't just the lack of flowers and organ music. It seemed to be a worship service rather than a celebration of a marriage."

"What would you have had them do?"

"I don't know—something to make it more special. Gretchen's a beautiful young woman, and I wanted to see her in an equally beautiful dress, not the same plain style she wears every day—and with an apron over it, for heaven's sake! And that little prayer cap over her bun. I so wanted to replace it with a flowing veil."

"Didn't you listen to what the bishop read from St. Peter—about not adorning one's outward self?"

"Yes, and I heard the one, too, about women needing to cover their heads. But a veil serves the same purpose, and if ever a woman is justified in adorning herself, it is on her wedding day. And she needs a train on her dress, too. If Gretchen had been wearing a train or a veil, Mary Sue would have had something to do, rather than standing there gazing at . . ."

Jonathan raised an inquisitive eyebrow. "Gazing at who? Or what? Did I miss something?"

"No, no, never mind. I'm through complaining, except about the lack of rings. A wedding ring isn't a form of adornment. It's a simple metal band, but it symbolizes the unbreakable bond between husband and wife, which the bishop was also determined to emphasize. I suppose they are against symbols, too."

Jonathan was laughing at her now. "You know, my dear, you'd make a terrible Mennonite."

"I would, indeed! Except for the food, of course. I think they are holding places for us at the bridal table. And I spotted roast pork and cheesecake."

The dinner was still in progress when Mary Sue approached her mother and drew her away from the table. "We have a small problem," she explained.

"What's wrong?" Susan was instantly alarmed.

"I'm not sure what all Jamey has been eating this morning while everyone was engrossed in the wedding. But he's been very sick back behind the barn. He's not running a fever, but he has a violently upset stomach. I think he needs to be taken home before he has another vomiting spell."

"Wait. I'll get your father and round up the others."

"No, Mother. You can't leave yet. You are the parents of the groom. Who knows what else the Schwimmers have in store for you? I, on the other hand, am completely unnecessary and have been so all day. Eli has Sable Girl hitched to the smallest cart, and we can take him home. We'll never be missed."

"Absolutely not!" Susan glared at her daughter, all sorts of images swirling in her head. "How do you think it will look if the groom's best man and the maid of honor disappear in the middle of the festivities? Particularly when the groomsman is a . . ."

"A what? What were you going to say?" Now Mary Sue was glaring back at her. "Would it bother you if my escort were a nice little white boy?"

"Oh, Mary Sue! I don't want to get into an argument with you. But the answer is still no. I'll take care of Jamey. Perhaps the Schwimmers have a place he can lie down for a while, and they probably know a home remedy for an upset stomach. You can tell Eli to unhitch the horse. You two aren't going anywhere until we all do. End of discussion."

"Fine! But the discussion is far from over." Mary Sue's eyes narrowed, and she tossed her head in defiance. "You won't be able to thwart us forever, you know!"

"So there is something to thwart? I thought so. I will do whatever it takes, my darling daughter, to protect you from yourself. Now go back to your new sister-in-law and see if she needs you. But stay where I can see you, or I'll come hunting you down."

Susan felt her cheeks flushing as she made her way back to the table. She couldn't decide if she was angry or frightened. Jonathan looked at her curiously as she sat down. "Something's wrong. What is it?"

"Not now, Jonathan. It will have to wait until we are alone. I intend to finish out this wedding day with a smile on my face, But I'll tell you one thing. I don't care how hot or tiresome Charleston may be in the summer, we are going home, just as soon as we can get packed up and out of Aiken."

The rest of the guests had settled down to serious eating, and Eddie and Gretchen had failed to notice the slight upheavals among the Grenville clan. "They don't deserve to have anything distract them from the enjoyment of this day," Susan announced to her charges. "So, Jamey, you will quit eating, and you will not throw up again. Do you understand?"

He looked abashed as he nodded and swallowed hard.

"As for you, Mary Sue, I want you to look at me. I'm smiling, and I want you to smile back every time our paths cross."

"I suppose I can fake it if you can."

"Sarah, you need to quit looking terrified. No one is going to come charging into this party and string your boy up for looking at a white girl. No one else noticed what you did. At a wedding, people look at the bride, not the best man."

"I don't even understand what's going on," Becca complained. "What did we do?"

"Nothing. You did nothing, dear heart. But I really need you and Robbie to lose yourselves in the crowd. Go help with Charlotte's brood and keep them occupied with some of the children's games, please. Just stay out of the way and don't draw any attention to the rest of us."

"I feel like Becca. I'm obviously guilty of something, but I have no idea what I did." Jonathan frowned at Susan. "Are you making trouble out of whole cloth?"

"No. We have a problem, but it will keep until we can deal with it in our own kitchen—I hope!"

Chapter 23

Mary Sue Takes Charge

July 11, 1868

The truce held during the long drive back to the farm. The younger children dozed, and the grown-ups seemed occupied with their own thoughts. Susan breathed a small prayer of thanksgiving when everyone was safely home.

"I'll take care of unhitching the horses and getting them rubbed down," Eli offered as the carriages drew into the yard.

"I can help," Mary Sue volunteered.

"No, you can't. I need you to help Sarah put together a light evening snack. If we don't eat something now, everyone will be hungry by midnight."

"Yes, ma'am." Mary Sue's voice was controlled but cold.

"Let's get some milk and butter bread for the little ones so they can get along to bed. Then we're going to have a family meeting. I don't want this situation to fester overnight."

"What situation?"

Robbie grimaced at Becca. "Shhh! You know how these things go. You'll eventually hear all the details and more than you want to know. But not before Mother is ready."

For the next hour or so, the family worked through the routines of setting the long kitchen table, bringing out cold dishes from the larder, and helping Charlotte put the smaller children to bed. No one had anything much to say, except for the occasional "Excuse me" or "Pass the salt."

At one point, Jonathan and Hector disappeared but soon re-emerged from the basement, carrying bottles of their very own scuppernong wine made from the previous year's crop. "It's been a long, dry day among all those Mennonites," Jonathan commented. "Besides, I suspect we'll need a touch of this before the night is over."

Susan glared at him for a second and then gave him a wry smile. "At least it's not that vile peach schnapps you buried in the yard for six months."

"We may get to that later."

"Can I have a taste? Just a little sip?" Jamey, apparently recovered from his earlier upset, turned to Hector with his request, but his mother wasn't in the mood for any of his tricks tonight.

"No, you may not. Furthermore, I don't want you eating anything else. Have a drink of cold water if you are thirsty and then get along to bed."

"But I'll miss the family meeting."

"It needn't concern you. Now go!"

Jonathan drew a breath and then let it out with a small sigh. It would do no good to interfere, he realized. Susan was working up to a cold, controlled rage and there was nothing to do but let it play itself out.

Eli was whistling softly as he entered the kitchen, still shaking the water off his hands after using the outdoor pump. "Sorry I took so long," he whispered to Sarah. "Is there something left to eat, or are we ready to go home?"

"While you are here, Eli," Susan said, "I have something to say to everyone, and I'd appreciate your attention. Would you sit down for a moment?"

"Yes, ma'am."

"Some of the family may not be aware of it, but Eli and Mary Sue came very close this afternoon to making a spectacle of themselves."

"Mother!"

"No. I intend to have my say. Don't interrupt. When a young man and a young woman start making cow eyes at one another, people notice because they look ridiculous. And when they decide to slip off in the middle of an event to be alone with one another, it's only a matter of time before they get themselves caught in a compromising position."

"I don't know what you . . ." Eli looked puzzled as he glanced from Mary Sue to his mother.

"Oh, yes, you do. I can see how weddings can put romantic thoughts into the heads of young people. It's a normal reaction. And I'm also aware the two of you have been spending almost all your waking hours together down in the barn or in the pasture with the horses. Under normal circumstances, I would probably indulge you. Every one of us has probably had at least one summer romance. But in this case . . ."

"In this case, one of us is black! Why don't you just come out with it? Did you think we hadn't noticed?"

"Mary Sue, you need to show your mother some respect," Jonathan cautioned.

"Mother, please. May I speak?" She wrinkled her nose in her father's direction and then continued. "You are talking about what you think you know, but Eli and I are the only ones who really know what is going on. Give me a chance to explain rather than sitting here listening to unfair accusations."

Jonathan wiped the sweat from his forehead and ran a finger under his snug collar. He grimaced, shook his head in frustration, and then unbuttoned the tight paper collar and thrust it away from him. He had always hated quarrels, and this one appeared to be getting ugly. It was time for him to intervene if he hoped to see this night end in peace.

"Your daughter has a point, Susan. Let's hear her out before you pronounce sentence."

Susan glared at him, her lips clamped tight against the words she wanted to hurl across the table at him. Only her years of training as a dutiful wife kept her from doing so. She gave a curt nod in Mary Sue's direction without meeting her eyes. "All right. Go ahead. Tell us all about this . . . relationship."

"Let me start with one reminder." Mary Sue stood and her seriousness drew the attention of everyone at the table.

"I have always told you I am not interested in marriage. I remember making an announcement right here in this kitchen when I was about twelve. Father was trying to convince me all little girls had to learn to cook and clean in preparation for finding and winning a good husband. All I wanted to do, even then, was to break out of that mold and become a horsewoman. And you, Father, bet me I would change my mind. Well, so far, you have not won the bet.

"I still know what I want to do with my life, and it has nothing to do with what was going on today. A young girl getting married in her apron, for heaven's sake! What kind of life does that promise her? Sweating over a wood stove and washing dishes under a rusty pump?"

"You may sneer all you like at housewifely duties," Susan said, "but you're not addressing the matter of what was going on between you and Eli today."

"But I am, Mother. You saw us looking at each other instead of listening to the marriage vows. But what we were thinking—and saying silently to each other—was that such an arrangement was not for us. And if we wanted to get away during the afternoon, it was because we were tired of smiling and making pleasantries about what a lovely couple Eddie and Gretchen were and how happy they were sure to be. Weddings! Bah!"

Susan was shaking her head in denial, but Mary Sue was far from finished.

"I love Eli. Of course I do. We were practically raised together. He was right there in the middle of my brothers, and I've always thought of him as a brother, not a cousin. I love Eli. I love Johnny and Eddie and Robbie and even Jamey, too, when he's not throwing up on my shoes. But of all my brothers—real and chosen— I love Eli the best, because we share a devotion to something the rest of you don't seem to understand.

"Grandmother Dubois gave me a little horse, and when I couldn't take care of it alone, I asked Eli to help. We became something of a pretend family—Sable Girl, Eli, and me. Not long ago, when I learned Sable Girl had birthed a foal, Eli referred to me as its grandmother. That's the nature of our involvement with each other. We're a kind of family. But we are not involved in some sort of storybook romantic relationship. We are engaged in planning a business partnership."

Jonathan was squinting and frowning at his daughter as if she were speaking in a foreign language. "You're right about one thing. I don't understand what you are talking about."

"We want to start our own stable—a horse-raising business. Sable Girl, Eli has discovered, is a very special breed, almost indigenous to South Carolina. She is a Carolina Marsh Tacky, descended from the horses that accompanied the first Spaniards to America centuries ago. People buy them for various purposes—families want them as first little mounts for their children, ladies prefer them because they are easy to handle, and farmers want them because they are strong enough to pull a plow in a muddy field. They've even been used as war horses. But because they were allowed to run wild in the Lowcountry after the Revolutionary War, they are in danger of dying out from lack of attention. We hope to save them. Our stable, when we can find a place for it, will breed, train, and sell horses like Sable Girl. Eli will take care of the animals, and I will take care of the business end—the recordkeeping and accounts. And if our horses meet the need we think they will, nobody is going to notice or care whether one of us is black and the other white."

For several minutes, silence settled over the warm kitchen. Mary Sue dropped her head, exhausted by her emotional speech. Eli looked around the room, hoping to see some smiles of approval. There were none. His parents and Mary Sue's had similarly stunned looks about them. Becca and Robbie were wide-eyed. Only Charlotte and Henry seemed receptive to hearing more, and eventually it was Charlotte who broke the silence.

"This all reminds me of another evening, not long ago, when Eddie and I broached the subject of The Greater Aiken Grocery Company. Ours was a similarly wild idea—seemingly beyond our grasp but eventually doable. And after your initial surprise, you gave us your blessing to continue with the plan. In fact, I remember Father calling it 'brilliant.' This proposal sounds no different."

She turned then to Mary Sue and Eli. "It'll take work and time. You'll need to do some research and explore possible locations. And you'll need a name—like The Greater Carolina Marsh Tacky Horse Breeders' Company! But I'm willing to bet you can do it."

Susan dismissed the idea with a snort. "You don't know the first thing about running a business, Mary Sue. As I remember, you barely managed to handle your arithmetic lessons. And as for Eli, he has no real education at all. Loving horses is not much of a qualification for restoring a dying breed." Susan closed her eyes, as if she could shut out the very idea of such an arrangement. But Mary Sue was not about to let her dream be crushed.

"I didn't say it would be easy, and we know it will take some time before we are ready to launch our efforts. But we're planning. In the short term, I want to stay here in Aiken when the rest of you go home, and . . ."

"No! There's no way I will allow you to stay here alone. I don't care what you say. Human passions have a way of taking over the best of intentions, and I won't—"

"Let me finish!"

"I don't want to hear anything more."

"Well, you're going to, whether you like it or not. I want to go back to school. From what Eddie has told me, Professors Anderson and Sams are ready to reopen their Female Seminary here in Aiken. You remember them, Father. Didn't you at one time talk about teaching for them?"

"Yes, they ran a fine institution, offering young women a chance for higher education, and they had applicants from all over the South—but that was before the war destroyed such ambitions."

"Eddie heard them give a presentation recently about their newest plans and passed the information on to me. They intend to address the problem of young women who now need to find a way to support themselves or their families. They will be offering practical training in various careers, not just finishing-school niceties. I want to enroll, starting this fall, if you will allow it."

"I don't —" Susan had barely started to speak before Jonathan held up a silencing hand.

"We will look into it. Your mother will need to know that you will have proper supervision at all times, curfews, and rules of conduct. And I will want to see their curriculum, to make sure that the instruction you will be getting will be suitable for your purposes. If we agree, you will have to work hard and convince us that your efforts are worthwhile. Now, can we please put an end to this discussion and get a well-earned night's rest—after Hector and I have one more drink?"

Chapter 24

Turning Plowshares
into Schoolbooks

July/August 1868

As much as Susan wanted to head back to Charleston on the day after the wedding, a precipitous move was not to be. Jonathan, in an uncharacteristic show of determination, announced over breakfast he hoped to be ready to depart by the first of August. "We will be home in plenty of time for me to arrange a teaching schedule for the coming school year," he explained. "But first, I want to take a side trip to Columbia and visit some of the people who are working on the state's new school system."

"I thought you were in a hurry to get home so you could connect with Benjamin Randolph."

"I'm eager to meet him, it's true, but he's no longer working out of Charleston. He's now a state senator, as well as the chairman of the South Carolina Republican Party, so he's in Columbia most of the time now. I want to find out what he has in mind in terms of start-up schedules, and I intend to offer my services, if I can be of use."

"That's a good idea, dear. Perhaps I will go along with you. I would like a chance to see for myself what kind of work Johnny is doing."

"Motherly interference is seldom a good idea. You would mortify him, Susan, by showing up to check on him. You need to stay here and make sure everything is in good running order before we turn the farm over to the children."

"That's motherly interference, too, isn't it?"

"Not at all. I would call it due prudence."

"But . . ."

"No, you're not going to Columbia. Do you understand me? I will take a look at the Dubois property on Broad Street while I'm there, but I will not hunt Johnny down and open up another opportunity for a clash of our wills. I don't intend to be gone long. When I get back, I will also have to deal with the problem of title in regard to Hector's land and talk to the professors at the Female Seminary. And while I'm thinking about schools, I'd like to look into day schools—or even a boarding school—for the boys as well. The school system back home will probably not be ready to take them. But I'll know more after I've been to visit the capital. I'll try to get us back to Charleston in early August. I'm not willing to leave here, however, until all these loose ends are taken care of, and I don't need anyone else getting in the way."

Charlotte and Henry listened to this exchange and realized they needed to assert their own plans.

"How long will you be gone, Jonathan?" Henry asked. "We need to return to Tennessee, but I would hesitate to leave Susan and the children here alone."

"Back to Tennessee? I thought you had decided to move here to the farm."

"We intend to do so, but transferring not only a household but also a large herd of cattle takes a good deal of planning. I'll have to arrange for a drover and several helpers, as well as wagons to carry our household effects."

"And as much as I love him," Charlotte added, "I don't trust him to see to the packing of my dishes and other breakables."

"I'd like to be headed back to Tennessee within the week. If we can do that, we should be back here before the first of September and Charlotte can get the twins settled in school."

"No problem. I'll take the morning train to Columbia and promise to be back by the weekend. How's that?"

"Good."

"Good for you, perhaps." Mary Sue had been listening to these squabbles with a clenched jaw. Now she glared at the assembled family. "Does nobody care what happens to me? I'm the one who needs to arrange to get admitted to school. I also want to help Eli look for a new location for our stables— before Henry's cows get here!"

"All right, Mary Sue. You are crying out to be recognized as one of the grown-ups. Let's see you act like one." Jonathan threw her a glance that dared her to defy him. "You take charge of getting yourself admitted to the Female Seminary. Take the small buggy and drive into Aiken today. Go see Professors Anderson and Sams. Find out what they need for the admissions process. Come back prepared to tell me what it's going to cost me, what living arrangements and supervision you will have, and what course work you will be doing."

"Fine! I'll have Eli drive me to—"

"You'll do nothing of the sort. You'll go alone. I need to know you can cope by yourself before I allow you to stay here. As for Eli, he can go off on his own and find an available piece of property for himself and the horses. You expect him to help you run this new horse business of yours? He'd better turn himself into a businessman pretty quickly."

"You don't think we can do it, do you? Well, we'll show you!"

"Good. I sincerely hope so. Now, does anyone know when Eddie and Gretchen are going to be able to move into their own house? They'll be wanting to move their things out of here in time for Charlotte and Henry to move in. We will need to get out of their way."

"I don't know, but I know I hate this!" Susan pushed away from the table and began stacking dishes together with a great clatter. "I feel as if I'm in the center of a wildly spinning wheel, and family members are flying off that wheel in all directions."

"I'm not going anywhere, Mama," Becca whispered.

"I know you're not, sweetheart. You're my own little house cat. You and I may be left all alone, but we'll have two melodeons to fill our hours. We can play lonely duets." And now Susan's eyes brimmed with tears.

"Oh, come on, Susan," Jonathan said. "Let's not make this any more melodramatic than it has to be. Families grow up, but children tend to be like bad pennies—they'll keep turning up. Wait till Christmas. You'll be trying to wedge them all into the house on Legare Street for the holidays. They'll all be back before you know it."

※

Jonathan returned on Friday afternoon, after having walked from the train station.

"Goodness, darling, you look absolutely exhausted. How was your trip? Was it as terrible as you look?" Susan bustled about the kitchen to disguise how happy she was to have him home. "Here. Have a glass of cool water and then tell me all about it."

"It wasn't terrible, Susan. I'm just hot and tired from the hassle of the train ride, and I probably should have let you know I was coming so someone could have met me." He looked around in puzzlement, noticing for the first time how abnormally quiet the house was. "Where is everybody, anyway?"

"Well, let's see. The boys are out in the woods, looking for the perfect tree. They've been begging Hector to help them build a tree house, but I told them they'd have to wait and get your permission."

"No tree house this year, I'm afraid."

"I hope not, but you get to be the authority who quashes the idea. Anyway, Charlotte and Henry have taken their brood out berry picking. Both blueberries and blackberries are ready, so I expect to see them coming in any time now, all covered in scratches and berry juice stains. Which is why you caught me elbow-deep in piecrust making.

"Becca is out with the chickens, and the Moreaus are all down in the barn. There's a young heifer who doesn't seem to understand that she is expected to nurse her firstborn calf. Eli came to get his father's help, and Hector in turn sent for Sarah, saying they needed a woman's touch. I'm keeping my distance from the challenge, although I'll bet there are a lot of cats hanging around, hoping for some spills."

"Have you seen Eddie?"

"Oh, he and Gretchen are hard at work on their new house. It's at the white-washing stage, I believe. They're staying at the Schwimmers, which seems to be part of the Mennonite tradition. Instead of going off to frolic, the newlyweds must stay close so their elders can supervise their adjustment to married life." Susan shook her head in dismay. "You were definitely right when you told me I wouldn't make a good Mennonite."

"Certainly not. But don't change the subject. Have you and Mary Sue reached any sort of peaceful settlement?"

"Well, she's not happy, but she's going to great lengths to prove there have been no shenanigans between her and Eli. Right now, she's in the front office, reading something."

"No, I'm right here, Mother." Mary Sue spoke from the doorway, one finger holding a place in a large and battered book. "Welcome back, Father."

"Hello, dear. Have you any news for me?"

"About school, you mean? Unfortunately, yes. It's not going to happen because I'm too early and too old." She shrugged and plopped down on a kitchen chair. "The two esteemed professors were quite polite and welcoming, but they admitted they don't have enough students yet to reopen the seminary. Apparently, they thought all they had to do was open the doors and young women would flock in, which didn't happen. So they're now proposing to open in about two more years and to limit their first classes to fifteen- and sixteen-year-old girls."

"So what will you do?"

"Educate myself! That's what Eddie did. He has all those agricultural books Grandmother Dubois gave him. I've been sorting through them, and I've found a lot on breeding and raising horses. You'll remember Grandmother gave me this one book on how to raise a colt, but I never really read it because . . . well, because Hector was in charge of our animals during the war and didn't want a twelve-year-old underfoot. But now, there's a new colt out there, and I intend to learn by doing."

"Fair enough, provided you come back to Charleston with us first and give Charlotte and Henry time to complete their move. Then, if they are still willing to have you, I'll approve of you coming back here to live and getting some firsthand experience in animal husbandry. Henry may be a good source of information, too, so it should work out well in the end."

Mary Sue nodded in somewhat sullen agreement. Then she opened her book on the kitchen table and pretended to get back to her reading.

Susan opened her mouth for a moment, preparing to interfere. Then she hesitated and turned back to her husband. "So much for the family report. We're all fine, and things are normal around here. I want to know what happened in Columbia."

"Quick news first. I didn't see Johnny. I did make an effort to find out where he was, but it turned out he was somewhere further upstate, keeping an eye on another seething cauldron of white discontent.

"I also checked on the house on Broad Street, or perhaps I should say I checked on the pile of rubble that was once the house on Broad Street. You remember the stories about how, when Sherman's army approached the city, General Hampton and others ordered all the stored cotton to be brought out into the streets. Then they lit it on fire as a gesture of defiance against the Union invasion. And when the wind came up, those fires spread to all the adjacent buildings."

Jonathan shook his head in dismay. "Some day, history books will say Sherman burned Columbia down, but the fires were really the result of Hampton's bad judgment. I can't say the story gives me much confidence in our son's chosen leader. But at any rate, there's nothing to be salvaged from the property your mother owned there. Best to just leave it abandoned until the city confiscates it. They can do with it as they will."

"Well, one less property we have to worry about. Did you see Randolph?"

"Briefly. No one in the official offices could help me get an appointment, but I finally managed to spot him on the street and accosted him like an ordinary panhandler, hat in hand. He seemed interested in my proposal but didn't have time to deal with it. Instead, he suggested I get in touch with Miss Towne and the Freedmen's Bureau chief, General Saxton."

"Who?"

"Miss Laura Towne. Don't you remember? She's the schoolmistress Sarah and Hector told us about—the one who took Annie in and trained her to teach in one of the slave schools."

"Ah, that's where I heard the name. But isn't she in Beaufort?"

"Well, specifically, across the river from Beaufort on St. Helena Island, where she runs something called The Penn School. But more important, Randolph has appointed her as Commissioner of Education for the Sea Islands. So if there is to be a school on Edisto Island, it will have to come with her approval. I thought I'd talk to Hector about going with me to St. Helena to pave the way, since he knows the people who will have to approve my plans."

Mary Sue looked up from her book, alert at the mention of the Sea Islands. "Excuse me. I think I'll take a break and go check on the new calf." She darted out the back door before her parents had a chance to object to her departure.

Susan was frowning at her husband. "Will it be safe for him to go back there? What about the Ku Klux Klan and the murder they were blaming on him?"

"That's what I want to talk to Hector about, but I think it will be safe enough. There haven't been any reports of Klan activity in the Sea Islands for some time now. Most of the trouble spots are in the urban areas, it seems, where former slaves are seen as a threat to the livelihoods of city workers."

"Oh, dear, this is all so confusing. Why can't life be beautiful and settled, the way it used to be?"

"Because life is never beautiful and settled, my dear. That's what keeps it moving and interesting."

Chapter 25

Turning Points

August 1868

As soon as she was out of sight of the house, Mary Sue broke into a sprint toward the barn. Eli, standing in the open window of the hayloft, saw her coming and leaped down to meet her outside. "Slow down," he said. "Don't want you upsetting Missy in there. She's one unhappy heifer."

"Sorry, but I had to get a message to you. My father is home, and he told my mother he is planning a trip to St. Helena Island. And he's going to ask your father to accompany him."

"St. Helena? Why would they be going down there?"

"Because Mr. Randolph told him to. It has to do with the new schools for black children, I guess. I don't know anything more than that, but don't you see? It's a great chance for you. You can ask to go along and then maybe find somewhere we can establish our stable."

"They'll never let me tag along. How would I explain it?"

"Tell your father you miss Annie and want to visit . . . No, tell him the truth! Tell both of them the Sea Islands are the natural home of the Carolina Marsh Tacky horses and you want to look into the possibility of finding land there."

"I don't know, Mary Sue. I think he'll discourage the idea."

"No, he won't. I've already told him no one around here would consider selling us property or giving a woman and a black man entry into their tight little world of horse people.

"So he knows we have to look elsewhere. Trust me—I know what moves my father, and nothing persuades him faster than total honesty. Now go on back to what you were doing and keep an eye out for him. I'll see to Sable Girl while I'm down here. I haven't visited with her and her colt recently."

By the time Jonathan strolled down to the barn, whistling to himself in anticipation of finally getting his school plans underway, Eli and Mary Sue had disappeared into opposite ends of the barn. Hector and Sarah, however, were still in the heifer's stall, glaring at her in frustration. And as Susan had predicted, several cats scurried beneath their feet to lap at the puddles of spilled milk.

"Welcome home, Jonathan," Hector said. "Taking a tour of the property?"

"Not checking up on you but actually looking for you. Can you take a break from the feeding lessons and come out where it's a little cooler under the trees? I have something I want to talk to you both about."

"Good. We need an excuse to get away from this stubborn gal for a while." He slapped the cow on her hindquarters, and then he and Sarah followed Jonathan to the small grove outside the barn. "What can I do for you?" Hector asked.

"Come with me to St. Helena Island."

"Oh, no, Mr. Jonathan. Hector can't go back down there!" Sarah's eyes were wide with the start of panic.

"Hush, woman!" Hector glared at her before turning back to Jonathan. "Why would you want to go there?" he asked. "And what do you need me for?"

Jonathan quickly explained his conversation with Mr. Randolph and the suggestion that he contact Miss Towne and General Saxton. "I figure you know them both, so it would help ease my way into their favor if you were to speak up for me."

"I'd be happy to introduce you, and I don't think going back down there would be a problem. I've been growing this beard ever since I got shot, because I didn't want to try to shave with my left hand. I don't think anyone would recognize me on the street. Besides, any Klanners still hanging around Beaufort would not be likely to cross over to St. Helena. The only white folks there are the school people and the plantation supervisors, and they're all Northerners."

"But . . ."

"Sarah, stop fussing at us. If I travel there in the company of a distinguished white man on a visit to General Saxton, nobody is going to interfere with me. I promise I'll be fine."

He turned back to Jonathan with a nod of acceptance. "When do we go?"

"Well, it'll take some planning. I figure we'll start packing up here so we can move back to Charleston by the end of the month. It would be a help to Susan if Sarah came to Charleston with us. Then once the family is reinstalled in the Legare Street house, we could leave the women to themselves, and you and I could find a way to get down to the Sea Islands. I understand the rail lines are still torn up south of Charleston, but we can take a carriage if necessary. That will also give me time to try to set up some appointments to meet with those who are in charge of the missionary schools down there."

"If I might suggest something—I don't know about Miss Towne's affairs, but I can write to Annie and ask when would be the best time to visit her. General Saxton, though, is always pretty busy. You might want to send a telegram to him suggesting a specific date for our visit."

"Good idea."

From the doorway, Eli's voice interrupted them. "Excuse me, Mr. Grenville . . . I couldn't help but overhear you. If you're headed for the Sea Islands, can I come along?"

"Why on earth would you want to do that?" Hector turned to stare his son into submission. "You have no business down there."

"Oh, but I do, Father. That's where the Carolina Marsh Tacky horses originated, and there are still herds of wild horses that have been there ever since the Revolutionary War."

"So?"

"Well, Mr. Grenville ordered me to go out and find a place for the stables we've been talking about, but there's nothing available around here, and this isn't a very good climate for our little horses, anyhow. The Sea Islands, though—they're perfect for them, and I thought maybe down there I could find—"

"Not a bad idea," Jonathan interrupted him. "Let's talk about this more over dinner tonight. Sarah, why don't you catch another chicken and go tell Susan to set three more places at the table."

"That depends on how Missy the heifer behaves," Hector cautioned as they walked back into the barn. "If she doesn't cooperate soon, I'm going to have to start bottle-feeding that calf."

"Oh, I don't think that's going to be a problem. Take a look."

In the cattle stall, Mary Sue stood quietly, holding the newborn calf in her arms. She was running her hands over the cow's neck and then over the calf, back and forth, until she had mixed their scents. Then, as the others watched, she held the calf to the cow's snout and rubbed their faces against one another. With one arm she hugged the cow and with the other she snuggled the calf, until the three of them were intertwined. Missy's wide cow eyes, which had been rolling in fright, slowly relaxed. Then she turned her head, and with a wet, sloppy tongue, she bathed Mary Sue and the calf in a long, motherly swipe. Mary Sue scratched two pairs of ears for a few more seconds and then lowered the calf to the ground, guiding his head toward the elusive teat as she squirted milk in the general direction of his mouth. He latched on, and the task was done. Missy the cow bent her head to look curiously at what was happening and then nudged her son into a more comfortable position for both of them.

"That girl!" Jonathan exclaimed with a smile. "She has a way with animals no one I know can match. I don't know where she learned it, but she's a natural. I think maybe it's time to quit discouraging her and help her accomplish what she is clearly cut out to do."

❧

Jonathan broke a family custom by not waiting for the end of the meal to drop a bombshell that would distract from dessert. Instead, he introduced the subject along with the mashed potatoes. Susan gave him the opening with a casual comment. "It's good to have you home, dear," she said with a smile. "The children will tell you that meals around here have been a catch-as-catch-can affair while you've been gone. You seem to inspire me to cook."

"Well, I'm grateful. We'll want to enjoy as much of this homegrown bounty as we can before we head back to Charleston in a couple of weeks. Of course, we'll get fresh seafood easily there, but vegetables and fresh blackberries tend to be in short supply."

"In a couple of weeks? Does that mean you've set a schedule?" asked Susan.

"Indeed. Here's what's going to happen—I hope. Charlotte and Henry are headed back to Chattanooga on Monday, correct?"

"Yes, sir." Henry nodded and looked relieved. He was anxious to get home.

"Good. Then we can use your room to start gathering and packing up what goes home with us. And that will help clear out some of the clutter we've managed to spread all over the house. Eddie and Gretchen can then start moving out the furniture and other items they want for their new house."

"Yes, like those antimacassars!" Becca giggled.

"Definitely!" Charlotte laughed at the wisdom of her little sister. "I certainly don't want them for my living quarters when we get back."

"Girls, you're being unkind."

"But honest."

"Let me continue," Jonathan begged, "although I happen to agree with you. The Grenville clan will depart the following weekend, and I have asked the Moreaus to go with us back to Charleston. We can use some extra hands along the way."

Susan looked at him with a question in her eyes, but he stopped her interruption with a shake of his head. "Let me finish. I'm counting on Eddie being available by that weekend to take over the running of the farm for at least two weeks. And after that, both Hector and Henry should be back here and in charge.

"Now, once we get to Charleston, Susan and Sarah, along with you children, will have to take on the tasks of reopening the house and getting everything settled and functioning again. Hector and I will leave almost immediately for St. Helena Island to meet with General Saxton and Miss Towne about the possibility of my taking charge of some of the Negro schools in the area. And . . ." He hesitated before making the final announcement. "And we will be taking Eli and Mary Sue with us to St. Helena."

"What?" The question came like a chorus from almost everyone at the table.

Mary Sue stared at her father, tears welling in her eyes. "You're serious? You're taking us both with you?"

"Yes, unless you'd rather not . . ."

"No, no . . . I mean yes . . . Or rather, of course I want to go, but why . . . ?"

"Eli, why don't you explain the argument you made to me—what's the great attraction of St. Helena Island?"

"Uh, well, first of all, the horses we want to raise? They come from there. After the Revolutionary War, Francis Marion—the Swamp Fox you used to teach us about—turned them loose in the Sea Islands where he had found them, and they've been there ever since. So if we're looking for fresh blood lines to add to our stables, that's where we'll find the breeding stock."

"But those are wild horses you're talking about. Won't they be dangerous?" Susan reached for the first argument she could think of.

"Every horse is wild at birth, Mrs. Grenville. That's why people talk about breaking them. But it's not much harder to break a horse taken from the wild than it is to work with a colt born on the farm. Besides, the climate is perfect for these horses. They need extra salt, so they thrive on the sea grasses. And their hooves are nicely adapted to slogging through the pluff mud. The Sea Islands provide an ideal pasture."

"Are there other horse farms there?"

"No, not as far as I know, but that's part of the advantage we'll have. And my sister Annie tells me in her letters there is a lot of farmland standing empty. It was bought up cheap by land speculators and carpetbaggers during the war. Then the new owners discovered how hard it is to grow cotton without slaves, so they gave up and went home.

"And finally, there's a market for our little guys. Many of the former slaves were able to buy up land—their promised forty acres—but the fabled mules? They never materialized. And our Tackies are better at pulling a plow than a mule would be, anyhow. There are all sorts of possibilities for a business like we're planning."

"All right. I'm convinced again," Jonathan said. "I've come to realize if you and Mary Sue are going to be business partners, she will need to have a say in decisions like this. So I'm going to take both of you with us. While Hector and I are meeting with people who would bore you, I expect you to use Annie as a guide and spend your time identifying the perfect location for your stable."

"Yes, sir!"

"Now, would someone pass the chicken, please? I have no intention of letting this fine meal go to waste. This is all good news. And even more important, there's blackberry pie waiting. Eat up!"

Chapter 26

Welcome to Beaufort

August 1868

*J*onathan sent an introductory message to General Saxton as soon as they were back in Charleston. Saxton replied to Jonathan's telegram with a friendly letter. It was not all good news, but Jonathan found it encouraging.

> *Dear Mr. Grenville,*
>
> *I read with interest your telegram proposing to come here to talk about what you can do to help educate the former slaves. We can always use help, especially from one as trained and experienced as you seem to be. I will be happy to meet you and discuss the possibilities.*
>
> *Unfortunately, I have to tell you Miss Towne will be unavailable. She is on furlough this summer—her first break since before the end of the war. She will not*

return from visiting her family in Philadelphia until late October. However, her friend and housemate, Miss Ellen Murray, is taking care of her business matters on St. Helena Island and will be more than happy to show you what they are doing with their Penn School and their new institution, the Frogmore School.

I also look forward to renewing my friendship with Hector Moreau. I am sure he will want time to visit his daughter, who is helping Miss Murray with clerical duties this summer, but he should also feel free to move about Beaufort. I have discreetly checked with the constabulary, and they tell me they have no further interest in pursuing Hector's part in the accidental death of a certain Klansman.

You inquired about accommodations. I should explain that, as the senior government official in Beaufort, I am expected to entertain all visitors, and my wife and I are amply compensated for doing so. You will be housed with us for the duration of your visit and take all meals with us, which serves to protect you from the dubious offerings of the local Beaufort Hotel. I assure you we will enjoy having you here, and Tillie will be particularly happy to have a young woman among our guests.

Travel arrangements are often subject to the vagaries of nature, so we will simply expect you when you arrive. If you come by ship, which I also heartily recommend, ask any of the draymen at the dock, and they will

be able to deliver you to our house on Craven Street,
where I also keep my office.

I look forward to our meeting and hope we can
reach a mutually beneficial arrangement.

Yours sincerely,

Rufus Saxton, General, U.S. Army.

"I'm quite encouraged," Jonathan confided to Susan. "It's
been a while since someone in the South was impressed
with my Harvard credentials. It's too bad Miss Towne will
not be there, but since General Saxton effectively runs the
Freedman's Bureau for the entire Lowcountry, I'm sure she
will concede to whatever he arranges."

"What's this about arriving by ship?"

"I had hoped to go by train, but there seem to be
some difficult detours down the line. One recent pas-
senger told me he had to travel from Charleston all the
way to Savannah and then make his way by cart back up
the coast to his destination. There is, however, a packet
boat—the *Varmin*, I believe it's called—that runs a regular round trip between Charleston and Beaufort. I was
hesitant because it leaves here in the evening and arrives
some eleven hours later, with passengers disembarking at
dawn. Furthermore, there are no sleeping accommodations. One simply sits up or walks the decks all night. Not
a pleasing prospect, but it may be the least uncomfortable
of several evils.

"Arriving first thing in the morning will give us another full day in Beaufort. We'll leave here next Sunday evening—that's August 9th—and depart from Beaufort on Wednesday the 12th. We'll be back before you know we're gone. And with good news all around, I hope."

❦

As their little party boarded the *Varmin*, Jonathan and Hector immediately moved to take possession of a long bench upon which they might be able to stretch out for some much-needed sleep. Eli and Mary Sue, however, could not be lured from the deck. It was the first nighttime sail for both of them, and they were reluctant to miss any part of it.

"I hope we get far enough away from land that we can see the full sunset," Mary Sue said. "I've always loved the evening sky colors, but it will be the first time I get to see them reflected in the water."

"Well, then, let's stay here on the starboard side, so other passengers don't block our view."

"And I can't wait to see the stars when we're far enough out to escape all the other light. I may stretch out right here on the deck to watch them."

"Uh, Mary Sue, I don't think . . ."

"What? That my father would approve of finding me on my back in the middle of the night?" She couldn't help but laugh at his caution. "You're right, of course. I'll look up, but I'll be dreaming of lying out there in the middle of the deck."

"While I watch from the rail! No matter how much fun this trip may turn out to be, we're not going to give anyone cause to question our relationship."

Eventually, everyone on board fell into some restless form of slumber, but Mary Sue was the first one awake to wait for the approach to land. She watched with curiosity as they neared the coastline of Hilton Head Island, still dotted with army tents and piles of munitions. Then they were sailing up the Broad River, and all the passengers began to stir, gathering their parcels and trying to smooth wrinkled clothing. "Will anyone be meeting us when we get to Beaufort?" she asked.

"I doubt it. General Saxton said to ask one of the cart drivers to show us the way to his house."

"Unless," Eli interrupted, "Annie turns up. I sent her a telegram telling her when we would arrive."

Then the ship was turning toward a long dock, and there at the end of the pier was a familiar face. Annie was jumping up and down with excitement and waving frantically to be sure they spotted her. Eli vaulted the rail to be the first to set foot on the dock. He swept his sister into his embrace and swung her around as he had done when she was much younger. For the next few minutes, the Moreau family was focused on no one but each other.

Mary Sue watched with a broad smile, although she was also feeling a touch of envy. "It's been hard on them, hasn't it? Being separated for so long, I mean. I can't imagine how I might have felt if you and Mother had dropped me off with strangers when I was only sixteen."

Jonathan nodded. "But remember, it was necessary. Hector was being pursued by people with a rope, and at that point the Klan wouldn't have hesitated to attack his wife and daughter as well. Hector did what he needed to do."

"Of course he did, but it still must have been difficult. I hope this short visit helps them all to restore their family."

❧

Tillie Saxton met them at the door of her Craven Street home. "Come in, come in! You must be the Grenville party. What a long night you have had on that packet boat! The General is most anxious to meet all of you, but he is tied up at the moment with a staff meeting downstairs. His orders are to show you your rooms and then feed you an enormous breakfast, so we will start upstairs. Follow me—ladies, here to the right."

She opened the door to a small room furnished with two narrow cots and ushered Mary Sue and Annie inside. "I'll have someone bring you a basin of hot water, and you'll find towels there on the credenza. As soon as you are ready, come back downstairs. You'll find a breakfast buffet in the dining room at the end of the hall."

Mary Sue grinned at Annie. "I'm so glad you're staying with us. We have so much to catch up on."

"When the general heard my family was coming, he insisted I be part of the visit. I'm very comfortable staying out at Frogmore, as you'll see, but everyone knows I've been a little homesick."

"I'm sure you have, but do you really like it here—on the islands, I mean?"

"It's awfully different from living in the heart of Charleston, but after a period of adjusting to the vegetation and bugs and swampiness, I've found it soothing and peaceful. Eli has written to me about your plans, if that's why you're asking. But everyone reacts differently to the Lowcountry. You'll have to decide for yourself."

Jonathan rapped on their door, interrupting the discussion. "Come on, girls. We're starving. Don't make us be polite and wait for you."

The breakfast spread was lavish and varied—fresh fruit, eggs, sausages and thick slices of bacon, biscuits, cornbread, porridge, fried potatoes, and hot coffee awaited them. They were still eating when a dapper little man burst through the door, his military uniform jacket half unbuttoned.

"Welcome to Beaufort!" he shouted over his shoulder as he helped himself to a brimming plate. "Hope your trip on what we affectionately call 'the Vermin' was not too uncomfortable."

"Not at all, sir. And we've managed to get enough sleep to carry us through a busy day here," Jonathan assured him.

"Good. Glad to hear it. And Hector—welcome back, although you appear to be a little worse for wear." The general frowned and nodded toward the sling that still kept Hector's wounded right arm close to his body. "May I ask what has happened to you this time?"

"Of course, sir. I was shot at, I'm afraid. I don't know if you heard the news about Solomon Dill down here, but . . ."

"Yes, yes. The black state senator who got himself murdered up in Camden. Don't tell me you were involved in that fracas!"

"I'm afraid so. I worked for him as a bodyguard of sorts, not that I managed to do a very good job of it. I was outside his house keeping watch, while he and his supporters celebrated his most recent election. His attackers took a shot at me from behind to keep me out of the way while they stormed the house. It's not a serious wound, but the bullet broke a couple of bones. I've been sidelined ever since, which is why I was free to accompany Jonathan on this trip."

"Well, good to see you, even if your wings have been temporarily clipped. Now, here's what I have in mind for you—I'd like to spend some time with you both this morning, Mr. Grenville, talking about your qualifications and how you propose we should approach the problems of educating the thousands of freedmen we are now responsible for. And I'm hoping Mr. Moreau can add some insights into that matter. I need to understand more about how our freedmen view their needs. Then after lunch, we'll take a tour of Beaufort and some of the schools we have managed to start here."

"So you're already in operation?"

"Actually, Beaufort is somewhat unusual because this is where the Gideonite missionaries first arrived in 1862. They immediately started schools here and then spread out to do the same through much of the Lowcountry. One of the most successful efforts has been the school of Reverend Solomon Peck and his daughter Lizzie. Peck arrived in January of 1862, even before the Gideonites. He financed his efforts himself—found himself a small empty house and began recruiting children off the streets. His classes have continued despite all the upheavals of the war and its aftermath, and many of his students are now providing good lives for their families. Several have become teachers themselves. I want you to meet him and hear his approach to conquering the problems of illiteracy. Then tomorrow, we'll travel out to St. Helena, where you can meet Miss Ellen Murray and see the results of the Penn School, which she and Miss Towne founded."

"Sounds fine," Jonathan said. "The Penn School—that's where you've been working, isn't it, Annie?"

"Yes, there and the new Frogmore School, which we'll be opening on the first of November. I'll be along to help show you around. I believe Miss Murray is expecting us all for lunch tomorrow." She looked at General Saxton for confirmation.

"Indeed. Most kind of her. But then, the folks on St. Helena have always opened their tables for those of us coming out to the islands from town. We trade the latest news for food. But what do you have in mind to do today with our younger guests, Annie? I'm afraid they would find our business discussions dull in the extreme."

Jonathan took a quick glance at his daughter. He had realized she and Eli were being completely ignored, and he was afraid she might not take kindly to being referred to as one of "our younger guests."

Mary Sue was looking straight at the general with her head cocked, but the tight-lipped smile on her face had not an ounce of humor in it. "Yes, Annie, will we be able to get on with our own business today?"

Annie took the question as her cue to put down her fork, wipe her lips, and stand up. "As a matter of fact, we need to get started. We'll be taking a small boat across the river. I've left a carriage waiting for us on the dock at Ladies Island so that I can give you a tour of the islands. Thank you for the breakfast, Mrs. Saxton. You'll excuse us?"

"Certainly. And I'll be eager to hear of your adventures over dinner tonight."

Chapter 27

The Lure of a Tomato Sandwich

August 1868

Annie led Mary Sue and Eli back along Craven Street to the dock area. She pointed across the river. "That's Ladies Island over there. It lies between Beaufort and St. Helena Island. There is a plantation I want you to see."

"All right, but how do we get there? There's no bridge and not a boat in sight. I hope you don't expect us to swim," Eli said.

"No, silly. We wait for a boat."

"When is it due? Or did we miss it?"

Annie shrugged. "One will be along sometime. There's a bench over here where we can wait."

"Sometime?" Mary Sue was not in a mood to be patient. "Do you mean this morning? Or sometime today? Or this week?"

"Sometime. I don't know when. I forget that you're not living on Lowcountry time yet."

"What's Lowcountry time?"

"It means that everything happens in due course. Clocks are a rarity around here. Nobody pays much attention to time. We get up when there's enough light to see where we're going. We eat when we're hungry or when food is available, and we go to bed when it gets too dark to see what we're doing. The boat will come whenever the rowers decide they ought to drop by and see if anyone wants a ride."

"But when are we supposed to be . . . wherever it is we're heading?"

"We're supposed to be there when we get there. The island's not going anywhere."

Mary Sue shook her head in dismay. "My father is going to hate this. He lives by his pocket watch."

"Then it's a good thing he's only here for a day or two. You, on the other hand, are thinking about living here, if I understand correctly. You'll have to get used to it. And when you do, you'll find you're a lot more relaxed. Lowcountry time keeps everyone happy."

Eventually a boat did arrive, and the three friends climbed aboard—Eli and Annie moving naturally, while Mary Sue stepped gingerly, clinging with both hands to the flimsy railing. Eli took pity on her and reached for her hand. "Come here to the middle of the boat. That way you can't see the water and it's steadier, too."

"Are you sure this thing will make it across the river? There's already water in the bottom."

"It be good, missy," the boatman answered. And it was. He nodded to his co-worker, and they swept their long poles in unison. In a matter of minutes, they were safely on the other side, and Annie was leading them to a carriage parked in the shade of a huge oak tree. Its horse stood asleep in his harness.

"Whose carriage is this?"

"It belongs to Mr. Eustis, who owns the plantation we're going to visit. This is what he does."

"What is?"

"Providing horses and wagons and carriages to people who want to get from one place to another. I picked up the rig this morning very early and drove it here. And now we'll take it back to him."

"Weren't you afraid someone would steal it?"

"Where would they go? It's a small island, and you can't get off it in a horse and carriage."

"He does this all on trust?"

"Exactly. We get along here because we trust each other."

"Wouldn't happen in Charleston," Mary Sue commented almost to herself.

❧

As they trotted along the narrow road, Annie filled them in on Mr. Eustis's background. He was a Bostonian, married to a woman whose Izard family originated in South Carolina.

Shortly before the war, he inherited a large cotton plantation from his mother-in-law. His wife would not hear of him selling it, but neither would she agree to live on it, claiming that the house was much too small for a family. When war broke out and South Carolina was threatened by a huge naval invasion, Frederick Eustis came south on the same ship with the Gideonites in March 1862, intending only to check on the plantation.

He discovered, however, that the caretaker and slave driver who ran the plantation for the Izard family had taken off in fear for their lives. The slaves, left to fend for themselves, had done so by plundering whatever they could find. Eustis realized that he had only two choices—he could abandon the plantation, or he could stay and run it himself. Because he knew nothing about growing cotton, he looked around for another use of the land and hit on the possibility of offering transportation to those passing through the islands. Gradually, he put together a stable of carriages, wagons, and saddle horses—all available for a price. He had been there ever since.

"Now he's ready to go home, but he's tied to the land because he feels responsible for the former slaves. They still live in their same cabins but spend their time now growing food crops for themselves and for the Northerners who live nearby. He also worries about what will happen to the animals that have served him so well. He needs to hand the land off to someone who will care for it and its inhabitants." She stopped and looked at her brother expectantly.

"You mean he is willing to sell the whole thing—people, animals, equipment included?"

"Well, not the people, surely!" Mary Sue protested. "We've moved beyond the idea of one man owning another."

"Yes, but whoever takes on the plantation will own the old slave cabins and the land the freed slaves are now farming as their own." Annie was now frowning in concentration as she tried to find the right words to explain the situation. "I didn't mean to imply that . . . that he owns the people living on his land. He feels he owes them something—a promise they can continue to live where they are and farm their old plots, a guarantee to protect them. You can understand that, surely."

"I guess so," Mary Sue agreed, "but it still leaves me with a guilty feeling."

"I think I get it," Eli said, "maybe because I was once a slave. Think about the word 'abandon,' Mary Sue. The old caretaker abandoned the plantation and its people. Mr. Eustis stepped in to make their lives better. Now he is unwilling to see them abandoned for a second time."

"So you're saying he might be willing to sell the land to someone he could trust to keep things as they are."

"Yes, exactly."

"Let's go see what all is involved."

Frederick Eustis met them at his front steps as Annie pulled the carriage to a stop. "Welcome, welcome," he said, as he helped the girls on the steps. "I have some lemonade and the makings of some tomato sandwiches on the porch, if you're hungry."

"Remember what I said," Annie whispered to Mary Sue. "We eat when food's available."

"I've never heard of a tomato sandwich," Mary Sue began. Then she caught a glimpse of the table. "And I've never seen a tomato so large!"

"Aren't they something extraordinary? My tenant Jerome grows them out in back of his cabin. Sweetest things you ever put in your mouth. Here, let me help you." Deftly he cut two slices off a rough-looking loaf of bread, smeared both with a soft homemade butter, piled on two slices of tomato, and sprinkled them with salt and pepper. The sandwich he handed Mary Sue dripped with juice and threatened to fall apart in her hands. It also invited her to gobble it as quickly as she could.

"That's the best thing I've ever tasted," she sighed.

"Tomato sandwiches come with the property." Mr. Eustis was laughing, recognizing his lunch offering had perhaps made the sale for him.

⁂

When the last drips of tomato and every smear of butter had been licked from their fingers, Eli stood and walked to the end of the porch. "This is the only house? How many rooms?"

"Only three. There's a bedroom, a sitting area with a table to eat on when it's too cold to eat on the porch, and a small office in the back, where I keep my records. That's why my wife would never move down here—not enough room for her. But there are, of course, other buildings on the property. I built a second place as sort of a guesthouse when I first arrived. It's directly behind this one, which is why you haven't noticed it. When the plantation had its full complement of slaves, they had lots of children. Miss Winsor, who came down with the Gideonites, wanted to start a school over here rather than make the children cross Chowan Creek twice a day. So I built them a house with bedrooms for two lady teachers and a big room at the back for a schoolroom.

"Then there's the cookhouse between here and the slave cabins, a chicken coop, a good-sized barn and stable area for all the horses, and down by the edge of the creek, we have a big storage shed, which the missionary ladies have been using for their food and used clothing distributions."

"I want to know about your horses," Mary Sue said. "How many do you have, and what kind are they? I'm sure someone has informed you we are thinking of starting a breeding horse farm in the area. So we need to know what our options are here."

"I'm never sure how many horses I have. They tend to wander in and out."

"Because you have them out on loan?"

"No, because there are so many wild horses on these islands. The ponies that live in the marsh have always been here, of course. They don't seem to mind wading out into the swamp, up to their hindquarters in the mud sometimes. But at the time of the Union invasion, when all the planters fled for their lives, any extra horses got turned loose to fend for themselves. Those that were strong enough, or clever enough, found shelter and a supply of sweet grass out there along the edges of the pluff mud."

"So how did they become your horses? Did you round them up or capture them one at a time, or . . ."

"They live in herds and move freely up and down the coast to find new grazing land. Sometimes, though, when there's a hurricane or when the weather turns cold and blustery, as it will even this far south, some residual memory stirs in them and they come trotting inland to check out any barn they happen to run across. It's not unusual to walk into a barn in nasty weather and see several faces you've never seen before. Usually they leave again when the weather clears, but sometimes they hang around. I don't believe in capturing them or forcing them into service. Once free, my policy has been to leave them free. But if they choose to stay, I welcome them. So by now, my stables are full of a mixture of breeds. I have everything from swamp ponies to thoroughbred stallions."

Mary Sue had been smiling at his descriptions, but she turned solemn again. "Are you selling the whole plantation?"

"I'm not sure I'm selling it at all. It's not really mine to sell, at least not without my wife's agreement. But here's what I am willing to do. If you think the two of you would be able to handle this operation, I'll let you have it for a year. More specifically, I'll lease it to you for the nominal sum of a dollar, to keep it legal. At the end of that year, we'll talk again."

"That easily? What makes you think you can trust us?"

"'Trust' is the proper word. That's how we do business down here. We have to be able to trust each other because we're so isolated from the rest of society. You say you are horse people, and I always trust horse people. You can have full possession of the land and the buildings, provided you take care of the animals and treat the other tenants on the land with fairness and respect. Within a year, you'll know if it's going to suit your purposes. If not, you can walk away, once I come back. If you've managed to organize a thriving horse farm, we'll try to come to some sort of agreement on what it's worth. Fair enough?"

"More than fair. But you probably know we've been accompanied on this trip by a couple of fathers who will want a say in what their delicate young children are getting themselves into. May we bring them by tomorrow to meet you and see the plantation?"

"Of course. Shall I have some more tomato sandwiches waiting?"

"Oh, yes. They are very persuasive."

Chapter 28

Sealed with a Handshake

August 1868

As they stepped out into the yard, Mary Sue was surprised to see how low the sun was hovering over the water. "I didn't realize how long we've been here. It must be nearly dinnertime."

Annie laughed. "It's not quite that late. The sun takes a long time to set around here, and dinner will be served whenever we get back. Nobody's going to ring a dinner bell at exactly six o'clock. Lowcountry time, remember?"

"Maybe so, but the precise Mr. Grenville will be checking his pocket watch," Eli agreed. "Still, maybe we have time to snoop around a little. I'd like a look at the barnyard and the livestock."

"Why don't you do that, while Annie and I look at the teachers' house. I'm thinking if we decide to do this, you'd live in the plantation house, and I'd take over the guesthouse. My mother would be happy with that arrangement."

The companionable laugh the two of them shared caught Annie by surprise. She glanced from one to the other and raised a speculative eyebrow. Ignoring the question in her eyes, Mary Sue caught her by the elbow and led her around toward the back of the house.

"Are you required to live at Frogmore in order to do your teaching?" she asked.

"No, not really. I needed to live somewhere, and Miss Towne thought I was too young to keep my own house. She took me in out of pity, I think."

"Could you live over here? I'd love to share the guesthouse with you. Maybe you could even start up the schoolroom again, if there are some children around."

"Oh, wouldn't that be fun! I'd get to see more of Eli, too."

"I think it will make a good selling point when we talk to my father."

The girls let themselves into the guesthouse and poked through the rooms and furnishings, until they heard Eli whistling as he returned from the yard. They stepped out onto the porch, meaning to join him. In a moment, however, Mary Sue gasped and stumbled to a stop. She was staring out toward the edge of the water.

"Eli." She waved a hand toward him but her voice was no more than an exhalation. "Eli, look. Out there. In the high grass." She reached out blindly for his hand and pulled him closer. "Do you see them? The Marsh Tackies. They're here."

They stood shoulder to shoulder, staring in wonder as the tiny figures waded through the marsh and disappeared. "It must be a sign—a sign we are meant to be here. Let's go tell my father we've found our place."

"How do we get back?" Eli asked his sister. "You surely can't leave the horse tied up near the dock until morning."

"No, but there's a small shed you didn't see. We'll un-hitch him and settle him into a comfortable stall for the night. He'll find water and hay waiting for him and be ready to go when we get back in the morning."

Conversation at dinner that night was monopolized by Mary Sue and Eli. They spoke in tandem, their words tumbling over one another as they described the Eustis plantation to Jonathan.

"The offer almost sounds too good to be true," Jonathan observed. "What do we know about this man Eustis? Can he be trusted, or is he trying to pull a quick deal to unload his plantation onto a couple of innocent children?" He turned to General Saxton for affirmation.

"Ah, Frederick Eustis is a fine man—often bowed under his load of responsibility. He came here not meaning to stay but could not bear to leave. Frankly, I'm surprised he's considering it now. He must believe your young people can handle the place, or he wouldn't offer it to them."

"Well, I still want to see it for myself. Can we stop there on our way to the meeting with Miss Murray?"

"On the way back, perhaps. We have no set schedule, but she said she is expecting us to stay for lunch, which implied to me our meeting should happen in the morning."

"See?" Annie whispered to Mary Sue. "Lowcountry time. It's vague, but it works well."

❧

Ellen Murray met the travelers at the Brick Church in which Laura Towne had begun her classes. "Imagine," she said, "five teachers, each with about thirty or more grubby little children who had never heard of school. There was a group in each corner of this sanctuary and one in the middle of the room. They were all talking at once, the children running from one group to another, some fighting, some crying. The miracle was, they were all learning."

As Annie had predicted, Ellen and Jonathan shared the same enthusiasms. They were soon chattering away without regard to the general's skepticism or the younger guests' impatience to be done with the whole issue of schools. Ellen led them across the street to the new Penn School, a three-section building that had been built in Philadelphia and then taken apart to be shipped to St. Helena Island and reassembled.

"All but the belfry," she added. "That was Laura's doing. She was determined to have a school bell and a place to hang it. Fortunately, there were some fine fellows in General Saxton's army who were willing to spend their free time building her a bell tower." She grinned so winningly at the general he could not help but smile back.

"Do you still have a copy of this past year's graduation ceremony?" he asked. "I suspect Mr. Grenville would like to hear about the demonstrations your students gave."

"I don't think I have any more copies of the program. Everyone kept them as cherished souvenirs, but I'll never forget the performances the children put on. They had read books on American history and on physiology, and they had contests to see who could answer the most questions from those texts. Others gave demonstrations of how they could write a sentence when they were told to use, say, two nouns, a verb, and an adverb in the predicate. My class read compositions they had written. And we also had demonstrations of mathematics, grammar, geography, and spelling. They were wonderful!"

"And this fall, you'll start all over?" Jonathan was curious about the plans to expand the school.

"We'll start over with our new students to bring them up to the same level, but now that we have two buildings, last year's scholars will move on to bigger and better lessons at Frogmore, where Laura will get to indulge her love of the classics and algebra. Come—I'll tell you what we have planned over lunch."

As the group made their way to the teachers' small cottage, Jonathan took the chance to confer with General Saxton. "You haven't given me any idea of what your staffing needs may be," he said. "But I'll tell you this. I want to be a part of what I see going on here. It's innovative and exciting and important."

"Actually, Miss Murray will have a better idea of our needs, since she works so closely with Miss Towne, who is in charge of all the Negro schools along the coast. Let's see what she has to say."

❧

Over a lunch of fish freshly pulled from the creek and slices of melon, which seemed to be the only crop ready at the moment, General Saxton raised the issue with Miss Murray.

"Mr. Grenville is obviously a fine scholar and educator, with many years of experience teaching American history to young men in Charleston and teaching his own family's slaves at a much different level. Where can you best use him, Miss Murray?"

"Your family is in Charleston, if I understood you correctly?" She turned to Jonathan, her head bent toward him as if she could hardly wait for an answer.

"Yes, we've recently moved back into the family home there, but if you need me to move somewhere else, I can . . ."

"No, no, actually, we need you in Charleston. You've met Benjamin Randolph, I was told."

"He was the one who sent me to you."

"Benjamin Randolph worked very hard after the war to set up schools in our major cities. Charleston has a goodly number, and they will be opening in November along with ours. But now that Reverend Randolph sits in the State Senate in Columbia, he cannot properly oversee schools so far away. We need help in Charleston, and we need it immediately. Are you familiar with those Negro schools, Mr. Grenville?"

"At this point, I only know what I've heard, I'm afraid. I know the American Missionary Society has sponsored the arrival of a great many teachers. They come with their own funding, most of them, so about all that's left to do is to make sure they have safe places to live."

"Can you do that?"

"Of course. Charleston is not as dangerous as you may have heard. One of the Northern teachers who lived alone had problems with the Ku Klux Klan this summer because she was outspoken about the need for black education. Klan members stomped about for a while, rattling the doorknobs and calling out insults, but there was no physical attack. They were more like silly schoolboy pranks being carried out by grown men who should know better. We'll house several teachers together, and there will be no trouble."

"What about curriculum?" General Saxton jumped back into the conversation. "I speak with some experience here, Grenville, having witnessed Miss Towne's struggles with some of her missionary teachers. You'll need to be clear from the start that we're interested in fundamental academics, not religious instruction. Time enough for that when the scholars can manage their letters well enough to read the Bible for themselves."

"A lofty goal, that! I'm not sure even I'm so advanced."

"But you understand . . ."

"Of course. I approach teaching with an overall principle firmly in mind—I remain convinced all children are equally capable of learning, so long as we offer them the material they need and want. There will be some who will be naturally inclined to scholarly pursuit, and I would want to get them reading good literature and writing compositions with proper rhetorical flourishes as quickly as possible. But there will be others whose interests tend toward business or agriculture or craftsmanship. For them, I would provide both lessons in the necessary mathematics and recordkeeping, and in manual skills, if that's what they want."

"Individualized instruction, then? Wouldn't that be hard to manage?"

"Perhaps, but not nearly as hard as it would be to take a natural-born artist and insist he complete grammatical exercises in place of the designs he wants to sketch. I believe schools should produce graduates who are capable of making their way in today's society, but I will not force any scholar to choose a path he does not want. And that goes back to your comment about religious instruction, I think. There will be a few budding preachers in the mix of potential enrollees, I'm sure. So I would let the fervent missionaries do their proselytizing among those who are most receptive to hearing it. The oters could get on with their sums."

Ellen Murray smiled broadly at Jonathan. "I am going to suggest to Miss Towne, and I know she will agree, that we make you a vice-superintendent of Negro schools in Charleston. It will be your job to oversee their efforts and keep them all on more or less the same trajectory. What say you?"

"I would be honored to do so."

"Good. Then let's consider it done. You will be paid from state funds, as the new constitution provides, but you will report directly to Miss Towne. You will want to go home and do some preliminary surveying of the situation. I'll get you a list of the schools. Then I'd like you to come back in late October to meet with Laura herself to discuss the particulars." She stood and held out her hand for a businesslike handshake. "Welcome aboard, sir."

꧁꧂

The other topic on everyone's mind played itself out over dinner that evening in the Saxton dining room. Tillie Saxton had been feeling rather left out of the adventures, so she took this opportunity to question Mary Sue and Eli about their plans for the Eustis property. Once again, they spoke over each other's words in their enthusiasm to explain their dreams.

"I have my own Carolina Marsh Tacky back at the farm in Aiken . . ."

" . . . but she didn't know that until lately. Now that we've discovered Sable Girl's lineage, we'd . . ."

" . . . like to work on breeding her with others to try to, to . . ."

" . . . bring the breed back toward its Spanish origins, depending on what has happened to the horses here."

"And we saw a whole herd of them this afternoon . . ."

" . . . silhouetted against the water's edge. They were so beautiful, and Mr. Eustis says that . . ."

" . . . some of them are tame enough to come right up and settle down in the barn."

"So we'll start with his animals, assess them, try to ascertain their breeds, and then start working on how we can best . . ."

" . . . manage the herd to have it produce the kinds of Marsh Tackies we can provide to farmers in these islands and . . ."

" . . . and ponies for children, and . . ."

" . . . more breeding stock."

"Oh, my word!" Tillie held up her hands in mock surrender. "You're making me tired listening to you. Is Mr. Eustis giving you a good price on the plantation?"

"We're leasing it for a dollar for the first year, to make sure we can manage. Then we'll discuss it further . . . that is, if Father approves. We haven't had much time since this afternoon to get his reaction."

"I'm impressed with the arrangement," Jonathan said. "It's fair and reasonable. When Mr. Eustis and I talked privately, the only concern he had was that you treat his former slaves well, and I was able to reassure him you both would do so. I offered the example you present in yourselves—a mixed-race couple, overcoming those odds more easily because you are also second cousins, but standing strong because you respect and love one another."

Mary Sue stared at him, unable to take in his offhand acceptance of an idea that had sent her mother nearly into fits of apoplexy. Then she burst into tears and ran from the room.

Chapter 29

Mary Sue and Eli

September 1868

Their Wednesday morning departure from Beaufort was subdued. The Saxtons, already focused on their next guests, waved good-bye without accompanying them to the door. On the dock, Annie hugged her father and brother, wishing she had accepted their suggestion to come back to Charleston with them for a visit. It had been tempting—she missed her mother more than she would admit. But the responsibility that made her such a good employee at the Penn School would not let her leave Ellen Murray without an assistant. "You'll be back in October," she whispered to her brother, "and we'll have lots of time to spend together after that." To her father, her secret message was, "Tell Mama I love her."

Jonathan and Mary Sue had boarded the boat immediately, each thinking ahead to what all must be accomplished in the coming weeks. Jonathan watched his daughter's still blotchy and swollen face, and wondered what he might do to lighten her mood. Her outburst of weeping last night had startled but also mystified him. He wasn't sure he wanted to know why she had been crying.

At last, Mary Sue broke the silence. "What are we going to tell Mother?" she asked. "I know you well, Father. I'm sure you already have a plan, but you'd better let me in on it so we present a united front."

"Well, I shall start by telling her all about my new title of 'Vice-Superintendent of Negro Schools.' She ought to be delighted to know I will be getting a regular paycheck and still be involved in teaching."

"I know she'll be happy about your new job, but that's not what I meant. What are we going to tell her about me and Eli?"

"The truth, of course. I'm quite enthusiastic about the opportunity that has been given to you, and I think she'll catch part of that enthusiasm. I'll stress the safety aspects— how you are going into this venture with a long trial period and that you've not gotten yourselves into deeper risks than you should. I'll tell her about how kind and helpful everyone has been, how Annie will come to live with you to provide companionship as well as assistance, how organized Mr. Eustis's plantation is, how relaxed everyone is, and how far removed Ladies Island seems to be from the racial tensions overrunning the rest of the state. I'm sure she'll be happy for you."

"Do you really think she's going to let her darling daughter go off to live with a former slave without putting up a protest?"

"Maybe not, but I'll see to it her protests come to me, not to you and Eli."

Mary Sue moved closer and rested her head on her father's shoulder. "Whatever would I do without you?"

"You would manage fine, I suspect, although I hope you never have to find out."

"What made you change your mind? About Eli and me?"

"I don't know I really had anything to change, my dear. I haveput been busy with my own thoughts and was not paying much attention to what you were going through. I apologize for that. It's too easy for a parent to keep seeing a child as too young to have real problems. I had not observed anything out of the ordinary and thought your mother was exaggerating the danger in which you were dabbling. But on this trip, short as it has been, I've been able to watch you closely. I've not only seen what your mother saw, I've seen you and Eli as a powerful team."

"And that's what convinced you?"

"That, and the unconscious performance the two of you put on last night. The way you finished each other's sentences reminded me of how your mother and I were in the early years of our marriage. People could hardly tell us apart—we thought and acted as one. That's exactly what you were doing last night."

"We're not getting married, Father. We're only starting a business."

"Much the same thing."

"No, it's not. As I told Mother, I love Eli, but he's like a brother—or my best friend. We're not courting or anything of the sort. I grew up hugging Eli, but now that we're older, we both understand the barriers between us. And that's all right. We can still work together." Mary Sue was wide-eyed with her attempt to appear earnest, but once again her father could see tears beginning to form.

"Darling girl, don't try so hard to deny what you feel. I think you and Eli are very much in love, even if neither one of you will admit it. The thought scares me, but I can't deny it. I think you're embarking on a difficult path and I'm worried about you, but I also believe you are strong enough to handle it."

"It's not fair! I should be able to love someone without being afraid to have anyone find out, because his life might be put in danger."

"You're right. It's not fair. The world is often not fair. But some places are fairer than others, and I think you'll both be safer on St. Helena Island than you would be in downtown Charleston. The former slaves in the Lowcountry have learned to trust those people—like Miss Murray and Miss Towne and Mr. Eustis—who have come to help them. You'll fit right into that pattern, and they will accept you as one of their own. Eventually, they will come to see your relationship with Eli as perfectly normal. And when they do, you'll be able to live however you choose."

"And that's why you approve of our move?"

"Yes, partially. I also think you have a good idea and a wonderful opportunity to put the idea into play. But the safety factor is what will convince your mother, so that's what we'll use." He turned away to look across the water, signaling the conversation had reached its limits.

Mary Sue, however, was not quite finished. "Papa?"

"Yes?"

"Thank you for understanding. I promise you we're not going to do anything stupid. We're not going to get married—at least not for a long while—and we're not going to have mixed-race children. Mother and I once had a good discussion about her grandfather and his slave mistress. And she helped me to understand why the added formalities of marriage and parenthood would have caused so many more problems for them. We'll be discreet and private about our feelings. If we can work together to accomplish something we both care about, that will be enough."

❦

Across the deck, Hector was having a similar conversation with Eli. "If you're going to do this, boy, I expect you to do it with every ounce of effort you can muster. Besides, we're going to have to convince your mother this is the right move, and I suspect she'll have a whole slew of objections we haven't even thought of."

"And what, exactly, does that mean?"

"It means you are taking on a man's responsibility, and you're going to have to grow up fast. Can you fill the shoes of a plantation owner who has been on the job for years? I think you have the skills to handle the livestock and manage the accounts—that sort of thing. But I'm not sure you can yet manage the stature you're going to need."

"Stature? I'm already inches taller than you."

"Stature is measured in more than inches, son. It depends on how straight your backbone is, how broad your shoulders are, how big a load you can carry without tiring, how high you can reach to accomplish your goals, and how low you can stoop to help someone less fortunate than yourself."

"Are you saying I'm not strong enough—not good enough—to do this?"

"No, I'm saying you haven't been tested yet. I'm saying you aren't even aware of some of the challenges you'll face."

"Like what?"

"You're going to need the cooperation of all the black men on that plantation. You'll need them to grow food and share it with you. You'll need their help with the animals. You'll need them to let you know when there are problems of any sort. You'll need them to trust you. Look at you—your skin is lighter than most of theirs. You're educated. You're in love with a white woman—"

"I'm not! We're only . . ."

"Yes, you are. Don't lie to me, boy."

"Well, even if I am, no one will ever have to know it."

"You're younger than any one of them, too, or you wouldn't say that. How can you make them respect you as the man in charge if they see you as someone entirely different from themselves?"

"I'll ask them to do things, not order them. I'll explain why I'm asking. And I'll thank them and reward them when they do what I ask. I think they'll get the message. If some of them don't, I'll try to find out why."

"Another thing—these same men are not used to having a woman who is helping to run the plantation. Eustis has been living there like a bachelor. How do you plan to make sure they show Miss Mary Sue the respect she deserves?"

"Oh, they've had white women around. Some of the teachers lived there during the war. And Mary Sue and Annie will be sharing the guesthouse, too. I'll try to set an example. I will always respect Mary Sue and let the men know she is knowledgeable and talented. And yes—I saw that raised eyebrow of yours—I'll be very careful never to give them reason to think she and I are . . . uh . . ."

"Messing around? That is what they are going to think, you know."

"Perhaps so, but I'll not give them a reason to think so."

"Be honest with me, son. Is there a reason?"

"No, sir. We both know a black man who gets caught with a white woman is asking for a rope. We've accepted that and won't be taking any chances. Annie's presence will help, I think. We'll make sure everyone understands we're not living together."

"All right. I won't belabor the point. I still think you have a very big job ahead of you. I hope you can handle it." Hector dropped the subject when he noticed the Grenvilles walking toward them.

"Are you two talking about the same problems we are?" Jonathan asked.

"Uh, probably, but . . ."

"So how are we going to make this move go as smoothly as possible?"

Eli let his breath out in a swoosh. Talking about logistics rather than love was something he could handle. "Mary Sue and I have had the chance to check out the plantation pretty carefully. Mr. Eustis is not taking anything back North with him. The houses come completely furnished and equipped, and so do the stables and the barn. We'll have to bring our personal things and some food staples and . . ."

" . . . the horses. Sable Girl is strong enough to make the journey, but what about Minkie?" Mary Sue caught her bottom lip with her teeth. "We can't leave him behind. He's too little."

"Who, or what, is Minkie?" Jonathan looked confused.

"Sable Girl's foal, of course."

"Rather a silly name for a horse, isn't it?"

"I know, and I'll have to change it once he's a yearling. But right now, he's soft and fuzzy and light brown—like a mink."

"And as valuable," Eli added. "He'll grow up to mate with some of the island Tackies and start a whole new line, I hope."

"All right. I think we can probably crate him safely. We'll bring the animals down from the farm to Charleston by train, give them a couple of days to rest, and then make the rest of the move by wagon. Minkie can ride in his train crate, and Sable Girl will trot along behind to keep an eye on him."

"How long will it take us?" Mary Sue asked. "Since I've only made the trip by water, I can't visualize how far we have to go."

"Maybe seventy-five miles or so. It'll take two to three days, I figure," Hector answered. "Sarah and I made it to Edisto Island in two days, but Beaufort's a fair distance beyond that. We'll have to stop and camp at least once. The road isn't bad, but there aren't any good-sized towns along the way."

"Oh, dear, I didn't realize it was that far."

"Don't look as if you're about to drop off the edge of the world, daughter. Actually, it's not that far when the trains are running. We can hope the rail line gets repaired soon. It probably won't happen in time for this initial move, of course, but later, visiting should be pretty easy."

"And we're going to do this . . . how soon?" Eli, too, was looking worried.

"The last week in October, I figure. That's when Miss Towne will be back. Remember, I would have to make this trip again whether you two were going to move to Ladies Island or not. You're not placing an unreasonable demand upon me. We're going to manage fine. But one thing—don't look so worried around your mothers. They'll pounce on any doubts you may have. Look excited and confident, and we'll make it so."

Chapter 30

A Death in Abbeville

Fall 1868

$\mathcal{H}$ector was happy to be back in his little house in Aiken. Things were more peaceful in the countryside. Even with the Grenville children setting up new households—Eddie and Gretchen in their new cottage, and Charlotte and Henry in the family farmhouse—changes took place at a more leisurely pace. The animals repeated their daily routines, the weather offered no sudden storms to upset outdoor plans, and the orchards produced their yearly crops neither too early nor too late. Occupying armies were no longer underfoot. And if newspapers carried occasional alarmist editorials, they arrived too late to make any difference to the day's routines.

Sarah was often occupied in the farmhouse kitchen, turning out batch after batch of late-season pickles and preserves.

"We have three households to provide for now," she argued when Hector tried to tell her she had done enough. "And Eli and Mary Sue will need to take some with them as well. I know you said their food needs would be pretty much met from the plantation's produce, but that Mr. Eustis fellow don't sound like he'd be much into making pickles."

Eli was busy from dawn to dusk, alternately working late in the barns and burrowing deep into the books Eddie had accumulated in the farm office. "I want to make sure I know how to keep track of blood lines and how to place a market value on livestock," he explained to his father. "The information is all here, but that won't help me much once we move to the island. I've got to get the details down now while I have the chance."

All was well until a letter arrived for Mr. Hector Moreau. Hector felt his mouth go dry as he turned the envelope over, looking for clues as to its import.

"Who's it from?" Sarah asked. "I've never known you to get a letter before."

"I never have, I guess."

"Well, open it. Maybe it's good news."

"Or bad."

"The Klan don't send no letters."

"Humph." At the very thought, Hector felt a twinge in his right arm. The wounds had healed well, but the surrounding muscles were not used to the tension and fear that now poured through him. He tried to disguise the trembling of his hand as he tore open the envelope.

"It's from Mr. Randolph," he said. "He must be looking for Jonathan." But his relief was short-lived. "No, he says . . . uh, he wants me to come campaign with him for the upcoming presidential election."

"I don't even know what that means. I don't pay no attention to things like elections. What does he want you to do?" Sarah dried her hands at the sink and then dropped into a kitchen chair as she stared at her husband. "I can tell this ain't good, but I need you to explain this election business to me."

"We're electing a new president in November to replace that fellow Johnson who got himself impeached not long ago. The Republican candidate is General Grant, leader of the Union Army during the war. His Democratic opponent is a man by the name of Horatio Seymour. I don't know much about him, but his vice-presidential candidate is Francis Blair, who's a nasty talker. Blair says the Democrats are going to restore white supremacy, remove all the Reconstruction governments now in place in the South, and get rid of all the semibarbarian blacks who spend their days lusting after white women."

"Hector!" She glared at him and jutted her chin toward the porch, where Eli was bent over a book. "Shhhh!"

"I'm not saying I believe that, Sarah. I'm only repeating Blair's campaign positions. That's why it's so important to help get Grant elected."

"But what's this fellow Randolph want you to do?"

"Travel with him. Help with the crowds. Watch his back. That sort of thing."

"Like you did for Solomon Dill? And nearly got yourself killed?"

"Not even close. Don't exaggerate. The Republicans used to have a great advocate and orator working for them—name of Thaddeus Stevens. But he died back in August, and now the other leaders of the Republican Party are trying to fill in for him. Randolph is scheduling a series of speaking appearances here in the upland region of South Carolina, and he wants me to join him."

"Why you?"

"Because he knows me through Jonathan, I guess, and because I live nearby. It won't be long—only a couple of weeks in October. I'll be back in time to travel with Eli and Jonathan to the Lowcountry, and that plan will get me off the hook in case Randolph wants more of my time."

"I still don't like the sound of it."

"Maybe neither do I, but I have to do it. We've come so far. We can't let it all go for nothing. I owe it to our fellow slaves."

❦

Once the last of the harvest was in, Hector turned the Aiken farm over to Eddie Grenville and caught a train for Abbeville. He had never visited there, but he was afraid he already knew what to expect. The clerk in the depot office grumbled when he stopped to ask the location of the Freedmen's Bureau.

"Downtown. Find it yourself. There'll be darkies loafing 'round the building, waiting for a handout. Just follow your nose."

Gritting his teeth to keep from responding to the suggested slur, he made his way downtown and eventually stumbled upon the building because of its prominent sign, not because of any lurking crowds.

"I'm looking for the Assistant Commissioner," he told the man at the door. "Senator Randolph sent me to do some preliminary scouting for a stop he'll be making here on his campaign tour."

"Yes, sir, we've been expecting you. Right this way."

Jonah Wainwright, the official in charge, stood as Hector entered the office, his hand extended in welcome. "Glad to have you here, Mr. Moreau. We can use all the help we can get. Abbeville's had a good deal of turmoil this summer—lots of unprovoked attacks on local blacks, former owners going after their old slaves, fights, rapes, kidnappings. You name it, we've seen it."

"Why is that? We haven't had that kind of trouble back in Aiken that I've seen."

"Has a lot to do with the local constable and his cronies, I think. They always side with local whites. And business has been bad—lots of former planters still suffering from losses during the war. They're out of work, hungry, sick, and they need somebody to blame. We're the targets."

Hector took a deep breath before commenting. In the recesses of his mind a little voice was asking why he had come and what he had gotten himself into. "I'm sorry to hear all this, but I was only sent to make sure arrangements were in place for Senator Randolph's visit."

"And that's what you'll be doing. But you need to understand that, while the meeting hall will be full of black men who idolize Mr. Randolph, the streets outside will be patrolled by white Democrats who have sworn to kill any Republican who tries to campaign here."

"That serious?"

"Yes, sir, I'm afraid so. We'll do everything we can to help you assure Mr. Randolph's safety, but . . ."

"But there are no guarantees?"

"Exactly. Even now—I've arranged for you to stay with one of our clerks who runs a boarding facility for traveling black businessmen. Security is tight there, and it will save you from having to make your way through the public establishments of a hostile town."

"I appreciate that. I was wondering where I could go safely."

"I'll walk you over there myself as soon as we close the office for the day. In the meantime, you might want to take a look at this list of offenses committed against black citizens of Abbeville and the final disposition of their cases. It'll give you a better idea of what you'll be dealing with."

Hector took the pages of carefully lettered depositions and settled himself into a corner to read:

REPORT OF OUTRAGES COMMITTED BY WHITES AGAINST FREEDMEN IN ABBEVILLE COUNTY, SO. CA. DURING THE MONTH OF JULY 1868

Name of offender: **Thos. Arnold**. *Date of outrage*: 3rd July 1868. *Person injured*: **Mary Williams**.

Nature of injury: beat her with a hoe. *Where committed*: Abbeville District. *Remarks*: warrant issued by J. P. but not yet executed.

Name of offender: **Mrs. Burnett** & her son. *Date of outrage*: 30ᵗʰ June. *Person injured*: **Chas. Moore** & wife. Nature of injury: Mrs. B. struck the wife & the son assaulted both with pistol. *Where committed*: Abbeville District. *Remarks*: Squire Merriweather <u>forced</u> to issue warrant against son; not yet executed.

Name of offender: **Alfred Blackwell**. *Date of outrage*: 22ⁿᵈ July. *Person injured*: **Lizzie Blackwell**. Nature of injury: choked and otherwise abused her. *Where committed*: Abbeville District. *Remarks*: referred to Squire Giles & not yet heard from.

Name of offender: Mr. **C. L. Cason**. *Date of outrage*: 19ᵗʰ July. *Person injured*: **Jr. McIntosh**. Nature of injury: beat him severely & sent him to jail on charge of attempt at rape on sister. *Where committed*: Abbeville District. *Remarks*: Warrant issued against Cason by Squire McCord on failure of Squire Sharp because Plaintiff had no land & could not give <u>white</u> security to prosecute.

Name of offender: **Albert Hamlin**. *Date of outrage*: January. *Person injured*: **Winnie Anderson**. Nature of injury: took her son off into Alabama. *Where committed*: Abbeville District. *Remarks*: reported on July 8ᵗʰ.

The list continued for several pages, but Hector did not need to read further. The pattern was clear. The injuries were assaults committed by whites against blacks. Cases were recorded and in some instances turned over to a white adjudicator. But the most common conclusion was always the same. No actions had ever been taken against the perpetrators.

Hector awoke on the day of Randolph's scheduled speech with a sense of foreboding he could not dislodge. He felt sure he had taken precautions to protect the senator from the moment of his arrival to the moment of his departure. A private carriage waited to transport him to and from the train station. Streets around the Courthouse meeting hall were barricaded against casual traffic. Doors to the meeting hall would be locked all the preceding day to be sure no unauthorized person was lying in wait for a chance to attack either the speaker or his audience. Burly guards were in place at the doors to screen every member of the audience for weapons. Randolph's local accommodations were a closely guarded secret, and only Hector knew his exact travel arrangements. But could anything stop a determined assassin? Hector feared the task was hopeless.

On the evening of October 15, 1868, Randolph spoke to an overflow crowd of admiring Republicans. Most of the faces were black, but a goodly number of white supporters had gathered as well. Mr. Wainwright had mentioned the town was home to a lot of carpetbaggers and scalawags, but Hector had not expected there to be so many. He stared at those white faces, wondering if any of them were really Democrats in disguise. One small part of his mind rebelled at singling out potential troublemakers by the color of their skin, but caution warned him that, if a shot rang out, it would not come from a black man. When the evening was over, he realized he had not really heard a word Randolph had spoken. Fear had drowned out all but the hammering of his heart.

The next morning, Hector himself drove the carriage that delivered Benjamin Randolph to the station. Randolph was to catch a train to Hodge's Depot and then transfer to the line that would carry him to Anderson, where he was scheduled to speak that evening. Randolph thanked Hector for his fine work and waved farewell as the train pulled out of the station. Hector's shoulders slumped in relief. But before the day was over, relief would turn to despair.

The report came into Abbeville over the telegraph lines. At Hodge's Depot, Mr. Randolph had boarded the Anderson train, but once he had claimed a seat, he disembarked again to speak to someone he recognized. Five men approached the platform, spreading out as if to encircle the senator. Three of the five stepped forward with drawn guns and fired directly at Randolph, who fell—dead instantly—onto the platform. The five men did not flee. They checked their handiwork to make sure the senator was dead. Then, according to the witnesses, they strolled to a nearby store. They chatted with other patrons, purchased a few sundries, and then came back out, mounted their waiting horses, and rode slowly away. Witnesses knew the five by name: "Big Bill" Talbert, the ringleader; the two other shooters, Joshua Logan and J. Talbert;

Langdon Connor, who discovered where Randolph was sitting on the train; and Fletcher Hodges, who offered a roll of bills to Logan and the two Talberts if they would shoot him. Yet no one moved to stop their departure. Senator Randolph's body lay on the platform awaiting its inquest, while the witnesses, both black and white, silently withdrew.

Chapter 31

New Revelations

October 1868

*S*usan was the first to see the news. She had picked up the day's *Charleston Mercury* from idle curiosity, but the first headline froze her attention.

BELOVED BLACK STATE SENATOR KILLED IN ABBEVILLE

MULTIPLE SHOTS FIRED ON RAILROAD PLATFORM

She skimmed the article quickly. Who was with him? Was anyone else injured? Were the perpetrators caught? Who was to blame? How would this news affect her husband, who had taken on his new job out of admiration for Senator Randolph? Did the article mention Hector Moreau? What about Johnny Grenville? She sighed with relief to learn none of her family members had been involved. Then she shook her head, ashamed she put the welfare of her family above the snuffed-out life of a good and generous man.

Jonathan was whistling as he came up the walk, warning Susan he had no idea of the devastating news waiting for him. She met him at the door, newspaper still in hand. At first, he failed to notice her expression. "What a wonderful day I've had, Susan! Four schools visited, and each one more exciting than the last. There really are some great plans afoot here in the city. I'm convinced we are going to make a huge difference in the lives of our . . ." His voice trailed off as he noticed her pallor. "What's wrong?"

She was momentarily struck dumb. Her mouth opened, but no words came from her lips. "You haven't heard." It was a statement, not a question.

"Heard what? What has happened? Is it one of the children? What?"

"Mr. Randolph. He's been . . . been shot."

"Shot? How bad is it? What did you hear?"

Still at a loss for the right words, she handed him the newspaper and watched his face as he devoured the article. She wondered if his thoughts were the same as hers had been—fear for those she knew rather than those she did not. But of course, Jonathan knew Benjamin Randolph. She could see him react to the description of the body left lying on the railroad platform. A muscle in his jaw jumped, and his clenched fists crumpled the paper.

"Damn it! Why are the good ones always the ones to die?"

For once, she didn't object to his strong language. It seemed entirely appropriate. "I don't know."

"Of course you don't know, because there's no answer."

"I'm so sorry."

He shook his head. "He should have known it was risky to travel unprotected. But then, this is supposed to be the United States, and the war is supposed to be over. The vaunted Fourteenth Amendment gave him the right to do as he pleased. And look where it got him. Damn it!" He slammed his fist against the wall, causing a small crack in the plaster.

Susan reached for his arm, but he shook her off. "Don't. I think I need to be alone for a while." He headed for his study, his refuge of habit when the world closed in upon him. At the door, he turned. "Hector wasn't there?"

"There's no mention of him."

"And Wade Hampton's group? Johnny?"

"Apparently not."

"I suppose we can be grateful for that." He started to close the door, not giving her much time to respond.

"Jonathan, wait. I think there's someone out on the piazza."

He frowned and cocked his head. But there was no need to listen more carefully. A fist pounding on the door and flashes of light left no doubt.

"Grenville? Open up! We want to have a little chat with you about the friends you keep." A harsh voice shouted over a background chorus of low grumbles, shuffling feet, and the occasional cough.

"Jonathan! Don't open it." Susan clung to his arm as he tried to reach for the lock.

"Would you rather I let them break it down?"

"Maybe I would. Better they break the door than attack you."

"It's the Klan again, Susan. I keep telling you, they are cowards. They're not going to attack me. We'll exchange a few unfriendly words, and perhaps they'll let slip something I need to know."

"With luck, they'll go away."

"Not till they've had their say, I'm afraid. But that's all they'll do—talk." Nonetheless, he turned back into his study and returned carrying his shotgun. He opened the door and jutted his chin at the nearest man. "You want to talk to me? Then step back and give me room to come out."

"Not going to invite us in, are you?"

"I only invite my friends to enter my house. And my friends don't show up with masks, ropes, and tarry torches. What do you want this time?"

"We were wondering if you'd heard the good news. Somebody put a bullet through the head of one of those pesky niggers who keep messing with our elections. Went by the name of Randolph. Heard of him, haven't you?"

"I knew Benjamin Randolph, yes. A fine man who devoted himself to the welfare of others." Jonathan's jaw clenched with tension.

"Devoted himself to lining his own pockets, more likely."

"Niggers ain't human."

"Ain't got no morals."

"Prob'ly deserved to die."

Jonathan slowly raised his shotgun until it pointed over the heads of the Klansmen. "I'll listen to no more of this. Get off my piazza and move quickly, before my trigger finger loses patience with you."

"Aw, you ain't gonna shoot us. They say you're a peace-able man."

BLAM! The shot blew a hole in the plaster above their heads, showering everyone with bits of white dust and wood shavings. "Now move!" Jonathan's face contorted into a snarl. "Move or you'll be picking buckshot out of your backsides for a week."

The Klansmen broke into a run as they cleared the stairs—all but a shadowy figure who now stepped forward to lay a hand on Jonathan's gun barrel. "You'd best give me that before you hurt yourself," the falsetto voice urged.

The anger still surging in his blood, Jonathan thrust the gun upward, breaking the masked man's grip. With his other hand, Jonathan reached for the piece of cloth covering the man's face and ripped it away. Shock stopped him before he could bring the barrel of the shotgun down on the intruder's skull.

"Alex! My God! Alex Croft."

"Yes."

"It's been you all along?"

"Afraid so, although I wish you had not discovered my identity."

"As a boy, you spent your summers playing on this porch, and we treated you with the same love and kindness we gave our own son."

Alex appeared unrepentant. "And I've treated you well since then. I've done nothing but try to keep you out of danger from my comrades."

"What has happened to you?" Jonathan's anger had drained, only to be replaced by a deep sadness as he stared at his son's childhood friend. "How did you get yourself mixed up with that uncouth bunch of thugs?"

"The war happened, Mr. Grenville. An invasion from the greedy North destroyed our homes, our livelihoods, our standards, and our values. Your army left us penniless and powerless, as well as sick and wounded. And speaking of your son, how is Johnny, anyhow? Too bad he had to lose a leg in our hopeless cause, wasn't it?" The voice was in its normal range now, but it was choked with bitterness.

The two men stood silently, staring at one another, unable to carry the conversation further—as if they had been speaking two different languages.

And into that silence stepped Susan. "Good. They're gone. Jonathan Grenville, did you blow a hole in my freshly painted ceiling? Oh, hello, Alex. We haven't seen you here in a good long while. How are your parents?" The polite Southern charm drilled into every Charleston belle took over, leaving Susan with a bright-eyed smile on her face, even in the midst of the debris of a shotgun blast.

Alex floundered. He suddenly felt twelve years old again as he stuttered an incoherent response to his best friend's mother. "Yes'm. They're, uh, fine, I guess."

"You might ask him about his mother-in-law, Susan."

"His . . . ?"

"Henrietta McLeod—Bodicia, intrepid defender of Confederate womanhood—your next-door neighbor and his mother-in-law." Jonathan turned again to Alex. "That's how you were able to appear and disappear without detection, wasn't it? You had your own little rathole, right next door."

Alex stared back without a word. There was nothing to say.

⁂

Three days later, Hector and Eli arrived by train from Aiken, bringing with them a wagon loaded with supplies, two old draft horses, and the two Marsh Tackies. Sable Girl had been trained to walk on a lead behind the wagon, while Minkie had his own straw-lined crate. Once everything was unloaded at the depot, they made something of an entourage as they headed toward Legare Street.

As usual, it was Susan who worried first. "Jonathan, what if Alex reports Hector to his friends? You know that horrible woman next door will tell him the Moreaus are here."

"Hector's no longer a wanted man, Susan, and as for the Klan . . . they seem to have gotten the message they are unwelcome. Besides, we'll not linger here. I need to get down to St. Helena to see Miss Towne and General Saxton before their schools open on the first of November. And Mary Sue and Eli are eager to get started as well. We'll be gone, and the

Klan will turn their unwanted attentions onto someone who doesn't shoot wildly at them with a load of buckshot."

Hector had been standing back, refusing to meet the eyes of his former owners. He dreaded the moment he would have to answer Jonathan's questions about the Randolph shooting. But the discussion of their departure caused him to brighten for a moment. "A little good news in that regard, Jonathan. On the train, we learned they have finally opened the tracks between Charleston and Pocotaligo. That'll cut almost two days off our travel time. Once we're all unloaded there, it'll only be three, maybe four, hours to Beaufort."

"Thank heaven!" Susan said. "I've been stewing over your plans to camp out along the road. That sounded very dangerous in these unsettled times."

"And the train ride will be much easier on the horses, too. How soon can we leave, Father?" Mary Sue's eyes were shining with eagerness.

"Can't wait to get away from your parents, eh?" Jonathan patted his daughter's arm to let her know he was teasing. "I'll stop by the depot this afternoon and see when we can arrange for a box car. But first, let's get these travelers inside and let the horses relax while they can."

While Eli and Mary Sue took charge of the animals and baggage, Jonathan and Hector settled into Jonathan's study for a talk.

"Tell me what happened, please," Jonathan asked.

"You probably know as much as I do. The situation in Abbeville was tense at first. A lot of folks didn't want a

Republican speaking in their courthouse. But we had guards, and there was no real trouble. I drove Mr. Randolph to the train station the morning after his talk and bid him farewell. He knew I needed to get home, and there was a new guard scheduled to meet him in Anderson. Not a breath or hint of trouble. I didn't even hear of the shooting until I reported to his office in Columbia."

"So you don't think it was a planned attack?"

"Not that I could tell. Maybe if I had traveled with him, I could have stopped him from stepping back out onto the platform at Hodge's Depot. Maybe if I'd been there, he'd still be alive. That's what haunts me, Jonathan."

"Or maybe the attackers would have boarded the train and shot you both. It doesn't do any good to play 'what if' with the facts. It happened, and we have to go on from there. I'll tell you this, though—this shooting has changed my mind about a lot of things. I can't sit back any longer and watch other people take all the risks. I'm tired—no, I'm ashamed—of being called a peaceable man. I'm an angry man, and I want to take a more active role in what's going on."

"What brought this on? Surely not Mr. Randolph's death?"

"No, not that alone. But I took on a batch of Klanners the other night. Threatened to shoot them and actually fired a shot into the ceiling of the piazza. And then I attacked that mysterious stranger who has been visiting me with vague warnings. I ripped his disguise off and found out who he is. And you know what? It felt good—really, really good. I felt younger than I have in years. I'm ready to take on this mess of a world and straighten it out."

"You're not thinking of giving up your new job of supervising the Negro schools, are you? You'll be needed even more now that Mr. Randolph is gone."

"No, I'll still do everything I can for the schools, but I'm setting out to become more involved in politics. I want to stand up and let others know what I believe. I'm trained as a public speaker. It's time I put that training to use somewhere beyond a classroom."

"Does Miss Susan know about this new resolve of yours?"

"No, and don't you tell her! She'll be the first to try to talk me out of it. But I have to act, Hector. I can't let others fight my battles for me any longer."

Chapter 32

New Alliances

Late October 1868

A t the depot in Pocotaligo, Jonathan and Hector asked directions to a livery stable, where they could rent horses to finish the trip. Eli and Mary Sue rehitched the old draft horses to the supply wagon and supervised the reloading of Minkie into his custom crate. The travelers parted on the outskirts of Beaufort. Mary Sue and Eli headed straight for the ferry dock, unable to wait any longer to reach their new property. Jonathan watched them until they disappeared around a corner. He blinked rapidly, making a faint pretense of wiping the sweat from beneath his eyes. "Go with God," he murmured.

At General Saxton's headquarters on Craven Street, Tillie Saxton once again met them at the top of the stairs. "Welcome back, gentlemen. Rufus is anxious to see you."

With her usual efficiency, she directed a servant to carry their valises to their room, while she led the two men into the dining room. The general had apparently taken over most of that space with stacks of papers spread across the table. He stood quickly, fussing in a futile attempt to re-button his jacket. He shook hands and then shoved the mess of paperwork into a higher stack, making room for Jonathan and Hector to enjoy a cup of coffee. He peppered them with a bevy of questions without pausing for an answer.

"How was your trip? Railroad functioning again, is it? And the children? Mary and Eli, wasn't it? Have you delivered them safely to Mr. Eustis's place?"

"We left them at the ferry. Truth be told, it broke my heart to do that, but they need to appear to be in charge from the beginning. It wouldn't do to have them arrive at the plantation with their fathers holding their hands."

"You're a wise man, Grenville."

"Maybe. I won't wait long to visit them, however. But first, I've been looking forward to getting your advice on a question of property rights."

"I'm not sure I'm your man, but tell me about it."

"Well, my wife and I have inherited a rather large amount of land scattered all across the state. But while we are entitled to take profits from it and required to pay taxes on it, the will itself prohibits us from selling it. The holdings must remain intact throughout our lifetimes and then be sold, with the profits passing to our children."

"An odd provision."

"Made by an odd old woman."

"Obviously."

"Now, some of the holdings are not a problem. A house in Columbia burned to the ground, so that's that. We live in the Charleston house, and two of our children live on the farm outside of Aiken. The business properties in Savannah are leased. The difficult decision is what to do with the plantations. I've always believed land should belong to those who put it to use. I fully supported General Sherman's decision to allow former slaves to claim the acres they had cultivated all their lives. In fact, much of our Edisto Island plantation is already in the hands of our former slaves, and they are doing well there."

"That's good to hear."

"Yes, but they are only temporary holders. They can't purchase the land because I can't sell it. And the other two rice plantations—one along the Ashley River Road beyond the Middleton holdings and one on the Combahee River— are pretty much lying fallow for the same reason."

"So your question is?"

"How can I make sure the land does not fall into the hands of people who will drive the current inhabitants off? My original idea was to lease allotments to former slaves for a minimal fee, perhaps a dollar a year, with the understanding they would keep the money they would be saving and then use it to purchase the land when it eventually goes up for sale."

"But they would have no guarantee . . ."

"I realize that. The other part of my daydream involved turning each of the plantation houses into a Negro school with the same arrangement—no cost for the use of the house during our lifetimes, with the savings ready to be used to purchase the school permanently at a later date."

"But again, you would be asking people to take an enormous leap of faith."

"If the holders deposited their money in the Freedman's Bank, it would be waiting when they needed it."

"No."

"No? Why not?"

"Because we can't trust the Freedman's Bank. It's too dependent on politicians for its very existence. We struggle from election to election to keep the Republicans in power, but you must realize what would happen to Negro money if the Democrats were able to seize control of the state. And one of these days, they will."

Jonathan stared at him. "You're serious?"

"Deadly serious."

"So what do I do?"

"Well, first, you give up the notion you can control what happens in the future. You want to do something to benefit the people who once worked your land? Then put them back to work on that land with assurances that, as long as you are around, they will not be driven off the land. Treat them as sharecroppers, but limit the rent you take from them to the amount you need to cover your taxes. Provide them with overseers to manage the cooperative use of the plantation lands and equipment, but make sure the overseers are decent men who share your goals and values. The Freedmen's Bureau can help you by providing a teacher or two for each plantation."

"But what if . . ."

"There are always 'what ifs.' All you can do is concentrate on the present, where you at least have a fighting chance of making a difference. That's the best advice I can give you."

"And that advice applies also to the Charleston schools, I take it."

"Of course it does. You open the doors to black children in Charleston, and you offer them the best education you can, for however many days they come to you seeking knowledge. That's how you change the world—in tiny increments, not grand sweeping gestures."

"I understand, and I agree. I'm anxious to talk with Miss Towne about the Charleston schools."

"Good. I've arranged for us to go out to Frogmore tomorrow morning. Laura Towne and Ellen Murray are working hard on their old plantation house, trying to make it habitable so they can move into it permanently. Ellen Murray is still offering a fish and watermelon lunch, and you'll be able to talk teaching with both of them."

"I assume that will also give us a chance to drop by the Eustis plantation and check on the new owners?"

"Certainly. For this afternoon, however, I've arranged for you to meet one of the most important men in this area—our very own congressman-to-be, Robert Smalls."

"Robert is in town?" Hector interrupted. "I've been hoping we would get to see him." He turned to Jonathan to offer an explanation. "Robert Smalls is the former slave I told you about—the one who stole *The Planter* right under the noses of the Confederate Navy and turned it over to 'Uncle Abe.'"

"Yes, I remember the name, but I thought he went into business with a sundries store. He's a congressman now?"

"He's running for the State Senate in the coming election," General Saxton explained, "and he's bound to win here in Beaufort. The rest of the state may not be too thrilled with him, but he has a strong political base here in the Lowcountry."

"Well, as I told Hector when we were planning this trip, I'm also looking for a way to contribute my bit to the political arena. Smalls sounds like the man for me to talk to."

❦

The reality of the man in question, however, took Jonathan aback. Robert Smalls had an overwhelming physical presence. He strode into Saxton's office that afternoon as if he were plowing through the air. He was not taller than Jonathan but perhaps twice as broad. His shoulders strained the seams of his coat, and the elaborate gold watch chain stretching across his ample stomach looked as if it were losing the battle of holding his expensive suit together. He wore a hat, perhaps for the sole purpose of being able to sweep it off and tip it toward the stranger to whom he was being introduced.

He pulled the proffered chair back several inches to allow himself to stretch out his well-shod feet. He hitched his trousers to give his knees more room to bend and wiggled several times to settle his hips into the restrictive dimensions of the wooden chair. An expensive cigar poked out of his shirt pocket, although he made no effort to light it. Instead, he removed his *pince-nez* and tucked it into the same pocket. Settled at last, he looked Jonathan up and down with a sardonic expression that suggested he was sizing up the man's character as well as his sartorial failures. Moreover, based on the black man's slightly curled lip, Jonathan was sure he had come up short on both accounts.

"So you're the new vice-superintendent of Negro schools in Charleston. Rufus, here, seems to think I can be of some assistance to you. What can I do to help?"

Jonathan was at a complete loss for a response. He glanced helplessly at the general, who graciously stepped in to cover Jonathan's befuddlement. "We were about to get onto the subject of funding the new schools. Robert, why don't you start there and tell us what's happening at the state level?"

"Well, as you may or may not know, this past summer's Constitutional Convention provided for state-funded education for all children, black and white."

"Yes, I do know that," Jonathan said. "I was in the audience when the finished document was read out for the first time."

"Were you?" Smalls sounded fairly surprised. "Out of idle curiosity or to some purpose?"

"I was there because I care about education, obviously. What concerns me, however, is that while the constitution specifies a poll tax to fund the schools, there were no visible provisions for collecting and administering that tax."

Smalls gave an elaborate sigh before he answered. "We couldn't take care of everything in one document."

Jonathan noticed his eyes had narrowed as he spoke. This was not a man who handled criticism well. "Of course not. And this school year will not be the first time I've started teaching without having any idea when—or if—money will be forthcoming. But I was wondering if you have any insights about when the legislature plans to implement the educational provisions of the constitution."

"That's why I'm running for the State Senate. I helped write that constitution. Now I feel obligated to see to it our promises are kept. It will happen, Mr. Grenville. I guarantee it."

"And I will support you in your efforts. Which brings another topic to mind—I have come to realize I have been sitting on the political sidelines for far too long. I would like to become more active in supporting the Republican Party and the causes it represents. What can I do to help you?"

"Oh, please. Not another political amateur! Politics may be a game, Mr. Grenville, but we don't need inexperienced players getting in the way."

General Saxton had been listening to the exchange without comment, but now he frowned. "I think you may be making an unfair judgment, Robert. You don't know Mr. Grenville well enough to pronounce him politically incompetent."

"Perhaps not, but the election is days away. Too late for a newcomer—especially a white one—to get involved."

Jonathan deliberately avoided reacting to the racial aspersion. "So what can I do to prepare myself for the next campaign?"

Robert Smalls took another long look at Jonathan, obviously running a mental assessment of his likely abilities. "I'll tell you what you can do, and you are perhaps the best person around to carry this out. Teach our black children about voting. You may not realize it—most white people are so familiar with the election process they assume the former slaves want to exercise the same rights. But in fact, many, if not most, ex-slaves have no idea what voting is all about. For generations, they've been punished for having an opinion. Now a white man tells them they have to vote, and their knee-jerk question is going to be, who does the white man want them to vote for?

"Let's start with the youngest children. Teach them about voting. Elect class officers. Help them understand they have the right to make a choice and that the majority wins. Stage little elections in the classroom. Have them elect a floor sweeper and a water carrier. Get two candidates for each position and make each of them give a short speech about their qualifications. And then carry out the election, complete with tickets and a ballot box. Make elections an integral part of their school experience.

"Then we hope they go home and teach their parents. And you might also make each school a safe place where those parents can come to learn the same lessons. Help the adults organize themselves into a political club, where they can practice voting. Bring in the candidates and let them speak about why they are running. Give our people ownership of the voting process, and it will become impossible to take it away from them."

Robert Smalls hoisted himself out of the chair. "I'm afraid I must be going. There's a Republican caucus taking place in the back room of my store, and I need to be there to direct the plans for our final campaign push. I hope we shall meet again, Mr. Grenville."

"I will make certain of it. I'm only beginning to understand how much I don't know about your people, and I'm willing to become your devoted student. Help me to understand what needs to be done, and I will follow your guidance."

The two men shook hands before Smalls turned to place his arm around Hector's shoulders. "Your former owner is a good man. I'm beginning to understand why you have remained his friend. Teach him well. We need men like him on our side."

Chapter 33

Farewell to St. Helena

October 1868

The following morning, Hector and Jonathan joined General Saxton on the mail boat headed for Fort Fremont on St. Helena Island. Horses awaited them at the fort, and they were soon trotting down a road Jonathan had not seen before. "I didn't realize this island was so tropical," Jonathan commented. "When we were here before, the Eustis plantation and the area around the Brick Church seemed well cultivated. But these trees look like they have been here forever, and I can barely see through the foliage on either side of the road. There's fog, too, isn't there?"

"Actually, that's primarily sea mist blowing ashore, although off on the right, there's a swamp that remains shrouded in fog most of the time," General Saxton explained.

"That's why black folk around here say the road to Frogmore is haunted," Hector added.

"Haunted?"

"Because of the Hanging Tree and all."

"Hanging Tree? You're losing me, Hector."

"Look up ahead. See that low branch extending out across the road? Legend says planters used to hang runaway slaves from that branch and then leave their bodies there to rot as a warning to other malcontents. When we get closer, you'll be able to see the rope marks all along the branch. Folks believe the souls of those murdered slaves roam this road at night because they did not receive a proper burial. They say that, at night, you can see those souls take on the shape of balls of fire that float above the road and swerve away from you at the last minute."

"Swamp gas, more likely, but lots of folks still believe it," Saxton explained. "That's Miss Towne's house up ahead. She ridicules the idea of haunts at every opportunity, and I suspect that's part of the reason she's establishing her upper-level school way out here. It will force the students to get used to the road."

"I wish her luck," Hector said. "It'll take more than a school to erase the memories of black folk who witnessed the hangings."

⚘

As they neared the clearing, the lady herself appeared, accompanied by two very wet dogs. "Morning, General! You almost caught us having a swim!"

"Laura Towne! You were not actually swimming in that lagoon of yours?"

"No, but Cash and Leo were. And one of these days I'm going to join them—although probably not in late October. Oh, look out. They're going to . . ."

Before she could finish the warning, both dogs splayed their front legs and gave themselves a mighty shake, drenching her visitors.

"I do apologize. We don't normally baptize first-time visitors, but you'll dry off soon enough. Come up onto the front piazza, and we'll find you a seat in a sunny spot."

Jonathan was grinning as he followed the determined little lady up the rickety front steps. Annie had once said Laura Towne was one of the homeliest women she knew, but that when you talked with her, you forgot she was not beautiful. Now he understood how people came under the force of her personality.

The chairs on the porch were scarred with age, but they displayed soft cushions in bright colors. A makeshift table of planks held a motley collection of glasses, a pitcher of lemonade, and a plate of cookies. "Sit and make yourselves comfortable," Miss Towne said. "And do try one of these ginger cakes. Miss Charlotte Forten taught our cook to make them as a treat for the officers stationed at Port Royal."

The lady herself moved about the porch restlessly, as if her world were too full of chores that needed to be taken care of. She brushed away a speck of dust on the shelf, bent to pluck a spent blossom from a plant growing near the steps, and straightened a stack of books. Now and then, she pushed out her lower lip to blow a wisp of graying hair from her forehead. But through all her activity, her face carried the remnant of a smile.

"How are our schools in Charleston?" she asked, turning to Jonathan. "The general wrote to me about appointing you as vice-superintendent there, but I really have not had time to follow up, especially with the news of Mr. Randolph's murder. Were you able to talk with him before his death?"

"Yes, fortunately, we managed a brief meeting. He was, of course very preoccupied with his duties as a state senator and with the campaign for the upcoming election, but he took time to pass on to me his notes on each of the schools he had established. So I have a good general idea of what the schools were doing at the end of the term and where we need to pick up in November."

Miss Towne looked at him appraisingly. "What will you require in the way of a set curriculum? How will you know where to start?"

"I'm afraid there's no answer to that question. Or perhaps it would be more accurate to say there are as many answers as there are children. I assume they will come to us from many different backgrounds, and I would hesitate to formulate a plan without . . . without knowing what they know. I taught the slaves on our plantations to read and write, despite the laws against it. I don't think I was the only one to do so. Some will be ready for advanced work, while others will have to start with learning their letters."

"But you're telling me the problems, not the solutions."

"All right. I want each teacher to assess the individual classroom—talk to the children, find out what they know—and more important, find out what they want to know. There's no quicker way to lose the interest of a young scholar than to bore him to death."

"So you're saying . . ."

"I'm saying we don't need to set a curriculum. The trouble with many teachers is they want right answers drawn from established facts. I want to hear questions. Only then will I know what to teach."

Saxton had been frowning as he listened to the discussion. "I agree we should teach these people what they need to know. I'm not sure, however, young children are aware of what they need."

"You might be surprised, General." Hector spoke up for the first time. "When I was Mr. Grenville's slave, I knew all too well what I wanted to know. I didn't know how I was going to learn it all until I talked to Mr. Grenville."

Miss Towne had her answer ready. "Ah, but you were a special case, Hector. We have to think about all children, not just the bright ones. From what I have heard discussed among the new members of our local boards of education, they are taking two very different approaches. One group argues we have been mandated to treat all citizens equally. So all children get an equal education.

"There are others who believe that by forcing black children to learn things like algebra and Latin, we are dooming them to economic failure. General Saxton and I have had this argument before. I believe in giving my little scholars what I think of as a good English education. The general tends to side with those who say our black children need to learn skills from which they can profit in the marketplace."

"It's hard to make a case these days against a goal of equality," Jonathan agreed, "but I don't know that 'equal' means 'identical.' With all due respect, General Saxton, I believe the marketplace will have important jobs for black men who know their Latin." Jonathan began to sound more sure of himself as the discussion progressed. "They will be the doctors, the ministers, the lawyers who help their people achieve economic and social equality."

"So are you advocating a standard English curriculum for all, or not?"

"No, sir. I'm saying I would offer that kind of academic training to those who want it and who prove themselves capable of handling it. And I would do it without regard for the color of their skin or their previous status as slaves. In the same vein, I would gladly train others—white or black—to be bricklayers or carpenters or fishmongers. If I am the teacher, I will ask the questions, determine what each scholar needs, and then do my best to help him get it. I can do no less."

◈

Late that afternoon, Jonathan and General Saxton returned their borrowed horses to the army fort and hired a young man to row them over to Ladies Island. "My head is swimming with all the discussions about pedagogy," Jonathan confessed, "but I feel well satisfied our Charleston schools are going to meet the high standards Miss Towne has set here in the Sea Islands."

"If they don't, she will not hesitate to let you know," the general said. "She is something of a force of nature, that one. I've had many an argument with Miss Towne over the years. Lost every one of them!"

At the Eustis plantation, they found business was already bustling. Eli met them at the gate, where he was supervising two men installing a hand-carved wooden sign that read "Grenmore Stables." He grinned at Jonathan. "Your daughter and I had a discussion about whose name ought to appear first in our new title. We finally drew straws, and she won— as she usually does."

General Saxton was laughing. "As I was saying, Jonathan, there are some women it doesn't pay to argue with. Your Mary Sue sounds like she's another one of them."

"Talking about me, are you, Papa?" Mary Sue came dashing around the corner of the house, looking disheveled but smiling broadly. "I'm so glad you stopped by before you left for home."

She grasped his arm and pulled him toward the house. "You should see all the welcome gifts we've received today. Annie arrived first with baskets of fresh bread and a whole ham. But then our tenants and their wives started coming, each of them bringing fresh produce or eggs from their own farms. I can't imagine how we're going to eat it all. So many eggs! Can I make you an omelet?"

"Heavens, no, child. We just finished lunch. But it sounds as if you've been made very welcome."

"Oh, we have. I expected the tenants to like Eli, of course, but I wasn't sure how they would take to a white woman having part ownership of the land. It doesn't seem to have bothered them at all. There are a couple of women my age, and we've already found common ground. Oh, and look! One of them brought me a kitten." She stooped and reached under the table, pulling out a rather bedraggled tabby cat. "His name is Charley, and he'll be the first of many stable cats. Horses really like cats, you know."

"Named after your sister?"

"Oh, dear, no! I wasn't thinking about Charlotte at all." Her hand instinctively flew to her mouth, and then she giggled. "I hope she won't mind. I was really thinking of Charleston, where all this started coming together."

Jonathan could not keep from staring at his daughter's transformation. A week earlier, she had been a neat and proper young woman with a tendency to pout and brood. Now she had hay in her hair, manure on her shoes, and a smudge of soot on her nose. But her eyes sparkled and her smile was wide.

"You are happy with your decision, I take it?"

"Yes, Papa. We're going to be fine here. And Sable Girl and her foal like it, too. Before he left, Mr. Eustis had part of the lower pasture fence extended out into the marsh. He said it might help our new horses adjust to the area. So we put Sable Girl and Minkie out there this morning, and they waded right out into the pluff mud. They're going to smell terrible when they come back to the stable, but right now they're out there munching on sea grass and looking as if they have lived here all their lives. They seem to recognize their home ground."

"Speaking of horses," General Saxton interrupted the family reunion. "I have a message for you from Miss Laura Towne. She is quite interested in hearing more about your experiments with the marsh ponies. She has this colt—Saxby, his name is, although she swears she didn't name him after me. At any rate, it seems their old mare Betty jumped the fence a couple of years back and headed off to find herself a beau. Miss Towne has no idea where she went, but she came back in a day or so, looking self-satisfied. Several months later, she gave birth to Saxby, who has turned out to be a somewhat wild and difficult colt—leaps and rears at odd moments. He looks strange, too, with short legs and a stocky little body. He's much smaller than his dam."

"Sounds like a Marsh Tacky," Eli commented as he joined the group. "Is that possible?"

"I suppose it is. Old Betty could have wandered off into the pluff mud instead of visiting a family farm. Rumor says there's a whole herd of marsh ponies living around Hunting Island. If Saxby's sire was one of the ponies from the marsh, it would explain his appearance and maybe even his wild streak. So Miss Towne says to tell you if you are interested in Saxby, you should send her word with Annie, and she'll be happy to bring Saxby over to let you meet him. And if he turns out to be part of the breed you are interested in, Miss Towne is willing to loan him out at stud for you."

"Wonderful! We'll do that soon." Mary Sue turned to grin at her father again. "See how things are working out, Papa? This is the best possible move we could have made."

"I hope that continues to be so, daughter. But please re-member, you are not all that far from Charleston if you need us."

"Of course. And we'll visit. We're not going to fall off the edge of the earth." Then her face started to crumble. She swallowed hard before she asked, "When do you leave?"

"Very early in the morning, I'm afraid. We'll be riding our livery horses back to Pocotaligo and then catching the northbound train around ten o'clock. So, yes, this is farewell, I'm afraid. Can I have a hug before we leave? And Eli—take care of my little girl, you hear?"

"Yes, sir. I'll keep her safe for you."

Chapter 34

Old Sheldon Church

Late October 1868

At Pocotaligo the next morning, the travelers learned that their train, in true Lowcountry fashion, would be at least an hour late. Hector pulled his horse to a stop before they reached the livery stable.

"Jonathan?"

"What is it, Hector? You look troubled."

"Not troubled, but . . . if the train's going to be running on Lowcountry time, there's something near here I'd like you to see. Would you be willing to ride with me a couple of miles outside of town?"

"Certainly. A ride will fill in the time. Where are we headed?"

"The Old Sheldon Church. Are you familiar with it?"

"No, I can't say I am."

"Well, it was the first parish church around here, built in 1745 to serve all the plantations of what is now Beaufort County. The British burned it down during the Revolutionary War, but the parishioners eventually rebuilt it. I remember it from when I was a child. The DuBois family used to come over from Edisto Island for services about once a month."

Mist still hung over the narrow road as Hector led the way. As he had on St. Helena Island, Jonathan once again felt he had been dropped back in time to an era when this was a primeval forest. Hector pulled his horse to a stop and pointed off to the right. And out of the mist, the shattered remains of the church began to reveal themselves.

"My God!" Jonathan exclaimed. "It looks like the ruins of an ancient Greek temple."

"It was a temple of sorts. That's what it was meant to be. And in the 1840s and 1850s, it was a sight to behold. I still remember the poetic way Massa Dubois would describe it. What now appear to be four freestanding columns across the western front supported an elegant portico, which was topped by a multi-petalled rose window set in a triangular pediment. Six attached columns forming five bays ran down the north and south sides. When the church was in its prime, the wood-framed windows of each bay were topped with perfect semicircular arches. The walls were three-feet thick. The brickwork was something called 'Flemish Bond,' which alternates the short and long sides of the bricks to weave an elaborate pattern. And, of course, as you see now, the grounds were guarded by an almost magical circle of live oaks draped in Spanish moss."

"The brickwork is wonderfully complicated, isn't it?" Jonathan was studying the walls at the edges where the windows had once filled the gaps. "Master craftsmen were at work here."

"Slaves."

"Are you sure? It takes a lifetime to learn how to do this kind of masonry."

"Well, slaves had a lifetime to spend. They made the bricks, too. White men didn't do that kind of manual labor down here in the Lowcountry."

Jonathan stared at Hector for a few seconds, trying to determine whether he was serious. Then he leaned against one of the pillars, folded his arms across his chest, and said, "Tell me what you remember of the church before it was destroyed."

"We'd have to leave the Edisto plantation very early to get here in time for morning services. Carriages would be lined up on both sides of the road. The ladies were all dressed in their hoopskirts and parasols, and the men in tails. Everyone glided across the grass as if their feet could not be allowed to touch the ground. Slaves were not permitted in the church, of course, but we could stand outside to listen to the preaching and the music of the harmonium."

Hector's eyes had a faraway look as he reminisced. "When the service was over, people whose ancestors were buried here assembled around their family plots, and the rest spread out across the lawn. We slaves scurried around to lay out an elegant picnic lunch for the family. Then we retreated across the road to a small clearing where we could eat our cold cornbread or maybe hope to snare a rabbit or a squirrel. It was a time for visiting and business dealings and courtships—sometimes lasting for most of the afternoon."

Caught up in the spell Hector was weaving, Jonathan looked around in wonder. He touched one of the freestanding pillars as if to reassure himself it was real. "What happened to it? The building, I mean," he asked.

Hector's voice turned rough. "War happened. War always seems to happen. The Union fleet sailed into Port Royal Sound, and all those elegant planters turned tail and fled for their lives. Sheldon Church stood here all through the war, safe from bombardment but not from neglect. Weeds and brush took over the yard. Vagrants broke open the great west doors to seek shelter inside. Someone stole the harmonium and sold it to some people in Beaufort."

"The Yankees, you mean?"

"I don't know. I thought I saw it once in a Presbyterian Church but was afraid to say anything. Were there Yankee soldiers roaming around here? Maybe, but I don't know that, either. I do know the window glass got itself shattered somehow, and the doors stood open to the weather. Dry oak leaves blew in through the openings and filled the sanctuary. And then in 1865, a single spark ignited the dry leaves and grass and burned the building out for the second time."

"Sherman? On his March to the Sea?"

"That's what most folks think, but I'm not so sure. General Sherman was brutal in his drive to conquer, but he was not an unholy man. You know that, too, from what happened on the Aiken farm. No, sir, I suspect it was God himself, hurling down a bolt of lightning to punish the foolishness of His people. And what the fire did not destroy was carried off by destitute and desperate people trying to rebuild their own poor dwellings."

"It's beautiful and tragic all at once. I'm glad you brought me here, but why was it so important to you to have me see it?"

"Because I see it now as a symbol of what has happened to South Carolina. Because it has a message people like you need to hear."

"People like me? What does that mean?" Jonathan's frown reflected his indignation.

"People who think the war is over now. People who think they have won a victory. People who think life can go back to being normal, and everything will be all right." Jonathan could not mistake the bitterness in Hector's voice, but it shocked him and left him without an answer.

Hector slapped a tree trunk in frustration. "All day yesterday, and again this morning as we rode, you've been congratulating yourself on how well things are going. You plan to use your new schools to take our poor, ignorant black children and teach them how to be the equals of white children—as if that were the only standard of intelligence. You and Miss Towne and General Saxton—you all think schooling will be the answer to the problems of the black community."

"It will be, Hector. Once your people learn to read . . ."

"I learned to read a long time ago, Massa Jonathan, but it hasn't changed what's penned up inside of me—the pain, the frustration, the hatred, the despair . . ."

Jonathan was angry now. "Don't you refer to me as 'Massa' ever again! That's not fair after all I've done for you."

"Yes, Massa. I'se grateful!"

Jonathan clenched his fists and walked into the center of the burned-out church. He looked toward the remains of the altar, hoping it could somehow spread its peace over both of them.

But Hector was not ready to let the discussion drop. "You all believe the brand new government of South Carolina will follow through on what's written on a piece of paper," he said. "You expect them to provide free and equal education for all, so everyone can be equal. Well, this burned-out church here says it's not going to happen. This ruin says once you let something be destroyed, you can't put it back together again. And that applies to countries as well as buildings."

"But it can't be wrong to hope our nation can recover its former glory."

"It's wrong if you don't understand what caused the problem in the first place. And it's wrong if you don't take responsibility for that problem."

"I? I didn't start that war."

"No? Maybe not directly, but your attitudes did. Look, even now, you talk to a black man like Robert Smalls and offer him your political help, as if to suggest he needs your advice. And you don't understand why he rebuffs you."

"I was only trying to be helpful."

"Because you cannot see him as your equal, any more than you can see me as your equal."

"You are my friend, Hector, and a member of my family."

"Am I? You have spent the last four days traveling with me through the countryside where I grew up. You've been meeting people I have known all my life and asking white men questions about the former slaves—questions I could answer because I am a former slave. And through it all, you have barely acknowledged my existence unless you needed me to do something menial for you. You preach equality and you expect it of others, but you don't practice it. And it's that sort of failure to live the message you profess that is going to doom all efforts to put this state back together again."

"I've never . . ." Jonathan started to protest his innocence but realized he did not know how to explain himself.

"Old Sheldon Church stands in my mind as a symbol of your kind of wrong thinking," Hector continued. "It's fitting, in many ways, that you first saw the church as the ruins of an ancient Greek temple. You are a historian. You should be able to understand that Greek civilization collapsed from the same sort of deeply seated beliefs that doomed the ideals upon which the United States of America was constructed. Both countries preached democracy and equality, and at the same time, both practiced and accepted slavery as part of the natural order. Both fell apart under the strain of that contradiction. What better to represent them both than the remains of shattered temples? That's what I wanted you to understand. That's why I wanted to bring you here."

Unable to handle the accusations and the depth of emotion that prompted them, Jonathan remounted his horse and rode back to the train station in silence. Hector followed, without further attempts at conversation. The balance of power had somehow shifted between them, and neither man knew what to do about it.

Chapter 35

Race Riots and Klan Trials

1868-1871

For almost a year, Hector and Jonathan avoided confronting one another. In Charleston, Jonathan worked hard in his role as vice-superintendent of black schools. During the mandated six months of school, he tried to place the younger children into grade-appropriate classrooms. He insisted they learn to read and write standard English, master the basic operations of arithmetic, and receive lessons on the history and political structure of the United States of America. For older children, he organized vocational training to help them become self-supporting. During the times when regular schools were not in session, he opened the buildings and made teachers available to teach the adults of the community. And for every age level, he tried to implement the suggestions Robert Smalls had made about teaching blacks to vote.

Hector and Sarah returned to their small farm outside of Aiken. Hector's services as a bodyguard were less frequently needed after the election in November 1868, and he was free to work more closely within his own community. Despite the overwhelming victory of Grant and the Republican Party, individual black men were still facing the possibility of bodily harm when they tried to exercise their new right to vote in local elections. The threat from the Ku Klux Klan was ever-present, and the establishment of a government militia did little to counteract the danger.

In the Uplands of South Carolina, local elections were still marked by violence and deception at the polls. Democrats tried to prevent blacks from voting by threatening them when they entered the polls. They handed out fake tickets and physically blocked the path to the ballot box. The *Charleston Daily Courier* described the process as "running a gauntlet." Hector was determined that, before the next national election, his people would understand the voting process, be able to identify the valid Republican ticket by color or by design when they arrived at the polls, and be prepared to push their way through to deposit their tickets in the right ballot boxes.

Hector, too, had listened carefully when Robert Smalls outlined what Jonathan could do within the schools to make sure new black citizens became effective voters. He realized black churches could perform much the same role. Under his direction, the small African-American church he had helped to establish in Aiken became a center for adult education and for the effective exercise of voting rights.

When the Grenvilles returned to the Aiken farm for the summer, Hector was eager to meet with Jonathan again and discuss what he had accomplished.

"Our little African Methodist Episcopal Church has become the center of the black community," he began. "I suggested we start a kind of political club to keep our members informed of what the Republican Party was doing. The idea went over well, and it soon became a group offering social events. Wednesday-night suppers proved popular and greatly increased our attendance. And now the gathering also provides assurance that members will help one another in times of crisis, such as illness or the death of family members."

"That sounds like an interesting progression. I wish my school classes on voting were so effective."

"I think the real key is that the lines separating religion from political action have begun to blur. Our people see voting as one of the obligations they owe to one another and to their faith. What begins as a political rally can turn seamlessly into a revival meeting, and our worship services frequently end with a call to political action."

Once again, Jonathan was not prepared to follow Hector's lead. "But the United States was founded on the principle of separation of church and state. It sounds to me as if you may be treading dangerous ground by combining the two."

"It's who we are, Jonathan. In the minds of my people, political action is a religious duty. I can't even imagine how you can separate the two."

"We know from history that it is dangerous to allow the Church to control the State. That's how Europe ended up fighting so many religious wars."

"Religious wars? That's a contradiction in terms."

"How so?"

"Because religion teaches us to love one another. Wars teach us to hate. Which lesson would you rather have us pass along to our children?"

"That's not the point."

"That's exactly the point. You may not approve of our pastors advocating political decisions, but the fact remains that, by the time the next national election occurs, the black citizens of Aiken will be prepared to run the gauntlet to the ballot box. And they will be voting their consciences. I will not ask any less of them."

Both Jonathan and Hector believed they were doing what they could to further the goals of black enfranchisement. As the Fifteenth Amendment made its way through Congress and the various state legislatures, they both were making sure the voters would be ready when their rights were guaranteed. Their methods, however, remained at odds. Hector was the political activist. His support of the Republican Party tended to overlook the corruption and behind-the-scenes deal making that marked a decline from the original goals of the Radical Reconstructionists. He wanted to see his people seize power through the electoral process and then turn the functions of government to their own advantage.

Jonathan, on the other hand, still took a paternalistic approach. He encouraged those who consulted him to vote for the Republican Party because he saw it as a defender of freedom. He had never lost his admiration for the Founding Fathers and their lofty goals for America. His efforts to turn the former slaves into voters assumed they would then vote to support that original idealistic model. Could these two men ever reconcile their approaches? There was no easy answer.

During the elections of 1868, a disturbing trend had developed. The Democrats campaigned on outspoken demands for a return to the days of white supremacy. Denying the federal government had any power to regulate what happened in South Carolina, they called upon the Ku Klux Klan to use any methods necessary to keep blacks from voting. The Democratic candidate for governor, William D. Porter, had refused to campaign on their platform, although he still managed to gather almost a quarter of the votes. Violence washed over the state. Blacks were dragged from their beds in the middle of the night, beaten, and hanged for the sin of intending to vote. The Klan had, in effect, become the terrorist branch of the Democratic Party.

Robert K. Scott, the Republican candidate, offered the black men of the state an opportunity to join the state militia. He provided them with weapons, access to local armories, and a mandate to prevent the activities of the Ku Klux Klan wherever they occurred. Most whites saw his policy as a way of buying black votes for the Republican Party. It also frightened those who had long feared slaves would someday rise up in arms and slaughter their masters.

The riot at Chester, South Carolina, in March of 1871 was one of many examples of what happened when the Klan and the black militias crossed paths. In Chester County, the militia began patrolling the roads at night to intercept any Klan activity. The Klan retaliated by trying to break into the home of the militia captain. Although the attack failed, the militia responded by marching into Chester to draw more ammunition from the local arsenal. And that in turn alarmed the whites in Chester, who sent out a call for reinforcements from as far away as North Carolina. The resulting clashes between the two sides were almost inevitable.

A careless shot from a militiaman who only managed to wound himself in the leg prompted the white townsmen to take up position near the town depot. Tentative peace talks almost convinced both sides to leave town, but the militiamen only went about five miles before taking up their defensive positions again in a small church. The next day, a troop of experienced Confederate veterans drove them from the church and scattered them in all directions. In disgust, the governor ordered the militia to be disarmed, which in effect, gave the Klan total control over the town and its black residents.

When the Grant administration moved to send federal troops into the most troublesome southern states to rid those states of the scourge of the Ku Klux Klan, Jonathan was delighted. He was even happier when federal enforcement of the law led to grand jury indictments being brought against the offending members of the Ku Klux Klan. He followed every detail of the trials that took place from December 1871 to January 1872 in Columbia, South Carolina. Surely, he thought, if the Klan could be stopped, the problems of racial violence would solve themselves.

In the middle of those trials, the various branches of the Grenville family came together in Charleston for a Christmas celebration. Mary Sue and Eli came up from the Lowcountry, and Hector and Sarah came down from the Uplands. Jonathan and Hector approached their discussions warily.

"Have you been reading the transcripts of the testimony?" Jonathan asked.

"Not often. It seems to me the witnesses are all saying the same thing. They admit they were there when a black man was attacked, because everyone knows it. But none of them admit they were responsible. Someone else was always the guilty party. The witnesses never handled a whip or strung a rope or participated in a beating. How convenient!"

"But, Hector, the important thing is seeing the names out there. The worst offenders are being made to answer for their crimes. There's to be no more hiding behind masks and the protection of darkness. That alone is enough to put an end to their depredations."

"Do you really believe so?"

"Of course. Look at Alex Croft—the day I ripped off his mask and called out his name, my visits from him and his KKK buddies stopped. They cannot stand being identified."

"That may well be," Hector said, "but it doesn't mean they have changed their minds or their hearts. You've simply driven them underground. They will re-emerge to trouble someone else."

"But if we shame the ringleaders . . ."

"Nothing changes unless you wipe them out. Look at the figures, Jonathan. In this trial alone, there were originally two hundred and twenty indictments. Out of that number, how many pleaded guilty? Do you know?"

"Actually, I do. I believe there were fifty-three who pleaded and accepted guilty verdicts in exchange for escaping any fines or prison sentences. But five of the worst offenders have already been brought to court . . ."

"Leaving some one hundred and sixty-two others against whom all charges seem to have been dropped or postponed, no matter that the grand jury found them all guilty as hell."

"The bad publicity may be enough to put an end to the Klan. I saw an article in the paper the other day that said General Nathan Bedford Forrest, the founder of the first Klan, has repudiated their actions."

"Because they were stupid enough to get caught, not because of what they did. Mark my words, Jonathan. They may reappear as the Society of Delicate White Rosebuds, but they will be back. They will still believe in white supremacy, and the haters will still hate."

Chapter 36

The Combahee Rice Strikes

1872–1876

Jonathan was once again a man in love with his work. The Negro schools of Charleston overflowed with eager scholars of all ages. There were few books to be had, and teachers sometimes went without pay, but grateful parents stepped in to be sure those teachers at least ate well. Disciplinary problems soon faded, because children were too busy with their lessons to make trouble. Jonathan had proved to be an effective administrator, and he was welcomed in each school he visited.

Susan could scarcely contain her relief. After years of struggling with frustration and feelings of inadequacy, her husband now hurried out to work every morning, eager for the challenges the day would bring. And if he was late getting home in the evening, he still had a bounce to his step when he came up the front stairs. He often worried about the lack of financial support for the schools, she knew, but he remained convinced his new partners in this educational enterprise would find a way to provide what was needed.

"Look at what this city has done!" he exclaimed one Saturday morning as he scanned the day's newspapers. "Charleston Harbor has finally been cleared of all those ships of the Stone Fleet the Yankees sank there to block our shipping routes. Now all three channels are open to ocean-going ships, and trade passing through our port is bound to increase. The Savannah and Charleston Railroad line is running normally again, making travel easier. Construction of our new Circular Church is going apace. We'll soon be back in its sanctuary. New businesses are opening every day. Even our new mayor, John Wagener, is contributing to our general prosperity by providing much-needed financing for the College of Charleston. I tell you, Arthur Middleton was right when he predicted all Charleston needed after the war was a group of caring citizens to help the city prosper."

Despite herself, Susan raised an eyebrow at his enthusiasm. "Not all growth is good, Jonathan. I heard someone remark the other day that the west side of Bay Street between Elliott and Tradd is occupied by nothing but bars and bordellos."

"Sounds like something our neighbor Henrietta MacLeod would say."

"Actually, it wasn't her at all. It was a black man, shaking his head at the foibles of these new white folks moving into town."

"He should have been praising the advances of his own people rather than criticizing others."

"As you have just done!" Susan was laughing at her husband, something she might not have done in earlier years.

"I'm serious, Susan. Our black citizens are doing very well for themselves. As the *Daily Courier* pointed out the other day, our police force is now made up of an equal number of blacks and whites, and there are over five hundred black firemen. Those are former slaves who are accepting responsibility for making our community better and safer. And now that we are educating their children, their futures will be even brighter."

⟨∾⟩

Trouble, however, was already beginning to make itself felt. Word from Europe warned of economic crises abroad. In Congress, bitter fighting raged over the issue of returning the United States to the gold standard. Paper money was disappearing from circulation, and silver coins were losing value. Real wages dropped, as more and more immigrants arrived to take low-paying jobs. Cotton and grain prices plummeted, leaving farmers to suffer losses of up to half their income.

Rumors of massive corruption in the Grant administration threatened to bring down the Republican Party. During the presidential campaign of 1872, newspaper reports revealed that the construction of the eastern part of the

343

transcontinental railroad was being financed by a fraudulent company created by the Union Pacific Railroad itself. One of those involved turned out to be Grant's vice-president, Schuyler Colfax. Grant promptly dumped him from the ticket, but not before it became known that Colfax had bribed members of Congress to approve contracts granted to Crédit Mobilier, which was a company wholly owned by the same railroad officials who were doing the contracting. The great financial bubble of economic growth attributed to railroad expansion proved to be nothing more than a get-rich-quick scheme for those who were already wealthy, and the whole idea of a transcontinental railroad now appeared to be based on an unprofitable financial projection.

A devastating blow fell on Black Thursday—September 18, 1873—when the bank of Jay Cooke and Company collapsed over the construction of the Northern Pacific Railroad. The government had granted millions of acres of free land upon which to build the railroad, relying on promises the costs would be covered by the issue of railroad bonds. When those bonds proved to be worthless, the whole scheme fell apart—as did the economy across the country. In Charleston alone, sixty businesses were forced to close their doors during the following months. On June 29, 1874, the Freedman's Savings Bank officially went out of business, still owing over two million dollars to its trusting depositors. On one disastrous day, 5,300 blacks and 300 whites lost their life savings.

"General Saxton warned me this might happen," Jonathan remarked, as he finished reading the newspaper accounts.

"How did he know?" Susan turned away from playing her melodeon. Music no longer seemed a fitting accompaniment to the day's affairs. "Was he part of the corruption?"

"No, certainly not. But he was worried the Freedman's Bank was not making sound investments of the money coming in. He thought they should be making standard loans secured by real property. Instead, the managers were investing in shaky bond issues like those that brought down Crédit Mobilier. He also feared they were spending too large a portion of deposited funds on new branch banks and other operating expenses. He actually predicted if customers ever started demanding to take out their money, the bank would have to close its doors because the funds were no longer there. And that seems to be exactly what has happened."

"Will the people who work our lands lose their money?"

"Undoubtedly. I haven't encouraged the exclusive use of the Freedman's Bank, but for many people it seemed a whole lot safer than keeping their extra money in an old sock."

"Is there anything we can do?"

"Probably not a great deal, although this article in the *Daily Courier* suggests there will be an appeals process by which depositors can reclaim some of their funds. I think it would be a good idea to send Hector around to all our properties to talk to those involved. We can make sure they follow through and do everything possible to get their money back."

345

There was to be no easy recovery from this economic disaster. For the next two years, Jonathan struggled to find ways to help the wage earners on his properties. He argued down attempts by his plantation supervisors to reinstitute the old practice of paying workers in scrip rather than cash. "There will be no company stores on my lands," he declared. "My employees will receive their pay in common currency and be free to spend their earnings anywhere they like." At the same time, he encouraged workers to reach higher levels of production so their incomes would not suffer from falling grain and cotton prices in the marketplace. Still, labor unrest lay beneath the surface.

One evening in early May 1876, Hector Moreau arrived unexpectedly at the Legare Street house. When Jonathan answered the knock at the door, his first reaction was to look up and down the street for signs of Klan activity, but all was quiet. "Come in! Come in, Hector. What brings you back to Charleston? No trouble at home, I hope."

"No, nothing like that. But there is trouble brewing down on the Combahee River. Strikes are springing up on rice plantations all along the river over economic problems, and Robert Smalls has asked me to look into the demands the workers are making."

"Are our River View Plantation people involved?"

"Not yet, so far as I can tell, but they will be soon. The call is out among black wage earners to unite their efforts to bring about change."

"And what, exactly, is it they want to change?"

"Well, it seems the plantation supervisors up and down the river have agreed to cut wages. From now on, workers are going to be paid forty cents a day rather than fifty cents."

"I haven't heard anything about a wage cut," Jonathan grumbled.

"Maybe your overseer hasn't seen fit to tell you. The strike leaders seem to be telling the workers the decrease is the idea of big businessmen from the North—northern Democrats— to make up their losses from the falling price of rice."

"So there's a political element to this as well?"

"Appears to be. With an election coming up this fall, there's an increased effort to make sure all Southern blacks vote Republican."

"They usually do, don't they?"

"Yes, but . . ."

"But what?"

"That's changing now. After the Freedman's Bank went broke, lots of our people put the blame on Washington Republicans."

"And rightfully so."

"Yes. But the Republican Party cannot allow black voters to desert their candidates, so this strike effort is designed to stir up hard feelings against the Democrats."

"You're sure that's what's going on?"

"That's how Mr. Smalls explained it to me. And he has evidence to back it up. He's getting letters like this one from a rice farmer named Monday. He gave me a copy:

I got tuh vote de 'Publican ticket, suh. We all has. Las' 'lection I voted de Democrack ticket an' dee killed my cow. Abum, he vote de Democrack ticket; dee killed his colt.

"So what's your job when you get down to the Combahee region? What does the congressman expect you to do?"

"He's hoping if I start with our rice plantation, I'll find people I know from the old days of slavery. He wants me to talk them down from violence directed against other blacks. If labor conditions are unfair, all workers have the right to strike in order to force better conditions. But at the same time, workers have a right to keep working if they don't want to strike. He calls it 'Right to Work.' I'm supposed to tell them freedom gave them both rights, and we must all respect the worker's right to choose between them."

"Do you think you can convince them?"

"Seriously? No, I doubt it. But Mr. Smalls says we have to try, because the alternative is much worse."

"And what is the alternative?"

"That the governor will call in the militia to put down the strikers, which would add more violence to the mix. Mr. Smalls says it would be a white supremacist's dream— black militiamen killing black strikers because they are attacking black workers who only want to keep their jobs. Black-on-black violence allows white men free rein in the name of putting an end to the violence they stirred up in the first place."

Jonathan was shaking his head in despair. "The whole thing is a nightmare. I don't want you getting mixed up in it."

"I'm already mixed up in it because I'm black. You can't help me there. I'll be careful, Jonathan, and I agree with Mr. Smalls—I'm in a good position to try to talk some sense into the people involved. I have to try."

Chapter 37

Trouble in the Uplands

Summer 1876

A week or so later, Hector reappeared at the Grenville door. He looked tired and disheveled, Susan thought, as she let him in. She tapped on Jonathan's office door to let him know and then scurried to find Hector something to eat.

"What's happened, Hector? Did you manage to put a stop to the nonsense on the rice plantations?" Susan was smiling as she asked.

"I wouldn't call it 'nonsense.'" Hector scowled at the Grenville's continuing misunderstanding of the situation. "The issues were—and are—very real. But to answer your main question, yes, things are a bit more settled on the Combahee at the moment. I won't make any promises for the future."

"So how did you manage it?"

"It took both my efforts and those of Mr. Smalls, who showed up two days ago to help. The most important agreement was that nobody wants to get the militia involved. That's a solution that only looks good on paper. When you examine the reality, you realize these local militias are untrained, often unarmed, and usually have a stake in the argument. The congressman is on his way back to Columbia right now to make sure the governor does not let them interfere and make things worse."

"And what about the original dispute?" Jonathan asked.

"The strikers have agreed to accept the pay cut for the time being, with the provision that, when and if the market price of rice goes up, their wages will also increase. And in return, the plantation managers have promised to pay only in cash, never in scrip. The strikers have also accepted the 'Right to Work' principle—that while each man has a right to strike if he feels he is being treated unfairly, he also has a right to continue working while the protests go on. That's the big step toward controlling the violence, although I think it will take some time to make an impact."

"I am relieved."

"Don't be. I still see a threat of violence everywhere I look these days. Right now, I'm on my way back to Abbeville to try to contain a potential outbreak there."

"Abbeville? I'm surprised you would be willing to go back. The death of Mr. Randolph must still haunt you."

"Of course it does, but Mr. Smalls seems to think I can be useful there as well, because I know several of the leading townsmen who have become embroiled in the latest murders."

"Murders? In Abbeville? Oh, wait, you're referring to the Harmon family, I suppose. I was reading about that case. But they lived in Edgefield County, not really in Abbeville."

"Close enough that the hearings are taking place in the Abbeville courthouse. The Harmons, as you probably read, were an elderly white couple who could not accept the idea of free blacks. Mr. Harmon needed workers for his farm, but he insisted on forcing them to sign labor contracts reminiscent of the old Black Codes. He offered to pay at a rate of $100 a year but would not pay anything until the end of the contract year. And the laborer who left before the end of the contract would receive nothing. That's why a small group of his workers decided to teach him a lesson. They beat him with a dogwood stick at first and attacked his wife. Then, frightened by how badly the old folks were injured, they cut their throats and set the farmhouse on fire."

"Horrible!"

"Horrible? Yes, but also incompetent. Despite their use of kerosene to set the fire, the house burned so slowly that all the evidence was still intact when the authorities arrived."

"You sound disappointed in them," Jonathan said.

"Not disappointed. Sad. Those who committed the murders were ignorant and frustrated, helpless in the face of unfair treatment. They admit they looted the house after the murders, finding a couple of pistols and a little jewelry. But mostly they carried off clothing and foodstuffs, things they desperately needed for themselves. They even brought their wives along on the night of the attack, not expecting the argument to escalate. And they are so scared, they've been testifying against each other ever since the first one was identified."

"Do you intend to defend them?"

"No, nothing will save their wretched hides at this point, but Mr. Smalls is concerned about the publicity the case is attracting. The local authorities have assembled a jury of citizens from Edgefield to conduct an inquest. The Abbeville coroner has examined the evidence, and the hearings are being conducted in the open because so many people from all around the area have assembled to hear the testimony—five hundred yesterday, according to reports."

"What can you do?"

"Maybe nothing, but I need to be there. I've borrowed a horse and intend to travel through the night. With luck, I'll arrive before the final sentencing. The six perpetrators will be taken to the edge of town and shot. That's certain. And a huge crowd will be on hand to witness the whole thing. That's when the real danger will arise—from whites seeking more blacks to punish and from other blacks seeking vengeance for their fellows."

"It's too horrible to contemplate."

"You keep saying that, Jonathan, but it's the reality of the world we seem to have created. You remain blissfully oblivious to the disasters all around you. One of the reasons I wanted to see you tonight was to warn you not to bring your family to the farm this summer."

"Why not? We've never had any problems there—except for that one day when Sherman's army passed through."

"It's a different place now. The population has shifted. The Uplands were an inviting destination for many plantation Negroes who were free for the first time to find a new place to live. And the white people, the ones who thought themselves above the fray of the war, now find themselves in the minority. The two sides are desperately afraid of each other, and as a result, Aiken is a dangerous place to be right now. That whole side of the state is dangerous."

"I can't believe that."

"No? Did you finish reading this article?" Hector picked up the newspaper and turned to the second page. "Here's what the Charleston papers have to say about tomorrow's outcome."

Events in Abbeville and Edgefield prove that lynch law is justified. Blacks are passionate, heedless, and have only a narrow sense of moral responsibility. Violent crimes require swift punishment, and justice is not available yet in South Carolina. Our civil government, in the hands of carpetbaggers, scalawags, and ignorant blacks, does not yet provide security to our citizens. The time has come for the People to save themselves.

"'The People' means white people, of course. This is a call for more violence. I would prefer you avoid the area, if possible. Now I need to move on. Heed my warning, Jonathan."

❦

Jonathan did not want to accept Hector's view, but he watched in alarm during the next few weeks as violence continued to escalate in the small towns of upland South Carolina. "You can't put a finger on any one cause," he grumbled to Susan, "and the upcoming election season is not going to make things any better. Governor Chamberlain has always been a supporter of civil rights for former slaves, so you would expect him to carry the black vote. But now he's losing his popularity with the whole Republican Party by making blanket accusations of corruption."

"He's right, though, isn't he? Government scandals surfaced under Governor Scott, and Chamberlain was a member of his inner circle. He knows who's been on the take, and I have to admire him for trying to expose the corruption."

"But he's doing so by allying himself with the Democrats, and that does nothing but make him more enemies."

"Blacks will support him anyway, won't they? I've read his outspoken statements against lynch laws."

"Maybe they will—maybe they won't. I know they don't like his quickness to call in the militia whenever trouble brews."

"You're just as quick to criticize, Jonathan. What's your solution to clashes based on race?"

"The same as it's always been. Each side has to be willing to make concessions to the other."

It was a forlorn hope. July 4, 1876, marked the end of any possibility of settling the disputes amicably. Trouble started when the all-black militia of Hamburg, South Carolina, chose the holiday to practice some drilling exercises in the center of the small town. As they marched, a carriage driven by Thomas Butler and Henry Getzen, farmers from outside the town, came down the street. Demands issued from both sides.

"This is a public highway. Get your black hides out of the middle of the street," snarled the carriage driver.

"There's plenty of room along the edge of the road," the militia commander replied. "Drive around us. We are engaged in official military training here."

Eventually, the two white farmers guided their horse and carriage through the middle of the militia's formation and drove on, leaving hot tempers behind on both sides.

On July 6, the farmers appeared before the local court and brought formal charges against the militia captain for obstructing the highway. Thomas Butler hired his cousin, Matthew C. Butler, as their lawyer, and Matthew demanded the immediate removal of the militia from the town. But outside the courtroom, the issue was already being taken out of the hands of the local judiciary. The Butler cousins and Getzen had used their time well to spread word of a possible insurrection. Even as the formal charge was being read, large groups of armed white men from surrounding towns began to assemble in the streets outside. Most were members of political or "rifle" clubs, organized to enforce their own favorite rules.

By July 8, the twenty-five militia members had taken cover in their stone armory, where they were joined by a dozen or so other black citizens of the town, including the town marshal, James Cook. White riflemen milled about outside. Shots rang out from both sides, and no one could testify as to which side fired first. After the first volleys, one combatant on each side lay dead. Shortly thereafter, a group of white men arrived from Augusta, a town that lay across the river. Behind them, they were dragging a small cannon left over from the war. They primed, pointed, and fired it, blowing a hole in the wall of the armory. The black men inside scattered, except for Cook, who lay dead. Four militiamen were grabbed as they came out and summarily executed. Then the white men turned their rifles on the rest of the fleeing blacks, killing two more of them, taking several as prisoners, and wounding others.

Demands for justice came from both sides. Whites claimed the militia represented a threat to public safety. Blacks declared they acted only in self-defense. The local magistrate trying to adjudicate the case was a talented and well-educated black man. Prince Rivers had escaped from slavery during the war and had sought asylum by joining the First South Carolina Colored Regiment. Colonel Thomas Higginson later commented that if black men ever formed their own country, Prince Rivers would surely become their king.

In this case, however, Rivers had little hope of holding a fair trial. Despite obvious prompting from the judge, witnesses against the militia refused to testify that the militia was nothing more than a bumbling group of black men who represented no danger to the public. Those who were accused of firing the fatal shots claimed that every death had been justified to protect the innocent citizens of the community, but at the same time they all denied that they had even been present. And outside, a white mob still waited, their presence a silent statement that only one verdict was acceptable.

Charleston newspapers would later declare there could be no excuse for the killing on either side. Democrats warned that the Hamburg massacre was a direct result of government in the hands of ignorant black men who knew only one solution to all problems. At the Legare Street house of the Grenville family, however, all such reports were meaningless. Only one short telegram mattered.

HECTOR MOREAU DIED OF INJURIES SUFFERED IN HAMBURG ON JULY 8 TAKING HIM HOME PLEASE NOTIFY FAMILY MEMBERS JOHNNY

Jonathan stood in the open doorway, the flimsy scrap of paper clutched in his trembling hand.

"Jonathan, who was at the . . . ? What's wrong? Jonathan? Tell me!"

He handed her the telegram and closed his eyes against her own agony. "Start packing our things. I'll go to the telegraph office and send word to Eli. We need to be in Aiken."

Chapter 38

Those Who Mourn

July 1876

Eddie met the family at the Aiken Depot when their overnight train arrived early in the morning. They silently embraced, no one able to find the first words in the face of such unspeakable tragedy.

At last, Jonathan turned to Eddie. "Is Johnny still here? I want to know exactly what happened."

"He's in town somewhere. He probably spent the night at the church or at the Democratic office. He wouldn't stay at the farm. He said he expected to be unwelcome as the bearer of bad news."

"His role goes deeper than that. I want to know how he always managed to be at hand when Hector was wounded."

"You don't think . . ."

"I don't know, but I need to confront my son."

"He was right, then, in choosing to stay away," Eddie said. "Sarah is at the farm. She and Charlotte and Gretchen have laid out the body in the parlor, and mourners will be coming along soon. None of us needs that kind of confrontation right now. I hope you'll respect the occasion."

The harsh rebuke from the usually soft-spoken Eddie stunned his parents, and they finished the trip in silence.

When they arrived at the farmhouse, Susan hurried inside. She found Sarah in her accustomed place, working diligently at something on the stove. "Sarah, darling, you shouldn't be out here cooking. The girls can handle everything in the kitchen. You need—"

Sarah whirled and glared at Susan. "What do you know about what I need? You've never been a widow. Your daughter knows, but you don't. Just leave me be!"

"No, I can't do that. Come, let me give you a hug."

"Don't need no hugs, 'cept from my husband, and he ain't gonna be passing them out anymore, thanks to you white folks."

"Sarah, no, we're family. We loved Hector as much as you did."

"No, you didn't. You couldn't love him like I did or need him like I did. You gots your own husband standing there in the doorway. But you keep him away from me. He's the reason we're all in this place today."

"Jonathan? This isn't his fault. We didn't even know until last night . . ."

"He started all this." She jutted her chin into a belligerent grimace as she pointed to Jonathan. "He freed us and then piled all his expectations on top of us. He wanted us to be educated Negroes. He wanted us to be part of your family. He wanted us to show the world how black folk and white folk could get along. And we tried. Hector tried. He worked so hard to do whatever Jonathan wanted him to do. Hector wanted to make Jonathan's dreams come true, but he couldn't. Up to his last dying breath, he pleaded for peace, but it didn't come. Instead, somebody shot him, and now all those fancy dreams of equality and cooperation are meaningless words. Like Hector, they ain't nothing but dust now."

Susan watched helplessly as Sarah turned back to the stove and began beating whatever was boiling in the pot. Jonathan led the way back into the parlor. "You may want to see the body in private," he suggested.

"It's not a 'body'! That's our own Hector lying there, and it's too soon for him to be dead. Too soon." Her tears were flowing now, and she blindly reached for a chair, fearing her legs would no longer support her. "Sarah thinks I don't care, but I do. Oh, how deeply I do!"

"She'll come around. Give her time. And let your own grief come out now, so you can be stronger for her when she's ready for your support."

"Is she right, Jonathan? Are we at fault for what has happened?"

"I don't know. I thought freedom was the answer, but maybe it wasn't. I gave Hector his freedom and assumed he would be the better for it. But ever since we first came to Aiken, he has been trying to tell me there were things I did not understand about his people. He tried to warn me. He understood dangers I couldn't even recognize."

"Freeing the slaves was the only right thing to do! I can't believe the war was fought for nothing. The abolitionists and supporters of emancipation were all wrong? President Lincoln died in vain? I refuse to believe freedom is wrong."

"Freedom isn't wrong. But I suspect we asked the wrong questions about it. We talked in terms of 'freedom from' things like bondage and slavery, freedom from having children sold away from their parents, freedom from chains and whips and shackles. Freedom from all those things was a worthy goal. But we forgot to talk about what the freed slaves would have the 'freedom to do.'"

"I don't understand."

"Freedom doesn't matter if you are not free to find a good job and earn a decent living, if you are not free to travel without someone questioning you about your destination, if you are not free to buy a house to shelter your family or own your own land. It doesn't matter that the constitution says your children must be educated if schools will not allow them to learn. It doesn't matter that black men have the right to vote if white men block them from reaching the ballot box. We gave them freedom, but we failed to grant them the privilege that has to be a part of freedom."

"So we made their lives more difficult?"

"In some sense, we made their lives impossible, and that is a burden we will have to live with."

"And we killed Hector?"

"Sarah's justified in thinking so, at least in these first days. I suspect she's desperately trying to make sense of what has happened. She has to find someone to blame. She also has her own patterns of grief to work through, and they may be very different from what we would expect. She'll move beyond all this eventually, but you'll need to give her time."

❧

As the day moved on, Susan and Jonathan learned how different the black rituals of death could be. By noon, women from the African Methodist Episcopal Church of Aiken had begun to descend on the farmhouse. None paid any attention to the white inhabitants of the house. Their focus was entirely upon Sarah, who accepted their ministrations with a willingness to surrender and allow herself to be cared for. They came dressed in finery to honor the deceased, and they came bearing food to sustain both family and visitors throughout the mourning period. Some brought their aprons and took over the kitchen. Others referred to as "nurses" spent time near the casket, reaching out to comfort those who mourned. Outside in the yard, their husbands collected to tell stories about Hector's life and to sing spirituals about the journey on which he was now embarked. In one corner of the yard, a small troop of drummers practiced their beats, while others prepared a bundle of torches.

Now and then, Sarah moved out onto the side porch to watch the road for signs of an approaching carriage. Susan found her there alone at one point and dared to approach her again. "You're waiting for your children, aren't you?"

"Yes, of course I am. Your Eddie has taken the carriage back to the station in case they come in today. We can't have a funeral until they get here."

"The afternoon train arrives around four o'clock, but they may not be here until morning, you know."

"I know Eli will be coming as quick as he can. I need him here to lean on. That's why we have sons—to lean on when all else fails us."

"Believe me, I do understand. Would you like me to watch the road for you and come get you when they arrive?"

"No. I don't need your help."

Hurt beyond words, Susan went inside and took refuge in the guest bedroom to cry out her frustration and sorrow at the apparent loss of her dearest friend.

The mourners continued their activities until full darkness fell and the last train whistle had made it clear the travelers from St. Helena would not arrive until the next day. Then some of the mourners departed, while most of the nurses and a few of the cooks made themselves comfortable in the parlor to watch out the night.

"We could move to the inn for the night," Jonathan suggested. "Get a good night's sleep and a good breakfast. Be better prepared to handle whatever tomorrow brings."

"No. I need to be here. I can't explain why. I just do." Susan and Jonathan shoehorned the boys in with Charlotte's brood and made room for Becca on a chaise longue in their own room.

❦

Eli, Mary Sue, and Annie arrived the next morning before anyone was awake. Susan came downstairs to find Annie on the parlor floor next to the coffin, curled into a ball and sobbing with huge gasping gulps. Susan immediately reached for her and pulled her into a tight embrace.

"There, there, poor little girl. Cry your heartache away." She rocked her back and forth. "I think I know how lost you feel. It will help to remember the good things about your father. He gave you a wonderful inheritance. He left you the strength of his love, and that love will sustain you through all life's crises. He was so proud of you, Annie. When he came back from St. Helena the last time, all he could talk about was how much you had grown up and how you had become a role model for all your little scholars. He said he thought that, of all of us, you had done the most to help your people succeed after the war."

"D-did he really s-say that?"

"Yes, he did, and more besides. He said, of all his accomplishments, you were the one who would earn him a star in his crown when he got to heaven."

"I want him to be proud of me, but I don't see how I am going to get through even this one day."

"By leaning on your mother and your brother. You are all suffering the pain of a tremendous loss that can only be eased by sharing your love. Don't hide your tears from your family but share your grief. You need each other."

"Thank you, Miss Susan. I'll try. Eli's taking it hard, I know. He's out on the porch because he said he couldn't stand looking at Papa's body."

Susan moved to look out the front door. Eli stood at the porch railing, head bowed, hands gripping the top rail as if it were about to break and hurl him into an abyss. Behind him, Mary Sue waited for his spasms to pass. Then she reached out gently and touched the back of his neck with a soft pressure that made no demands but only gave reassurance. In return, he tipped his head back to lean into her touch.

How they love one another, Susan thought. Perhaps this horrible loss will make everyone realize how important it is to keep that love alive. She blessed them both.

Soon the house was alive with people coming and going. Since the last of the mourners had arrived, the Moreaus' church friends sprang into action again. Cooks set out a breakfast to tempt even those who did not believe they could swallow.

A party of gravediggers arrived for direction. They called on Sarah to make decisions about where Hector would like to lie, and she became almost animated as they discussed the relative virtues of the top of a small hill as opposed to the shade of a mighty oak. "I like the hill," she said. "I want his spirit to be able to see the sky and the steeple of the church reaching up to the clouds. Perhaps in the fall, we can plant a small tree nearby to provide comforting shade as the years pass."

"Reverend Blackwell is here!" someone called. "Sarah, can you talk with him about the service? Do you want something held here, or at the church, or at the graveside?"

"I want to move Hector to the church today, so all his friends can visit. But services? Only at the graveside, I think. And with all due respect, Reverend, I don't need to hear any sermons on this day. Only the words of the Lord to give me direction and song to lift Hector's spirit toward heaven."

"We can do whatever you wish, my child."

"I want our usual procession at dusk—pallbearers carrying the casket, accompanied by blazing torches, the sounds of marching feet, and the voices of those who loved him raised in the soft chanting of prayers."

"Yes, ma'am."

"And we will bury him with the traditional rituals of his Gullah ancestors, sharing the task of covering the coffin with dirt and marking the grave with conch shells and some of his favorite possessions. We will send his soul back across the water from which he came and let darkness fall over his grave."

Chapter 39

Family Ties

July 1876

The hour was late, but no one was willing to put an end to the day by going to bed. It had not been a good day. Funerals seldom are. But there had been waves of love, old friendships renewed, family ties strengthened, memories dredged up from a long-forgotten past, hugs, and music to soothe the soul. The younger children drooped with exhaustion, but no one was willing to banish them to their beds, not tonight. The older children scrounged through the kitchen, tasting leftovers and putting together unlikely combinations of cold chicken and chocolate cake frosting.

Eli and Mary Sue returned from the barn where they had been brushing down the horses and putting away the carriage hitches. They smelled of wet hay and horse sweat, but both were more relaxed now that they had had some time to re-engage in their normal activities.

In the parlor, thoughtful parishioners had rearranged the furniture to fill the space where the coffin had once stood. They had removed the candles and opened the windows to let in the freshening night breeze. Family members sat close together, not talking much but enjoying their togetherness. Conversations seemed casual but touched for the first time on unanswered questions.

"I was moved to see that Congressman Smalls attended the burial. Hector would have appreciated his recognition," Susan said.

"There were other government officials present, too—even Governor Chamberlain. I suspect Hector never knew how much his work was valued in Columbia," Jonathan added.

"It's too bad we never think to say 'thank you' until a person has passed beyond hearing it."

"Oh, I believe he heard it," Sarah smiled.

"You know, I even thought I saw our Johnny at the gravesite, but when I tried to move around to where he was standing, he had disappeared."

"He was there, Mother. I saw him, too," Charlotte said. "I don't understand why he seems to be avoiding us."

"I can explain it," Eddie said. "I talked to him right after he brought Hector's body home. He was afraid someone would think he had been involved in the Hamburg Riot."

"So you said, Eddie. But isn't that a natural assumption? Of course he was involved somehow. How else did he know Hector had been shot?"

"Yes, he was there but not as a rioter. He's one of General Hampton's new Red Shirt guards. Hampton is above all else a politician, and he does not want the upcoming election enflamed by lynching or murder or armed insurrection. He created the Red Shirts to settle racial arguments and put an end to violent clashes before anyone gets hurt—if they can. In this case, they failed. But when Johnny realized Hector had been shot, he took leave of his duties to bring him home."

"Why not tell us, if that's all there is to his involvement?"

"Johnny has his problems, Father. He is not the same young man you sent off to war all those years ago. He loses his temper easily, he suffers from nightmares, and he's often in real physical pain. He can't handle emotions. But he's doing his best to stand up for what he believes."

"Which is . . . what? He spends most of his time cavorting with white supremacists, from what I can tell."

"Yes, he does, but I believe him when he says he is trying to show them how to compromise—a lesson he learned from you."

"Bah! There are better ways."

Susan laid a hand on her husband's arm. "Enough for tonight, Jonathan. Tonight is a time for us to love one another. If we can't do that, we'll not accomplish much else of value."

❧

Sarah had deliberately turned a deaf ear to the conversation because she did not want to hear it. Instead, she was watching her children and taking comfort in having them both under the same roof with her, even if only for a little while. Susan sensed her preoccupation and pushed the conversation in a new direction.

"What will you do now, Sarah? I know it's too early for you to make any final decisions about your life, but perhaps you'd like to come back to Charleston with us for a while?"

"Oh, no, Susan! I don't want to go anywhere. I intend to stay right here. I have my own little house—the one Hector built for me with his own hands. He wouldn't want me to go anywhere else. He knew I'd be safe there, and there's where I want to stay."

"I've been thinking about this, too, Mother," Annie said. "Why don't I plan to stay here with you for a while? We can live together and do things and—"

"No! I don't want that, either. I love you, Annie, but you can't give up your own life for me. I won't let you do that."

"I won't be giving up all that much. The school on St. Helena can get along without me, and most of the children I've been teaching on Ladies Island are grown up now."

"I'm all grown up now, too, and I don't need anyone to take care of me."

"But you'll be lonely."

"Yes, I will. That's part of being a widow. But I need that. I need time to come to terms with Hector being gone. I won't be able to understand the loss so long as people keep trying to shield me from it. I need some time alone, so I can learn how to stand on my own."

Annie had been perched on the edge of her chair as she made her offer. Now she leaned back, frowning and wishing she could come up with a better argument. In hopes of enlisting Eli's help, she looked around but couldn't find him. Then a small movement from the porch revealed that he and Mary Sue were having their own private conversation.

Sarah followed her daughter's glance and also realized what was going on. Maybe it's time to stir things up and draw attention away from me, she thought. "Eli? Where have you gotten to?" she called.

Flustered, he poked his head back in the door. "What is it, Mother? Do you need me?"

"As a matter of fact, I do. Come in here, and bring that young woman with you."

Now Mary Sue was blushing as well, but she tried to cover it by quipping, "We were trying to let some of the barn smell blow off."

"We've been talking about our future plans," Sarah said. "My plan is to stay put, right where God planted me. But what about you? How's the Grenmore Stables business? Are you both still intent on staying on St. Helena with your horses?"

"Yes, of course. We're doing a great business. We're slowly building a stable full of Carolina Marsh Tackies. We won't ever deliberately go out and capture a horse in the wild, but every winter, one or two of the island's herd wander up to the barns in search of food or shelter. And when they see what great care we have to offer, they usually decide to hang around. We've added several new blood lines to our breeding program, and I think we're pretty close to discovering what the original Spanish horses looked like."

"And we have more customers than we can handle," Mary Sue added. "Our young horses make great ponies for children, and when the horses get a little older, they make good farm animals for local farmers. I have a waiting list for Sable Girl's next foals."

"That's all well and good, but it ain't much help to me right now."

"We'd be happy to have you come live at Grenmore, Sarah. I'm sure Eli would be grateful for your cooking rather than the haphazard mess Annie and I manage to make of the job."

"That's not the kind of job I'm looking for!" Sarah looked from one of her children to the other, giving them the kind of look she had used to discipline them when they were toddlers.

"What I need right now is grandbabies—grandbabies I can love to pieces and raise up to think their grandmammy can do no wrong. Cuddly little brown grandbabies to give my life a new meaning and purpose. And I ain't seeing anybody doing nothing to make that happen. Ain't gonna happen with you two living in separate houses. And it ain't gonna happen with Annie playing chaperone for your odd living arrangements. And baby horses ain't gonna do the job."

"Mother!"

"Don't you 'Mother' me, Eli Moreau. You know the two of you have been in love ever since you were children. You just ain't been brave enough to admit it. And furthermore . . . furthermore, it was your father's dream that one day the two of you would be able to marry without fear and without criticism. He didn't get to see that day, but when I go to join him at the Pearly Gates someday, I want to be able to tell him it happened at last."

For long seconds a shocked silence reigned. Then Susan took a deep breath and stood up. "I agree. A wedding is just what this family needs."

"Wait! Wait one minute, both of you!" Mary Sue's face had gone white, although a flush of anger was spreading across her cheeks. And the tears she had managed to hold back all through the funeral now ran uncontrollably down her nose and dripped from her chin.

"You can't do this. Eli and I are all grown up. You no longer control us and what we do. You have no business interfering with our lives. When you first realized we were falling in love, you told us it was dangerous and impossible. You said that because Eli was black and I was white, the world would never accept us. We believed you, and we went along with your decision. Do you have any idea what it has cost us to work together every day while hiding our feelings and refusing to give into them? Do you? And now you're changing your minds? After eight years of preventing us from loving one another? What gives you the right? And if there is ever to be such a suggestion, I want it to come from Eli, not from his mother—or mine!"

Eli reached for her arm, but she jerked away and fled from the room. Her footsteps pounded on the staircase, and a door slammed with terrible finality. Eli glared at both Sarah and Susan. "If I have lost her, I will never forgive either one of you, ever!"

"Don't be melodramatic at this stage, Eli," Susan suggested. "The next move is definitely up to you. You need to go after her."

"She went to her bedroom. I can't . . ."

"Why not?" Jonathan now entered the discussion. "I won't come after you and beat you for courting my daughter. But I might do it later, if you end up breaking her heart."

"Go on, boy," Sarah added. "But here, take this with you." She held out a small handkerchief-wrapped bundle.

"What is it?"

"It's your great-grandmother Ernestine's ring. The ring Pierre Antoine Dubois gave to his slave mistress to bind her to him for all time, even though his own family would not let him marry her. Pierre was your great-grandfather, and Mary Sue's as well. Ernestine gave it to Thomas before she died with the instruction that it should stay in our family, and he gave it to me. I can think of no better use than to unite Pierre's two great-grandchildren."

Eli took the handkerchief and unwrapped the ring. It was plain, simple, and elegant, a wide gold band inlaid with multicolored stones—a ruby, an emerald, a sapphire, and amber and topaz in various shades. "It carries its own message, doesn't it? It's perfect for Mary Sue—but not tonight. We've had more than enough emotion for one day. Tomorrow will give us a new beginning."

Chapter 40

Blessings upon the Day

July 15, 1876

 li found Mary Sue the next morning exactly where he knew she would be. Still looking grim, she was pitching clean hay into the horse stalls as if it had tried to escape and was now being punished. Several of the horses, the whites of their eyes showing, had withdrawn into the backs of their stalls to avoid the onslaught. Chaff filled the air and hung in the early-morning beams of sunlight.

He approached her carefully, trying not to startle her into any further rage. "Did you sleep?" he asked when he caught her glance.

"I must have. Don't remember. Are you here to help? I need another bale tossed down from the loft." She turned away, but he was not to be put off.

"I'll take care of it later. The horses will be fine. Right now, I'm more concerned about you."

"I'll be fine, too. You aren't required to worry about me."

"Yes, I am, because I love you."

She glared at him, then shook her head. "Please don't."

"Please don't what? Worry about you? Love you? What?"

"All of that."

"Can't help it. I do, and I do. In fact, that's why I'm here—to talk about the I dos."

"No, Eli, please."

"Yes. And put down that pitchfork for a little while. I'd rather not be impaled, even if by accident. I have something to show you."

Her lower lip was beginning to jut out. She sniffed and blinked rapidly but then did as he asked. "There. You're safe, temporarily. Now, what do I have to see right this minute?"

"This." He held out his closed fist and then slowly opened it to reveal Ernestine's ring lying in his palm. "Have you ever seen this?"

"No. It's a ring, but I don't recognize it."

"It's a family heirloom. Our great-grandfather, Pierre Antoine Dubois, had it created especially for Ernestine. You do remember reading his diary, don't you? You were devastated when you read that he and his dearest love were not allowed to marry. Didn't he mention a ring in the diary?"

"I don't think so, no." She was staring at the ring with awakened curiosity. "It's unusual, isn't it?"

"I thought so, too. And then I realized what it shows. It's not an engagement ring or a wedding ring. It has no central stone, no focus, no top or bottom. It's a continuous band of stones of all colors, no one of them more important than the other—like us."

"How did you find it?"

"My mother had it. Ernestine wore the ring until her death. She left it to her son Thomas, with instructions it was never to leave the possession of the family. Thomas passed it to my mother, and now she has given it to me."

"Why? Why doesn't she wear it?"

"She gave it to me last night. She said it would be only right if it united the two branches of Pierre's family. That's you and me, you understand. Here, try it on. Let's see if it fits."

He took her unresisting hand and slipped the ring onto her finger. "Perfect!"

"No, not like this," Mary Sue pulled her hand away and removed the ring. "Take it back." She was crying again.

"But why?" Eli stared at her, unable to understand.

And then she managed a wobbly smile. "Because it needs to be our wedding ring."

⚘

They were late joining the rest of the family for breakfast, but they were both smiling as they came into the kitchen.

"There you are!" Susan greeted them eagerly.

381

"Did you save us anything? Coffee, at least?"

"There's toast. And bacon." Sarah moved back to the stove. "Find a place to sit down, and I'll cook you some eggs."

"While you're waiting, we have something to discuss with you," Susan said.

"What's that?"

"Well, Annie indicated last night she is not particularly eager to return to St. Helena, and your father has come up with a suggestion. You understand I am speaking for all of us here. How would you feel if Annie stayed in Charleston for a while? Jonathan is always in need of good teachers for his schools, and being in Charleston would make it easier for Annie to keep in touch with Sarah."

"I think it sounds like an interesting idea," Mary Sue said. "What does Annie say about it? For that matter, where is Annie?"

"Not up yet. That's why we took this chance to get your reaction before we suggested it to her."

"There you go again, Mother, making decisions for us as if we were still children. Annie's an adult. Ask her."

"Ask me what?" Annie asked from the doorway. "What have I missed?"

"Well, dear, we were thinking you might like to come back to Charleston with us and find a teaching job there."

"Whatever gave you that idea?"

"Last night you said you didn't need to go back to St. Helena, and . . ."

"I spoke out of love, in case Mother needed me to stay with her. But I have a whole life on St. Helena among people I have come to regard as family. I moved out of the guesthouse at Grenmore Stables a couple of years ago. I don't play chaperone for Eli and Mary Sue, either, and you don't have to find a place to stash me, as if I'm a family hanger-on. So, no—thank you, but no. I wouldn't dream of living in Charleston."

Eli cleared his throat. "If that's the end of that topic, we have something else to discuss with you. It sounds as if we still need to hold one of those famous family meetings."

"Before coffee?" Jonathan asked. He lifted the pot and gestured toward a stack of cups.

"Well, over coffee, perhaps." For a moment, Eli's voice failed him, and even his mother turned to stare at him, forgetting to stir the eggs. He reached for his cup and took a fortifying sip. Then the words came tumbling out, and Mary Sue joined him in another demonstration of their ability to finish one another's thoughts.

"We have decided to honor Father's memory by getting married . . ."

" . . . right away, while everyone is still here, and . . ."

" . . . before we all forget about how much we need one another."

"We thought we could hold the wedding here in the yard . . ."

" . . . rather than in either of our churches . . ."

" . . . so nobody feels excluded . . ."

" . . . sort of like what Eddie and Gretchen did . . ."

" . . . although maybe not with all the preaching . . ."

" . . . but with lots of music . . ."

" . . . and food."

Then chaos reigned. There was much laughter and hugging—with kisses for the women and congratulatory handshakes among the men. The eggs burned, but no one cared.

"When?"

"We thought—maybe Thursday?"

"That only gives us two days," Susan protested.

"My family can help," Gretchen offered. "They'll all remember Eli and Mary Sue from when we got married. And you know the Mennonites can really do weddings! The women will cook, and the men can bring over some of the benches and tables we used. It'll be easy. Leave the details to me."

"But no preaching. We've already had more than enough of that!" Eddie added.

"I promise, although you won't be able to stop my folks from singing."

❦

Thursday dawned clear and hot. Mrs. Schwimmer was already sweating as she unloaded her baskets from the wagon. "What is wrong with these English families? What don't they understand about summer weather? This is the second time one of them has insisted on getting married in July. They're plain foolish, if you ask me!" But her opinions had not stopped her from preparing a lavish wedding spread. She and her sisters soon had the tables loaded with a boiled ham, fried chicken, macaroni salad, bean salad, trays of fresh raw vegetables, platters of boiled corn, and a huge variety of fruit-laden desserts.

Both Pastor Blackwell from the African Methodist Episcopal Church and Reverend Cornish from the Aiken Episcopal Church were on hand to read the scriptures and offer their blessings, and many members of both congregations had also decided to attend. The biggest surprise was the arrival of Johnny. Eddie had taken it upon himself to find him and give him a brotherly lecture on his responsibility to support their sister. Johnny had risen to the occasion, again bringing with him Congressman Robert Smalls.

Upstairs, the women were busy concocting a wedding dress. Susan had found an embroidered lawn gown in the attic, and Sarah was still taking tucks in it here and there to make it fit. Susan disappeared for a few moments and returned in triumph, saying "Voilà! A veil!"

"Mother! That's a lace curtain."

"So it is, and on your head it will be a veil."

"I'll look like a child playing dress-up with the draperies."

"You are going to look like a lovely bride, Mary Susannah Grenville, despite your best efforts to behave like a stable hand. Now be still and let me figure out how to pin this veil to your head. I don't want you to lose it mid-ceremony."

From the bedroom window, Mary Sue watched the assembling crowd. "I can't believe this," she said. "Why are all these people so interested in our little wedding? It doesn't mean trouble, does it?"

"That's a happy crowd down there, Mary Sue," Gretchen assured her. "Don't worry. The people who are joining us today are those who want to see this new unified nation succeed. And this wedding is a symbol of that unity. They are here to cheer you on."

❧

And so they were. Reverend Cornish read from the Thirteenth Chapter of First Corinthians, Reverend Blackwell read the story of Jesus at the wedding, and several of the attendees looked around, hoping the passage presaged the arrival of the wine. The Mennonite choir, borrowing from a Methodist hymnal, sang a hymn of blessing for the wedded couple:

> *MAY the grace of Christ our Savior,*
> *And the Father's boundless love,*
> *With the Holy Spirit's favor,*
> *Rest upon us from above!*
> *Thus may we abide in union*
> *With each other in the Lord;*
> *And possess, in sweet communion,*
> *Joys which earth cannot afford.*

At last, the young couple turned to each other, and, following the example set by Eddie and Gretchen, they took vows they had written specifically for each other. Mary Sue stayed close to the traditional wedding vows, promising to honor her husband, work by his side, and respect him and obey him. She then repeated the vow of Ruth to Naomi: *"Entreat me not to leave thee, or to return from following after thee: for whither thou goest, I will go; and where thou lodgest, I will lodge: thy people shall be my people, and thy God my God."*

Eli's vows ventured further from the traditional, as he promised to love and cherish Mary Sue and then reminded her of their family connection. "Our great-grandfather, Pierre Antoine Dubois, had a dream he was never able to fulfill. He wished for a day in which all people would be seen and treated as equals. He even created a ring for his true love—a ring of many colors, all of them equal. I give you this same ring today, as a reminder that in our love, color has no meaning. With these vows, we thus take our great-grandfather's dream and make it a reality."

It was a moving ceremony, and even some of the most stoic of the attendees found it necessary to wipe away a tear or two. Then revelry prevailed. In the emotional turmoil of the past week, appetites had been poor. But now, in the joyfulness of this summer afternoon, ravenous hordes descended on the picnic tables. Outdoor games sprang up among the children, and the choir singers from both churches began a friendly competition.

The Episcopalians serenaded Mary Sue with "Beautiful Dreamer," and the black choir responded with "When You and I Were Young, Maggie." Johnny went back to the tables for a second helping and found himself greeted with "When Johnny Comes Marching Home." The black choir responded with Stephen Foster's "Old Folks at Home." But the highlight of the afternoon came when all the singers combined for a rousing rendition of the year's most popular song, "My Grandfather's Clock." By the time they had made it through a verse or two, almost everyone was joining in for the chorus:

Ninety years without slumbering
Tick, tock, tick, tock
His life seconds numbering
Tick, tock, tick, tock
It stopped, short, never to go again
When the old man died.

As the celebration wound down, Robert Smalls sought out Jonathan. "Are the newlyweds going back to the Beaufort area right away?" he asked.

"Early tomorrow, I believe. They have a large horse farm there, you know, and they can't afford to stay away very long."

"In that case, I will act immediately. I want to notify General Saxton about the wedding, if that's all right with you. His wife, Tillie, will certainly want to arrange a celebration there for all their friends. I want them to feel comfortable with their new situation from the beginning. And a lovely celebration there will spread the word in a positive way rather than letting normal island gossip take its course."

"Do you think their marriage will be accepted among the black community?" Jonathan asked. "I approve of the union—don't misunderstand me. But I can't help but worry that, somewhere down the line, Mary Sue will pay a heavy price for her decision."

"From what I've heard, she is a popular addition to the islands. There's very little hostility toward whites among the Gullah of St. Helena. Miss Towne and her people have always treated them well, and that has fostered good relationships. Besides, I trust your daughter, and you should, too."

"Oh, I do. I trust her judgment, or I would never have approved this marriage. It's others I don't trust."

"I fully understand your worry, but I think you can relax. You have a good reputation in the area, and so do these young people. They are going to be fine. And speaking of your reputation, I wanted to congratulate you, Mr. Grenville," he said. "I never doubted you were sincere in your concern for the Negro cause. But it is rare to find a white man who lives the cause he espouses."

"I have been accused of failing at that, I admit," Jonathan replied.

"Well, not today. This has been one of the happiest wedding days I have ever witnessed. Your son has filled me in on the relationship between your daughter and her new husband. I admire them tremendously. But I'm still curious about the Mennonite connection with your family. That's something I did not expect to find."

"That's my second son's doing. He married into the Mennonite family several years ago after going into the cheese-making business with his future wife's family. We've found them all very compatible and delightfully open-minded."

"Blessings on every one of you, my friend. After we get through the coming elections, I'd like to meet with you further. There are some matters on which I could use your guidance. You're still running the Charleston Negro schools, are you?"

"Yes, sir, and I'll be glad to work with you. Anything I can do to help."

Jonathan watched as the congressman rejoined the party traveling back to Columbia. Smalls turned once and raised a farewell gesture. But Johnny never looked back. As if on cue, a small, dark cloud passed over the sun.

Chapter 41

Wade Hampton and the Red Shirts

August 1876

*H*enrietta McLeod was working in her garden when the Grenvilles arrived home from Aiken, keeping one eye on her weeds and the other on anyone who stirred on her quiet street. "Welcome home," she called, as the Grenville carriage pulled up. "Did you have a nice time wherever you were?"

"We were attending a funeral," Jonathan snapped at her.

"Oh my, I'm dreadfully sorry to hear that. Someone near and dear to you?"

"Family."

"Not one of your children, surely? I know our Alex has been terribly worried about your son Johnny—the one who was wounded in the war?"

"Jonathan," Susan whispered. "Come away. Don't answer her. She does that to people—keeps asking questions to tie them up in knots."

But Jonathan pulled away from her cautionary hand. "Don't you have enough business of your own to worry about, Mrs. McLeod? I have no intention of discussing our sorrows with you so that you can put them in your newspaper."

"Oh, I would never do that! So it was your Johnny, then?"

"No, it wasn't. I'm sure you are disappointed to hear that."

"No, not at all. There are always some family members we don't want to talk about, aren't there?"

This time Susan grabbed his arm and pulled him firmly toward the door.

"That woman is a menace!" he exclaimed.

"She is that," Susan agreed, "which is why we must try to avoid her rather than egging her on."

"I can't help it. She and that son-in-law of hers seem to take perverse delight in harassing our family."

"It's because you're still the 'Damned Yankee,' dear, while she is the flower of Southern womanhood." Susan was hoping to jolly Jonathan out of the black mood that had settled over him after the wedding, but it did not work.

"I'm happy Annie decided not to move to Charleston," he said. "I wouldn't want her living here where she would be subjected to cruel remarks by that woman. It'll only be a matter of time before she finds out who died. Huh! She probably knows already, come to think of it. Alex, I'm sure, still keeps track of dangerous blacks like Hector, even if the Klan has been put out of business."

He turned toward his office, a sure sign he wanted to be left alone. At the doorway, however, he turned to have the last word. "And I'm no longer a Damned Yankee, my dear. I'm a Damned Scalawag!"

⁂

In the days following their return to Charleston, Susan continued to worry about Jonathan's altered mood. He headed off every day to work on preparations for opening the Negro schools in November, but he was finding more to criticize and less to praise. He read the papers diligently as the electioneering heated up, frequently grumbling under his breath as he did so. He was also corresponding frequently with Robert Smalls and other Republican stalwarts—long, worried letters scribbled late at night.

"Are you fearful about the outcome of the election?" she asked one evening.

"Yes, actually I am. Accusations about the corruption under Governor Chamberlain are increasing, and the accusers have ample evidence to back up their statements. I'm afraid the Democrats are going to be stronger in the election than anyone expects."

"But surely the black population will vote Republican as they always have."

"I wish I could believe that, but I don't. We're seeing real defections to the Democratic Party, especially concerning the governor's race. Now that General Hampton has officially declared his candidacy, his popularity is soaring!"

"What does that man do to the people around him?" Susan wondered out loud. "We've seen for ourselves how deeply loyal Johnny is to him, but if he can also attract the black vote . . ."

"Right now, I'm most upset about the new term the Democrats are applying to their policies."

"Which is?"

"'Redemption.' They are calling themselves the Redeemers and promising to save the South from the terrible fate losing the war has brought upon them."

Susan turned to the keyboard of her melodeon and picked out the beginning measures of one of her favorite hymns, "I know that my Redeemer liveth . . ."

Jonathan grimaced as he recognized the music. "Exactly. Redemption is a Christian idea. It implies a savior, and that's how the Democrats are portraying themselves. Hampton's also the epitome of the fine Southern gentleman. Toward both his former soldiers and his former slaves, he takes a paternalistic approach. He promises to take care of them, and in these days of economic uncertainty, being taken care of is terribly important."

"That's how democracy works, isn't it? People vote for those officials and policies they think will improve their lives."

"Yes, of course it is, but in this case, the promises are lies."

"Are you sure?"

"I am! Hampton's making grandiose statements about his intentions. Just the other day, the paper quoted him as saying—wait, here it is.

I will be the governor of the whole people. I will support black suffrage and public education. If any white man thinks I will grant privileges on the basis of color, he is wrong. I promise only to enforce the laws, encourage prosperity, and run an honest government.

"What's wrong with that? I might vote for him myself, if I could vote."

"Nothing, on the face of it. But while he was saying it, his campaign manager, Martin Gary, was sending out his bands of armed white men to round up blacks who intend to vote Republican. And whenever they found them, they were beating them senseless. Hampton is never around when acts of violence take place against his enemies. He can pretend innocence or ignorance, but I don't believe either argument. Hampton intends to steal this governor's race by whatever means it takes."

"And our Johnny is involved?"

"He is, and I can barely swallow the bitterness that rises in me when I think about it."

"Have you tried talking to Johnny? Telling him how you feel?"

"And how do you think I could do that? You've seen for yourself how he avoids us. He puts in an appearance at family functions but disappears before anyone gets a chance to talk to him."

"But at least he comes. He's been at both our children's weddings, as well as bringing Hector home twice. I think he's reaching out to the family but doesn't know how to start the conversation."

"Or maybe he's ashamed of himself."

"No, I don't think so. He has never been one to deliberately do something he knows is wrong. He has a good conscience, that boy. We raised him that way. But the soldier's experience—it did something to him."

"It certainly did!"

"No, Jonathan, I don't mean the obvious wound. Our family observed the war from afar. It affected us, yes, in terms of our livelihood, but a soldier—he saw the war from the inside, and it must have looked very different. I can't really imagine how it must have been, but I know Johnny has a haunted look in his eyes that wasn't there before. It's as if he has seen sights and places whose horrors we cannot even imagine. And those memories from the past alter the way he sees the present."

"Well, I would like to alter the way he sees the present, too, but I haven't had a chance."

◈

On the evening of August 25, 1876, the Democratic Party held a torchlight parade through downtown Charleston. At the head of the parade rode their candidate for governor, General Wade Hampton, favored son of South Carolina's once wealthiest family. Behind him came a troop of former Confederate soldiers, all wearing identical red flannel shirts. And behind the mounted troops came a ragtag army of supporters on foot, some dressed in red shirts or jackets, others sporting red scarves or red bands on their arms. And from every throat came the identical shout: "Hurrah for Hampton!"

Among the soldiers, of course, rode Johnny Grenville. As the procession continued down Meeting Street toward Broad, he scanned the crowd, wondering if anyone from his family had ventured out to see what was going on. When the parade broke up on the Battery, he hesitated. The flickering flames of the torches reminded him of a similar evening in the past, when fear of a spreading conflagration had sent him riding headlong to make sure his family was safe. He spurred his horse and sprinted toward Legare Street.

As was still his custom, Jonathan was watching the last fading light of the day from the front piazza. The drum of hoofbeats pulled him out of his reverie, and he craned his neck to see who was coming. The figure was so familiar that Jonathan, too, was momentarily reminded of the night of the Great Charleston Fire.

"Johnny?"

"Yes, Father. I haven't come for a long visit, but I needed to stop by and make sure you all arrived home safely from Aiken."

"You have time to sit for a spell, surely. We haven't talked for a very long time, and I've missed you."

"Have you? I would have thought you were glad to have me out of the way."

"Most certainly not. Now, what are you doing in town?"

"You missed tonight's triumphant procession, I gather. The Democratic Party was introducing Charleston to their candidate for governor."

"I heard there was going to be a Hampton parade, but it didn't occur to me you might be in it. Is that why you are wearing a . . . that red shirt? Was it the parade dress for the evening?"

"It's not a parade uniform, Father, as you undoubtedly know, but I'll indulge your pretense of ignorance. The red shirt has become a symbol for the Democratic Party."

"In Mississippi, I understand, a red shirt is the uniform of armed bands who have replaced the Ku Klux Klan."

"The wearing of a red shirt began as a way to ridicule those who wave a bloody shirt to illustrate their exaggerated tales of violence against carpetbaggers, scalawags, and black Republicans. We wear it now as a symbol of our pride in the Old South and as a statement of solidarity against the depredations of Republican rule over Southern states."

"Noble words. High-flown ideals. Until they become symbols of violence, fearmongering, intimidation, and murder."

"If it takes violence to put an end to the evils of Reconstruction, as you people refer to your practice of destroying every vestige of Southern civility, then so be it."

"Hector Moreau died defending the rights of black men to be free, to receive an education, and to have a voice in their own government. I thought you would respect that."

"I respect his views, but Reconstruction has failed, Father. Republican government has collapsed under the weight of its own corruption. Education has not managed to put a dent in black ignorance. The enfranchisement of blacks has destroyed the economy of whole states. The Democratic Party must be allowed to take over and redeem as much as we can of the Old South. Or else, everything we fought for, every Southern son who died, every limb lost—was in vain."

"You believe that?"

"I don't believe it—I know it to be true."

Jonathan was saved from making an intemperate reply by a squeal as Susan stepped outside. "Johnny! Oh, how good to see you. Come here, let me hold you for a minute. Goodness, you feel thin! Are you getting enough to eat? Can I fix you some supper?"

"Mother, stop. I'm fine. And no, I don't have time for supper. I only came by to say hello and let you know I am in town. I'll be here for several days, I think, but I'll have to check with General Hampton to see if I can have a little time off. Right now, I need to get back to Democratic Headquarters. I ducked out on the parade on a whim, but my absence will be noticed. I'll see you again soon." He started to turn away and then weakened. He gave his mother a big-hearted hug, rocking her back and forth, and kissed her forehead. Then he turned to his father with his hand extended. "I hope we can agree to disagree, sir."

"We will have to do that," Jonathan replied, but he took the extended hand and then clasped his son's arm in a partial embrace. "Come back soon."

Chapter 42

Riots and Elections

The weeks leading up to the November elections were full of horrors. From all over the state—indeed, from all over the South—came reports of riots, ambushes, lynchings, and deaths. On September 6, one of Hampton's Democratic Clubs held a rally in Charleston, with J.R. Jenkins, a black Hampton supporter, as its featured speaker. After the meeting, a group of Republicans made threats against the Democrats, and a riot followed. Army troops were called out from the Citadel to handle the problem, which they did by surrounding Jenkins and his men with a protective cordon.

The Democrats might have dispersed peacefully, but the Republicans were ready for a fight and began shooting their rifles into streetcars and looting stores along King Street. The Charleston police stood by, unable to handle the mob, while citizens on both sides sought to protect themselves. The *Charleston News and Courier* reported that, by the next day, "it was impossible to purchase a revolver in the city, the stock being completely exhausted."

Johnny returned to visit his parents on Saturday, ostensibly to reassure them the trouble had not been the fault of Hampton's Red Shirts. "We held a peaceful meeting at Hibernian Hall last night to inform voters of General Hampton's promises," he reported. "People listened, asked civil questions, got their answers, and went home. We did not anticipate any further trouble and got none."

"And you did not start the riot that broke out on Wednesday?" Jonathan's expression suggested he did not believe a word of what he was hearing.

"No, sir, we did not."

"Wasn't the invitation to Mr. Jenkins a deliberate attempt to be inflammatory?"

"No, sir. Mr. Jenkins is a free man. It doesn't matter what color his skin is. He has a right to support whatever candidate he chooses, even if you don't agree with his choice." Johnny's lips curled into a derisive smile, but Jonathan refused to be baited into a different argument.

"I disapprove of your Red Shirts, and I don't trust any of you. I know—and you know—that your merry little band takes great delight in intimidating black voters. You ride your horses dangerously close to them. You attend their rallies and stand in silent, threatening judgment of them. You block them from the ballot box, and, yes, you drag them out of their beds and beat them to a pulp whenever you think you can get away with it. You're the KKK dressed in a different colored shirt!"

"Jonathan!" Susan exclaimed. "Stop it. This is your son. He's not evil."

"He is a member of an evil group. I cannot forgive that."

❧

Jonathan became more and more morose as he read the daily reports from across the state. In Aiken County, two black men attempted to rob a white woman and her son. The attackers beat them severely before the woman managed to grab her husband's shotgun and run them off. When the two robbers were identified, however, a group of some forty black men protected them and fired upon those who tried to arrest them. Fears of further violence caused two former Confederate generals to organize their own local militias, which, of course, only escalated the trouble. Four more deaths followed. Ambushes and property damage did not end until federal troops arrived in Aiken to deal with the violence.

The next week, a similar situation arose in nearby Ellenton. As soon as the federal troops withdrew, local blacks began to set fires on white property and ambush solitary travelers. This time, the local militias managed to kill some thirty-nine blacks before order was restored.

In October, the Democrats scheduled a huge political rally in Cainhoy, a short ferry ride northeast of Charleston.

They agreed to share the stage with their political rivals, but only if both sides came unarmed. The Democrats complied, but the black Republicans hid weapons in the swamp and retrieved them at the first sign of trouble. Only one black person died as a result of the ensuing battle, but six Democrats were killed and sixteen were wounded.

A few days later, six men wearing red shirts were attacked by two black men who came out of a cotton field with rifles. In that skirmish, even the coroner was wounded. And at Mt. Pleasant, a black mob threatened to kill every white man in town. They didn't follow through, but the white citizens were so terrified they gathered in a single house for protection.

"Surely, Jonathan, this violence will subside once votes are cast," Susan said, hoping to soothe his increasing agitation.

"Do you think so? Rumor says black voters will be stopped before they get to the polling places. Red Shirts will block the way to every ballot box. Forgers are already falsifying the tickets themselves, so the names in big letters at the top look legitimate, but the ones at the bottom of the ballot are for the opposite party. Voters not used to reading will be deliberately misled by the colors or pictures on the tickets. No, Susan. I'm afraid the election will only be the beginning of more—and worse—trouble."

On Tuesday, November 7, Jonathan was up early. "I'm going to vote," he told Susan, "and then I plan to stay around and become one of the poll watchers. If I'm going to try to help our black citizens with the voting process in the future, I need to see the obstacles they face."

His walk took him to a small boatmen's meetinghouse on the bank of the Ashley River, not far from the ruins of Charleston's original fortifications. Much of the neighborhood had not been reclaimed after the fire of 1861. Burned-out houses were now overgrown with brush and brambles, the cobblestone street giving way to weeds and mud. Almost nothing moved, except for the occasional waterfowl or passing boats. Near the meetinghouse itself, red-shirted men stood on the street corners. They watched Jonathan's approach without reacting—casual, hands in pockets, apparently unarmed, but threatening because of their silence and stillness.

Jonathan ignored them as he climbed the steps to the open doorway. Inside, every candidate seemed to have carved out a small space for himself and his supporters. Democrats were all decked out in something red—a hat, a sash, an armband, or the ubiquitous shirt. Republicans, in contrast, were formally dressed. At the central table, officials checked voters against their lists of registrants. Jonathan was given an immediate nod, but he heard others being rudely questioned or asked to prove their identity.

"Pick up your ticket from the party of your choice, sir. And once you've marked it, deposit it in the proper ballot box up there at the edge of the stage." The clerk smiled and nodded off to his right. "One of Mr. Hampton's fine young men will see to it you have all the right papers. And they'll get you a cup of coffee, too, if you'd like one."

Jonathan stared at the man long enough to make him uncomfortable. Then Jonathan deliberately turned in the other direction to seek out the Republican candidates. Behind him, he heard someone snarl, "damned carpetbagger," followed by the unmistakable sound of a throat clearing and a soft plop as someone spat in his direction.

"Worse," came the reply. "I know him. He's a damned scalawag. Married into the Dubois family a long time ago—long enough to know better."

Jonathan made his way to the ballot box and then lingered close enough to be sure the Red Shirts who were milling around were not blocking the way to reach the stage and deposit one's ticket. Some black voters noticed his intervention and decided to join the effort. And before long, they had created a protective cordon between the two sides of the room. They, too, stood silent, relaxed, casual, unthreatening to anyone who did not try to move them. Jonathan smiled to himself. Sometimes, he thought, scare tactics can work both ways.

When the last votes had been cast and the polls closed, the guardians of civil liberties dispersed. In town, however, tensions increased. At the local telegraph office, small crowds gathered, hoping to hear early returns from other parts of the state and country. Although the presidential race loomed large, most voters were more concerned with the outcome of the gubernatorial race.

The *News and Courier* had come out at the last minute in favor of Hampton for governor because of his stated policies of inclusion, but at the same time, the editor predicted no former Confederate general could win an election in a city with a black majority.

"If so, Jonathan, why does the newspaper editor favor him at all?" Susan once again turned to Jonathan for explanations.

"Well, if you look at the way Hampton has organized the Democratic Clubs, you'll see some interesting moves. He advocated recruiting members at age sixteen so they would grow up in the Democratic Party. He promised club members would provide transportation to the polls for both blacks and whites. He encouraged each of his white followers to take on the responsibility of persuading one black voter to support the Democratic ticket. He repeatedly called out Republicans for lying about their actions, and he encouraged everyone to support local candidates, rather than Yankee carpetbaggers who were only out to make money. He vowed to enforce the Thirteenth, Fourteenth, and Fifteenth Amendments, and promised equal treatment for all. His speeches have been reasonable and therefore persuasive, especially to an editor who is tired of seeing his city tear itself apart."

"But Hampton was responsible for much of the violence that occurred here."

"Not exactly. Hampton did an amazing job of holding himself aloof from any bloodshed. And when violence could be blamed on the Red Shirts, they appeared to be under the command of only Martin Gary, who has never shied away from shedding a little blood for the sake of a political goal."

"And what about the presidential race? The papers I've read seem to think the Democrat Samuel B. Tilden will defeat the Republican Rutherford B. Hayes for President of the United States. Is that possible?"

"I'm afraid so," Jonathan said. "Northerners are tired of focusing their attention on lingering problems engendered by the war. They are unwilling to pay federal troops to keep order down here. And they blame the Grant administration for the corruption that has led to financial ruin for so many investors. No matter which one wins," Jonathan added, "I fear we have seen the last of federal support for the policies of Reconstruction."

"Maybe not," replied Susan, the eternal optimist. "Hayes may have been trying to keep his policies a secret lest he give his enemies more ammunition to use against him."

But there was to be no easy or quick answer. Tilden clearly won the popular vote, since Northern voters were growing weary of the constant turmoil in the defeated South. But the Electoral College was a different matter. When all the ballots were counted, Tilden led Hayes by nineteen electoral votes. But there remained twenty uncounted delegates, seven of them from South Carolina, whose own elections were disputed. Both parties claimed victory in each contest. In the end, backroom politics prevailed. The final agreement gave the presidency to Rutherford B. Hayes, but only after the Republican Party had formally agreed to withdraw all federal troops from the southern states and end all programs of Reconstruction.

In South Carolina, both parties similarly claimed to have won the race for the governorship. Hampton showed a winning margin of about 1,100 votes across the state, but Republicans argued the black vote had been suppressed by the illegal activities of the Red Shirts, particularly in the Upcountry. For nearly six months, Governor Chamberlain refused to vacate the governor's office, and he could not be forcibly removed because of a twenty-four-hour guard posted by federal troops. When President Hayes completed the withdrawal of all federal troops in 1877, however, Chamberlain fled the state, leaving South Carolina in the clutches of Wade Hampton, who had, indeed, "waded to victory," just as one of his campaign slogans had promised.

"That's it." Jonathan proclaimed. "Ten years of work destroyed. Thousands of blacks disenfranchised. Madmen in charge of the insane asylum, as they say."

"What will you do?" Susan asked.

"Hampton has promised to support public education—not that I believe him—but he can't break his promise immediately. Besides, our schools are already open. We've paid the leases for our buildings, and our supplies and books are in stock. Most of our teachers are funded by private corporations. We should be fine for the rest of this year. But after that? No one knows. I fear public schools for Negroes will have disappeared before the next election."

"And then what will you do?"

"I don't know, Susan! Don't badger me. I don't know."

Chapter 43

When All Else Fails

*S*chools opened in November for the new school year without any legislative funding in place and with no sign that free public education was any longer a priority within Governor Hampton's administration. Jonathan also worried about the latest scandal on the political horizon. In October, Robert Smalls had been arrested on an accusation of bribery. According to the charge, he had taken $5,000 from a printing company to see to it that the company received a state contract. The alleged bribe had taken place in 1872, when Smalls was a member of the South Carolina Senate.

Was he guilty? In a letter, Miss Laura Towne maintained that the Democrats were charging a Republican first, hoping to distract voters from discovering that a Democrat was really the offender. Smalls denied the charge, and when a court sentenced him to three years of hard labor, Governor Hampton stepped in with a pardon in time to let Smalls take his elected seat in the United States House of Representatives.

Nevertheless, Jonathan saw the court action as an omen— a sign of just how far the new Redeemers might go to strip political power from those who supported the Republican Party. He had dithered for several months, trying to decide what course of action would be best for his family. Then he made an appointment to see his old friend and lawyer, Arthur Middleton.

"I need to determine my legal status in regard to the plantations my wife and I inherited from Mrs. Dubois," he began.

"I thought that was all settled. The estate moved through probate without a question. Every property listed in the will came back into your possession for your lifetime, just as Mrs. Dubois specified. At your request, one of our clerks has been handling the financial dealings on those properties. Several of the buildings have long-term leases to business owners. The plantations are being worked by tenant farmers or sharecroppers under the direction of overseers. None of them are producing enormous amounts of profit, but they are paying their own way, which is all you asked."

"But, specifically, I need to know about the Edisto Island plantation, Harbor View. Is the main house occupied? How many tenants are there? What are the terms of their leases?"

"Well, for exact amounts, you will have to speak to the clerk."

"Then get him in here, Arthur. I'm not questioning your management, but these are details I need to know immediately."

"What's going on, Jonathan? I've never seen you so agitated."

"I'm planning to move my family out of Charleston. If necessary, we can return to our farm in Aiken, but I would rather start over on the Edisto Island property, if we can arrange it."

"But why?"

"Because my position as vice-superintendent of the Negro schools is about to disappear into the rubble left by the last election."

"I don't think that's really . . ."

"I don't want to hear your denials, Arthur. I'm sure you voted for Hampton, and you were certainly entitled to do so. But I cannot function under his administration because I do not trust him or his cronies to keep his campaign promises. I have fought these public battles long enough. I used to say I was a peaceable man. I avoided political arguments. Then I took on public responsibilities, because I still trusted the world to come out right in the end. But recent events have disabused me of that belief. I am retiring from the fight."

"To do what?"

"To become a peaceable man again."

"You're not really a farmer, you realize."

"No. I am a teacher, and that's what I want to do with the rest of my life. I have long dreamed of opening a private academy, one in which I offer lessons to scholars who need them, regardless of their skin color or ability to pay. The plantation house at Edisto will make a perfect setting for a school. Our own children are nearly all grown now and out of the house, so there will be plenty of room for us to share our living space with a schoolroom or two. And with a little bit of luck, the rest of my lands will provide the financing, so I no longer have to rely on the good will—or good sense—of politicians."

"I see. In that case, let's find out what Mr. Lytle can tell us." He stepped out of the office for a few moments and then returned, trailed by a bespectacled young man juggling a stack of record books. "The Edisto plantation house, Lytle. Is it occupied?"

"No, sir. It was closed up when Mr. Thomas Moreau died, back in '67. All the contents are still there. The furniture has been protected by dust covers, and the overseer keeps an eye on its condition."

"Is it ready for occupancy?"

"I should think so, sir, once it gets a good cleaning—windows washed, little things like that."

"And the agricultural acres attached to it?"

After some frantic shuffling of papers, Mr. Lytle found the right book. "Here it is, sir. Some 200 acres remain under cultivation—mostly small vegetable crops instead of the former cotton fields. Those acres are divided into five 40-acre tenant farms, each one with its own small house. The tenants—who are, I believe, all former slaves of the plantation—raise whatever crops they choose and share the resources of the main barnyard and outbuildings. They pay a small leasing fee of $20 at the end of the year and keep the rest of their profits to support their families."

"Perfect. Then if you could arrange for the cleaning, Mr. Lytle, and notify the tenants of our imminent arrival, my family and I would like to move into the plantation house at the first of the year."

"Yes, sir." Lytle gathered his papers and scurried away.

"Satisfied?" Arthur Middleton asked. "I hope this new plan will be successful for you."

"I'm sure it will. This is the first time in years I have felt optimistic about the future."

Jonathan was actually whistling as he left the Middleton Law Offices. He walked home by a circuitous route, passing many of the locations that had been a part of his life in the past—the Croft Mansion, where he and Reverend Croft had shared coffee and concerns about their sons' futures; the Meeting Street location of the Apprentices' Library Society, where he had begun his teaching career; and the rubble of Logan Street, where no one had yet cleared the evidence of the great fire that destroyed his family's first home. As he passed each one, he bid it a silent farewell. Then, with a renewed bounce to his step, he burst through his own front door.

"Susan? Prepare to migrate!"

⚞⚟

"Migrate? Where are we going now?"

"We're moving back to Edisto Island and Harbor View Plantation."

"What are you going to tell the children?"

"What children? The last I looked, our youngest was nearly twenty. Both boys are away in college, and . . . Becca . . . well, Becca is such a housecat we can just carry her along. She's past the marriageable age by now, and she has few, if any, friends. She probably won't even notice."

"Don't be cruel, Jonathan. She does have friends in Charleston. Perhaps she'll want to stay here and keep this house up. We can't sell it, and someone will have to take care of it. Becca needs a chance to make a life for herself, and it would give the boys somewhere to come during school holidays."

"Fine. We'll give her the choice—the boys, too, for that matter. I'm not trying to run away from them. I'm just trying to run toward a new life for us."

"But, but . . . the old plantation house? Is it even livable? We haven't seen it since the Yankee invaders drove you off the island in 1862. In fifteen years, it could have reverted to jungle. And what are we going to do there? How will we live? Where will we . . . ?" Susan's voice was rising higher and higher, taking on more than a hint of hysteria.

"Susan, the plantation house is fine. I've just come from Arthur Middleton's office, where I asked the very same questions. They assured me that Thomas lived in the house during the war and took good care of it. When he was killed, the overseer had everything closed up—perishables removed, furniture covered, entrances sealed. All it's going to need is a good cleaning. The law clerk who handles our properties is arranging for the details right now. You don't have to worry about a thing."

She had no intention of being put off so easily. "Jonathan, I have gone along with these sudden decisions of yours before. You moved the household to Edisto when you lost your first teaching job, even though you had no idea how to run a plantation. Then you dragged us off to a farmhouse in Aiken without any preparation for the hardships of living off the land. You decided to return the family to a war-weary, half-empty Charleston, and we adapted again. I'm tired of moving. I thought this house would be our home for the rest of our lives. You promised . . ."

"Things change, Susan."

"But I don't change—not easily, at any rate. What on earth has gotten into you this time? I thought you said Governor Hampton would protect the Negro schools. And if so, you have a job to do here."

"I said he wouldn't change things immediately. But make no mistake—with the Democrats back in charge, free public education for blacks has become a dead issue. There will be no more government money coming in. I can keep one eye on the schools here for the rest of the term, if they last that long, but then I'll be out of a job again."

"But how does moving back to Edisto help? Surely you can't go back to being a cotton planter!"

"No. I'll be free at last to follow the dream I've talked about before."

"Which is?"

"To open my own school—The Grenville Preparatory Academy."

"For blacks or whites?"

"Both, I hope, and girls as well as boys, you'll be happy to hear. I plan to take anyone who shows me a desire to learn and an ability to deal with abstract thinking."

Jonathan watched Susan's face as she struggled to keep from rolling her eyes. He had long wished she shared his passion for higher education, but he had come to accept the fact that she did not understand. He waited for the inevitable objections to follow.

With a tight-lipped smile, she nodded. "You'll just snap your fingers and make it happen."

"Not so easily. I'll start with one or two little scholars, perhaps. But word will spread, especially among my educator friends in the Beaufort area."

"All those people I've never met—like Miss Towne and Ellen Murray and that Saxton fellow . . ."

"General Saxton, yes. I'm sure he'll send promising students my way. He knows all the prominent families living in the Lowcountry. And you will meet them, once we get settled on the island."

"And while we wait for these unidentified students to show up, will there be anyone else around? Or will we be the only inhabitants of a deserted island?"

"Susan, you're making it sound like you're being dragged to the edge of the known world. Many of the old planter families returned to Edisto after the war. Our own section has five tenant families who lease fields on our land. It's a growing, recovering region. And best of all, you are forgetting that your daughter and her new husband live not far across St. Helena Sound. We'll be surrounded by friends, probably more so than we are here."

"What about a building for the school itself? Are you planning on refurbishing that old ramshackle schoolhouse again, or will these little scholars be grubbing around in my parlor?"

"I don't expect them to be 'grubbing around' anywhere. I think you're being deliberately provocative. For the foreseeable future, I'll only be taking day students, not boarders . . ."

"Thank heaven for small favors!"

"Their studies will take place wherever I set up my office. You needn't be troubled by the students at all."

"And exactly when is this all going to happen? Should I be upstairs right now, packing my valise?"

If Jonathan had looked closely, he might have realized his wife was close to tears, but he was too wound up in his own impatience and enthusiasm to notice. He simply plunged ahead with his plan. "We could have our things organized for the move by the fifteenth of December. If you remember, we promised Eddie and Gretchen we would go back to Aiken for Christmas, and we said we would be there early enough to witness the grand opening of The Greater Aiken Grocery

Company. We'll then set out for the Lowcountry, perhaps arranging to spend the New Year's celebration with Mary Sue and Eli. Immediately after the holidays, we will move into Harbor View, where we will take a leisurely approach to settling in. I don't expect to welcome the first students until at least Trinity Term and possibly not until Michaelmas."

"I don't even know what those words mean."

"Sorry. They correspond to the school divisions used in England. Trinity Term runs from sometime in April, depending on the date of Easter, until the end of June. It's the third session of the school year. Michaelmas Term starts the new school year and runs from October through mid-December, and Hilary Term begins in mid-January and finishes in April, again, depending on the date of Easter."

"It's confusing, but I'll try to remember. I have other things on my mind, however, like deciding what we pack and what we store. May I take my melodeon to Edisto?"

"Of course. You may take anything you like, so long as it is packed and ready for shipment by the end of the year. In fact, the melodeon is an excellent idea. I may want you to offer music lessons, particularly if we get some female students."

"You make this all sound so easy," she grumbled. "I hope you realize how much work it will be."

But the discussion was over, and she knew it.

Chapter 44

The Greater Aiken Grocery Company

December 1877

Jonathan, Susan, and Becca arrived in Aiken on December 15. Eddie met them at the train station and then headed the wagon out of town in the wrong direction.

"Where are you going?" his father asked, as if his son were still a child. "We need to get home and settle in."

"You promised to be here for the grand opening of the store, and it's happening right now. I only came into town to pick you up. I have to get back, and you are coming with me. Your trunks have been packed for days. They'll wait another few hours."

With a determined look on her face, Susan did her best to hush her husband's grumblings. "He's so proud of what he's accomplished, dear. Please let him have his day."

The grassy space in front of the new store held several carriages, the horses happily munching away as they waited for their owners. The building itself looked much like a barn, except for the long railed porch across the front. "By the week-end, we'll have the porch filled with Christmas trimmings—pine boughs, holly, wreath-making materials, mistletoe, and the like," Eddie explained. "I see the porch as something like a roadside stand. We'll fill it with whatever is most plentiful and seasonal—maybe flowers and bedding plants in the spring, lots of vegetables and summer fruits as they ripen, and then in the fall, we'll add apples, nuts, pumpkins, gourds, Indian corn, and baled hay. We want to catch people's eyes as they come down the road and then lure them in to see all our other goods."

"It's very attractive, dear, although it's too bad you have a hill right behind the building. With more space back there, you might have been able to put in some demonstration garden plots."

"No, Mother, that hill is actually part of the building. You'll see how we use it when we get inside. Come on."

Eddie led them through the sliding doors, waving to Gretchen to join them. She came running from the back of the store, smiling to welcome her in-laws. "What do you think?" she asked. "Isn't it all wonderful?"

"We haven't had a chance to look around yet. But, surely, you children don't produce and supply everything you have for sale here. I was expecting something much simpler," Susan said.

"No, most of this building is rented out to various suppliers in the area. It's truly a cooperative venture. Let me show you, while Eddie checks on a customer in the dairy section. Over here on the right, we have baked goods. Several women in the Mennonite community contribute to our inventory of pies, cakes, and breads. Each one of them used to make two pies at a time. Now they make four and bring the extras to us. A couple of the young girls take turns working the counter and keeping track of how much money we owe each baker. Don't those mince pies look heavenly?"

"They do, indeed."

"And then further along this side, we have our cheese display. This section is the responsibility of my three uncles, all of whom are experienced cheese makers from the Old Country. Uncle Karl, you remember Eddie's parents. May they sample a bite from the new wheel of Swiss Emmenthaler?"

"Ah, *ja*! Please to taste." The oldest of the three bearded men behind the counter took a huge knife from a rack, deftly cut a wedge from the center of the wheel, and then shaved it thinly to pass out samples to everyone within arm's reach. "Is good and nutty, *ja*?"

"Give a slice of ring bologna to go with," one of the other uncles suggested, reaching into the back cabinet and pulling out a coil of dark sausage. "We eat these together ever."

Jonathan was finally beginning to smile. "Those are both excellent!" he exclaimed. He was about to suggest they needed a good glass of wine as an accompaniment but decided not to risk it. Instead, he turned to look at the back of the building. "What's back there?" he asked. "I see a counter but . . ."

"That's what Eddie has been anxious to show you. Here he comes now, so I'll let him take over."

"Welcome to our dairy and meat department!" Eddie greeted them with a wide sweep of his arm. "Henry and I came up with this idea to give us some cold storage space. The back of this building opens up here to a cave cut into the hill you saw behind us. It's well shored-up with beams, but because it's underground, the temperature tends to be constant—cool enough that milk products don't go bad and meats can hang and age properly. Customers tell us what they want, we disappear behind the hanging canvas, and reappear like magic with their orders."

"Interesting. I've seen small cold cellars but nothing of this size."

"So far this winter, it's working well to protect our products from freezing during the really cold snaps. We'll have to wait to se how it does during the summer, but we're prepared to bring in chunks of ice from a nearby icehouse, if necessary."

"You seem to have thought of everything."

"We've been planning this for a long time, Father. You taught me well."

"Too bad he didn't teach himself to do more advance planning," Susan mumbled under her breath.

Becca had wandered off to explore the offerings on her own. Now she turned back to Gretchen. "These shelves of goods on the left—who supplies them?"

"In the back area here, we have barrels of things like flour, sugar, cornmeal, hominy, grits, sorghum molasses, and the like. We order those from a local mill. But the front shelves are stocked with all kinds of home-canned goods. We have pickles, chow-chow, various vegetables pickled in brine, and also lots of jams and jellies. Can't you guess who does those for us?"

"Well, I could see items like those red beet eggs and sauerkraut coming from your Mennonite ladies, but . . ."

"Who made your jams and jellies when you lived here as children?"

"Sarah did, but . . . Sarah? This is what she's doing?"

"Yes, she and some of the women from her church. They manage to keep us well supplied. And I think they are enjoying it immensely. They also grow most of the vegetables you see in the baskets there in the middle of the floor. It's mostly potatoes and onions and turnip greens right now, but in the summer, we'll be overflowing with garden produce. They bring their items in, and we pay them as customers make their purchases. And if some of the vegetables start to look a little wilted, the ladies just take them back home and fix them for their dinners."

Susan laughed. "That sounds like Sarah! I'm grateful you have found something useful for her to do."

"It's not kindness on our part, Mother Grenville. She is doing more for us than we could ever do for her. She has created bonds of friendship between our people and the black community. Her church ladies feel they are a part of this store, so they encourage their neighbors to shop here. Look around. Our customers are about evenly divided between blacks and whites, and you'll see them exchanging pleasantries and recipes, too, if you eavesdrop on some of the conversations."

"I am overwhelmed with admiration for all of you. I remember the night when Charlotte and Eddie first broached the idea of a grocery company with their father. We both thought it was nothing more than a youthful pipe dream. Yet here it is, brought fully to life and flourishing. But speaking of Charlotte, where is she in all of this?"

"She's our accountant, of course, the one who keeps the books up to date and pays the bills. She can do those things at home and in the evenings, which is a good thing because she has her hands full of children who are growing up too fast. Feeding them is a challenge she can handle only because she's part owner of a grocery store."

Susan smiled and then caught her breath as she started to calculate. "My goodness, the twins have turned sixteen, haven't they?"

"Yes, and the Pickford children are right behind them. Martha is fourteen and Richard celebrated what he called 'the big thirteenth.' They are all old enough to help with chores on the farm when they are not in school, and we plan to put them to work here at the store next week for the Christmas Week rush. Still, Charlotte always seems to be juggling several balls at a time—school programs, after-school lessons in cultural things like music and languages, mealtimes, housekeeping, accounts, payments to suppliers. I don't know how she does it, although she handles it all with grace. I suppose she learned it from you. And speaking of children, where are your youngest?"

"Not so young anymore, I'm afraid. Robbie and Jamey are both at Harvard. They'll be arriving by train, probably the day after tomorrow."

"Meanwhile, we need to get you settled." Eddie stepped in to interrupt the conversation. "Henry has finished the last meat order of the day, so he is ready to drive you and your wagonload of luggage out to the farm. Gretchen and I will join you all for a family dinner as soon as the store closes at six."

"Oh, dear, I hadn't finished exploring everything you have on offer." Jonathan was eyeing a wine display in the back corner.

"Never fear, Father. You'll be back here several times. The store will be very busy during Christmas Week, because we plan a series of specials and holiday tastings. We've lured you here on a false pretext, you see. We really need extra shop clerks."

"I wouldn't miss it! You can let me handle the wine samplings."

❧

The farmhouse was a welcome sight. "The old place looks prosperous," Jonathan remarked as the wagon came to a stop in the yard. "Better than when we lived here during the war."

"We've had time to do some work on it since then, sir," Henry replied. "And lots of help, too," he added, as a swarm of grandchildren descended upon the visitors.

While the young men unloaded the wagon, Charlotte came to the side door and waved for her mother to come inside. Susan allowed herself to be dragged to the kitchen by her granddaughters. "You have to come see who's here!" they squealed.

She stopped in the doorway for a long, warm embrace with her oldest daughter. "It's always good to get back to the country," she commented, "but seeing you here is the best part. The house looks wonderful, and I see your touch on everything. You've made it your home."

"I'm happy that you are pleased. But come on into the kitchen, and you'll see I've had more than a little help."

"Sarah! Of course! Every time I come to the farm, I find you in this kitchen cooking something. You're not supposed to be working here anymore." The cousins exchanged hugs. Then Susan held Sarah by her shoulders and gave her a long, searching look. "How are you, really?"

"I'm fine, Susan, and I'm cooking because it's what I love to do, so don't you go fussing at me. I'm not here all the time—just when I know you're coming." Then she gave a sheepish little grin. "Or when I need to borrow your children to keep me company."

Sensing the two women needed some time alone, Charlotte corralled her daughters and Becca. "Come, girls, I need you to help me set up the dining room for dinner. We're going to have a full house."

"You've been very lonely, I know," Susan said, turning back to her longtime friend.

Sarah's eyes were a little misty, but she gave Susan a determined smile. "No, not always. There are times when it's hard being alone, but I need those times, too, to make room for the memories. Most days, I'm at my house working on things for the store. And my church friends are in and out all day long, bringing me their preserves and their crops. We have time to visit and gossip and turn out some good eats, too. You know me, Susan—let cucumbers begin to ripen, and I start filling barrels with pickles. And we won't even talk about apples and applesauce."

Susan laughed at the memory of their first pickle experiments during the war. "All right, I understand. But I'm also happy to know Charlotte and Eddie are keeping the family ties close."

"And Johnny, too." Sarah added. "He's a big help."

"Johnny? You've seen him?"

"Sure I have, all the time. I find him hanging around my house once or twice every week."

Susan swallowed to dislodge the sudden lump of jealousy blocking her throat. "I . . . I didn't know he had much free time, what with his job with the governor."

"Oh, dear, you folks are still feuding, aren't you?"

"No, I wouldn't call it feuding, exactly. But every time he does come home, he and Jonathan find something to disagree about, and one or the other of them gets huffy. I think Johnny has decided life is easier when he doesn't have to talk to us at all. We haven't seen him in months."

Now it was Susan's turn to blink away her tears.

"I know," Sarah said. "He's told me about it. Can I be open with you?"

"Aren't you always?"

"No, not when I'm afraid I'm going to hurt you. But I can't bear seeing this split in your family. If I've learned anything from Hector's death, it is that we can take nothing for granted. If you love someone, you have to tell him—right then—because you may never get another chance. And if someone needs help, you help right away, before it's too late."

"All right. Say what you have to say."

"You and Jonathan expect Johnny to remain your little boy. But he's not, Susan. He's a grown man, one who has seen more and suffered more than either of you ever have. He sees the world differently than you do, as well he should. He lives in a different world, one you can't begin to understand. And if the two of you would quit trying to push this grown man back into the good old days when he was your little boy, you might start seeing him for what he is."

"Which is?"

"He's a good man, Susan."

"He's a white supremacist."

"No, he's not. He's a realist. He sees the current political atmosphere for what it is, not what it should be. And he knows the only hope of changing things depends on cooperation between those who want to return to the past and those who want to leap into an ideal future of brotherly love."

"And exactly how is this cooperation supposed to happen?"

"It starts with teaching both sides to live in the present, where they can find a common meeting ground. So that's what he's trying to do. He listens to both sides, and he doesn't condemn either side. Eventually, he hopes others will learn to do the same."

"It doesn't sound like there's been much progress to me," Susan grumbled.

"Your son gave me some very good advice when I was first grieving over Hector. He said I couldn't live in the past because it was gone. Nothing of the past would ever be the same again, he said. But he also warned me against looking far into the future and being afraid I couldn't cope with what it would bring. He told me to live today as if it were my only day—one day to do what I could to be happy, to help someone, to appreciate the beauty around me. He was right. Living one day at a time is what gets me through this widowhood business. And it's what gets him through the work he does. He settles for little advances, little changes, hoping some day all those little steps will pave the way to a better world.

"You and Jonathan, though—you want it all now. You want to see everyone living in the ideal world suggested by all those constitutional amendments you fought for. And you forget that those rules only say how things should be. They are the long-term goals, not some magic formula that will change men's minds immediately and forever. The sooner you both understand that, the better off we will all be."

Susan nodded but had no words for a response.

"And you can start tonight—when Johnny shows up for dinner."

Chapter 45

A Lowcountry Boil

January 1878

On the train ride back to Charleston, Susan stretched her arms above her head. "Peace and quiet at last," she sighed. "Oh, but it was a lovely Christmas. I felt like a child again—helping people to make wreaths, sampling cookies, decorating everything that didn't move, watching snow fall on Christmas Eve!"

"And working ourselves to a frazzle at the store," Jonathan grumbled.

"Don't be silly, Jonathan. You loved every minute of it. Every time I looked for you, you were back there at the wine counter pouring little samples for customers and telling stories about your famous buried peach brandy."

"And it was so much fun to have everybody together again," Becca added. "Except for Mary Sue and Eli, of course. I missed them."

"I think the best Christmas gift of all was seeing how happy everyone is," Susan said. "The store left me flabbergasted. It's such an accomplishment for a group of young people to have put together. And they all enjoy what they are doing. That's the first rule for success, I think."

"Maybe that's what's going on with Johnny, too. He seemed both content and mature this Christmas," Jonathan said.

"As Sarah reminded me, our children often behave the way we expect them to. We treated him as an adult, and he behaved like one."

"Perhaps so. I'm moderately encouraged about him. And after seeing the grocery, I'm even more anxious to see the horse farm," Jonathan added. "From what Mary Sue and Eli described last summer, it sounds like their business is booming, too. That would be two successful family ventures out of three. Then it will be up to me to pull off the third with the Grenville Preparatory Academy. Who says people in South Carolina can't do anything but grow cotton?"

"Which leaves only me, with absolutely nothing to show for my first twenty-five years." Becca spoke softly as she stared out the train window, but the pain in her voice made the words echo around the compartment.

"Not everyone has to create a new company, darling girl. You have much to offer the world."

"Such as?"

"Your kindness, your gentle humor, your ability to empathize with the feelings of others, your quick observations, your skill at expressing yourself."

"Do you think . . . No, never mind."

"What?"

"I wonder if I could be a writer. I've always loved reading stories of other people's lives. Do you think I could write something others would enjoy reading?"

"Why not give it a try? You'll never write a novel if you don't put the first words on paper."

⁂

The Grenvilles had only a few days to prepare for the next part of their journey, and Susan spent most of it worrying about leaving Becca alone. "She's such a little homebody," she fussed at Jonathan. "She's never really been away from the family, not even overnight. And this house is so big. What if she's terrified?"

"As you once reassured me, she's not going to be alone. The boys will be here for most of January, and Johnny promised to stop in as often as he can. Mrs. Henderson will still be coming to work every day, and Sammy Hawkins will still be living above the stables. She's going to have very little time on her hands if she intends to keep this big house running and write a novel at the same time."

"I hope she doesn't turn to that horrible woman next door for writing advice. Henrietta McLeod would love to get a foot inside this door so she could nose around."

"I don't think you have to worry, my dear. This is one case in which Becca's shyness will serve her well. Now come on, Susan. She's twenty-five. Let go and give her a chance to learn how to be a woman rather than a little girl. Remember Sarah's advice. It worked with Johnny, and maybe it will work with Becca, too."

❧

Susan stared out the train window and shuddered slightly.

"Cold?"

"No, feeling a little uneasy."

"Still worrying about Becca?"

"No, worrying about me." She gestured at the window. "There's nothing out there, Jonathan. Nothing but pine trees and overgrown brambles and mud holes. I haven't seen a bird or an animal, let alone a real live person since we left Charleston. No houses, no crossroads, no cleared farmland. The whole area is wild and deserted. How are we going to live down here?"

"There are real towns, I promise you. We're not there yet. This is the Lowcountry, remember. It's full of marshland and creeks wandering their way to the shore. The railroad line had to be built fairly far inland to keep it on firm ground. Edisto Island is about fifteen miles off to your left. And, no, it hasn't moved. You never approached it from this angle before."

"Sorry. I'm nervous about the move, that's all."

"I know. But look—we're coming in to Pocotaligo now. We get off here and hire a wagon to take us into Beaufort."

"Do the children know we're coming?"

"Of course. I suspect they'll meet us on this side of the ferry dock to help with the crossing."

"The ferry? Crossing what?"

"The river. You do remember that Beaufort is on Port Royal Island, don't you? It takes a boat to get anywhere from there. Unless you'd rather try swimming, of course."

Susan glared at him in frustration but decided not to answer.

❧

"Mother!"

Susan hardly recognized the young woman who swept her into a bear hug. "Mary Sue! Look at you! You're glowing. You're thinner than I remember. Everything about you is different—and beautiful."

"I'm happy, Mother. Marriage agrees with me. Come on—I can hardly wait for you to see our place. Here, let me help you onto the ferry. This ride terrified me the first time I did it, but now it's like walking down the street. Come onto the center of the ferry where the ride is a little smoother. The men will be driving the horses and wagons onto the deck, so we need to stay out of the way."

Susan stepped gingerly to a place on a bench and held tightly to the edge of the seat. "Is it far?"

"No, just deep," Mary Sue laughed. "The road's right over there—see?"

Even Jonathan gasped when they approached the Grenmore Stables gateway. The little cluster of buildings he remembered had been transformed into a sprawling expanse of piazzas and porticos shaded by graceful leafy canopies.

"Do you like it?"

"It's gorgeous! But how . . ."

"Welcome to Grenmore!" Eli called as he came around the corner of the building. "Sorry I couldn't meet you at the dock, but we had a foundering horse here. She's better now," he said in an aside to Mary Sue.

Then he turned to Jonathan. "Not quite the old plantation you remember, is it?"

"No, it certainly isn't. Did you completely rebuild it?"

"No. If you look closely, you'll find the skeletons of the old houses. We started by connecting them with breezeways and then added the piazzas all the way around to make it look like one long building. We did move the cookhouse, so it could connect with its own passageway in the back."

Mary Sue jumped into the conversation. "I like to think all we really did was give the old plantation a little love. The original buildings looked like someone was camping out on their way to elsewhere. We wanted it to be clearly our home. We planted the myrtles because they grow so fast and spread out to provide shade—and flowers, too, in the summer.

"Now, come in. You'll be staying in our guest wing, which was at one time the guesthouse that Annie and I shared. You're welcome to make yourselves comfortable here for as long as you need to, so long as you don't mind sharing the space with Charley the cat. The guest bed is his favorite sleeping spot."

"It's lovely, dear, but we can't stay long. We have a house of our own to open up."

"I know, but it will take longer than you think."

"Why? What's wrong?"

"Oh, I didn't mean to alarm you. I don't know there's anything wrong with your house. But you'll want to take your time getting things unpacked and put away. I know how long it took me to settle in when we moved here. There will be times when you need to get away from the mess for a while. Think of this as your temporary home. You can come and go as you like. It's time for me to learn how to mother you for a while. Besides, I'm going to need the practice."

"Practice?"

"Being a mother." Mary Sue giggled.

Susan took a couple of seconds to register what she heard. Then she gasped and threw her arms around her daughter. "Oh, my dear, I'm so happy for you!"

"Now aren't you glad you are going to be living nearby?"

"I certainly am. When are you due?"

"Next summer. Late July, probably. But that's a long way off. For right now, I have other plans to deal with."

"Such as?"

"Well, we thought we'd have a quiet New Year's Eve dinner here tonight. But tomorrow, we've invited some of Father's friends as well as our own for a New Year's Day get-together. It'll give you a chance to meet everyone we talk about. You're going to be part of the Lowcountry now, so you might as well see how we do things."

"That sounds like a lot of work!"

"Not at all. You'll see."

❧

The next morning, Susan and Jonathan awoke late to the sounds of voices in the yard. Two men with shovels were digging a shallow hole at the edge of the yard, while others were chopping wood and piling it nearby. "Fire pit," Eli explained as he passed by. Not far away, others were setting up sawhorses and topping them with wide planks to form a table. A third work detail was constructing what looked like the skeleton of an Indian teepee. And on the back porch, several women, including Annie, were scrubbing clam shells and roughly chopping vegetables under the close supervision of Charley the cat.

"I thought Mary Sue said that kitten was going to be a barn cat," Susan laughed.

"Well, he had different ideas. He runs the place now. He's definitely a Lowcountry cat."

"What is all this?" Susan asked.

"Preparation for a Lowcountry Boil," Annie explained.

"That word!" Susan shook her head in puzzlement. "I hear people using it to describe everything."

"Lowcountry?"

"Yes."

"It simply means something like 'this is how we do things here.'"

"And how did you manage to hire so many workers on a holiday morning?"

"They're not workers, Miz Susan," Annie said. "They're guests at the party. This is a community affair, and these are our neighbors. The party starts with the preparations and won't end until the last scrap has been cleared away. That's how we do things down here."

"But Mary Sue said she was having a New Year's Day celebration. I thought . . ."

"You thought finger sandwiches and tea cakes? No, not here. Our parties are much more fun."

And so it was. By early afternoon, a fire was blazing in the new fire pit, and the teepee held a huge iron pot suspended over the flame. Water was slowly coming to a boil. Across the yard, Eli had brought out several ponies and hitched them to a central pole, where they walked around in a circle, giving rides to any child brave enough to climb aboard. Neighbors wandered in and out of the yard, greeting each other and welcoming the new travelers. Pitchers of molasses water, lemonade, and cold tea offered refreshment. White guests from Beaufort mingled easily with black tenant farmers from Ladies Island, and white teachers from St. Helena hugged their black students and chatted with their parents.

A signal the water was boiling sent several ladies scurrying to the back porch. Then back they came, bearing trays and bowls. Chunks of onion and little potatoes went into the pot, followed by chicken pieces and slices of pepper-flecked sausage. A little later, one of the cooks added broken cobs of corn, along with liberal doses of salt and pepper, sprigs of unidentifiable herbs, and some lethal-looking red powder. And finally came the clams and shrimp still in their shells.

"How do you tell when it's done?" Susan asked, standing on tiptoes to peer into the pot.

"Mostly by when the chicken starts coming off the bone and the potato skins burst open."

"And then what? How does this all get from pot to plate?"

"Plates? Who needs plates? You'll see." Mary Sue was having a great deal of fun as she watched her parents shed their Charleston assumptions.

"Food's up!" came a shout. Several men with long-handled shrimp nets surrounded the pot, scooping up whatever bits and pieces they could catch. They carried them over to the scrubbed tabletop, dumping everything unceremoniously into a pile.

Quick hands darted toward the table, choosing a chicken leg or clam or shrimp. Shells, bones, and corncobs began to pile up at one end of the table. Fingers were definitely better than forks, the newcomers decided, and licking fingers was as efficient as napkins. The cooks kept adding more items from the pot until even the hungriest of the guests held up their hands in surrender. Then the pot was tipped over to pour the remaining broth on the flames, sending up a final cloud of fragrant steam. The huge pot itself was carried to the table to receive the remains of the meal.

"See? Quick, easy, delicious." Mary Sue was beaming at her parents. "Everybody's happy. Nobody had to work too hard, and cleanup's a breeze. Best of all, everyone had fun, and nobody was left out. Welcome to the Lowcountry!"

⁂

As the well-fed crowd began to disperse in search of a much-needed nap, General Saxton and his wife, Tillie, sought out the Grenvilles. "I can't begin to tell you how happy we are you are bringing your talents to the Lowcountry," he said to Jonathan. "Your new school will fill an important gap in the quality of education we are able to offer to the area's young people."

"Thank you, sir. I'm hoping to be of service."

"We were wondering if you and your lovely wife would grace us with your presence for dinner on Friday evening. I am bringing together several interested parties for an important discussion. Robert Smalls will be joining us, we hope, as will Miss Towne and Miss Murray from the Frogmore School and several other educators from around the area."

"As far as I know, our children have nothing scheduled for us. Susan?"

"We would be delighted, General."

"Then we will look for you around half past seven. You know the way, I believe."

"I do. And thank you."

"What do you suppose that is all about?" Susan whispered to Jonathan as they turned away.

"I have no idea, but it promises to be an interesting evening."

Chapter 46

A Slight Change of Plans

*L*ater, Jonathan could not remember much about the dinner Tillie Saxton served that night. Something with chicken and rice, probably, but he was only guessing. He did remember thinking about how many distinguished people there were around the table. At the head of the table sat General Rufus Saxton, a Medal of Honor recipient, and his lovely wife, who had always been called the most beautiful woman in Beaufort. Laura Towne and Ellen Murray might not have been quite so famous, but they were certainly well-known in abolitionist circles. And then there were the politicians: Congressman Robert Smalls, newly released from jail after the governor had issued him a pardon; Justus K. Jillson, state superintendent of schools from 1868 to 1876; and his successor, Hugh S. Thompson. Among all those worthies who seemed to know one another well, Jonathan was feeling very much the out-of-place country bumpkin. And from the look on Susan's face, he could tell she was also intimidated. Both of them sat quietly, absorbing the fascinating conversations swirling around them.

"I'm delighted to see you out and about, Mr. Smalls," Miss Towne commented. "The last we heard of your little altercation with the law, you were about to be sentenced to three years' hard labor in a cotton field."

"All too true," he said with a shrug. "And I was imagining my mother saying, 'See, Robert, I told you that you might need to know how to hoe cotton when you grew up.'"

"And now you're free again and about to resume your seat in the U.S. House of Representatives. How did you manage it?"

"Well, the judge knew someone had been paid $5,000 to grant a favorable printing contract to a company owned by a Republican with a shady reputation. But no evidence existed as to who received the bribe. The prosecutor dragged in a known felon and offered him a deal if he would point to me as the guilty party. Everyone, including the judge, knew it was a trumped-up charge, but it was a quick way to discredit me."

"Just to keep you out of Washington?"

"Apparently so. But then people started to say the real culprit was a Democrat, which would have embarrassed the current administration. So the governor stepped in and pardoned everyone involved in order to get the case out of the public eye. End of story."

"Such shenanigans!" Tillie exclaimed. "Is that the way Southern politics always work?"

"I wouldn't put all the blame on the South, my dear," the general answered. "Politics have always been a dirty game. But that's why we are assembled here tonight—to lure another innocent civilian into the fray."

Jonathan glanced around the table, wondering whom the general had in mind. Then slowly, he realized everyone was looking at him. Too astonished to speak, he could only cock his head in the general's direction and wait for an explanation.

"As I'm sure you know, Mr. Grenville, South Carolina's educational system is one of the worst in the land."

"Uh, well, it certainly needs improvement, but I've been very encouraged by the provisions in our new constitution," Jonathan responded.

"You shouldn't be," Mr. Jillson interrupted. "Mr. Smalls and I wrote that section of the constitution, and we're not encouraged. There's not a hope in hell—begging your pardon, ma'am—not a hope of ever seeing any of our provisions actually come into being. Why, in 1870, the state only allotted me twenty-five cents per student to run all our schools. We have no system to raise taxes. Even when the state appropriates more money for schools, it never materializes. We can't pay teachers, and there's no money to provide oversight of what goes on in the schools themselves. You know that, surely, Mr. Grenville. When was the last time you were paid for your job in Charleston?"

"Well, uh, several years ago, actually, but I didn't take the vice-superintendent's job for the salary."

"No, you wouldn't, because you are an honest man. That's why we need you."

"To do what?"

"To teach our teachers."

"I don't understand what you want from me."

"Look, Mr. Grenville. Many of our problems are inter-related. For example, we are never going to have schools where blacks and whites learn together. It won't work," Mr. Thompson said.

"But didn't South Carolina College open its doors to blacks several years ago?"

"Yes, it did. And all the white students, along with almost all the white faculty, promptly quit, leaving a few lonely black boys wandering around Columbia wondering what had happened to their promised education. Now our new state government has closed the school completely so they can reopen it as an all-white institution. Nobody really cares if blacks don't have schools or teachers. Educated blacks don't make good field hands, and what's worse, they make voters who are too smart to be bamboozled. Ask Robert here."

Smalls made a face at Thompson before agreeing with him. "You're right, of course. And if truth be told, most blacks would prefer to have black teachers and black schools. But that's not going to happen, either. There's little money for education, and what there is goes to white schools and white teachers. Maybe you didn't see the same problem in Charleston, Mr. Grenville. There, I understand, the American Missionary Association is still paying teachers to come down from the North to teach the ex-slaves. Isn't that so, Miss Towne?"

"I don't really know what's happening there anymore," she replied, "but I do know even the groups that funded Miss Murray and me in the past have lost interest in the cause. The reaction in Philadelphia is, the war is over so the need for aid should be over, too. If I didn't have a private source of income and a couple of generous friends back home, we'd be forced to close Frogmore this year."

"What I'm hearing from you is that you think the cause of black education is hopeless. What do you need me for?"

"Not hopeless, no, but in dire straits," General Saxton said. "The gap between black and white schools is widening, the state has given up all efforts to set standards in school districts, and illiterate hangers-on and political hacks have been issued licenses to teach in one-room schools. Meanwhile, the number of voters in the last election who could not read the names on the ballot increased to something like fifty-seven percent." Saxton looked from one serious face to another. "It's time for the people in this room to do something about the situation."

Now Hugh Thompson took control of the discussion. "Technically, I'm in charge. I'm the state superintendent of education now, and it's my responsibility. I want to start with teacher training. We'll never have good schools until we have good teachers. And people are not born knowing how to teach. They need formal instruction. I have had some encouragement from various schools and colleges around the state—places that may be willing to run training institutes for black teachers. But they want some assurance the trainees we send them will be prepared to learn."

"And that's where you come in, Grenville." Saxton smiled at him triumphantly. "You have announced you are going to open your Grenville Preparatory Academy on Edisto Island. But you haven't said what you'll be preparing your future students to do. We have a suggestion!"

"You want me to . . . prepare . . . young black people to go to teacher training institutes?"

"Exactly!"

"But what . . ."

"What do they need? Well, they'll come to you able to read and write and do their sums. If Miss Towne has her way, they'll know a little Latin, too. But they won't know how to be college students. They won't know how to make their way in a white world. They won't know how to speak without their Gullah rhythms." Thompson turned to Robert Smalls. "You probably understand the problem better than anyone, Robert. You have become an enormously influential figure in this state, but you were able to do so because Mr. McKay raised you with his own son and taught you how to live in a white world."

"Yes, he did. And I admit I sometimes succeed in what I try to do only because I happen to know which fork to use at dinner. And that I really know how to do," he said, patting his ample stomach.

He reached for another biscuit and then continued. "I find it sad that our society judges people by such things, but such is the state of our world. And even I stumble now and then. I remember one Washington luncheon for new congressmen. I ordered something from the menu called 'Turkey Wing Fricassee.' I was expecting small bites of turkey meat stewed in its own gravy—something I could eat neatly with a fork. What I got was a plate of dry white rice, topped by a whole fried turkey wing, moistened with just enough gravy to make it slippery. Ever try to cut up a turkey wing with a knife and fork?"

Even Susan was laughing. "Oh my, it must have been impossible. Did you manage to keep it on your plate, or did it go flying off across the table?"

"I held it down so it didn't get away, but I didn't get anything to eat off it, either. All I could do was nibble at the rice. Thought I was going to starve! And I'm a man who likes his food."

Jonathan pushed the conversation back to the question of his new school. "So you want lessons on how to survive in polite company and how to make small talk?"

"Yes, and they need to know other niceties, too. For example, for generations, black people were taught not to look a white man in the eye. To do so was seen as threatening. So now, most black people will go to any length to avoid looking directly at someone. And now a white man takes that as being . . ."

"Shifty? Dishonest?"

"Yes. So it sounds silly and simpleminded. But our future teachers will need to be taught how to make eye contact. They'll need to learn about fancy foods, proper dress, events in the news."

"In short, you want me to make them white? I don't think I'm comfortable with that."

"I don't want them to become white. I want them to be at ease around white people. There's a difference."

"I see another big problem with this whole proposal. I was envisioning a day school. I planned to recruit neighborhood children who could walk to our house and go home when their lessons were over. Our plantation house is quite large, and I was going to use two of the downstairs rooms as schoolrooms. But what you are proposing is not the kind of schooling one gets in a classroom. It will require immersion in a living situation. And I cannot impose that on my family."

"And the students would have to come from relatively far away, wouldn't they?" Susan asked. "I mean, we would have to have somewhere for them to stay."

"From what I understand, there are a number of unoccupied houses on Edisto Island. Perhaps we can find one to turn into a kind of communal house, where the students could live on their own. They could come to you during the day for instruction on various topics and then go back to their own house where they could practice their lessons on one another." General Saxton turned to Mr. Thompson. "Is that possible?"

"I don't see why not. We'll have to find someone who knows something about the situation on the island to help us . . ."

"I can be of assistance," Miss Towne volunteered. "A couple of our old associates are living on Edisto Island now. Mr. Alden helps with the general store, and Miss Hunn still teaches some young students. They'll be the ones to know about suitable quarters. I'll contact them tomorrow."

"Good. Are we set then? Mr. Grenville, will you take on this task for us, at least as an experiment?"

"I'll try. I'll need some time to think about what kinds of lessons to offer. And I'm thinking I would like to visit with some of Miss Towne's oldest Frogmore students, in order to see what problems we'll be dealing with. Organizing such a school is going to take time. I hope you don't want their training to start immediately."

"Take all the time you need. I think we can all pledge our assistance to help you along the way," Mr. Jillson said. "And thank you, sir. I am excited about the possibilities in this idea."

"Enough business talk for one evening," Tillie Saxton announced. "I have a caramel cake that's begging to be eaten."

"And I'll be the first to demonstrate proper fork usage," Smalls said with a nod.

Chapter 47

Lost Inheritances

*A*s Jonathan helped her down from the wagon carrying all their possessions, Susan's glance went immediately toward Edisto beach and St. Helena Sound, with the wide Atlantic beyond. The sea never changes, she thought. Perhaps that's why it's so comforting to come close to it.

Harbor View, the Dubois plantation on Edisto Island, had been Susan's summer home throughout her childhood. Because the back of the house and the outbuildings lay along the oceanfront, onshore breezes had usually kept the bugs away and tempered the hot Carolina sun. It was here she had first learned to read about faraway places, to imagine what might lie across that expanse of water, to dream. She came here to calm her fears and soothe her childish hurts. The front piazza, facing the river rather than the ocean, had always been her refuge from the issues of the day, and so it was even now. "May I take a few moments to absorb what it means to be back home?" she asked.

"Certainly. Take a walk along the water if you like. I'll see if I can find someone who can help with getting these boxes and trunks unloaded."

Once she and Jonathan were married, they had not come out here often. There were too many other demands on their time from Jonathan's job, their seven children, and the mundane details of keeping up their Charleston residence. But one fall visit stood out in her memory. It was November 1860. Jonathan was taking a new interest in the business of raising cotton. The children were happy and healthy. Life was good. She had stretched out on a chaise and stared out across the river, wishing she could freeze the moment in time. But it had been Election Day—the day Abraham Lincoln was elected president of the United States—and nothing was ever the same again.

She closed her eyes against the swirl of images filling her mind. More than seventeen years of pain and suffering— the horrible fire that destroyed their Charleston home, the coming of war, Charlotte's quick marriage and the equally quick death of her husband in battle, the birth of her premature twins, Johnny's enlistment and subsequent wounding, the years of struggling to feed their family on whatever they could raise on a small farm, the sight of an army marching against her house, the return to a bombed-out Charleston, and the turmoil of racial riots and Ku Klux Klan attacks. I've lost track of the girl I was, she thought to herself. I wonder if I can find her again by coming back here.

⁓

Her practical nature drew her attention to the problems at hand—the need to open up the house and let the sea breezes waft through it, to get the wagon unloaded, to check the rooms and identify any immediate needs. Shaking her head to dislodge the unpleasant memories, she hurried back to the house. The work crew had done a thorough job. The outside of the house needed to be whitewashed to hide the stains of too many winters, but the task could wait until summer. Inside, dustcovers had been removed and furniture polished. All we need are a few homey touches—maybe some books, a flowering plant, a bowl of fruit, and a tune from my melodeon, she decided. I'm going to enjoy being back.

Jonathan, however, was looking around with dismay. "I remember this house as being much bigger," he said. "How did we manage living here with seven children?"

"The house hasn't gotten smaller, Jonathan, but you're right. The property as a whole seems to have shrunk. Surely you noticed the old slave quarters are all gone. There used to be a long street of cabins along the shore, with little garden plots around them. There used to be a cookhouse where the slaves prepared meals for themselves as well as the family. There was a washhouse and several other outbuildings besides the stables. Now everything is gone, except for the stables."

"What happened to it all?"

"I'm guessing once the slaves were freed, they tore down the old buildings to get the materials to build their new houses on the 40-acre plots they claimed. Or maybe the Union army helped with the destruction. All I know is, most everything out there is gone, except for this one lonely little house."

"Maybe so, but I still seem to remember the family having good times, with plenty of room for everybody, including your parents."

"For one thing, when we came out to the beach with the whole family, we were expecting to be on holiday. The children didn't mind being crammed together on the sleeping porch because they spent all day outside. We had picnics rather than formal dinners, and nobody got dressed up or did any entertaining. And there's another factor, too. The first time you came out to see if you could manage as a cotton planter, you had nobody with you but Eddie. The rest of us were back in Charleston. It must have felt very empty to you, which would also have made the house seem bigger."

"I suppose you're right. I know the house hasn't shrunk. But it worries me. There are only four rooms on this main level—the two parlors and the dining room, and a small office. Upstairs, there are only two bedrooms besides the sleeping porch. Where on earth am I going to hold classes?"

"I assumed you were going to use part of the dining room as your lecture hall."

"Then where would we eat?"

"In the kitchen?"

"Is the warming kitchen still in the cellar?"

"Maybe. I don't know. This was your plan." Susan suddenly felt irritated. Sometimes it seemed to her Jonathan had a head full of magnificent dreams and not a drop of common sense. "Maybe you'll have to find somewhere else to hold the classes. What about the old schoolhouse?"

"As you once reminded me, it was pretty dilapidated even before the war. I was planning on having the slaves rebuild it until the invasion came along and we were driven off the island. By now it's probably nothing but a pile of old boards."

"You won't know until you go look. But don't go scurrying off right this minute. I would like to get us moved in first. I haven't even checked downstairs to see what storage areas are still functional. And we do need to figure out what to do about meals and food preparation."

"You're right, as usual. There will be more time to think about the school once we are comfortably settled in. You check the cellar, and I'll start bringing the trunks in."

❦

"Jonathan? Jonathan! Help! Please help me!"

Her screams sent Jonathan racing back into the house. In the butler's pantry off the dining room, he found the pocket door opening onto a dark, gaping hole beyond. And from that dark space came Susan's sobs. Jonathan grasped the doorframe for support and peered into the darkness. Familiar stair steps led downward. But on the third step Susan balanced precariously, her arms outspread to brace herself on the walls of the stairwell.

"Susan. I'm here." He fought to keep his voice soft and calm. "Try not to move, but I need you to talk to me. What lies ahead of you?"

"Nothing!" She was gasping for breath, panic threatening to overtake her last vestiges of control. "The stairs are gone, Jonathan. There's nothing. Only the broken edge of a board and then . . ."

"Can you lower your left hand about six inches to the railing? Just slide it down the wall till it comes to a stop."

"I have it."

"All right. Now I need you to test the railing by trying to shake it. Not hard. You only want to see if it is still firmly fastened to the wall."

"It doesn't move."

"Good. Keep holding onto it, but otherwise don't budge. I'll be right back."

"No, Jonathan! Don't leave me!"

"I need a strap to fasten up here, so I don't tumble down to join you. I'm not sure there's room for both of us on one step."

"I can't laugh."

"Please don't. Just keep breathing—nice and slow. Count to two hundred and I'll be back."

Sprinting back to the wagon, he grabbed one of the canvas straps that had secured their load of boxes. He tied it securely to the leg of the heavy oak dining table and then fastened the other end around his waist.

"I'm back, Susan. Are you all right?"

"I . . . I'm hanging on."

"Good. Don't look behind you." He stretched himself out on the floor and then eased the upper half of his body through the doorway. He braced his left arm on the top step, trying not to put too much weight on the shaky structure. Then he reached out with his right hand toward Susan.

"Take a deep breath now and hold it. I'm going to touch your right arm, and I don't want you to jerk when you feel my hand. Ready?"

"Y-yes." He heard her inhale. He turned his hand so it caught the underside of her wrist in a tight grip. "Now turn your hand to clutch my wrist. There. Good. I have you, and we are both tethered to the dining room table. We're not going to fall. Trust me."

"I do."

"I want you to back your way up the stairs. Don't turn around. Lift your right foot until you feel the tread of the step behind you. Then I'll give you a slight tug to help lift you. Don't let go of the railing until your foot feels firmly planted. Now the left foot. Good. Slide your hand up the railing until it's comfortable. Now the next step. Right foot first, then left, then move your hand again.

"Let's rest a minute." Jonathan was now on his knees to give himself more leverage. "Breathe deeply. Only one more step to go and you'll be safely back in the dining room. Ready?

Right foot. Left foot." As she took the final step, Jonathan threw his free arm around her waist, and they both rolled toward the middle of the room.

"Can I cry now?" she asked in a shaky voice.

"Not until I close this damned door! All right. Now, cry all you like, and I think I'll join you."

They sat on the floor for several minutes, clutching each other as the terror oozed away. Then Jonathan helped Susan to her feet. "Let's go out on the piazza for some fresh air," he suggested. "What was that terrible smell down there?"

"I don't know. Rot? Mold? Pluff mud? Dead fish? Dead bodies? Not a kitchen, certainly."

"Maybe all those! Is there another way into the warming kitchen or the rest of the cellars?"

"Back before . . . when we still had slaves . . . the cook brought food from the cookhouse into the warming kitchen through a door next to the cistern. It must still be there."

"Let's go look, if you're up to it."

The back of the house was a jungle of debris buried by growing weeds and brambles. "There, I think," Susan said, pointing to a darker spot along the wall. They pulled away the vines and rubble to reveal a gaping hole in the cellar wall.

"My God!" Jonathan gasped in shock.

"What in the world happened to the door?" Susan asked. "There was no battle here. No cannon fire."

"No. But look along the wall. That's a high water mark. There must have been a small tidal wave during a nearby hurricane. Maybe a storm surge. Some of this debris is flotsam and jetsam, seaweed, sand—the kind of accumulation you usually find along a dune. It looks like a huge wave came ashore here and dashed up against the house. The door to the cellars was the weak spot—wood rather than concrete—so it gave way first. It could have happened years ago. And there's no telling what all might have washed into the lower level of this house."

"Maybe it won't be too bad. We can get somebody to come and shovel out all the debris, and . . ."

"No, Susan. Don't think that, even for a moment. I'm afraid the house is destroyed. Look all along here. The foundation itself has cracked and shifted. I suspect the only thing that has kept the house standing is the fact that it's been empty. A wrong movement inside the building could bring it all down, like the stairway. It's gone. We can't stay here, not even for tonight."

"But what will we do?" She was sobbing now. "We have nowhere to live, no land, no place for your school, no . . ."

"We have each other. Hush now. I'm going to reload the wagon, and we'll head back toward Beaufort. I know a nice little inn about halfway—in Yemassee, which is next to the railroad station at Pocotaligo. We'll have a nice dinner, get a good night's rest, and then return to the horse ranch. Remember, Mary Sue said we could come back and forth as long as we needed to."

"I know she said that, but I didn't intend to have to do it."

"We don't have much choice. We'll rest. We'll get over the initial shock. And then we'll find a new home. Now let's load up. If we can get to Yemassee before dark, there's something there I want you to see."

Chapter 48

Why Ruins Matter

February 1878

This was the same road they had followed on their way to Edisto, but it seemed longer now because they were retracing their path. In the morning, they had been filled with anticipation; now only sadness and regret filled their hearts.

"Do we really have to make an extra stop on the way to your nice little inn?" Susan asked.

"Yes, we do."

"I'm emotionally exhausted."

"I know, but this is important." Jonathan guided the horses down a narrow road overhung by ancient live oak trees.

"There doesn't seem to be anything out here but woods. And we haven't seen another soul on the road. Are you sure you're . . . ?"

"I'm sure."

Knowing when she was beaten, Susan quit protesting and closed her eyes against the occasional glimpses of the setting sun. She had almost drifted off to sleep when she felt the wagon leave the road and bump to a stop. At first, she saw nothing. Then, off to her right, a late beam of sunlight caught the glistening edge of a granite tombstone.

"A graveyard? Jonathan, for goodness sakes! I am not in the mood for a cemetery, and I don't care who might be buried here. Some other day, perhaps, but not after what I've been through today."

"Precisely because of what you've been through today," Jonathan declared. "You are getting down from your seat, and then you are going to turn around and let your eyes adjust to the fading light."

Grimacing at him, she did as she was told. She turned with hands on hips, as if daring anything interesting to show itself. And then she gasped. "What . . . what is that?"

"What does it look like?"

"It looks like one of those Greek temples in your history books."

"Close!"

"What's it doing in South Carolina?"

"Not much of anything. Existing."

"Jonathan! Stop it! I'm too tired to think or play games. Why are we here?"

"Come on, I have a story for you, but I want you to hear it while we walk around the grounds." He took her arm and steered her first to a row of freestanding columns. "They look pretty useless, don't they? But look at the rectangular shape behind them. Use your imagination for a moment. Picture a roof on the building, then add a triangular lintel above these columns and connect it to the building, so you have a wide, sheltering porch.

"Now come through the doorway. Off to either side, imagine those pointed arches filled with colored glass. At the far end of the rectangle, you'll see a raised stone. Place an altar upon it. What have you now?"

"A church, I suppose. But if I were in need of a church, it would be easier to find one that's already built."

Ignoring her comment, he turned her around and led her back through the columns. "Stand here and look out over the grounds. Fill the emptiness with the ghosts of people long passed. See the women in their elegant hoopskirts and parasols, the gentlemen in their cutaway tails, the slave women in their turbans, and the little dark-skinned children chasing one another."

"And then?"

"Nothing is triggering a memory? I thought you told me you once read your grandfather's diary."

"My grandfather? You mean Pierre Dubois? Yes, I read some of his diary when Mary Sue was curious about him and Ernestine. I don't see what that has to do with . . . this, or today, or anything, for that matter."

"I read the diary, too. I'll bet you didn't know that, but Mary Sue was apparently sounding us out long before we had any idea she and Eli were involved. But it's beside the point. Do you remember one particular line? It said, 'I am a despicable man.'"

Susan frowned, and then, clearly, she remembered. "This is the church? The one where Pierre allowed his wife to insult his mistress and her child? No! But what happened to it? If I remember the diary correctly, they had come here because it had just been rebuilt after the English burned it down."

"It burned again, apparently right at the end of our own little war. I didn't know it, either, until Hector brought me here several years ago. He was upset with me because I was satisfied with having the war over. He said I didn't understand that black people's problems were not finished. He said I was content with the status quo, while he was still fighting the same old battles against inequality. And he compared the political situation in South Carolina to ancient Greece. I can still hear his exact words.

> *It's fitting in many ways that you first saw the church as the ruins of an ancient Greek temple. You are a historian. You should be able to understand that Greek civilization collapsed from the same sort of deeply seated beliefs that doomed the ideals upon which the United States of America was constructed. Both countries preached democracy and equality, and, at the same time, both practiced and accepted slavery as part of the natural order. Both fell apart under the strain of that contradiction. What better to represent them both but the remains of shattered temples?*

"So when I saw today how upset you were because your old home at Harbor View was about to collapse, I knew you needed to see this place. I wanted you to understand that your grandfather's South Carolina—that lovely place where you grew up—is gone forever. And not only is it gone, it represents an idea, a way of thinking, that must never be allowed to return. Our collapsing house, like this burned-out church, serves to remind us of what we must never again allow ourselves to become."

Susan turned away. She stood silent, staring at the ruins. Then she began to wander through the old graveyard, trailing a finger here and there across a monument. Wisely, Jonathan watched her but did not speak or urge her to hurry through the journey she was on. As darkness began to settle on the scene, she returned to him, taking his hand.

"It's beautiful here. It has the same sort of beauty I found on the beach this morning, before . . ." She tilted her head and looked up at him. "Was that really only this morning? It seems much longer. Maybe because so much has been lost. We need ruins in our lives, don't we? They serve to drag us out of our past and push us toward a better future, one that will not need to collapse."

❧

The next morning, they drove the rest of the way to Ladies Island. Mary Sue and Eli both came running when they heard the wagon pull into the yard. "Mother! Father! What are you doing back so soon? What's wrong?"

"Everything, I'm afraid," Susan answered. "Our lovely plantation house has proved to be unlivable."

"But didn't the overseer say it was fine?"

"Yes, and it looks fine from the road and the river. But around back, where the sleeping porch and the yard face the ocean, there has been massive damage."

"Fire?"

"No. It looks like a storm surge hit the back wall and destroyed the foundation," Jonathan explained. "The cellars are now full of debris and pluff mud. The house itself is slightly tilted off the foundation, and the old slave yard has been wiped away. Wasn't there a hurricane along there a while back?"

"I remember one," Eli said. "Back in '74, a storm twice brushed the coast of Florida and then went back out to sea. Everybody around here relaxed. Then it turned a third time and came inland between Beaufort and Charleston. It wiped out all the inland rice crops just as they were ready for harvest. Killed a couple of people, too, as I remember. At the time, it never occurred to me, but it must have passed right through your Edisto property."

"That could well have been what happened. The damage is several years old, from the looks of the building."

"In any event, here we are, back again, needing shelter until we can figure out where we go next. I'm sorry to impose upon you," Susan said.

"Don't be silly, Mother. You are always welcome."

"I'm going to go see General Saxton this afternoon," Jonathan said. "He needs to know right away that my plans for the school have met a setback. And I'm hoping he may have some suggestions."

"We're going to see him," Susan corrected him. "This is our problem, and we'll manage it together."

❧

Tillie Saxton met them at the door of her Beaufort townhouse. "How odd to see you!" she exclaimed. "The general was talking about you at lunch not an hour ago. Did you somehow know he was worried about you?"

Jonathan was puzzled. "Did he know we . . ."

"Jonathan, my good man!" the general's voice boomed from the stairwell. "You have come upon a wish!"

"I don't understand," Jonathan said. "I'm here to bring you a serious problem, but you couldn't have known . . ."

"No, I'm the one with a problem. I was wondering how I was going to get in touch with you."

"This is all terribly confusing," Susan said, turning to Tillie. "Can we get them to sit down and talk one at a time?"

In the parlor, General Saxton took the lead. "My house—my problem first," he said. "I have received a disturbing communiqué from Hugh Thompson, the superintendent of schools. He has been talking to the governor, and they have decided any training for black teachers must take place in an urban setting. The governor says it won't do to send those prospective teachers out to Edisto Island where they will be in a familiar countryside environment.

He wants them exposed to city life. So he is suggesting we establish our proposed school here in Beaufort, where the students will have more opportunities to interact with white cultural activities. He doesn't seem to understand you are the key to this preparatory training and are firmly committed to . . ."

Jonathan had started to laugh, and once he started, he found he could not stop. Soon Susan joined him, while the Saxtons watched in complete befuddlement.

"What's so funny?" the general demanded.

"Nothing. Everything. Oh, my!" And the Grenvilles were off again, grinning at one another and giggling with a touch of hysteria.

"I'm sorry, General Saxton," Jonathan finally gasped out an apology. "It's that we have come to tell you that we are not moving to Edisto Island after all."

"What?"

"We drove out to the island yesterday and discovered the house and lands have incurred heavy storm-related damage. The outbuildings are gone, and the house itself has been nearly knocked off its foundation. The place is a total loss, and we have nowhere to go and nowhere to establish the school I promised you."

"So there's no school?"

"No school. And we came to ask you if you had any ideavb where we might find a new place here in Beaufort. I was prepared to apologize for misleading you and your friends the other evening."

"And you have no place to live?"

"Well, we're staying with our daughter and her husband for the interim, but we cannot impose on them long. Besides, they have an annoying cat that keeps trying to sleep in our bed! We'll either have to find a new place here in Beaufort or return to Charleston."

"And we don't want to do that," Susan added. "It's time for us to have a fresh start—maybe by trying to live on Lowcountry time."

Now Saxton looked at his wife, and the two of them began to laugh. "This is the most ridiculous conversation I have ever had," Saxton sighed.

Tillie was nodding. "Providence sometimes reigns," she said.

"What?"

"Let me start over," the general said. "My house—my problem, remember? Hear me out this time. I received two letters today. One, as I have told you, demanded we move the preparatory school for black teachers to Beaufort. The other was a letter of resignation from an old friend, Reverend Solomon Peck. After some eighteen years of self-financed service to the former slaves of this community, he has decided to return to Philadelphia because of ill health."

"Reverend Peck? I remember him from an early visit here. He's a fine gentleman. I'm sorry to hear he is ill."

"That's right. I had forgotten you met him. Let me remind you of his story. He was the first teacher to arrive in Beaufort. He came on his own with no sponsorship, only a desire to teach. Beaufort at the time was deserted, except for some abandoned slaves. Their owners had all fled ahead of the Union invasion. Solomon looked around town and found two abandoned houses near downtown. No one claimed them despite his inquiries, so he commandeered them for his own humanitarian purposes. The smaller but more elegant of the two he turned into a home for himself and eventually for his daughter and a couple of her friends who came to help him with his teaching. He turned the other building into a schoolhouse, with classrooms upstairs and down.

"He has taught Negro children and adults there ever since. As soon as the war was over, he made another attempt to find the owners of the properties, but no one ever came forward. Several years ago, the provisional state government formally granted ownership of both buildings to him. And now, because old age is making it impossible for him to continue his mission, he has charged me with finding his successor. I think I have succeeded."

"But two houses? I don't know that I can afford to take on that . . ."

"The buildings are free, Jonathan, as they were when Solomon found them. It's the responsibility you must be willing to accept."

Chapter 49

Rebuilding the Dreams

December 1878

In December, Susan decided to throw a party. "I know how you feel about holiday folderol," she told Jonathan, "so I'm not going to call it a Christmas party. But we have so much to celebrate this year and so many people to thank for enriching our lives. I'd really like to entertain everyone—perhaps on the fifteenth. That's the Sunday after the Michaelmas school term ends. We have never had a housewarming for our new residence. We've never celebrated the opening of the Grenville Preparatory Academy. And we haven't formally introduced our new granddaughter to our friends. I'm thinking of an informal afternoon open house, where guests could drop in, sort of on Lowcountry time.

"There are also people we need to thank for their service. We might never have gotten the school off the ground if it hadn't been for the assistance of Reverend Peck, who stayed on to help with the remodeling and repurposing of the school building. He leaves for Philadelphia on the twentieth, and we need to bid him farewell. Similarly, the Reverend Doctor Joseph Walker is retiring at the end of the year as rector of St. Helena's Episcopal Church. And Robert Smalls is completing his term as a U.S. congressman."

"Robert Smalls lost his election bid, Susan. I'm not sure he would see the occasion as one calling for a celebration."

"On the contrary—Laura Towne tells me he is thinking of taking an extended trip out west, to Arizona, perhaps. She says he is seeing this loss as an opportunity to distance himself from local disputes and concentrate on the needs of his own people. From what I understand of his new purpose, he's looking for places where black people could settle and begin new lives, without the stigma of servitude following them."

"I can see you've already worked out all the details. You're not really asking me, are you? You're making a pronouncement."

"Well, I wouldn't do it if you didn't approve, but . . ."

"Fine. On one condition—you promise not to turn this special occasion into an annual tradition."

"Of course not. These are unique events, so we won't need to do it again next year, unless . . ."

"And no holly. I hate those prickly leaves!"

"You're a seasonal grouch, Jonathan Grenville, but I love you anyway." She kissed him on the nose and scurried off to begin her preparations.

She started with handwritten invitations to all their friends and neighbors. She asked her former cook, Gemma, to provide a menu of drinks and finger foods. She alerted Maggie, the twice-a-week housekeeper, to plan to work an extra day on Saturday, December 14. Mary Sue volunteered to have Eli cut magnolia branches and pine boughs to decorate the house. Susan's own music students would provide background music on the melodeon. "But not all Christmas carols," she cautioned the girls. "My husband hates Christmas. He'll need some popular tunes to keep him jolly."

❧

It was a lovely affair, designed in every way to cement the Grenvilles' new role within Beaufort society. The Saxtons were honored guests, of course. Tillie stepped right in to help with the hostessing tasks. The general had invited the two gentlemen who had planned the teacher training program to accompany him. Mr. Jillson and Mr. Thompson were eager to praise the efforts that had gone into opening the new school, and to Susan's surprise, they had brought the governor, Wade Hampton, with them to assess the first year's accomplishments.

"I hope you don't mind my crashing your party, Mrs. Grenville," the governor said as he bowed over her extended hand. "I feel as if we have already met, thanks to your wonderful son, who has become something of my right hand in this administration. A woman who is married to an inspiring teacher and is the mother of a brilliant up-and-coming political figure deserves our highest praise. Thank you for having me in your home." He bowed again and moved in a noticeably straight line for the punch bowl.

From behind her left ear, Jonathan whispered, "Do not ever tell a soul you invited a Democrat into my home."

"Hush, Jonathan. He's not the only Democrat here. Some of them are perfectly charming people. And they seem to admire you, so be grateful."

❧

It was Robert Smalls who held the floor for much of the afternoon. Regardless of their political affiliation, everyone in the room recognized Smalls as the most influential citizen of Beaufort. People invariably asked him for his reactions to recent events and his predictions for the future of the nation. Because he was both a pundit and a seasoned political campaigner, he was only too happy to oblige. He regaled his listeners with stories of congressmen who fell asleep during hearings and showed up for crucial votes with their clothes half undone. Black Republicans were not the only political buffoons, he assured his listeners.

With only a little encouragement from Laura Towne, he soon plunged into the story of one of his recent campaign adventures. "I was scheduled to make a little speech at Gillisonville. Lots of nice people there—reasonable people. They had scheduled my speech for ten o'clock in the morning, and they had the podium set up in front of the grocery store, right there on the main street. But as people were gathering, here comes a troop of about 800 mounted Red Shirts." He hesitated as he noticed that the governor himself was listening to his story.

"Beggin' your pardon, Governor, but they were your men, I believe. They were whooping and yelling, and every few minutes a few of them would break off from the troop and go racing down a side street to harass some black man because he was wearing a hat. They were slapping some of the black women, too.

"I held up my hands to keep my followers from going after the troublemakers, because that wasn't going to help the situation. Then the leader of the troop announced he wanted half my speech time to talk about my opponent. I told him to go ahead, because I was no longer intending to speak at all. Well, they gave me ten minutes to make up my mind whether I wanted to speak. I went into the grocery store and about forty of my people followed me in. We locked the door, lined up behind the counters, and pointed our guns at the door, waiting for trouble.

"Sure enough, when ten minutes were up, the Red Shirts started trying to break down the door and threatening to set fire to the whole building. Then they started shooting into the building, but they didn't hit anybody. In the meanwhile, the rest of my followers had scattered, raising the alarm that Mr. Smalls was cornered and in danger. And pretty soon, people started coming in from all parts of the county, and they were armed with whatever they could grab—hoes, axes, sticks. By six o'clock in the evening, there were a thousand Negroes marching on Gillisonville, and the Red Shirts took off, all except for twenty armed men who promised to take care of me if I tried to get on a train out of town. Well, I did get away, but I had to run for the train after dark and jump on the tender."

"But you still lost the election, Smalls," Wade Hampton commented.

"Sure I did, Governor, but I don't mind. The Democrats played dirty tricks and openly bragged about it. Now everybody knows it was not a fair election. We Republicans will have an easier time of it in 1880, thanks to all their pranks."

"Or maybe by 1880, we will have found a better way to conduct ourselves," Hampton suggested. "May I have a minute to make a couple of important announcements? This will interest you, Mr. Grenville."

Susan was afraid the political discussion was about to get out of hand, but Jonathan nodded. "You have the floor, sir."

"Mr. Jillson, Mr. Thompson, and I are here today to celebrate the success of the new Grenville Preparatory Academy. Until now, college-level classes have been closed to young black men and women who were thinking about becoming teachers. Mr. Grenville's new school offers the first step in their preparation. But where will they go from here?"

Hampton stopped for a moment and looked around the room, as if waiting for an answer. Then he smiled and continued, "I am pleased to announce my administration has agreed to help finance the following programs. In 1880, Wofford College in Spartanburg will hold a summer training institute for new teachers. The next year, Furman College will follow suit, and Bettis Academy, in Trenton, will also offer training to black teachers, following the pattern set here at Grenville's institution. By 1882, the University of South Carolina will begin to hold its own teacher training institutes and will begin offering regular college classes for all teachers in 1883. We are on our way to a better educational system for South Carolina, my friends, and I'm proud to say it started here in Beaufort."

Cheers and applause broke out across the room, and Susan looked up at her husband, beaming to see him recognized at last. Jonathan, a bit embarrassed by the attention, broke the mood by announcing, "I've refreshed the punchbowl. Let's save any more political discussions until you've all had a chance to sample it. Maybe we can take a vote to see if it passes muster."

❦

Mary Sue and Eli spent much of the afternoon in one corner of the parlor, watching with pride as their newborn daughter held court among her many admirers. Every woman in the room made it a point to hover over the softly lined bassinet, gently touching a finger or smoothing the peach fuzz topping the tiny head.

"She's going to be a real beauty. Look at those deep, dark eyes. She's already seeing things we can't even begin to imagine."

"Look at her smile!"

"Babies don't smile. That's gas!"

"No, it's not. When she's really happy, she smiles and flashes her dimple. See? Like that."

"Have you decided on a name?"

"Oh, a long time ago. This is Miss Ernestine Rose Moreau."

"Lovely."

Reverend Walker, who had presided over Beaufort's Episcopal community since before the war, watched until the admiring women had moved on. Then he approached the young couple. "Have you thought about a christening ceremony for your daughter?" he asked.

Mary Sue saw a muscle twitch in Eli's cheek and laid a cautionary hand on his arm, but he shook her off. "As I'm sure you know, Reverend," Eli said, "there are people in town who have questioned the appropriateness of baptizing a mixed-race baby in their churches. They may coo over her in a setting like this, but when it comes to Sunday morning, it's a different story. My own AME congregation would prefer us to have a private ceremony, and I know you are well aware that your own white parishioners would object if we showed up at your baptismal font."

"That may well be, son, but those views are not the opinions of God. Nor do I support them." Reverend Walker hesitated and then plunged on. "I know something of your story. Your father-in-law has told me of your and your wife's relationship as distant cousins, both descended from the same great-grandfather. And I also know for whom this baby is being named. With that background knowledge, I have a proposal for you.

"I understand that the ruined old Prince William's Parish Church on Sheldon Road has a special significance in your family. It was the site where the original Ernestine was betrayed by your great-grandfather. If you would allow me to do so, I would be honored to baptize your daughter at the ancient altar of the Old Sheldon Church, thereby helping to redress that betrayal."

Mary Sue looked up at the elderly man with tears running down her cheeks. "I think our great-grandfather would approve."

"Then let us assemble on the first Sunday of the New Year at noon on the grounds of the Old Sheldon Church. I shall be retired from St. Helena's by then and answerable only to God, but my ordination remains a holy responsibility. I will bring my vestments and a container of holy water. We will christen your beautiful daughter there in the eyes of God and all those you choose to invite. And if the weather allows, perhaps we can have a picnic on the grounds."

⚭

When the party was over, the punchbowl drained, and the last crumbs eaten, Jonathan put his arms around his wife and pulled her close. "It was a wonderful party, Susan, and it accomplished more than you may realize. Do you remember an old dream of mine—the one where I would grow old in a professor's office at Harvard?"

"How could I forget your story? It was so sad, and I still regret you didn't get the chance to be a part of that college scene."

"But that's my point, Susan. Don't you see? The picture I painted for you was someone else's reality. This new school here? It's my reality. This is what I have to contribute to the world. And it's much more important than I ever dreamed possible. I learned that today.

"And I realized something else, too. We belong here now. The town has taken us into its midst. In our home, Republicans and Democrats, white people and black people, the young and the old—all found acceptance and common ground. I feel as if we have made a beginning, the start of reconstructing our own small influential circle. I see a bright future ahead for us all. But just in case there turns out to be more trouble ahead, perhaps we'd better plan on holding another one of these affairs next Christmas."

Thank You For Reading!

Dear Reader,

I hope you enjoyed *Yankee Reconstructed*. I really enjoyed resurrecting the story of Jonathan and Susan and tracing their progress as the children grew up and the country faced new challenges As was true of the first book in this series, the setting and the events are based on historical fact. Several real historical figures appear, although the family and most of the characters are creatures of my own imagination. What fun it has been to take them through a series of absolute disasters and once again bring them safely out of harm's way.

As an author, I love feedback. You, the reader, are the reason I keep writing. So, tell me what you liked, what you loved, even what you hated. I'll enjoy hearing from you. You can send me an email at schribercat4@yahoo.com or visit me on my website at katzenhausbooks.com

Finally, I need to ask a favor. If anything in this story has touched you, or inspired you, or caused you to see an issue in a different light, I'd appreciate a review of *Yankee Reconstructed*. As you may know, reviews from readers like you are the life blood of an author. Your comments have the power to make or break a book. If you have the time, please return to the website where you found the book, and leaave your comment, so that others can share the same experience.

Here's a link to my "Carolyn P. Schriber's Author Page" on Amazon. You'll find all of my books here: http://www. amazon.com/-/e/B003ZM9GVE.

Thanks again for spending some time with me, and with Jonathan and Susan.

Gratefully,

Carolyn P. Schriber